CRISIS: BLACK

CRISIS: BLACK

J. A. DAVIS

VIREO / RARE BIRD • LOS ANGELES, CALIF.

This is a Genuine Vireo Book

A Vireo Book | Rare Bird Books
453 South Spring Street, Suite 302
Los Angeles, CA 90013
rarebirdbooks.com

FIRST TRADE PAPERBACK ORIGINAL EDITION

Set in Minion
Printed in the United States

10 9 8 7 6 5 4 3 2 1

Publisher's Cataloging-in-Publication data
Names: Davis, John Alvin, author.
Title: Crisis : black / J. A. Davis
Series: A Rex Bent Thriller
Description: First Trade Paperback Original Edition | A Genuine Vireo Book | New York, NY; Los Angeles, CA: Rare Bird Books, 2017.
Identifiers: ISBN 9781945572722
Subjects: LCSH Terrorism—Fiction. | Doctors—Fiction. | United States. Navy. SEALs—Fiction. | BISAC FICTION / Thrillers.
Classification: LCC PS3604.A9585 C85 2017 | DDC 813.6—dc23

Agnes "Sissy" Barr Davis

San Rafael & Tiburon, California

Thank you for all the love, for opening our eyes to all the beauty in the world through travel, and for struggling to provide us with the finest education. Packing up and moving every two years, finding new schools and decent, affordable housing, coupled with all of the challenges along the way, were met with such strength and determination. Given Dad's lengthy and frequent deployments, heaven only knows how you found the courage to raise four little rascals.

Dad's nomination for the Congressional Medal of Honor in the late 1950s would have, in your words, "changed our lives." In a desolate part of the Pacific, hundreds of miles north of Oahu, Soviet helicopters laden with torpedos and depth charges circled overhead and watched as the USS *Greenfish* (SS-351) snagged the Soviet's first satellite. This occurred at a time in which the United States was lagging far behind in the Space Race. In broad daylight and at periscope depth, the risk of being blown from the waters was imminent and the intelligence gathered for our great nation during the Cold War, invaluable. Squelched sixty years ago for national security reasons, perhaps President Trump would be kind enough to consider reopening his nomination. As a casino developer in Atlantic City in the early 1980s, Dad met with DJT on several occasions and always spoke very highly of him.

Your beauty, warmth, and charm shall surpass the test of time. Your smile and laughter are as memorable as the bartender's inevitable question to you when asked if you would care for another martini:

"*Yes, please. You can't fly on one wing!*" Cheers, Hummingbird!

INTRODUCTION

DETERMINED TO RENDER THE East and West Coasts of the United States uninhabitable, driving Americans inland and our great nation into obscurity, radical Islamic terrorists are confident that all infidels will soon be wiped off the face of the earth.

From their clandestine base in Whiskey Bay, LA, all is proceeding as planned. Their only concern is a recalcitrant emergency room physician, Dr. Rex Bent, who became suspicious and notified the proper authorities after treating blue, bloated, and grossly disfigured Asian sailors—all of whom, died suddenly and violently.

With their coup de grâce in jeopardy, the radical Islamic terrorists realize that not only Dr. Bent but also his wife and confidant, Trissy, must be eliminated without raising suspicion. Pursued and hounded like traitors who have betrayed their country, the Bents are in a race against time, determined to discover the significance of "Prussian Blue."

THE ACTION FROM **CRISIS: BLUE** *CONTINUES.*
THE CONCLUSION IS THRILLING!

CHAPTER 1

THE STARS AND THE moon were exceptionally bright, but the light from the heavens could not penetrate the sinister haze that had engulfed Whiskey Bay. The cool night air mixing with the warm waters of the Bayou had generated a boggy mist that drifted skyward, occluding the clear skies. All sound seemed to be trapped and amplified within the cold, damp, foreboding cloud. Guards armed with AK-47s nervously patrolled the grounds of Camp Eagle. The sound of crushed limestone grinding beneath their feet was heard with every step, as was the occasional striking of a match. However, each man was ill at ease for there was no doubt that the sound and smell of a horrifying death permeated the air. Loud, bloodcurdling shrieks preceded by a sudden splash, momentarily interrupted prolonged periods of eerie silence, as predators stocked, captured, and then devoured their prey. Each time, the guards were startled. These gruesome sounds reverberated, making it impossible to locate the direction from which the kill had occurred. Hearts raced, weapons were raised higher and triggers squeezed tighter, as each man twisted quickly to the left and then the right, straining to see into the darkness.

The sounds of the nightly struggle for life and death on the Bayou could not be appreciated from within the command center. The dimly lit structure was bathed in a pulsating blue glow, as computer screens continued to yield valuable intelligence essential to the success of their evil plans. The excitement of the attack on Grand Central Station had subsided earlier in the evening. All was quiet in the den of terror, with the exception of the sounds of fingertips striking plastic keypads and the creaking of the wooden floorboards as Mohammad paced back and forth. With his hands clasped behind him and his chin held high, he appeared to be a supremely confident general, yet he remained deeply concerned that forthcoming operations could be compromised and his brilliant *coup de grâce* would never materialize.

All of the terrorists had turned in, with the exception of two men working the Internet from within the command center. They feverishly pursued the job of exchanging intelligence with activated cells, managing ongoing operations as well as collecting and transferring funds, as per Mohammad's explicit orders.

"Mohammad, there is traffic from the *Amazonas*. She is experiencing engine trouble. Her position is thirty miles east of Key West. She is on the surface and the crew is attempting to effect repairs," Azul announced, reading the disappointing report on his computer display.

"Not again!" Mohammad shouted. "Will that diesel boat ever reach its destination?" he asked himself quietly, shaking his head in frustration, wondering why they had purchased the old decommissioned submarine from the Brazilian Navy.

"Azul," Mohammad growled, "please forward the following reply:

'*Captain Pompeii, we are anxiously awaiting your arrival in New York Harbor. Get that submarine submerged and making way, immediately!*'

We can't allow the Statue of Liberty to stand forever, now can we, Azul?"

"Absolutely not, Mohammad," Azul agreed as he finished typing the message before hitting *send*.

"The wire transfer of funds to Saudi Arabia has been confirmed," Beezor announced.

"Excellent," Mohammad responded as a door to the command center slammed shut.

"Mohammad," Yassar said, attempting to gain his leader's attention. But Mohammad continued to pace back and forth, unaware that his second-in-command had entered the room. Mohammad's cell phone began to beep. He grabbed the communication device and flipped up the screen.

"Mohammad," the leader announced in a deep, rough voice.

At that moment, Mohammad looked up and noticed Yassar standing next to him. He quickly placed his index finger to his mouth. Yassar understood that he was to remain silent.

"Allah is with you, Zia. Call tomorrow night when you're in position and prior to the execution of our plan," Mohammad instructed, terminating his brief conversation.

"Yassar, all is proceeding quite well. Zia is in Phoenix and assures me that he will be in Los Angeles by six o'clock tomorrow morning."

"I have more good news, Mohammad," Yassar announced with great pride. "I heard from Sahib only moments ago. He and his men are positioned at Agnes Dollar Restaurant on San Francisco Bay. It is a stormy night but ideally suited for their mission. He assures me that, within hours, the monument erected by and for the infidels will crumble into the sea."

"Indeed, that is good news. Ideally, I would have had all of these attacks coincide with our nuclear scenario. However, I now believe that the problems we have endured and the subsequent delays in the execution of our plans have worked to our advantage. Panic and fear, followed by mental and physical exhaustion, followed again by panic and fear, will have a synergistic effect. The fatigue will be cumulative, effecting thought and rationale. We will strike again and again until the United States of America has been destroyed," Mohammad voiced with confidence.

"Allah is great! Our message to the United States and the world will be unmistakable. Believe in Islam and our cause or you and your families will experience a painful death," Yassar added.

"Yassar, we have thirty thousand gallons of nuclear waste, which the North Koreans have been kind enough to provide. I have no doubt that these deadly radioactive isotopes are anxiously awaiting a new home. Have you had any luck procuring additional tanker trucks?" Mohammad inquired.

"Unfortunately, we have not. We were lucky to have quietly obtained the one tanker, which is now headed toward Los Angeles. I'm confident that, over time, we could steal the additional seven tankers as you had requested, but I fear this action would arouse too much suspicion. Alternatively, with your permission, may I suggest that we substitute the tanker trucks with U-Haul vans? There are several advantages to doing so and I could have the vehicles here by early afternoon," Yassar stated.

"U-Haul vans?" Mohammad thought for a moment before continuing.

"How interesting, that's a brilliant idea. There's no doubt that these vehicles would go unnoticed, but how difficult would it be to convert the vans to achieve our goals?" Mohammad began to pace the command center.

"Not difficult at all. Home Depot has large metal drums on sale, all the connections we would need, and even lead shields," Yassar replied.

"That's remarkable! Only in America," Mohammad chuckled.

"I even have a discount card," Yassar laughed before continuing to brief Mohammad in greater detail. "I have thoroughly investigated this possibility. The configuration of a sixteen-foot U-Haul truck is such that four drums can easily fit within the bed. Each drum would be secured and rigged to drip nuclear waste at any desired rate. Just as importantly, I can have the conversion completed and the nuclear wastewater on board by nightfall," Yassar added.

"Excellent! Would there be enough room in each vehicle for additional cargo, such as explosives, shrapnel, and ball bearings?" Mohammad inquired, stroking his chin.

"Absolutely," Yassar responded proudly.

"Well then, proceed with leasing the vans. After the vehicles have slowly dispersed their deadly cargo throughout the selected cities, each is to be exploded at a soft, densely populated target. We must ensure the maximum number of casualties," Mohammad insisted.

"Which cities are we targeting?" Yassar asked with great interest.

"Washington DC, New York, Atlanta, San Francisco, Los Angeles, San Diego, and Houston," Mohammad answered.

"The plan is brilliant!" Yasser exclaimed.

"Within a matter of weeks, the East, West, and Gulf Coasts will be uninhabitable, driving the infidels inland and the United States of America into obscurity," Mohammad proclaimed.

"Mohammad," Beezor announced. "We just received a message from Captain Asaki. It appears that a United States navy destroyer is shadowing the *Il-sung*. They've ordered that 'the *Il-sung* come to all stop and prepare to be boarded.'"

Mohammad and Yassar looked at one another. The concern was evident on each man's face.

"What is the present position of the *Il-sung*?" Mohammad asked.

"The cargo ship is approximately eight degrees, fifty-six-point-one minutes latitude and seventy-nine degrees, thirty-three-point-three minutes longitude," Beezor responded, bringing up his chart of the Caribbean before continuing. "That would make her approximately sixty miles north-northeast of Colón and the entrance to the Panama Canal." Beezor pinpointed the location and drew a circle around it.

Mohammad was suddenly filled with rage.

"The *Il-sung* is in international waters. How dare the infidels be so bold! Beezor, forward this response:

'Captain Asaki, should the Americans board your vessel, the mission that you and your gallant men have sacrificed so much to complete would fail. To yield to the infidels would bring great dishonor to you, your family, and North Korea. Resist and, if necessary, fight to the death.'"

"If the Americans capture the *Il-sung*, I don't believe they could trace the ship back to Whiskey Bay," Yassar assumed.

"You may be right, Yassar. But do not underestimate our enemy. The Americans are clever bastards, directed by an evil God. They could very well find hints as to our location, such as a nautical chart, which would lead them directly to Camp Eagle," Mohammad responded with concern.

"I see."

"Your orders have been forwarded, Mohammad," Beezor announced.

"Very well. Beezor, please inform me immediately of any reply from Captain Asaki and of any American traffic referencing the *Il-sung*."

"Yes, Mohammad," Beezor replied sharply. Mohammad's cell phone began to beep once again.

"Mohammad," the leader of the terrorist movement answered. In the silence of the moment, Yassar could see an intense anger suddenly overwhelm Mohammad. His facial expression and body language left no doubt that the information Mohammad was receiving was not good.

"GeeHad, listen to me. Do not panic! Discard your computer, your files, and any evidence that would lead the authorities to Whiskey Bay. I want you and your advisors to be at Camp Eagle by tomorrow afternoon. Is that understood?" Mohammad stated emphatically, impatiently waiting for a reply. Mohammad placed his hand over the receiver and disclosed to his trusted friend, "It appears that Dr. Bent and his wife have been killed despite my explicit orders not to do so." He secured his cell phone.

"I completely understand, GeeHad. It's not your fault. Again, be here tomorrow afternoon and bring all those who have worked so hard on your behalf. It's time that we have a celebration."

◆

"As I had predicted, Yassar, the deaths of the American physician and his wife have aroused great suspicion. The FBI, the CIA, and the local authorities have announced on TV that they will descend upon the town of Carencrow tomorrow! Furthermore, they vow to leave no stone unturned!" Mohammad complained bitterly.

"These setbacks are indeed unfortunate," Yassar acknowledged as Mohammad turned and walked away. Again, the room fell silent. With his hands clasped tightly behind his back, Mohammad began to pace. Minutes later, Mohammad's anger appeared to subside and the pacing stopped. He had regained his composure. With his head held high, he turned back toward Yassar.

"Allah has spoken to me, Yassar. Nothing else is to go wrong. Prepare a sumptuous feast for GeeHad and his people tomorrow night. After that, GeeHad is to be killed, and those who have followed him bound and gagged. Each will then be placed in a U-Haul van for a ride of their lives. This honorable sacrifice is far more than these partial believers deserve. Allah is great. Death to the infidels!" Mohammad shouted, the strength of his voice shaking the walls of the command center.

Chapter 2

It was early evening in Carencrow, Louisiana. What had been a brisk but clear wintry day had turned more hostile as the temperature continued to plunge and the winds gained speed. With the moon reflecting the sun's light, low-lying clouds cast eerie shadows on the raging Cajun River. The frigid water appeared to be boiling and a thick mist whipped skyward as the levies struggled to contain the turbulence of the mighty tributary. This force of nature was unstoppable. Virtually everything in its path would be consumed as the muddy waters made their way toward the Gulf.

Only minutes before, Rex and Trissy had been given no other option but to attempt to cheat the river from claiming two additional victims. The hostile body of water had aided in their escape from an unforgiving judicial system and a certain trip to the gallows. They were now miles downstream and both continued to cling to the improvised flotation device Rex had created with his scrubs.

"Trissy, swim time is over. Let's head to shore!" Rex screamed above the loud thunderous sound rumbling from the river.

"Wow, what a ride! We can't possibly get out now. I finally learned how to dodge all the floating debris," Trissy joked while struggling toward shore as a multitude of heavy, life-threatening objects continued hurtling downstream.

"Here we go," Rex said, grabbing Trissy's hand, pulling her toward him.

"Thanks, I could feel the undercurrent sucking me under," Trissy replied.

"My legs are starting to cramp," Rex complained, as every muscle began to spasm with the slightest movement.

"I can't feel my arms or legs but the water sure does feel warm," Trissy shouted moments before she also started to cramp.

The pain intensified with each kick and scoop of water as they fought for their lives. Their body temperatures had dropped so dangerously low that their thought processes had become more and more irrational.

"Rex, I'm not sure we're going to make it!" Trissy yelled. Although the riverbank was a mere ten yards away, safety appeared to be an unobtainable illusion and the river ruthlessly determined to claim more victories.

"Keep kicking. We're almost there!" Rex insisted but the strength in his kick and the movement of his arms had slowed dramatically. Finally, in desperation, he put his feet down and touched river bottom. The water depth was only five feet. The current was swift, but at least he had a toehold on survival. He pulled Trissy toward him, grabbing her around the waist. Together, they slowly struggled onward. Fatigued, frozen, and gasping for breath, Rex and Trissy collapsed on the muddy shoreline.

"I—hate—cold— water!" Rex yelled as a puff of condensation billowed forth with each word.

He fully expected a reply from Trissy, but she lay quiet and motionless. Steam rose from her body as the cold air consumed what remained of her bodily warmth.

"Trissy, Trissy, are you all right?" Rex shouted, staggering to his knees. He reached over and grabbed her wrist. She had a strong radial pulse.

"Yes Rex, I just needed an opportunity to wallow in the mud," Trissy replied sarcastically, her teeth chattering as she slowly rose to her feet. "You know how women are about beauty and the importance of a good mud bath."

"Well then, I suggest you stop wallowing and we find a warm shelter before we freeze to death," Rex blurted out before slipping backward, suddenly tumbling into the deep, putrid muck.

"Rex, have you no sense of balance?" Trissy joked, fighting to stay upright on the treacherous riverbank. She extended her hand to help her husband to his feet, but he was unaware of her kind offer.

"I'm having a little trouble here. I can't feel my feet and I can't feel my ass! However, overall it has been a rather enjoyable evening," Rex remarked, crawling through the mud and onto the grassy embankment.

When he was finally able to erect himself, Trissy surveyed Rex's nearly naked lily-white body, which was now coated with thick splotches of Louisiana slime. He looked so helpless standing on the riverbank in his underwear, clutching his deflated scrubs. Trissy was speechless, but after a few moments of silence, she reacted instinctively.

"Ah Rex, you have skid marks in your new underwear!" Trissy blurted, much to Rex's chagrin.

"You don't say! Come on, doll, let's get out of here," Rex said, taking Trissy's hand as they staggered up the levee.

The lights from several camps were soon visible. Rex noticed the outline of a darkened structure nestled among several large cypress trees. Suddenly, a gust of wind pushed them in that direction. As the wind howled and the trees swayed, Rex and Trissy stomped through a thick bed of fallen leaves.

Their bodies had instinctively shut down nearly all blood flow to the extremities in an effort to keep their vital organs warm and functional. The muscles in their legs were so starved for oxygen that they remained partially contracted. Each step was exceedingly painful as they slowly made their way toward what appeared to be a vacant home.

"What's that?" Rex asked, looking at the ground. He suddenly stopped and bent over. While struggling to catch his breath, he pointed.

"I don't see anything except dead leaves."

"Trissy, I think we've hit the mother lode," Rex shouted, suddenly veering to his left.

"A Jacuzzi!" Trissy screamed with joy. Within seconds the protective, heat-retaining cover was off, revealing an oasis that had evolved from a rather rebellious California culture. "Fire this bad boy up, by gar!" Trissy insisted, climbing into the tepid bath.

"As you wish, my love. Surf's up and your lifeguard is now on duty—Wahoo!" Rex proclaimed, twisting all the knobs on the control panel. Moments later, a bright underwater light came on and there was a loud, deep rumbling sound, followed by a multitude of tiny bubbles.

"Ah," Trissy sighed as the heat penetrated her body. She was immediately overwhelmed by a tingling sensation as blood vessels dilated, restoring vital bodily fluid to oxygen-starved tissues while the pores in her skin began to pop open. Slowly she slipped in deeper and deeper until she was nearly totally submerged. With her head above water and her neck extended, resting against the rounded edge of the Jacuzzi, she gazed skyward. For a moment Trissy remained motionless, captivated by the warm tranquility and mesmerized by the stars above.

"Make room for Daddy," Rex shouted, jumping in. The subsequent tsunami he created had no effect on Trissy. As the tidal wave rolled over her face and her body swayed violently in the turbulence, she remained in a Zen-like state.

"Damn, that's hot!" Rex quickly made a hasty retreat, exiting the boiling pot. "Now I know how lobsters feel!" Rex plopped his fanny down on the edge of the Jacuzzi. With only his lower legs submerged, he looked down at the liquid adult playground. The clear water had been replaced by river muck. The bright, white light was now nearly obscured and the surface appeared to be a thick bed of slowly percolating mud from which bubbles struggled to break the surface.

"Rex, stopped splashing," Trissy requested after emerging from her trance.

"I'm sorry, my love. I'm having difficulty deciding if I should die from hypothermia or third-degree burns," Rex confessed as Trissy sat upright and turned to face her husband.

"Rex, you're not going to die, so please move away from the light and slip into these soothing waters," Trissy insisted.

"Perhaps you're right," Rex responded reluctantly as he found the courage to slowly and carefully slip into the scalding waters. However, after five minutes, Rex had had enough. With his body warm and his leg cramps resolved, he was certain that the time was right to explore his new surroundings.

"Trissy, I'm going on a recon mission. Please give me your clothes."

"Rex, you're not feeling frisky again, are you?"

"Trissy, are you insinuating that I may be in the mood to jump your bones?"

"Well, the thought had crossed my mind, and knowing the male species..." Trissy replied with a smile as she quickly removed her clothes, tossing them onto the grass.

"I assure you that my intentions are, at present, more than honorable," Rex replied seconds before her beautiful breasts broke the surface, short-circuiting all logical thought. "But then again, given the exhilaration of running from the law and our near-death experience, it's important to live life on the edge and take advantage of every opportunity," Rex rationalized as his underwear was quickly discarded.

"Ah, the warm waters are rather appealing." Rex roared passionately as he slipped back into the Jacuzzi, edging closer to Trissy.

"Rex, no hanky-panky," Trissy pleaded, worrying that the owner might emerge from the adjacent darkened home at any moment.

"As I recall, Wikipedia states that the term 'hanky-panky' refers to shady activity and specifically excludes foreplay and sex," Rex replied genuinely, putting his right arm around his wife, stroking her nipple with his left hand and passionately kissing her neck.

"How fortunate," Trissy sighed with delight. Her fear of discovery quickly vanished as Rex stroked her right breast with the hand he had strategically placed only moments before.

"Unlike the mud-wrestling monotone hermaphodites who work the front desk in the ER, you're absolutely beautiful, even when you're covered in Cajun River muck," Rex admitted while gently massaging her soft breasts.

"That's reassuring, but just when did you see those two prehistoric sisters covered in mud?" Trissy moaned as Rex began stroking her erect nipples.

"That's not important," Rex replied elusively, his hormones beginning to rumble.

"Trissy, you feel so good!" Rex moaned, kissing her lips. Trissy's pelvis slowly started to sway back and forth, as she reached down and grabbed his penis.

"Wolf!" Trissy howled, as she started to nibble on Rex's ear.

"That's no wolf, it's a big bad sperm whale," Rex proclaimed with pride as she gently stroked the engorged mammal.

"You're not on the endangered species list are you, Mr. Whale?" Trissy moaned, straddling his hips.

"Yes, in fact he is. That's why Mr. Whale needs lots of love and nurturing," Rex admitted, placing his hands on Trissy's hips, feeling her sensually stimulating rhythm.

"How long can Mr. Whale stay down?" Trissy asked, rubbing Rex's rather stout penis between her legs.

"Oh, on a good day, Mr. Whale can stay submerged for hours if his blowhole remains shut, and even longer after a 'Happy Pill,'" Rex admitted, retreating to the security of Trissy's voluptuous breasts.

"Um, that sounds rather optimistic."

"No, indeed, and let me assure you that Mr. Whale is up to the challenge."

"We shall see. By the way, how deep do whales dive?"

"We're about to find out!"

"And where do whales swim when they're submerged?" Trissy questioned while rubbing Mr. Whale against her groin.

"In the ocean, but it's a little-known fact that they prefer deep, dark, underwater caves, " Rex moaned.

"Oh—ah, well then, clearly it's time for Mr. Whale to begin exploring," Trissy sighed, slipping the creature from the deep into her warm, moist, and inviting cave.

"Ah, now that's a perfect fit," she moaned, rhythmically swaying back and forth, slowly at first to control the depth of penetration.

"Well, I suppose I could hold off a little while longer before going on that recon mission," Rex rationalized as Trissy placed her hands firmly on Rex's hips.

"Leave me now, Mr. Whale, and your whale of a tail will be left with just the tail," Trissy declared, moving her hips faster and more forcefully.

"Well then, I have no doubt that he would look rather funny swimming around with just a giant tail," Rex groaned, gently tugging on Trissy's long wet hair, raising her chin and exposing her slender neck.

"Um," Trissy sighed as Rex moved his tongue up and down her neck.

The muddy waters of the Jacuzzi were now showing signs of renewed life. In addition to the multitude of tiny bubbles breaking the surface, there now appeared to be a respectable tidal surge and rather substantial standing waves.

"Oh!" Rex moaned as Mr. Whale started to throb and thrash about. Once again, Rex placed his hands on Trissy's sensitive breasts, gently massaging her nipples with his fingers. The stimulation proved to be overwhelming. The bumping and the grinding quickly became more frenzied. With each pelvic thrust, Rex penetrated deeper and deeper as the surrounding waters continued to surge.

The moaning and groaning became louder and the sounds of ecstasy began to merge. As Trissy dug her fingernails into Rex's skin, he reached down and placed a tight grip on her hips. He could feel her firm cheeks rhythmically contract and then relax with each movement. Rex forcefully pulled her closer with each forward thrust as he continued to probe deeper and deeper into Trissy's insatiable underwater realm. Instinctively, he constrained the range with which her hips swayed backward. Now was no time to slip out and leave the safety of the cave.

Suddenly, there was a loud rumbling sound, followed by a deafening boom.

"Trissy, I don't want to raise any concern, but the tectonic plates are about to shift—violently!" Rex stuttered as the waters unexpectedly receded.

"Yes, Yes, YES! I can feel them moving!" Trissy screamed.

"Oh, Oh, OH!" Rex screamed moments later just as a massive circular tsunami, originating from ground zero, surged well beyond the confines of the cement enclosure. Without warning, the pelvic thrusts ceased. Rex could feel Trissy's cheeks contract forcefully and her death grip intensify. Moments later, the cave suddenly but rather expectedly collapsed.

"Ah!" Trissy and Rex sighed simultaneously. The hugging and kissing continued for several minutes in silence as each struggled to catch their breath.

"Wow!" Rex exclaimed, his entire body tingling.

"Um-huh!" Trissy moaned before dismounting and releasing the stunned marine mammal back into the wild.

The steam rising from the Jacuzzi was whisked away by the prevailing winds. Exhausted but satisfied, Rex and Trissy leaned back and stared at the stars, which were now bright, bold, and pulsating.

"I'll be back momentarily, my love," Rex announced, much to Trissy's surprise. He quickly gathered their wet clothes and stumbled toward the darkened structure twenty yards away.

"Don't be long," Trissy insisted, still sighing in ecstasy.

Chapter 3

Rex left the warm and relative safety of the Jacuzzi, walked onto a wooden patio, and attempted to open a sliding glass door.

"Damn, it's locked," Rex complained.

"Surely there's a key hidden somewhere..." He threw the wet clothes onto the deck and looked under the doormat, but there was no luck.

"Ah-ha, success," Rex blurted enthusiastically, lifting an adjacent flowerpot and finding a small brass key illuminated by the stars and the moonlight. Soon he was inside the home and fumbling for a light switch.

"There it is!" Rex announced, flicking on the panel of switches adjacent to the door. The kitchen, the living room, and the patio were now awash in light.

"Wow, nice pad! Let's just hope that there's no security alarm," Rex whispered before quickly searching the riverside camp to ensure that no one was home.

Several minutes later, he had the dirty laundry and their muddy sneakers churning in the washing machine.

"Warm and dry at last," Rex declared with great satisfaction after rubbing himself with the owner's fluffy white towel and slipping into his monogrammed bathrobe.

"I think I'll let Trissy swim for a little bit longer while I explore," he said to himself, grabbing a fresh towel and an extra robe for his frolicking mate.

Soon his interest focused on a door situated under the stairwell, adjacent to the living room. He immediately tossed the towel and the robe onto the nearby couch.

"Damn, security seems to be an issue in this home. Well, it's probably a wine cellar. If so, someone has to make sure that the bottles are properly stored, I suppose," Rex rationalized, searching the adjacent bookshelf for a key. He pulled out several books before his eyes focused on an evil-looking ceramic statue, depicting some grossly disfigured Asian god.

"You're as ugly as that potbellied North Korean dictator," Rex declared, lifting the bad luck charm from its roost and finding an oddly shaped key within.

"I'm having a rather decent run of luck," Rex announced in a congratulatory tone. "There we go."

The security bolt retracted with a 'pop' and Rex twisted the handle. As soon has the door opened, he was overwhelmed by an intense musty odor, which was oddly familiar. The light revealed what his well-seasoned olfactory system had sensed.

"Oh, my God!" Rex gasped, surveying the contents within the small closet.

Stacked to the rafters was an assortment of impressive explosives guaranteed to make any pyrotechnics enthusiast salivate. There were two small kegs of gunpowder, several sticks of dynamite, dozens of rockets, and a large cardboard box containing firecrackers.

"What, no pistols, rifles, knives, hand grenades, or wine? How disappointing!" Rex complained.

"Yet, with all these goodies I'll bet I could still put on an unforgettable winter celebration." Suddenly, he was struck by an idea, which would utilize this enormous firepower for the greater good of mankind: mainly him and Trissy.

"This is just with the doctor ordered! Enough explosives to defend our rather tenuous position and save our skins, should the authorities come a knocking," Rex announced with conviction, as he dragged a large box of fireworks from the closet and placed it next to the living room sofa.

"Look at this!" he said after discovering a role of coiled quarter-inch fuse. "Come to Papa," he insisted, rolling a keg into the light.

"First sex and now gunpowder. Thank you, Jesus!" Rex shouted as his raised his hands toward the heavens. For the first time in years, he felt like a kid in a candy store. All of his dreams were coming true.

Rex quickly stuffed the pockets of his newly acquired bathrobe with several sticks of dynamite and a role of duct tape before gathering a few rockets, the keg of gunpowder, and role of coiled fuse. He was all smiles as he walked outside and set the rockets down on a patio table.

"Good God, even the winds have died down. Keep those favors coming and I'll be sure to toss a little something extra into the collection plate this Christmas," Rex assured the guardian of the heavens and overseer of mankind.

With a renewed spring in his step, Rex walked over to a large pine tree adjacent to the camp. Utilizing the duct tape, he secured a stick of dynamite to one side of the tree in such a manner that, if detonated, would cause the tree to fall toward the house.

"Not my best work, but it'll have to do," Rex admitted as he cut a four-foot section of fuse. Quickly, he spliced one end of the fuse to the dynamite and left a remaining portion coiled on the ground. An adjacent rock ensured that any unexpected gusts of wind would not jeopardize the timing or the desired effect of his homemade surprise.

"What a perfect night for a fireworks display," Rex assured himself has he poured a rather generous mound of gunpowder over the coil and then proceeded to walk backward across the lawn, laying down a thick ribbon of the aromatic black powder in his wake.

"Rex, what in the world are you doing?" Trissy asked, resting her arms on the side of the Jacuzzi and watching him intently.

"Just a little late night gardening, my love. One can never be too prepared for bugs, slugs, or any other predatory varmint," Rex rationalized before reaching the stand of trees on the opposite side of the house, where he selected a pine tree and duplicated his detonation scheme.

"Well then, please close your robe," Trissy giggled.

"Yes dear," Rex responded instinctively, although the suggestion went in one ear and out the other without so much as touching any viable gray matter. Without breaking stride, Rex remained focused on his mission. Soon, trees on all four courners of the house were rigged to explode simultaneously and fall toward the invaders.

"I need to add a little razzle dazzle to this defense," Rex whispered as he thought for a moment.

"I've got it!" From the existing ring of gunpowder that now surrounded the house, Rex added two lines, each of which ran on either side of the patio.

"This should do just fine!" In short order dozens of rockets were stacked against the house and positioned such that the rocket-propelled explosives would crisscross twenty yards from the home. He then took great care to ensure that the fuses were deeply embedded in mounds of gunpowder.

"Rex, what's that smell, sulfur?" Trissy asked, sniffing the foul night air, which was not as pungent or as malodorous as the river muck yet still quite offensive.

"Gunpowder, my love," Rex said affectionately as he kept working.

"Gunpowder! Have you lost your mind?" Trissy asked, already knowing the answer.

"Yes, as a matter of fact. All that's left is one flickering brain cell, which keeps short-circuiting," Rex confessed without remorse.

"That's what I thought," Trissy replied, continuing to watch Rex madly set up his "unwanted visitor" reception.

"Trissy, please don't step on the line that I've laid down in the grass, don't drip on the gunpowder, and, whatever you do, don't rub those gorgeous thighs together. You may cause a spark that ignites the whole shebang!"

"All right, all right," Trissy responded, deciding it was time to retreat from the warmth of the Jacuzzi. "Rex, I'm turning into a prune. Would you kindly bring me a towel?"

"Certainly dear, coming right up," Rex replied before walking back into the house, where he immediately became distracted.

"I'm missing something. What is it? Ah yes, a means of escape among all the confusion," Rex quickly realized.

"Hum, I never looked in the garage. Maybe there's a tank," he thought optimistically as he remained intently focused on his mission.

"Rex, where's my towel? My skin's starting to prune and peel," Trissy complained, watching her husband dart back and forth in the house.

"Damn, there's nothing here but an old muddy four-wheeler," Rex complained, surveying the contents of the garage.

"I do believe there's a flaw in my battle plan… or is there?" he said, eyeing the four-wheeler once again.

Seconds later, he had the engine cranked.

"Half a tank of gas. Excellent!" Rex announced, placing the vehicle in gear as the garage door opened.

Rex quickly found a clearing in the woods hundreds of yards away from the house and adjacent to the main road. He turned the engine off and jogged back to his new and improved refugee home for wayward felons.

"Now, I need some way of detonating my 'welcome home greeting'… By jove, I've got it! When in doubt, go for the black gold!" A circle of gunpowder connected the front and the rear of the property with two branches leading to either side of the patio. Rex laid down one last swath of power from this circle into the garage, lowered the door, and locked it in position one foot above the cement foundation.

"I feel like 'MacGyver,'" Rex declared as he brushed off his hands before glancing at his watch. Only thirty minutes had elapsed. He closed his robe before confidently strutting back toward the living room.

Chapter 4

Rex looked out onto the patio. Trissy was naked and shivering. Her hands were cupped against the glass and she was staring into the living room but had not attempted to open the door.

"I'm sorry, little girl, but my wife and I purchased Girl Scout cookies last week," Rex joked after opening the sliding glass door.

"Rex, you're cruising for a bruising," Trissy growled, stepping inside.

"You're not the same girl I had sex with in the Jacuzzi earlier this evening, are you?" Rex asked, handing is mottled wife the towel that he had tossed onto the couch earlier.

"Rex, I'm hungry and I'm cold," Trissy complained as she quickly dried herself off. Instinctively, she gave Rex the "if looks could kill" expression, which had no trouble penetrating deeply into his soul. This was followed by "the golden moment of silence," which only compounded the danger Rex now faced from his feisty young wife of German descent.

"Rex, there's a very fine line between life and death," Trissy declared, while moving her index and middle finger in a scissor-like motion. Without question, this was a tragic fate Rex and Mr. Whale hoped to avoid.

"Man was born to live dangerously," Rex countered gallantly as he helped his half-frozen wife into a warm terry cloth robe. Although her lips were purple, her extremities were blanched, and her teeth were chattering uncontrollably, she still had her wits about her.

"Look Rex, a fireplace!" Trissy shouted with joy.

"Excellent idea, I could sure use some warm buns," Rex snickered. "Thank God, it's gas. I ran out of gunpowder," Rex announced. "Give me one minute and I should have his baby stoked."

"Just make sure the damper is open," Trissy reminded him.

"Damper? What damper?" Rex asked as the fireplace suddenly roared to life and an intense wave of heat rolled into the living room.

Trissy was immediately drawn to the flame. Rex, on the other hand, satisfied that no smoke was billowing into the living room, found his attention focused elsewhere. Adjacent to the kitchen was a rather respectable "watering hole," which included several of his favorite libations. Rex had poured two rather large snifters of Sambuca, a rather stout licorice-flavored liqueur.

"All that's missing are the coffee beans," Rex said, handing Trissy her glass.

"You know, those three little beans have brought us a great deal of luck in the past. Remember Rome?" Trissy asked, bringing the drink to her nose and sniffing the pungent, effervescent fumes.

"How could I forget the Italian beans and your hot American buns? Cheers, my love," Rex said as he and Trissy brought their glasses together in a toast.

"I meant the romance of the city. Oh, this is so good," Trissy added after taking a sip.

"That's right, now I remember," Rex replied nonchalantly, although the only things he could vaguely recall about Rome were the ruins and a grumpy waiter mumbling something about drinking the liqueur without the three beans bringing bad fortune.

"Rex, don't you find this camp a little bit eerie? Look at all the dead critters mounted on the walls. Every square inch is covered with animals of all sizes, all posed in bizarre and rather unnatural positions. How spooky, even their eyes appear to move!" Trissy gasped as she stepped away from the fireplace and cautiously moved about the room. She began to scrutinize the few pictures, which had been propped up on selected tables.

"I wouldn't worry about it," Rex responded without looking around to confirm Trissy's concern. "The home either belongs to an eccentric hunter, an enthusiastic taxidermist, or some psychotic killer. Besides, you've gotta admire anyone who has a Jacuzzi, a full bottle of Sambuca, and a doormat that reads: 'No Pets, No Children, and No Progressives.'" Rex concluded.

"Oh!" Trissy screamed, looking at one of the photographs.

"What is it?" Rex asked, spinning around quickly.

"Rex, you're not going to believe who owns this camp," Trissy gasped as she picked up one picture and looked more closely.

"Governor Babbling Blanco," Rex blurted, trying to focus on the news.

"Good guess, but thankfully, she's out of office. No, it's Dr. U. B. Fubar. The SOB who got you fired," Trissy revealed.

"Well then, I was correct. A deranged psychotic killer is the proprietor of this hunting and haunting lodge," Rex added without appearing to be phased by the gruesome discovery.

"He's in every picture, sporting the same shit-eating grin," Trissy voiced with anger and resentment.

"Given his recent divorce, I'm amazed he doesn't have his former wife and mother-in-law stuffed and mounted over his fireplace," Rex responded with an air of disappointment.

"That's because they're probably either still at the taxidermist or stored in the basement," Trissy replied.

"So that explains the smell in that small rancid room under the stairwell. I'll bet he's resected their brains and has their bodies cryogenically preserved. No doubt Fubar is anticipating a transplant," Rex added.

"I can see one brain, but where in the world would you find two brains? And what's the probability that each would admire a godlike saint?"

"Sheila would know from watching *Young Frankenstein* so many times. Personally, I think the local sewers are definitely out. So that leaves the brothels and the catacombs. However, not to worry, I feel confident that he would never choose your beautiful brain because it would take him too long to detach the halo," Rex reassured his gorgeous wife.

"Rex, you say the nicest things. Even though they're usually relayed under the oddest circumstances. I thank you for the compliment," Trissy said.

"Come, my love, and enjoy the spoils of an overpaid, egotistical neurosurgeon who suffers from 'cranal-anal-inversion-with-cardiodal-tendencies,'" Rex suggested as he motioned Trissy over to the couch.

"Now, that's a rather bizarre disease. I've never even heard of it," Trissy confessed.

"He has his head so far up his ass that his heart is beating his brains out," Rex clarified as Trissy howled in delight.

Chapter 5

Rex and Trissy sat comfortably on the plush leather couch in Dr. Fubar's living room at his secluded riverside camp. With their feet propped up on the coffee table, they appeared quite relaxed and, for the first time in days, did not have a care in the world. What could be better? They were warm and sitting in front of a cozy fireplace, sipping on a stout after-dinner drink awaiting the ten o'clock news.

"Rex, turn up the volume," Trissy insisted.

Suddenly, both were mesmerized by a roaming reporter's story. They took their feet off the coffee table, firmly planted their tootsies on the floor, and leaned forward.

"This is Tracey Brewster reporting live from the Cajun River in Carencrow, where a prominent physician and his wife are believed to have drowned earlier this evening," the reporter said, walking on a dirt road atop a levee and pointing toward the raging, merciless body of water below. "After an intense investigation by a multitude of national and local agencies, in addition to FBI SWAT teams headed by Special Agent in Charge (SAC) Sammy S. Richter, Dr. Rex Allen Bent and his wife, Trissy Rawson Bent, were arrested at their home on Mallard Drive earlier this evening on suspicion of masterminding terroristic plots against the United States. Reliable sources closely involved with this case have informed me that the evidence is overwhelming. This couple had intended to disseminate biological agents and then profit by investing in the pharmaceutical companies manufacturing the antidotes. There are also indications that they were closely affiliated with terrorist organizations abroad. On their way to jail, the police cruiser in which they were traveling rolled off the levee and into this section of the Cajun River. The police officer driving the vehicle miraculously survived after swimming to shore, but there was no sign of Dr. and Mrs. Bent. I'm joined now by SAC Richter," Ms. Brewster reported enthusiastically.

"Mr. Richter, what can you tell us about these alleged terrorists, their capture, their crimes, and now, their presumed death?"

"I am not at liberty to disclose all of the particulars of this case or the success of our extremely well executed raid. However, by eighteen thirty, both Dr. and Mrs. Bent were in our custody. With regard to their crimes, it does in fact appear that Dr. Bent and his wife were part of a sleeper cell, which had been activated to conduct horrific crimes against humanity. That's about all I can disclose at this time," SAC Richter answered, although prior to the camera rolling, he had shared with the rather attractive reporter exactly what he and his men had found in the home.

"I understand that biological agents and incriminating computer traffic were uncovered. Can you substantiate those findings?" Ms. Brewster asked.

"Well, now that the cat's out of the bag, I can truthfully share with you that computer traffic, which reflected the Bent's close association with terrorist organizations and fund transfers from terrorist groups, was discovered. Additionally, thousands of vials containing a dirty yellow liquid were found in Dr. Bent's office. I don't think there's any doubt that these vials contain deadly biological agents capable of killing hundreds of thousands of Americans," SAC Richter concluded with a gleam in his eye.

"WOW," the reporter blurted with well-rehearsed enthusiasm. "I understand that shortly after their arrest, the police cruiser in which they were traveling ran off the levee and tumbled into the Cajun River, where the alleged terrorists drowned. Do you have any comment with regard to that tragedy?" Ms. Brewster asked, pulling her coat tighter in an effort to protect her voluptuous figure from the cold night air.

"First of all, this was not a tragedy. Two vicious Islam-loving killers are presumed dead. However, they're not good and dead until I find their worthless carcasses. The second issue, which I'd like to clear up, is the fact that the police cruiser didn't merely roll off the levee. The police officer transporting the prisoners reported being rammed broadside by a large black truck," SAC Richter disclosed.

"Are these the tire marks here?" Ms. Brewster asked, pointing at the grooves in the dirt and gravel road.

"Yes. As a matter of fact, you can clearly see the cruiser's tangential skid marks and the deep rectangular divots in the soft shoulder where the vehicle dug in before being flipped. Now, what remains to be seen is whether this was a heroic gesture by some patriotic American, an indiscriminate act by a drunk driver, or Dr. Bent's accomplices attempting to shut him up."

"It appears that you have many unanswered questions, Mr. Richter," Ms. Brewster observed, batting her eyes.

"The FBI's work is never complete. We'll find the vehicle that struck the police cruiser and round up every terrorist and Islamic sympathizer in the seedy little town of Carencrow. However, for now our top priority is to find the Bents. Hopefully, they remained in the back of the police cruiser and drowned," SAC Richter exclaimed in a deep growel.

"Is there any chance that the Bents survived?" Ms. Brewster asked as she canted her head toward him, clearly impressed by the SAC.

"Possibly, so in addition to looking for the police cruiser, which may be miles down river by now, we intend to search every camp on both sides of the Cajun River."

"Just when do you intend to start your search?" Ms. Brewster asked.

"The manhunt is presently underway. Fifty men and women are involved in the search. By morning, we will have a hundred more personnel on the ground and several helicopters in the air. I assure you that we will leave no stone unturned. We'll find these traitors, preferably dead, but if not, their journey to the gallows will be swift," SAC Richter stated emphatically.

"Perhaps we've overstayed our welcome, Trissy," Rex suggested with the smirk.

"That arrogant son-of-a-bitch is bluffing!" Trissy huffed.

"Now SAC…" the reporter started to say before being interrupted by an FBI agent who whispered something into Richter's ear.

"We have a lead," SAC Richter announced with great emotion to the small crowd, moments before both he and the agent dashed off.

The reporter was somewhat shocked with the abrupt nature with which the interview had been terminated. She watched quietly as the agents entered a black, unmarked vehicle and quickly sped off. But she soon regained her composure as her producer nudged her onto her next story.

"In other news, Rula's restaurant is hosting a fundraising benefit for Asians who had been displaced by Hurricane Katrina. The event is scheduled to get underway shortly. Carencrow news reporter, Jeffery Caballero, is present at this black-tie affair," Tracey Brewster announced.

"Well, there you have it. The ratings-hungry bastards have flipped from terrorism to fundraising in one breath," Rex growled.

"Rex, be nice," Trissy requested as her husband huffed.

"And look, the reporters always have the same goofy smile whether talking about the end of the world or some gala event," Rex added as he thought for a moment. "Now, just how many Asians do you think were living in New Orleans at the time? I'll tell you. Take the number of Chinese restaurants and sushi bars, multiply times ten, and you'll arrive with the exact number, legal or otherwise. I'll bet it was one-tenth of one percent."

"Ugh," Trissy mumbled as she shook her head. Clearly, her suggestion had been ignored.

"Thank you, Tracey."

"Mrs. Chum, it appears that your fundraising event has been a spectacular success," Mr. Caballero concluded, standing under the veranda and watching the host greet the arriving dignitaries.

"Yes, we've been quite pleased with the response from the local and international communities, which have been so generous in helping our Asian brothers and sisters in need. As you can plainly see by the turnout, the leaders in Carencrow feel it's important to give back to those who lost everything in the storm," Chum replied, forcing a smile and attempting to sound sincere.

As Rex and Trissy watched this public relations sham unfold, Rex noted a big black truck with a heavy chrome bumper pass in the background. Steam was trickling from the engine compartment.

"That's it!" Rex shouted, jumping to his feet and pointing at the TV. "That's the truck that hit us!"

"Rex, are you sure? There must be a hundred black trucks in this town and they all look the same. Even the red necks driving them look alike."

"That's because of inbreeding, but there are very few black trucks sporting a heavy chrome battering ram, which just happens to be having engine problems on this very night. In fact, that massive shiny grill was the last thing I saw coming at us before the police cruiser was struck. Now that I think of it, that truck seems to be parked at Rula's every time we go to dinner at that North Korean soup factory."

"Rex, you're getting rather paranoid. Why would Chum and her North Korean buddies want us dead?" Trissy asked as her mind suddenly flashed back to recent events. "Just a few days ago we were attacked while driving home in the Mercedes. The assassins appeared to be of Middle Eastern descent. Tonight, I awaken to find WMDs planted in our home. We're arrested and once again an attempt is made on our lives, but this time presumably by Asian hit men. Someone wants us out of the way and there's little doubt that they would prefer us dead, but why?"

"Somehow, Trissy, we present a very real threat to the successful execution of their plans. I've got to believe that this sudden interest in our lack of well-being stems from my attempts to contact the CDC. Remember, everything bad has transpired over the last several days."

"You're right. The timing just can't be coincidental. Several of the nurses, including Mean and Evil, knew you were contacting the CDC because of the deaths of the Asian sailors and all the other mysterious occurrences in that Muslim-run hell hole, Carencrow Regional. Rest assured, those malicious, self-serving buzzards told their bosom buddy Teresa. She, in turn, probably relayed an embellished version of the events up the chain of horrors," Trissy surmised with ever-increasing confidence.

"If Joint Commission only knew that those two disease-laden buzzards had carried the deadly H5N1 virus, they would've shut down Carencrow Regional and we would've been trouble free," Rex chuckled, clearly pleased with his sense of humor and his description of Mean and Evil.

"Rex, be serious for once. Honestly, why do you think we're being attacked from so many different directions?"

"The only viable explanation is that Chum is in bed with GeeHad. As disgusting and visually unappealing as that relationship would seem, somehow the radical snaggletoothed Muslim and the aggressive North Korean with the patchy Chia Pet face are working together. It would appear that they have conceived and are presently implementing some bizarre anti-American plot."

"Of course, that would explain the violent argument between GeeHad and Chum we observed at the Rula's last Wednesday, while we were having dinner. It appeared to be a business deal gone bad, but perhaps they were discussing the Asian sailors and their sudden appearance at Carencrow Regional," Trissy concluded.

"Now, that's highly likely," Rex replied as the wheels started turning. "You know, the more I replay recent events in my mind, the more convinced I become that all that has transpired is not as independent and unrelated as one would first assume. Remember the sequence of events. Last week, several dead Asian sailors were either found floating in the Caribbean or washed ashore in Galveston. They must have died in transit while steaming toward a designated location in Louisiana.

Undoubtedly, the ship's cargo included weapons of mass destruction. While in port, other disease-ravaged sailors mysteriously appeared at Carencrow Regional seeking medical attention. Within an hour, each had died an agonizingly painful death. Furthermore, by the next day, all records of their existence had vanished. Concurrently, I contact the CDC to voice my concerns and shortly thereafter, it became apparent that we needed to be eliminated," Rex added, reinforcing the connection between GeeHad and Chum, painting a picture with the information he and Trissy had assimilated.

"It's all starting to make sense. But what in the world could have been on board that ship that could cause such serious burns and kill so quickly?" Trissy pondered.

"Trissy, you're a genius!" Rex shouted before giving her a quick kiss on the cheek. "I've got it!" he announced with great excitement.

"Rex, what is it?"

"The word 'burn' kept running through my mind. Your skin and the skin of all the victims was burnt. Undoubtedly, the Asian sailors died of radiation poisoning. You and your fellow nurses were so preoccupied taking care of the sailors that you all were exposed to the intense radiation emanating from their dying bodies. That would explain the nausea and vomiting, the redness of the skin, and the blistering. The longer the exposure and the closer the proximity, the greater the amount of radiation absorbed. Thus, the more dangerous and threatening the symptoms became. Clearly, this was not the result of a virus or chemical/biological agents as we had first thought," Rex concluded.

"You mean to tell me that I've had my goose cooked by these slimy bastards?" Trissy screamed.

"Yes, from the inside out and the outside in, by a rather nasty collection of rapidly decaying radioactive isotopes."

"Well then, Sherlock, how do you explain the blue-tinged skin, the bright blue emesis, and the bluish excrement?" Trissy inquired with the hint of sarcasm as she put down her glass and crossed her arms, impatiently awaiting an answer.

"I'm not sure, but I'll figure it out, eventually," Rex replied as he continued to think what polar opposites, such as Chum and GeeHad, could possibly have to offer one another.

"Well, you'd better hurry up, because we're running out of time."

"What could North Korea possibly offer Islamic terrorists? They have been testing nuclear weapons for years but by all accounts, every test firing has met with limited success. Surely, if North Korea had developed a viable weapon, they wouldn't just give it away," Rex shared.

"Maybe they're in the dirty bomb business," Trissy injected.

"There's no doubt that Kim Jong-Il would do anything for a dollar, but if North Korea is on the production side of this evil scheme, that would mean that GeeHad is on the distribution side."

"Rex, that makes perfect sense. The North Koreans make money selling the weapons and greatly increase their stature by eliminating a superpower without doing the dirty work. Then, the Muslims destroy western civilization, bury Christianity, and spread their religion," Trissy suggested.

"Well, that sounds rather ambitious," Rex replied. "However, I believe you're right. They've attempted to either kill or discredit us. Now, they're determined to destroy the United States and take over the world."

"Rex, clearly my beautiful Mercedes was not destroyed by road rage, my illness was not the result of an indiscriminate winter virus, and the attempts on our lives not the result of mistaken identity," Trissy growled.

"Also, I might add that the invasion, occupation, and subsequent seizure of our home was not the result of a failure to pay the mortgage. So what if the government found a few WMDs just lying around the house? What's the big deal? It's not as if we cheated on our taxes or tracked carbon footprints across the White House lawn," Rex rationalized before taking another sip.

"Rex, I'd say we have our work cut out for us. In a matter of days, we need to stop the destruction of the United States, prevent the deaths of millions of our fellow citizens, expose GeeHad and Chum as terrorists, and clear our good names. How do you propose we go about accomplishing these rather lofty goals in a timely manner?" Trissy asked.

"I'd recommend that we pay an after-hours visit to Rula's and then to GeeHad's office," Rex replied.

"Excellent ideas. We may just uncover the clues that expose those two terrorists," Trissy confirmed.

"It's clearly time to go on the offensive," Rex announced confidently.

"Absolutely, but I must insist that I'm granted the opportunity to return the radioactive isotopes to there rightful owner, in person," Trissy snarled, shaking her fist.

"It's definitely time to kick ass and then kick some more ass. No prisoners will be taken," Rex replied, lifting his glass to Trissy's in a toast.

"Agreed," Trissy affirmed, tapping her glass against Rex's to seal the deal.

Both quickly polished off their drinks.

"Let's get a few hours of sleep. Early this morning I need to retrieve my bag of tricks from our home before we commence this operation," Rex proposed as he started to devise a strategy.

Suddenly, the serenity of their evening was interrupted and their well-conceived plan abruptly placed on hold by a loud knock on the front door.

"Oh shit! Trissy, douse the lights!"

Chapter 6

It was a magnificent evening. There were no clouds in the sky, the stars were bright, and the waters calm. A warm, gentle breeze bathed the *Il-sung* in the salty night air. The North Korean ship had successfully completed its secretive twelve knots and was only sixty miles from the entrance to the Panama Canal. The vast Pacific and freedom lay only a day's transit away. The ship had delivered her valuable cargo as ordered and a hero's welcome awaited the captain and his crew upon their return to Wanson. However, all was not well. Only hours before, the *Il-sung* had been ordered to stop by the *USS Kidd*, a guided missile frigate. Captain Asaki stood silently on the bridge of the *Il-sung* with his first officer at his side, looking through his binoculars and analyzing this new threat. He had advised the North Korean Central Command as well as Mohammad of this danger and was awaiting their guidance.

"We were so close to vanishing into the Pacific, but now the *Kidd* is only fifteen thousand yards off our starboard quarter," Captain Asaki complained to his first officer, Lieutenant Wasabi, as he lowered his binoculars.

"Captain, we're in Panamanian territorial waters and the canal no longer belongs to the Americans. Surely we can't be forced to meet our aggressor's demands," Lieutenant Wasabi replied confidently.

"Unfortunately, that's not the case. The Panamanians remain quite loyal to the United States. Should we enter the first lock, I feel certain that our ship would not be advanced and we would remain trapped within the confines of the canal," Captain Asaki replied in disgust.

"Well then, what alternatives do we have?" Lieutenant Wasabi asked as he watched the running lights of the United States warship grow nearer.

"Our options are limited. We don't have the speed to outrun the frigate or the armament to stand and fight," the captain stressed, coming to grips with the tactical situation and attempting to develop a strategy.

"Captain, Mohammad's reply," a crewman from the communications shack announced, as he stepped onto the bridge and handed Captain Asaki a white sheet of paper.

The captain read the message quickly. "We have been strongly advised to fight," Captain Asaki announced with an air of disbelief as he handed the response to Wasabi.

"That's not possible!" Lieutenant Wasabi responded as he read and then reread the message."There's no doubt that we'll be branded as cowards if we don't go down with the ship, Captain," the first officer emphasized as Captain Asaki paced the deck.

"That's an accurate assumption," the captain simply replied.

"We've lost twelve good men while delivering the WMD, and now Mohammad expects the rest of us to die for their cause," Lieutenant Wasabi reminded Captain Asaki, who was well aware of the sacrifice and the hardship his men had endured.

"If the Americans search the *Il-sung*, they will quickly discover that our ship delivered the radioactive material."

"There isn't any doubt that our successful mission would be compromised, Captain," Lieutenant Wasabi agreed.

"The embarrassment the disclosure would present to our government and the shame that it would bring to our families is far too great a price to bear. Therefore, that scenario will never unfold," Captain Asaki stated emphatically as Lieutenant Wasabi frantically thought of viable alternatives.

"What's the depth at our present location?" the captain asked as the *Il-sung* kept steaming toward her destination.

"In excess of eight hundred feet, Captain," Lieutenant Wasabi responded.

"We have three and only three options, Lieutenant. We can run the *Il-sung* aground and flee inland, in which case we would be faced with surviving an attack from malaria-laden mosquitos and deadly snakes as we trek through the dangerous jungle. There's little chance any of us would make it to the Pacific alive, let alone survive the subsequent six-thousand-mile swim back to our beloved homeland. Alternatively, we could scuttle the ship and beg our captors for mercy. Yet the *Il-sung* could be raised from that depth and our secret uncovered. Furthermore, knowing how brutal a Democratic government can be, we would most definitely be hanged in short order. Lastly, as Mohammad has insisted, we fight," Captain Asaki proposed, outlining the unpalatable alternatives.

"Have we heard from the North Korean Central Command, Captain?" Lieutenant Wasabi asked as he came to grips with the direction he felt certain Captain Asaki would choose.

"No, and I wouldn't expect a reply. Communications are too easily intercepted and our orders prior to sailing were exceedingly clear. Above all, North Korea is not in any way to be implicated in the plan to destroy the United States."

"I understand, and the more I think of our alternatives, I believe that Mohammad is right," Lieutenant Wasabi concluded.

"Without question, we must honor our ancestors and our families. However, we will do so with dignity. The Americans will never set foot on the *Il-sung*," Captain Asaki assured his first officer.

"Captain Asaki, it has been an honor to have served with you," Lieutenant Wasabi replied with pride as he silently prayed for the safety and well-being of his wife and his two beautiful young children at home.

"Destroying the warship *Kidd* with our unarmed but seaworthy *Il-sung* appears improbable but not impossible, my dear friend. Battle stations!" Captain Asaki growled, as if destined for greatness.

"Helmsman, all ahead flank, right full rudder."

"Aye, aye, Captain."

"Come to course eighty," the captain ordered after looking at the compass and drawing a reciprocal bearing to the *USS Kidd*, which was now only twelve thousand yards away and closing rapidly.

"Lieutenant Wasabi, I want every explosive and all available fuel transferred to the bow. I intend to ram and sink the *Kidd*," Captain Asaki ordered, while the *Il-sung* started to lean precariously to starboard as she came to her new heading.

"Yes, sir," Lieutenant Wasabi responded smartly, with no evidence of doubt or hesitation in his voice.

"Communications, this is the captain. I need the following message forwarded to North Korean Central Command and the world, immediately:

'While engaged in peaceful trade, the unarmed cargo ship Il-sung was attacked in international waters by a United States ship of war. The captain and twenty-five of his loyal shipmates were killed.'

We must assure our honored place in history, Lieutenant Wasabi," Captain Asaki shared with smile of confidence.

"Shall we also inform Mohammad of our intentions?" Captain Asaki's lieutenant asked.

"No, he's aware that we have no other choice. He will soon be apprised of the course we have chosen after the media gets ahold of our message."

"We shall be victorious!" Lieutenant Wasabi declared with pride.

"If not, the *Il-sung* will fade away into the obscurity of a deep watery grave," Captain Asaki replied as he lifted a pair of binoculars to his eyes.

"Communications, please instruct the *Kidd* that we will make all preparations to be boarded," Captain Asaki ordered as his vessel steamed into harm's way.

Minutes later, one hundred pounds of explosive and ten fifty-gallon barrels of fuel had been lashed to the bow.

The *Kidd* and the *Il-sung* were now a mere 1,500 yards apart and closing rapidly. The *Il-sung*'s boilers strained to generate enough steam to meet demand. The gauges in the engine room were redlined and the ship was now making an impressive eighteen knots.

"*Il-sung*, this is the United States warship *Kidd*. This is your last warning. Turn to starboard, stop your engines, and prepare to be boarded," the order blared over the speaker on the bridge of the dilapidated old rust bucket.

Captain Asaki walked out onto the flying bridge and lifted the binoculars to his eyes. The *USS Kidd* had turned slightly to port and given her bow wake, unquestionably increased her speed. It was evident that the captain had to make an adjustment in the *Il-sung's* course.

"Come right to seventy," Captain Asaki ordered calmly, as he maneuvered his ship to her destiny. He anticipated that at any moment the *Kidd* would turn hard to port in order to avert a collision.

Suddenly, the *Kidd's* five-inch gun began to fire. Captain Asaki could see flames leap from the barrel of the forward mount. Almost instantaneously, two columns of white frothy water rose from the sea, splashing onto the *Il-sung's* deck. The projectiles had struck the water less than ten yards off her port bow. The ship shuddered with the force of each explosion but her forward momentum was not deterred. Captain Asaki remained determined to keep the bow of the *Il-sung* pointed forward of the warship's intended course.

"Come right to fifty-five," Captain Asaki ordered. The *Kidd* had indeed initiated a hard turn to port as he had predicted. Binoculars were no longer necessary. The *Il-sung* was less than eight hundred yards away and closing rapidly.

Moments later, the darkness of the night was penetrated by several blinding flashes of light. The *Kidd's* forward and aft five-inch guns had begun firing in rapid succession. Multiple projectiles struck the *Il-sung* forward, amidships and on the bridge, ripping massive holes in her hull and superstructure. The ship shook so violently that she appeared to be lifted from the sea. Fires raged and thick black smoke suddenly engulfed the cargo ship. The *Il-sung's* forward momentum stopped nearly instantaneously. She was listing thirty degrees to port and her bow was now submerged. On the bridge, a dazed Captain Asaki found himself sprawled out on the deck. The navigator's table was ablaze and a thick grayish smoke filled the bridge. He wiped the blood from his face and slowly rose to his feet. The devastation was unimaginable. Glass was everywhere and metal had been twisted into bizarre configurations. The man-made materials, which had given life to this mistress of the sea, were quickly being consumed by fire and the resultant pungent odor made him gag. As pervasive and noxious as these charred remains where to the senses, they were overshadowed by the smell of death. The bodies of the signalman and the helmsman were nearly unrecognizable. The helmsman's head appeared unscathed but lay several feet from his body, while the signalman's limbs had been severely mangled and his chest cracked wide open as tall flames consumed what remained of his flesh.

In the dim, flickering light, Captain Asaki could see his lieutenant lying motionless. The captain rushed to his aid. As he knelt down beside his trusted friend, the captain could see that he was still breathing but had been mortally wounded. His intestines were eviscerated and the loops of bowel protruding from his bloodied abdomen appeared to swell before his very eyes. One leg was missing and the other twisted awkwardly behind his back.

"Captain, shall we abandon ship?" the lieutenant asked softly.

"No, my good friend, I shall not give that order," Captain Asaki replied, grasping Lieutenant Wasabi's hand tightly. The first officer's pupils were dilated and his eyes were glazed over. It was as if he were looking beyond him and into a different world.

"We have brought great honor to our families and our country," Lieutenant Wasabi whispered. "It has been a pleasure to have served..." he started to say with his last breath before his body went limp. Almost immediately, his lips became cyanotic and his skin took on a ghostly, mottled appearance. Captain Asaki hesitated for a moment. His eyes started to well up as he recalled all the memories they had shared over the many years spent sailing the seas. His lieutenant had always remained intensely loyal. Captain Asaki said a short prayer before releasing his grip and staggering to his feet.

In a matter of minutes, his bridge had been destroyed, lives had been lost, and his ship was sinking. His sadness was quickly replaced by anger. Through the smoke, he could make out a faint outline of the *USS Kidd.* The *Il-sung* was now listing forty degrees to port and lying deeper in the water.

The *Kidd* was a mere five hundred yards away, but Captain Asaki felt confident that the *Il-sung* would take her many secrets to the grave—until he realized that a boarding party had been launched. A small skiff, containing half a dozen men, was plowing through the calm seas. Soon the well-armed men would be aboard. This was clearly unacceptable.

"No!" Captain Asaki screamed as he raced to his stateroom. Under his bunk he quickly located the Type 68 pistol, which he had stashed away many years ago. "Not only should a captain go down with his ship, but he should also take as many of the enemy with him as he can. Long live North Korea!" Captain Asaki shouted, as he slipped the magazine into the butt of the gun and slid a round into the chamber. He grabbed a box of ammunition and scrambled back onto the starboard side of his ship to repel the invaders.

By this time, the boarding party had made their way alongside the mortally wounded cargo ship and several ropes had been tossed up and over the side. In short order, the metal cleats attached to the end of each rope snagged a secure portion of the *Il-sung*'s deck. The ropes were pulled taut and two American sailors began to scale the side of the dangerously listing ship slipping deeper and deeper into a watery grave. Fires were now raging out of control and the rusty old cargo ship was rocked frequently by internal explosions. The smoke, which billowed from all her wounds, played havoc with visibility, but the gentle night breeze occasionally whisked away the plumes, creating a window of opportunity.

"These pirates will pay with their lives for attempting to board my ship!" Captain Asaki screamed, and as the smoke cleared momentarily, he took aim at the men scaling the *Il-sung*. He popped off eight rounds in quick succession.

"Take that, you heathens!" the captain shouted with glee as one of the bullets found its mark. Donald James, an American sailor, suddenly released his grip on the rope he was climbing and fell back into the water, dead. In an instant, the captain was shrouded once again in a dense layer of black smoke. Several of the sailors on board the skiff discharged their automatic weapons in the captain's general direction, while others assisted their fallen comrade.

Finally, one of the *Kidd*'s sailors made it on to the deck. There would be no time to search the ship. He slipped off his black backpack and unloaded a small Geiger counter. Moments later he had gathered the invaluable information he had been sent to obtain. The thin black needle pegged to the left. The *Il-sung* was indeed the ship that had transported nuclear material to terrorists operating within the United States. Quickly, the sailor slung the backpack onto his shoulder, climbed over the side of the ship, and slid back down the rope. As soon as his foot hit the deck of the skiff, the coxswain slipped the engine into reverse and opened the throttle. As the small boat backed away from the dying ship, the entire boarding party kept their weapons trained on the North Korean cargo vessel.

Moments later, the coxswain briefly stopped the engines before shifting into forward gear and once again opened the throttle while he turned the wheel. As the small boat quickly spun around before racing back to the *USS Kidd*, the prevailing breeze once again swept away the smoke, exposing the man who had taken their shipmate's life. However, Captain Asaki was dead, his lifeless body draped over a railing, the superstructure behind him splattered with his blood.

Seconds later, the *Il-sung* turned turtle, exposing her entire hull, and the fires were suddenly extinguished. The cargo ship moaned violently as her stern was lifted out of the water. Her propellers appeared to be churning helplessly in the warm salty air. Several underwater explosions could be heard and the seas seemed to boil as the *Il-sung* slipped beneath the tranquil Caribbean waters on a magnificent starlit night.

Chapter 7

"Oh no!" Trissy screamed, leaping from the couch.

Again, there was a loud knock at the front door of their newly adopted home.

"I knew we shouldn't have had the Sambuca without adding the three coffee beans for luck!" Trissy whispered loudly as Rex fumbled for the remote control.

"I know. I know! I'll kill the lights. Grab our clothes and the sneakers!" Rex insisted as the television screen went dark and he scrambled toward the backdoor. But there was no response. Trissy was long gone.

Quicker and more agile than her husband, Trissy was already headed toward the rear of the house while successfully extinguishing every light in her path. Her heart was racing and each time the heavy fist collided with a flimsy front door, it seemed to skip a beat. However, she reacted instinctively. Her thoughts were clear and her actions precise. The gray ominous veil of deception brought on by the hypothermia had been lifted. Gone as well were the excruciatingly painful and debilitating leg cramps. Trissy dashed to the laundry room and flung open the dryer. The tumbler was still spinning and the green scrubs started to flop out, with more and more clothing greeting her with each rotation.

"Thank God they're dry," Trissy whispered as she rapidly gathered the laundry using the hue cast by a dusky appliance bulb.

Rex crawled to the lighting panel adjacent to the back patio door and flipped all the switches off. Suddenly, the living room, the kitchen, and the patio went dark. With the exception of the gas fireplace generating radiant bursts of blue, orange, and red flames, there was little illumination. In one fluid motion, his hand continued down to the sliding glass door, which led to the patio. There was a subtle click as the lock on this flimsy see-through barrier was secured.

Just as quickly as it had begun, the incessant bone-rattling pounding at the front door ceased. Rex was now keenly aware of the beating of his heart, which generated a thundering pulse. With the exception of a whooshing, flickering sound produced by the updraft in the fireplace, all was silent.

Suddenly and unexpectedly, the patio door started to rattle. Rex hugged the adjacent wall, attempting to remain out of sight. Soon, the rattle turned into a violent movement in which the aluminum frame began to grind and twist. Rex looked down at the kitchen counter where earlier he had noticed a butcher block housing an assortment of rather fine German cutlery. He quickly selected a razor-sharp fourteen-inch weapon with a serrated blade. He held the knife tightly in his right hand and, with his arm flexed, was ready to strike. There was no doubt in his mind that the glass was about to shatter. As a former Navy SEAL, Rex had played these hunter-killer games before. He was well aware of the importance of patience and timing in the successful execution of the kill. He would wait for his quarry to take one step into the home before driving the knife deep into his heart.

Trissy was startled by the loud rattling sound coming from the living room. It appeared to grow more intense and threatening as she made her way down the darkened hallway. She stopped suddenly and slowly peered around the corner and into the large darkened living room. Her eyes immediately triggered on the movement outside. There was a massive figure, which appeared to grow in size as the light from the fireplace cast shadows, magnifying the large man's stature. She was shocked at the amount of force the intruder exercised in his attempt to gain entry.

Suddenly, the loud noise resolved and all was relatively quiet with the exception of a low-pitched creaking sound as the thin sheet of glass slowly took on additional strain. From the corner of his eye, Rex could see a circle of steam form on the window, which quickly grew in diameter. Rex could not visualize the man, but he most certainly felt his presence as his weight bowed the glass pane inward.

From Trissy's vantage point, she could see the intruder cup his hands and place his face against the thin glass pane. She was overwhelmed by a spine-tingling sensation as the hairs on the back of her neck rose at the site of the grossly contorted caricature peering into the living room.

Then, just as quickly as the threat had materialized, the circle of steam vanished and the man was gone.

Rex released the death grip he had on the handle of his lethal weapon. The tension in the air eased for a moment as he looked around. He noticed Trissy in the far corner.

"Stay low and follow me," Rex whispered, pointing toward the other side of the house. He placed the knife in his mouth, fell to his knees, and crawled through the kitchen and into the hallway, which led to the master bedroom. Trissy was hot in pursuit with one arm tightly wrapped around their warm clean clothes.

Once in the windowless hallway, Rex knew they were out of sight of prying eyes.

"Here, you may need these," Trissy suggested, handing Rex his mud-stained, battle-worn scrubs.

"Thanks," Rex replied as they both stood to put on their clothes. Within seconds the change was complete. In a rapid flurry of arm and leg movements, their damp robes had been discarded and replaced by warm scrubs.

"Damn, my sneakers are still wet," Rex groaned, kneeling down to tie his shoelaces.

"Rex, don't complain. Mine are, too. Now, either there's a blue light special or we're surrounded," Trissy surmised as she saw the flashing blue lights penetrating both the front and rear windows of the home.

"Christ!" Rex gasped as the interior of the home suddenly became awash in a dull blue, interrupted by blinding flashes of white light.

"Well, what do you think?" Rex asked.

"What do you mean, what do I think?" Trissy responded in amazement, unsure as to whether Rex had grasped the seriousness of their situation. "I think we're in big trouble," she stressed before their predicament suddenly took a turn for the worse.

"This is Special Agent in Charge Richter of the FBI. I strongly suggest, Doctor, that you and your wife surrender immediately. The home is surrounded and I assure you that this time there will be no escape. You have only five minutes in which to choose life or death," Richter announced over a microphone as he peered over the hood of his vehicle parked in close proximity to the Jacuzzi.

"I must say that the persistent little bulldog is rather blunt. How in the world did they find us so quickly?" Rex wondered.

"I don't know, but there is one thing for certain. Richter is not pleased with us," Trissy emphasized.

"Well then, I suppose it's time to execute Plan B."

"What happened to Plan A?" Trissy asked, trying to analyze Rex's newfangled coding system.

"Plan A is outside and ready to be executed. Now, all we need is Plan B, which in turn, should lead us to Plan A," Rex replied with a sense of pride and confidence.

"Rex, you're losing me. Don't you need Plan A to get to Plan B?"

"That's the standard, mundane thinking in the civilized world north of the equator. I'm thinking out-of-the-box, south of the equator, where booze is cheap, sunshine is plentiful, and everything spins harmoniously in the opposite direction," Rex replied.

"Surely you're joking. Rex, please tell me you're joking," Trissy insisted as she watched Rex struggle for a response.

"Huh," Rex mumbled while stroking his chin.

"Huh?" Trissy gasped in self-doubt as she began tapping her foot on the floor, expending nervous energy before deciding to take another tack. "Well then, just what exactly does Plan B consist of?"

"Dr. and Mrs. Bent, you have two minutes in which to decide if you will die in the electric chair or from lead poisoning. Personally, as traitors and terrorists, I would prefer you both go down in a hail of bullets," Richter announced before clipping a magazine into his automatic weapon and releasing the safety. The FBI agents and various police officers, with their weapons at the ready, started to chuckle. They truly enjoyed SAC Richter's John Wayne style of law enforcement.

"That does it. There'll be no Christmas presents from us to that inbred turkey!" Rex responded trying to make light of a very real threat.

"Stay focused, Rex. Plan B, what's Plan B?" Trissy prodded.

"I'm thinking, I'm thinking," Rex growled, while rubbing his forehead.

"Well, think faster!" Trissy insisted, watching Rex open a hallway closet.

"Here we go," Rex announced rather nonchalantly as he handed Trissy a stack of fluffy white towels.

"I'm already dry. What do you expect me to do with these?" Trissy asked, trying to see over the top of the stacked cotton gifts.

"Trissy, it's time that we send the SAC a smoke signal," Rex insisted, pushing down gently on the top of the stack of towels, revealing Trissy's beautiful eyes.

"This is a diversion that I learned from our good old friend, Chief Black Cloud," Rex made up as he tried to build his case. He could clearly see that Trissy was not buying the story, so he immediately decided to embellish the attributes of someone they both knew quite well. "I'm sure that boy could put his ear to the ground and know exactly how many police cars were surrounding this home," Rex continued.

Trissy looked bewildered, her concerns immediately apparent. "Rex, Chief Black Cloud, although a good nurse, was a paranoid schizophrenic who was miserable to work with because he always brought bad luck to every shift. Even when he wasn't drinking firewater, he was hearing voices and believed everyone was out to get him. Don't you remember?"

"This is SAC Richter. You have ninety seconds left before we open fire."

"Trissy, I realize that now is not the time for true confessions, but I suddenly feel overwhelmed by an intense sense of paranoia myself. I can now clearly see where Chief Black Cloud was coming from. I, as well, am tortured by the visual and auditory hallucinations. I keep seeing a very territorial bulldog barking through a bullhorn and the bowed-up bastard keeps announcing that he's out to get us," Rex relayed, much to Trissy's surprise.

"Rex, we've gone far beyond the realm of probability. We're now in the absolute certainty range. He is out to get us!" Trissy assured her husband.

"Not to fear, my love, now is the time to face our demon. I can clearly see that this situation calls for desperate measures. With a few bells and whistles, of course," Rex added as he calmly leaned forward and pushed the panic button on the alarm system above Trissy's head. Suddenly, the home was flooded by the loud, irritating pulsating siren.

"Trissy, stuff the towels into the fireplace!" Rex yelled.

"What?" Trissy screamed, dropping the towels and pressing her hands against her ears.

"Stuff the towels into the fireplace!" Rex screamed over the unanticipated intensity of the deafening decibel-shrieking speaker just above them.

"What?" Trissy yelled, fighting to preserve her eardrums and her sanity.

"Christ, seventy seconds," Rex mumbled to himself after glancing at his watch. Valuable seconds were ticking away. He had to act quickly. Rex gathered the towels, scurried past Trissy and dashed into the living room. Hidden behind the couch, he rapidly stuffed the towels into the fireplace.

"Mission complete with thirty seconds to spare," Rex announced with pride before looking at the large cardboard box containing packages of firecrackers he had positioned adjacent to living room couch.

Instantaneously, the fire roared to life and a thick grayish black cloud engulfed the cozy living room. Rex coughed and gagged as he grabbed the box, turned it on its side, and kicked it away from him. A good portion of the contents fell onto the hearth in close proximity to the heat and flames.

"That will have to do," Rex concluded before scrambling back into the hallway where he grabbed Trissy by the arm. Together, they quickly made their way into the garage where the sounds from the alarm system were not as intense or bone-jarring.

"Excellent," Rex shouted, observing that the garage door had remained locked one foot above the concrete floor and the thick line of gunpowder he had laid down earlier had not been disturbed.

"What in the hell is going on in there?" Richter shouted in an attempt to be heard over the obnoxious alarm.

"It appears that they've set the place on fire," one of his men concluded as they watched the black smoke billowing from the chimney before rolling off of the roof and onto the lawn.

"I can't see a damn thing in the living room anymore, with the exception of an occasional flickering dull flame," another law enforcement officer complained.

"Well, I surely won't lose any sleep knowing those two maggots burned to death," Richter shouted, grinding his teeth in disgust while lifting the bullhorn. He realized his threat would not be heard but felt compelled from a PR standpoint to issue additional warnings.

"You Muslim maggots have fifteen seconds," SAC Richter boldly announced.

"Thanks for the countdown," Rex announced appreciatively. As he reached into his pocket, he looked back into the hallway. A thick cloud of black smoke was rapidly rolling toward the garage. He was quickly running out of time and it was imperative that he execute his plan before the FBI agents had a chance to open fire. He had no doubt that his Neanderthal nemesis would blink in the confusion, which would surely follow.

"Ten seconds, you maggots!" Richter screamed as Rex pulled a matchbook from his pocket and struck the wooden fire stick against the rough gritty edge.

"Get down low, Trissy," Rex insisted as the flame came to life and his watch alarm started to chime.

"Obviously, Rectal Richter needs to invest in a better chronometer. His timing's off," Rex criticized.

"Trissy, Plan B is now underway. When I say 'go,' crawl under the garage door and sprint into the woods where our chariot awaits. Whatever you see, whatever you hear, don't look back!" Rex instructed before tossing the lit match onto his improvised fuse.

The gunpowder ignited and the flame quickly raced out the garage toward prearranged explosive destinations. All that was left was a wide charred line and an intense smell of burnt gunpowder.

The smoke from the crudely stoked fireplace quickly engulfed the garage. Trissy and Rex started to cough as they inhaled the noxious fumes. Both remained crouched low. As Rex gazed into Trissy's eyes through the haze, he could plainly see that there was no sense of fear or concern. All that was revealed was an intense concentration and a strong will to survive. Trissy had tuned out the loud constant wailing sounds, which had continued to announce the activation of the home security and now the fire alarm. She patiently awaited Rex's signal. They were both focused and determined to avoid capture.

Suddenly, there were four loud explosions in rapid succession.

"GO, GO, GO!" Rex yelled at the top of his lungs.

Trissy sprinted to the garage door and quickly slid underneath. Rex followed a split second later. Once clear of the metal barrier they scrambled to their feet and took off running through dense clouds of smoke. As they successfully dodged large fallen tree limbs before reaching the forest, each was keenly aware of the multitude of explosions, bright flashes of intense light, and loud whistling sounds that seemed to follow them into the darkness.

"This way, Trissy," Rex whispered loudly, darting past her. He could see the clearing ahead where he had hidden the four-wheeler earlier in the evening.

"Yes, the beast is still here," Rex announced with great satisfaction before straddling the odd-looking vehicle with the wide knobby tires. As he fired up the chariot and revved the engine, Rex felt empowered as the adrenaline surged through his system. He was back in his element, playing cat-and-mouse games. The transition had been complete. The warrior, who had sacrificed so much to become a healer, had been transformed back into a warrior. He truly enjoyed combat and the struggle for life and death. Most importantly, once again he was overwhelmed with a youthful feeling of immortality.

"Rex, you put on one hell of a fireworks display," Trissy gasped, emerging from the forest, staggered toward the vehicle. "I'm exhausted," she added, struggling to catch her breath.

The explosions and the flashes of light had ceased, but both were once again aware of the irritating, nerve-racking sounds generated by the alarms.

"Well, thank you, Trissy. Let's just hope they don't send us the bill!" Rex replied as Trissy hopped on board.

"Now, before I forget, let me assure you that neither Plan A nor Plan B were disappointing. However, for a moment there, I must admit that I had my doubts," Trissy confessed as she placed her arms around Rex's waist.

"That's certainly reassuring," Rex responded.

Seconds later, the muted sounds of multiple explosions could be heard as the firecrackers ignited. Almost simultaneously, the sounds intensified as small arms fire erupted from outside the home. Automatic weapons, shotguns, and rifles were being discharged at an unimaginable rate, penetrating the wooden facade and shattering glass.

"It sounds like World War III just erupted," Rex announced with great joy, as an awesome high-pitched sound of rolling thunder filled the frigid night air.

"Well, you've got to give Richter all the credit. The brainless pit bull does more than just bark," Rex added before pausing for a moment to reflect on their harrowing escape. Suddenly and unexpectedly, Rex started to laugh uncontrollably.

"What's so funny?" Trissy insisted upon knowing.

"Nothing but more pleasant auditory and visual hallucinations, my dear. I can see and hear Dr. Fubar's reaction to the changes our quirky destructive design team has brought to his exquisite egotistical little hideaway. For some reason, I don't think he'll be pleased!" Rex howled, slipping the four-wheeler into gear.

"Oh, I never thought about that. Perhaps we can send him something nice for Christmas," Trissy chuckled.

"Absolutely, do you think he would appreciate receiving Richter's rather large head mounted on a silver platter?"

"Rex, how gruesome."

"My sincerest apologies," Rex snickered while slipping the clutch.

"I'm telling you, Rex, hours ago the world thought we were dead. Now, we're in big trouble and it all started after we angered the gods! Never, I repeat, never, ever drink Sambuca unless those three little beans are floating on the surface," Trissy insisted.

"Excellent advice, my love," Rex replied as he opened the throttle.

The wheels began to spin and the rear end started to fishtail in the soft dirt. Moments later Rex and Trissy were off, racing into the darkness toward a safe haven, yet to be determined.

Chapter 8

The narrow, windy, tree-lined state highway was littered with tributes to victims who had lost control and failed to negotiate the many unexpected turns. It was ten thirty in the evening. A canary yellow Hummer raced down the darkened blacktop at a speed that was far too excessive. The adjacent shoulder was soft, the danger hidden beneath a layer of fallen brown leaves. As the heavy vehicle slowly drifted off the main path, the sandy shoulder gave way, grabbing at the tread of the wide, unsuspecting tires. Suddenly, the rear end fishtailed slightly, but the driver never lost control, nor did he ever let up on the gas.

"Crap!" Dr. Fubar growled, when he felt his vehicle shimmy. He'd been in the operating room when he received a distressing call informing him that his highly prized river camp was on fire. He immediately dropped his instruments and abandoned his patient without saying a word. The nurses were in shock, as was his young patient with a massive brain tumor, who lay on the operating room table under-anesthetized yet paralyzed. The patient could hear everything that was going on but was unable to move. With his cerebral spinal fluid drained, the not-so-good doctor had just completed sawing through the top portion of his skull. A chisel and wooden mallet completed the job. With just a few taps, the calvarium popped off, exposing the diseased brain. Unexpectedly, the operation was placed on hold—indefinitely.

"I'll return to Santa's little workshop in a few hours," Dr. Fubar thought as he sped down the deserted road. "In the meantime, my obedient OR elves will either ignore my absence and mind the shop or suffer horrific consequences," the neurosurgeon chuckled, while thinking of all the power he wielded. This power was the result of being the top income producer for the hospital. Patient outcome be damned, Carencrow Regional would protect him at any cost and he knew it.

Dr. Fubar was bound and determined to reach his camp, which lay only one more mile down the road. With his mind now clouded by anger, he never noticed passing his four-wheeler heading in the opposite direction.

"Wasn't that Fubar?" Rex yelled to Trissy.

"Could have been," Trissy screamed back over the roar of the engine and the deafening windy turbulence.

"I certainly hope he doesn't mind us borrowing his four-wheeler," Rex snickered as he gave the commandeered toy a little more gas.

Dr. Fubar slammed on the brakes. The tires screeched as they strained to rapidly slow the massive, style-less rectangular beast. The smell of burnt rubber was in the air as the Hummer turned to the right and onto his limestone drive. His speed was still too excessive but, in his haste, Dr. Fubar depressed the gas pedal even further. The back of the Hummer quickly slid to the left.

"Shit!" the neurosurgeon screamed, attempting to regain control by turning the steering wheel to the left, but he had run out of time and road. The gas-guzzling ironclad plowed into a large pine tree, which had mysteriously fallen across the path leading to his home only moments before. There was a loud explosion as the mass of metal was twisted into a new and more aesthetically pleasing configuration. The ornate chrome grill was ripped off before the wheels had even attempted to negotiate the man-made obstacle. The forward momentum was such that the vehicle momentarily left the ground, but something so ugly was never meant to fly. The force of the impact sheared off the front axle and bent the frame like a pretzel. When the vehicle came to rest, the front end was angled at forty-five degrees and the headlights pointed toward the heavens. Unfortunately, you couldn't kill this ill-tempered mean SOB. Given the severity of this accident, the gods had refused to claim Fubar's sorry soul on this fateful evening.

"Goddamn it!" Dr. Fubar shouted in disgust before starting to cough excessively after inhaling the irritating plumb of powder, which had coated the recently deployed airbag.

"Son of a bitch!" the notoriously arrogant and egotistical physician screamed as he attempted to crawl out of his demolished road demon. However, given its newly found orientation, every time he flung open the driver's side door, it immediately slammed shut. After several attempts, he was finally successful in extricating himself from the outrageously expensive metal death trap.

Dr. Fubar moaned as he collided with the ground. He lay motionless for a moment to ensure that he had not broken anything in the fall.

"My Hummer, my beautiful Hummer," Dr. Fubar cried, dusting off his scrubs and surveying the damage. Steam billowed from the contorted hood and there was a loud hissing sound as escaping radiator fluid suddenly vaporized upon striking the hot engine.

But his grief was short-lived. His accident went unnoticed and the sound of gunfire erupted once again as the FBI agents decided to pump more rounds into his lush camp. Weapons were discharged without aiming and fired as rapidly as possible. Dr. Fubar parted two large bushy branches as he climbed over the fallen tree, which now proudly displayed the newly acquired Hummer ornament. As the dense clusters of pine needles separated, a maddening scene came into view. Persistently irritating blue lights kept silently flashing and there appeared to be several unmarked cars and police cruisers surrounding his camp. At least a dozen men were using their vehicles as shields and shooting at his home.

"What in the hell is going on here?" the exasperated self-proclaimed demigod shouted as he attempted to understand why his home was under siege.

"Stop! Stop! You're destroying my camp!" Dr. Fubar peered through the smoky haze that engulfed his hideaway. The sounds of shotguns and automatic weapons being discharged and the shattering of glass, along with the sight of the pulverized wooden exterior, were almost too much to bear. He staggered out from behind the fallen pine tree in a state of shock and madly began to wave his arms to gain the officers' attention. No one took notice, so Dr. Fubar ran toward the back of his property where there appeared to be more activity.

"You sorry bastards!" the angry neurosurgeon screamed, continuing to wave his arms. Suddenly, the gunfire ceased. The camp was now surrounded by a magnificent silence, which was only broken by the sound of each man reloading his weapon and the now hysterical Dr. Fubar beating on the hood of an unmarked FBI vehicle.

"You fucking sorry bastards! You've destroyed my camp!" Dr. Fubar yelled. His anger had now turned into an insatiable rage evidenced by the multiple deep dents he had placed on the hood of the Ford.

"Get down!" one of the agents demanded.

"I'll kill the son-of-a-bitch who's behind this outrage!" Dr. Fubar threatened, waving his index finger at the agent hunkered down behind the vehicle.

"Thibodeaux, Coubereaux, restrain that man," SAC Richter ordered, watching the aggressive behavior of a madman in fluorescent orange scrubs.

"Goddamn it! Get off of me, you horny bastards!" Dr. Fubar mumbled as they took him down. A rather large knee kept his face firmly planted in Mother Earth. Yet, he continued to struggle as his arms were twisted behind his back. The handcuffs were placed with flawless precision and he was pulled to his feet in one fluid motion.

"I'm the son of a bitch in charge of this operation. If you have a problem with the way I'm conducting business, then I suggest you get it off your chest—NOW!" Richter growled, wiping his face clear of the tobacco juice, which had rolled down his chin.

As the son of a hard drinking, hard fighting roustabout, Sammy Richter had spent all his summers working in hot, humid, and unforgiving oil fields in Texas. Born and raised in Houston, he had attended Kinkaid High School before heading to Texas A&M and later, the FBI Academy. Always mission-oriented, Richter never learned how to relate to his fellow man. He never married, never socialized, and each year became meaner and meaner. He truly had become one ornery son of a bitch!

"I want your badge. Your ass is mine!" the physician threatened as he spit dirt and grass from his mouth.

"We'll see 'bout that. What's your name?" Richter demanded.

Dr. Fubar's nostrils started to flare and he made a grotesque snorting sound as he started to breathe faster and deeper. "Never have I been so humiliated. I'm close to royalty in this town, and now I'm being treated like a common criminal!" he yelled, then tried to intimidate Richter by silently staring him down.

"Last chance, Howdy Doody. Give me your name or suffer the consequences," Richter insisted, grabbing Dr. Fubar's scrub top, twisting the material and yanking him closer for a little "face time."

"Fubar, Dr. Ulysses B. Fubar," the defeated physician conceded as Richter released his grip and pushed him away.

"Well, Mr. Fubar, perhaps you can tell me what you're doing here on such a fine evening."

"That's *Dr.* Fubar," the arrogant neurosurgeon responded curtly.

"Well, I suppose anyone can have delusions of grandeur. But you still haven't answered my question. What in the hell are you doing here tonight?" Richter demanded, his patience quickly wearing thin.

"This is my camp and you're trespassing on my property," Dr. Fubar growled.

"Are we now? Well then, Doctor, perhaps you wouldn't mind giving us a guided tour of your fine camp," Richter requested as the fire trucks arrived and struggled to gain access to the property.

"No Goddamn way! Not until I see some ID," Fubar demanded.

"I'm the Special Agent in Charge of the FBI's investigation on terrorism in Carencrow. The last name is Richter," the SAC responded, flashing his badge.

"Thibodeaux, Coubereaux, follow me and do ensure that the good doctor tags along," Richter added as he walked off toward the camp.

"Chambers, you and your men enter through the front. We're going in the back."

Dr. Fubar was strong-armed along as he continued to resist the agents. Richter stepped onto the patio. The sound of glass crunching beneath his feet was magnified in the darkness. The sliding glass door had been reduced to a few dangling angry shards. The large flames in the gas fireplace had subsided. The towels had been totally consumed, yet smoke still filled the living room.

"What kind of doctor are you, anyway?" Richter asked as he turned toward his prisoner.

"A neurosurgeon, a brain surgeon to you laymen," the ego-inflated doctor responded. "And I am the finest neurosurgeon in the country," he added without hesitation.

"Ah, you don't say. Lead the way, Jethro," Richter insisted as he motioned to Dr. Fubar to enter the camp.

"The light switch is on the wall to your left," the doctor said after being shoved forward.

"That's all I expect, just a little cooperation," Richter announced after flicking the bank of switches upward. "Well, I'm amazed you don't have an electrical problem," he added as the lights came on.

Even with all the smoke, the destruction was now more than evident and truly overwhelming. The fine sofa appeared to have been shredded by an angry animal. Stuffing was everywhere. The walls had suffered a similar fate. Large sections of drywall were missing and plaster scattered throughout.

"Ah, my mounts!" Dr. Fubar screamed as he looked at the tattered remains of the trophies he had traveled the world to hunt. "You bastards have killed my animals, my beautiful animals."

"Yea, well, get over it," Richter suggested.

"Thibodeaux, go to the left, Coubereaux, to the right. And for Christ's sake, turn off the Goddamn alarms!" Richter screamed, snapping his fingers.

"What's the code?" Thibodeaux screamed to the now dejected doctor as the alarms continued to wail.

"One-nine-five-four," Dr. Fubar disclosed reluctantly.

SAC Richter's men disappeared in an instant to search what remained of the camp.

Suddenly, there was a large crash as the front door imploded.

"I believe that's Chambers who has come a-knockin'," Richter snickered.

"What do we have here, Doctor?" Richter asked, noticing two glasses on the coffee table.

"That coffee table was clean when I was here two days ago. Someone's been in my camp," Dr. Fubar concluded with anger and disgust. "And they've had the balls to drink my liquor," he added after noticing the shattered bottle with a familiar label lying on the rug.

"Doctor, I'm sure you're well aware of the penalty for treason. Now, I want you to think very, very carefully. Have you directly or indirectly supported terrorist activities against the United States of America?"

"You must be joking. Absolutely not!" the insulted physician replied in no uncertain terms.

"Well then, has this camp ever been used to harbor terrorists?" Richter demanded.

"You're fucking insane," the neurosurgeon shot back.

"Now, correct me if I'm wrong, but I believe it's the second cervical vertebra that is shattered after a short drop from a long rope," Richter shared, recalling what he had learned from a Clint Eastwood movie. He spit a wad of tobacco-stained saliva onto the living room floor as he awaited the reply.

"That's a hangman's fracture, and I'm brilliant at repairing the injury, should the victim survive," Dr. Fubar growled angrily after observing the Richter's barnyard etiquette.

"But, my arrogant friend, the question is, are you good enough to operate on yourself?" Richter asked with a shit-eating grin, which revealed his tobacco-stained teeth.

Chambers, Thibodeaux, and Coubereaux returned to the living room.

"Anything, gentlemen?" Richter asked.

"No, sir," Chambers and Thibodeaux responded in unison.

"Not that it means anything, but I found two wet bathrobes lying in the hallway," Special Agent Coubereaux disclosed.

"Don't even tell me that they were using my fucking robes!" Dr. Fubar screamed.

"My, aren't we rather high-strung, doctor," SAC Richter chuckled. "Thibodeaux, gather the robes and have those crystal glasses dusted for fingerprints."

"Yes, sir."

"Dr. Fubar, you're not friends with a Dr. Bent, are you?" Richter inquired rather nonchalantly.

"I recently crushed that bastard like a fly after he had the balls to confront me," Dr. Fubar relayed without remorse.

"I see. Well, just to make your day complete, we believe he's been hiding out in your house," Richter disclosed, anxiously awaiting a volatile, high-spirited reply.

"Bent! If that bastard is behind this disaster, I'll hunt him down like a dog and kill him with my own fucking bare hands!" Dr. Fubar shouted as his face turned red.

"We'll get Bent, but you're not going to get the chance for two reasons: Number one, that's going to be my pleaure, and number two, you'll be behind bars," Richter relayed joyfully as he looked at the shattered trophies dangling precariously from the wall surrounding the fireplace.

"No…!" Dr. Fubar screamed, as every fiber in his body started to spasm.

"Chambers, I expect this animal refugee camp to be examined with a fine-tooth comb. Rip apart what remains of the damn thing, if you have to," SAC Richter barked.

"Yes, sir," Chambers responded affirmatively while smiling at the doctor.

Dr. Fubar looked at Richter with disbelief as he rattled and tugged at the handcuffs on his bound wrists. With his hands firmly secured behind his back, he realized that this nightmare was real. In all his years he had never encountered anyone as cold, calculating, and arrogant as he.

"Come, my petulant neurosurgeon. You have an appointment with the gallows. And as your judge, jury, and executioner, I'd like to assure you that I look forward to your death by hanging!" An angry but satisfied SAC Richter growled as he stormed past the prisoner and out the sliding glassless door of Dr. Fubar's newly remodeled camp.

Chapter 9

As Rex and Trissy raced down the dark narrow highway, Rex could see several vehicles ahead speeding toward them, sporting an endless line of silent blue flashing lights.

"Oh, Christ, reinforcements!" Rex shouted into the wind, as he slowed the four-wheeler they had recently absconded from the arrogant self-appointed aristocrat, Dr. Fubar. Instinctively, Rex pulled as far over onto the soft shoulder as he dared and doused the headlights, hoping they would go unnoticed.

"Damn," Rex cursed as the handlebars were suddenly and unexpectedly nearly ripped from his grip. He fought to maintain control of the off-road all-terrain chariot as the right front wheel hit the loose sand lining the blacktop.

The threatening vehicles rapidly grew closer. There would be no time to veer off into the dense woods. Suddenly, bright lights blinded Rex as the lead vehicle turned on its high beams.

"Trissy, get down," Rex yelled, leaning forward in an attempt to blend in with the frame of the four-wheeler. Trissy never heard Rex's words but followed his actions. However, the contrast between the green scrubs and the bright red Polaris stuck out like a blue light special at an underfunded police convention.

Two black unmarked vehicles and three police cruisers soon shot by. In his rearview mirror, Rex could see several of the police cruisers struggling to come to a stop. Their aspect changed quickly as the red taillights faded and the white headlights illuminated the woods.

"I told you we were in big trouble!" Trissy shouted to Rex after looking over her shoulder. She had no doubt that the police would soon be in hot pursuit.

"That does it. We're getting camouflaged scrubs for Christmas," Rex replied as he carefully maneuvered the four-wheeler back onto the blacktop.

"I'm open for suggestions," he added.

"Well then, open the throttle and get us the hell out of here!" Trissy ordered, holding on to him tightly.

"Will do," Rex shouted with gusto as he gave the thirsty engine a large gulp of gas. The four-wheeler responded immediately. As the speedometer rocketed past eighty, Rex wished the noisy beast had wings. However, that was not to be. Knowing that the officers would radio ahead to set up a roadblock, Rex struggled to think of some viable means of escape.

"Rex, there's a dirt road a half-mile ahead, on your left," Trissy shouted into the deafening wind.

"What?"

"Dirt—ROAD!" Trissy yelled, pointing to her left.

"Gotcha," Rex shouted. Moments later he spotted the narrow turnoff.

Rex slammed on the brakes. He could feel the rough unforgiving asphalt grind down the knobby rubber tread. The four-wheeler started to fishtail as the vehicle continued to slide forward. Rex let up on the breaks momentarily in order to regain control.

"We're not going to make it!" Rex yelled after realizing that his speed was still too great to safely negotiate the abrupt turn. But they were simply out of time. He had to take the chance.

"Lean!" he shouted as he shifted his torso to his left while twisting the handlebars in the same direction.

Trissy screamed as the unstable four-wheeler suddenly became precariously balanced on its two right wheels. She leaned to her left and increased her death grip around Rex's waist, fully expecting to flip at any moment.

The four-wheeler continued to slide in the dangerous high-speed turn as it left the asphalt and ran onto the dirt road. Instantaneously, the left wheels slammed down and the vehicle started to spin. Several hair-raising moments later, Rex regained control. They had survived the death-defying maneuver. Rex was clearly proud of their success.

"I enjoy the smell of burnt rubber on a bitterly cold winter evening," Rex shared with Trissy as the four-wheeler came to a stop.

"Yes. Well, we all have our quirks. Personally, I would enjoy a warm fire and a stiff nightcap," a shivering, teeth-chattering Trissy replied as her body struggled to replenish the heat lost on their windy jaunt.

Rex and Trissy could hear the sound of sirens growing louder and turned around, hoping they had evaded the threat. Through the cloud of dust they had created, they could see the police vehicles race by the obscure turnoff. The sounds of sirens faded momentarily but then quickly intensified.

"I'd say we need to get a little bit farther down this road," Rex suggested, turning on the headlights and opening the throttle. He was certain the law enforcement officers had seen the plume of dust, which marked their exit from the highway. Without question, the police had turned around yet again.

"Good idea," Trissy said. The tires spun, throwing more dirt and gravel into the air before gaining traction.

Soon, the four-wheeler was flying down the small access road. However, the seldom-used road was littered with large deep potholes, and whenever the four-wheeler slammed into a rutty depression, Rex and Trissy were violently jerked forward, forcing them to fight just to keep from being launched from their seats.

"Flying over the handlebars and subsequently being run over by this heavy ATV would not be a pleasant way to end our flight from justice," Rex shouted, swerving to avoid a menacing pothole only to come face-to-face with a more challenging obstacle: a giant sinkhole.

"Oh!" Rex and Trissy screamed in unison after the four-wheeler briefly went airborne before touching down in the twenty-foot-wide crater. Rex never let off the throttle. The off-road vehicle bounced once and then flew out the other side. However, once again, gravity prevailed, and the vehicle came crashing down with a loud snap, followed by the grinding of metal with each subsequent bump in the road. Now, more than ever, Rex and Trissy could feel their spines crack and compress with each jolt.

"Christ, now what?" Rex shouted as soon as he noticed that the vehicle was not riding as smoothly as it had previously.

"It's the shocks," Trissy yelled.

"Ah," Rex responded, shaking his head while continuing to look forward in order to anticipate the unexpected.

The police vehicles were now rambling down the dirt road at high speed with lights flashing and sirens wailing.

"Faster, Rex, they're gaining on us!" Trissy shouted, looking over her shoulder.

"It's not possible!" Rex yelled, giving the four-wheeler even more gas. "Damn!" he shouted in disgust when he suddenly noticed that the road ahead stopped abruptly. He hit the breaks and frantically looked in all directions for an escape route. The woods were dense on either side. As the four-wheeler slid to a stop, Rex thought they had run out of options until his eyes focused on a large, steep grassy knoll that lay ahead, hidden in the shadows.

"Hold on and lean forward," Rex shouted as he revved up the four-wheeler and started to climb the hill. They could hear the collisions behind them as the police vehicles ran into one another after being faced with the insurmountable sinkhole.

"Rex, I'm slipping!" Trissy shouted, holding on for dear life.

"Hang on, Trissy, we're almost there!" Rex yelled encouragingly as he fought to keep the vehicle from flipping and losing forward momentum.

Just when he thought he had control of the thousand-pound beast on the steep terrain, Rex reached behind with one hand to grab Trissy, but she was gone.

"Oh no!" Rex shouted as the four-wheeler rounded the top. He immediately slammed on the brakes, put the vehicle in park, and ran toward the location where he had lost Trissy.

"Don't you think this state has enough levees?" Trissy gasped and as she slowly crawled up the last five feet of the man-made barrier.

"Everywhere, with the possible exception of New Orleans. Trissy, are you all right?" Rex asked as he extended his hand to help his wife up.

"Yes, but I'm certainly lucky that I didn't tumble all the way down this massive mound," Trissy replied as she brushed the dirt and grass from her hands.

"I just knew you would be. You younger women have a tendency to bounce and not break!" Rex said joyfully. They embraced at the summit until Trissy became distracted by what lay beyond the levee.

"Oh no! Are we ever going to lose sight of this damned river?" Trissy complained as she looked down at their nemesis: the raging Cajun River.

"Possibly, but not in our lifetime, my love," Rex replied as he noticed several officers on foot attempting the scale of levee.

"It's time to go. We've clearly worn out our welcome." They scrambled back to the four-wheeler and hopped inside.

"Hold on," Rex said as he placed the vehicle in gear and opened the throttle.

"You don't have to tell me twice," Trissy assured her husband, as she wrapped her arms firmly around his waist.

Once again, they appeared to be out of harm's way. However, from out of nowhere, a bright white spot light shone down from the dark skies while, simultaneously, headlights appeared on the levee in the distance.

"Helicopters and police cruisers, won't the men in blue ever give up?" Rex complained as he observed the lights growing closer from each direction.

"Rex, there's absolutely no way that I'm going back into that river. So don't even think about it in our plan of escape," Trissy stated emphatically.

"Yes, dear," Rex responded as he veered off the levee and slowly eased the ATV into the low-lying woods.

"Wouldn't you know it, marsh!" Trissy moaned after hearing a splash.

"That's what the environmentalists would have you believe. I'll bet we have some leaky levees. Knowing Louisiana's reputation for cost-exorbitant, crony-fed construction, the contractors probably used cheaper, more porous dirt," Rex concluded as he continued to zigzag through the rough, wet terrain.

Minutes later, Rex and Trissy were covered from head to toe with a thick layer of mud, which had been churned up by the wide tires.

"What a god-awful smell!" Rex complained as he wiped the cold black muck from his face. "Oh! That's even smellier than river mud," he added.

"I didn't think it was possible but you've got that right," Trissy replied after she stopped gagging. "If the dinosaurs didn't die from a meteorite striking the planet, then they most certainly keeled over after inhaling this wretched decay."

"It reminds me of the noxious odor coming from a patient with a GI bleed. The gut-wrenching aroma first permeates the air before it engulfs and then asphyxiates anyone and everyone in close proximity," Rex theorized as he tried to keep himself from vomiting.

"Rex, I'm frozen, hungry, and nauseous," Trissy complained. "Can you get us out of here?" she asked.

"Absolutely. All your desires shall be granted momentarily, of that I assure you," Rex replied with confidence, although he knew they were lost.

Several hours later, the four-wheeler finally climbed up and onto dry ground situated adjacent to a large area in which the underbrush had been cleared but the tall pine trees remained untouched. Rex turned off the engine and surveyed the terrain.

"Stay quiet, I'm sure the police have setup some type of perimeter. Let's make sure that Rectal Richter isn't lurking in the brush, waiting to spring a trap," Rex whispered as he looked for glowing tobacco embers or the flames from a match, indicating the presence of their nicotine-addicted predators.

Rex and Trissy waited patiently. They were both overwhelmed by a deadly silence, which was broken only by the nocturnal creatures that inhabited the wooded marsh. Fifteen minutes later there had been no light or visible movement.

"I think the coast is clear," Rex whispered as Trissy noticed a large linear mound of dirt to her left.

"Oh NO, the levee! Will we ever escape its grasp?" Trissy moaned, as she looked down at the dry patch of earth and shook her head in frustration.

"Apparently not," Rex replied with a chuckle.

"Rex, I know you were never a Boy Scout, but please tell me that we haven't been traveling in circles," Trissy pleaded as she began to shiver.

"Of course we haven't. I know precisely where we are," Rex replied as his eyes strained to make out a faint structure nestled among the trees.

"And exactly where would that be?" Trissy asked, realizing full well that there was more than just an element of doubt in Rex's voice. After being raised with three older stubborn knuckle-butt brothers, she clearly recognized the "I'm lost" tone. Over the years, Trissy had come to the conclusion that this was a genetic flaw afflicting the male species from all corners of the world.

For several moments, Rex found himself speechless as he struggled to find the appropriate response.

"Why, Rula's! My love and our table awaits, assuming we can break into Chum's quaint North Korean hideaway," Rex replied, recognizing the restaurant they frequented.

"Not that I'm complaining, but I thought we were going to pick up your toys on Mallard Drive?" Trissy asked as she dismounted the four-wheeler.

"Think of this as a detour and a welcome surprise after a rather pleasant late night drive in the country," Rex replied painfully as he attempted to walk off the unique and unpleasant soreness gained from spending hours on the noisy, vibrating redneck chariot.

Chapter 10

SAC Richter walked from Dr. Fubar's camp up onto the levee that restrained the unforgiving Cajun River. With his hands clasped behind his back, he stood silently and watched three-foot rolling white-capped waves rush by. The deep rumbling sound generated by the massive body of turbulent water was hypnotic. He briefly admired this magnificent but deadly force of nature.

"There's absolutely no way Dr. and Mrs. Bent could have survived a ride down these rapids. Yet, I continue to feel their presence. I'll find those bastards and when I do, I'm going to kill 'em," Richter promised himself as he scanned the shoreline for evidence. But his concentration was broken momentarily when one of his men approached unnoticed.

"The Carencrow PD had no luck apprehending the subjects on the four-wheeler. They lost them on an old abandoned dirt road," Special Agent Stacey Burley, an eighteen-year veteran of the FBI, relayed with frustration to her boss.

"Incompetence is no excuse for failure," Richter growled, the anger evident in his voice.

"The officers gave it their all. In fact, three of their cruisers collided at high speed and sustained heavy vehicle damage. Two of the officers were pretty badly shaken and the third is in critical condition. All were taken to Carencrow Regional Hospital," Burley fired back in their defense.

"Do you think I give a damn, Stacey?" Richter snarled.

"Pardon me, sir?" the special agent asked in disbelief, not knowing why Richter had suddenly become so hostile. Although the two had known one another for years, the special agent had always thought of Special Agent Richter as a strange bird. Richter had no friends and no family that anyone knew of. He was cold and always condescending. Yet, she had chosen to ignore his narcissistic personality disorder on more than one occasion. There was no doubt that he was a highly successful field officer, but no one could understand how he had advanced so rapidly within the agency.

"I understand that there were two riders on the four-wheeler. Did the police get a glimpse of what they were wearing?"

"As a matter of fact, they did. Both were wearing green scrubs," Special Agent Burley disclosed.

"I knew it!" Richter screamed above the sound from the thunderous Cajun River.

"Knew what, sir?" Burley asked the volatile SAC, who seconds ago had been depressed and angry but now was elated and optimistic.

"The Bents are alive!" he screamed, clenching his fists and shaking his hands.

"Possibly, but we've found no evidence that they were in Dr. Fubar's house or even on the grounds."

"Trust me, Burley, they're alive, and once the submerged police cruiser is found, we'll have our proof," Richter relayed with unwavering certainty.

"Yes, sir, but personally I don't think we'll ever find the police cruiser. Assuming that the Bents somehow made it out of the submerged vehicle, their bodies won't surface for another three days. By that time, they'll probably be floating in the Gulf, miles offshore," the special agent replied realistically.

"Burley, I'll dredge every inch of this river and troll the entire Caribbean if necessary until I find their mangy carcasses. However, under no circumstances am I going to wait for any damned 'floaters,'" Richter assured the special agent after sensing an element of doubt in Stacey Burley's voice. Her words infuriated him simply because "doubt" was a sign of weakness.

"Yes, sir," Burley replied grudgingly. She knew there was no sense in arguing with her tyrannical boss.

"Don't you understand what in the hell is going on here?" Richter asked condescendingly, not giving the special agent a chance to respond. "Our national security is at stake and time is of the essence. These fugitives may possess the information necessary to crack this Carencrow case wide open. Furthermore, my means of extracting the truth are quite effective. I can assure you that within hours I could achieve all of our goals. More specifically, the much-needed intelligence would be obtained and the Bents pronounced dead from natural causes," Richter growled enthusiastically.

"Yes, sir, I'll ensure that we redouble our efforts. We'll find the Bents dead or alive. In the meantime, I'd like to check on that critically injured Carencrow police officer."

"Bullshit! We're at war and as in any war there will be attrition. Injury or death is to be expected on either side and I will not tolerate any pansy-ass crying over the dead or dying. Winning is everything. There will be no compromise and failure will not be tolerated. You're not going to check on the injured police officer because I need you here," Richter stated in a loud and degrading manner.

"But—" the special agent began before promptly being interrupted.

"Burley, my rules are quite simple. Perform and produce or get the hell out of my way and find yourself some obscure pasture in which to graze until your pension comes to fruition. Do you understand?" Richter barked.

"Yes, sir, I read you loud and clear," Special Agent Burley responded affirmatively although angry at this unjustified personal attack. For the first time in her career, she felt threatened and tempted to strike back until she soon realized that this threat was coming from a short-statured power-hungry nut no one could please.

"Do I have your loyalty, Burley?" SAC Richter inquired as he impatiently awaited a response.

"Absolutely," the special agent responded, gritting her teeth and biting her tongue. She was tempted to tell Richter to go "stick it" in a career-ending verbal lashing but instead found herself eating crow and sucking up her pride. She thought about her husband and three lovely children who needed her support. Most importantly, she was only a few years from retirement. She had no other choice but to remain silent.

"Excellent, now, where were we? Ah yes, I recall, the capture and eradication of the Bents. Brief me on the success of the helicopter, which we were fortunate enough to get up at this obscene hour."

"The whirly-bird pilot thought he caught a glimpse of the fleeing four-wheeler. However, there was no true confirmation. They searched a ten-mile stretch on both sides of the levee and the river before knocking off. They'll be airborne again at daybreak to resume their reconnaissance," Special Agent Burley replied while looking at her watch. "And that should be two and a half hours from now," she added.

"Are you sure the damn pilot had his eyes open?" Richter growled.

"Most assuredly," the special agent shot back just to appease her boss.

"They're out there and I know those traitorous bastards are alive. The elusive Dr. Bent was a Navy SEAL. No one else could have given us a Rambo-style greeting and then escaped right under our very noses. I'm going to catch those fucking assholes if it's the last thing I do!" SAC Richter groaned, shaking his fists in the air.

"As you instructed, we have two perimeters established; one at five miles and the other at ten miles. Furthermore, the major roads are blocked and we're searching all vehicles entering and exiting the area. We'll get 'em, it's just a matter of time," Burley responded with confidence as she watched the antics of a madman.

"Damn right we're going to get them. Now, where do we stand in regard to our ground search?"

"We have four five-man teams searching the east and west sides of the river. Two teams started at the point of entry where the police cruiser rolled into the river, and two teams started approximately two miles down river. I instructed the search parties to turnover every rock and look behind every tree," the special agent assured her boss as she noticed a number of flashlights in the distance along the riverbank swinging back and forth. She was sure it was one of her search teams.

"Excellent," Richter replied as both became aware of a large dog barking. Within minutes, Sergeant Schnapps, the reliable and extremely friendly Golden Labrador retriever involved in the search of Dr. Bent's home earlier that night, was barking and digging vigorously at the muddy shoreline twenty yards away. In close pursuit were his officer trainer and the other four members of the search team.

"Good boy, Schnapps, good boy!" Sergeant Jones could be heard shouting above the turbulence generated by the river as he praised his loyal companion and fellow police officer.

The team immediately illuminated the area with their torches, searching for clues.

"Schnapps may have something," Special Agent Burley assumed as she observed the frenzied canine at work.

"It's about time," Richter replied as his frustration mounted.

Suddenly, Schnapps abandoned the shoreline search and started scurrying up the levee, sniffing all the way.

"Jones, did you find anything?" Burley queried as Sergeant Jones fought to restrain the dog as his strong four-legged friend kept pulling him toward Dr. Fubar's camp.

"Yes, as Schnapps so diligently pointed out, this section of shoreline is highly unusual," Sergeant Jones responded.

"In what way, Sergeant?" Richter asked.

"We've examined the river bank for miles. The mud and grass at the water's edge appears to be relatively smooth with the exception of this ten-foot area in which the mud is all churned up. Most importantly, there are fresh footprints and handprints on the muddy shoreline," Sergeant Jones answered before being tugged down the levee and toward the camp.

"I want molds made of the footprints and handprints," Special Agent Burley shouted to Sergeant Jones, who was now a good fifty yards away.

"Will do," the exhausted sergeant acknowledged as he struggled to slow down the energetic canine.

"How interesting, Schnapps has provided us with even more overwhelming evidence that validates our theory that the Bents are, in fact, alive and well. I want their heads on a platter, Burley. Is that perfectly clear?" Richter screamed.

"Absolutely, nothing would give me greater pleasure," the special agent replied as her stomach began to churn.

"Now, I want your men and the local authorities notified that the Bents are alive. Instruct all to remain extremely diligent and report anything suspicious."

"I'll get right on it," she replied emphatically as her cell phone rang. "Burley," the detective answered.

"Where are you? Were there any bodies found? Have you thoroughly searched the vehicle?" the special agent asked, listening intently for the response to all her questions. She then conveyed the good news to her superior.

"We've located the police cruiser. It's as if the vehicle rolled up onto the river bank, demanding to be found," the special agent announced.

"Excellent, we'll be right there. Instruct your men not to let that cruiser out of their sight," Richter growled as he and Special Agent Burley scrambled down the levee and toward Dr. Fubar's home, which had recently been vacated by the fire department.

"King, we'll be there in five minutes. Please keep a close eye on the vehicle," the special agent requested before she hung up, all the while scurrying to keep up with the SAC.

"Stop lagging behind, Burley," Richter shouted over his shoulder as he continued his mad dash. "Did we find the bodies?"

"No, sir, but after digging through the mud that had collected inside the vehicle, two sets of handcuffs were uncovered; each open and vacated," the special agent disclosed.

"I knew the fucking bastards were alive!" Richter shouted as he rushed around several downed trees, which conveniently blocked the driveway and access to the rear of the house.

"You were right," the special agent conceded as she caught up with her boss.

"Damn right I was!" Richter shouted as he made his way around to the front of the house and toward the last obstacle.

"What in the hell is a Hummer doing stuck in that pine tree?" Richter shouted.

"I believe Dr. Fubar had difficulty finding a parking space," the special agent chuckled, looking at the twisted canary yellow vehicle precariously lodged in the downed tree.

"Well, he certainly won't have that trouble again, at least not from a dungeon. That's another asshole I'm going to fry," Richter assured the special agent, as they approached a waiting black unmarked sedan. "Now, let's roll! I want to see that police cruiser!" Richter demanded as he opened the rear passenger door.

"Yes, sir. By the way, Leslie Valentino had insisted that she be notified immediately of any new lead in the search for the missing couple. Shall I inform Ms. Valentino of our finding?"

"Over my dead body. The farther that bitch stays away from me, the better. She's a nuisance and I'm not going to put up with her crap, regardless of her stature in this operation. Do I make myself perfectly clear, Burley?" Richter barked before hopping into the vehicle.

"Loud and clear," the special agent replied as she opened the front door and jumped in. Both doors slammed shut simultaneously as the vehicle lurched forward.

"Ms. Valentino! How did you..." Richter gasped, as he searched for the appropriate words, while Special Agent Burley turned around, pretending to be surprised.

"Let me remind you once again, Special Agent Richter, that this national security matter calls for a team effort utilizing the talents of a multitude of agencies. I, as your superior, must insist upon your unwavering loyalty and full cooperation. Do I make myself perfectly clear?" Leslie demanded to know in a deep tone, which left no doubt that she had overheard Richter's conversation with Special Agent Burley.

"Yes, ma'am," Richter replied as he stared out the window, thinking of ways to escape the Valentino wrath.

Stacey Burley turned back around in her seat, snickering quietly as the vehicle sped away.

Chapter 11

Rex and Trissy had abandoned their four-wheeler at the edge of the marsh and were cautiously walking through a forest of large pine trees. It was 4:00 a.m. The winds had subsided but the temperature continued to drop. The stars were unusually bright, and when the light from the heavens penetrated the ragged pine needle canopy, Rex and Trissy could see wisps of condensation from each breath billow forth before the exhaled moisture quickly faded into the shadows.

"Damn, it's cold. I'm beginning to wonder if I'll ever warm up," Trissy complained, shivering uncontrollably.

"I think the temperature is just right," Rex replied as he crept along unfazed by the invigorating night air.

"Huh," Trissy gasped, wrapping her arms tightly around her chest and strutting briskly.

"Rex, would you please pick up the pace?" she pleaded as she surged ahead.

"Don't worry about the mule," Rex complained. With each step his knees cracked, his thigh muscles contracted violently and his butt throbbed. Undoubtedly, the four-hour excursion on the redneck chariot had not been kind to Rex or his rapidly deteriorating body.

"What a sweet smell in the air," Trissy observed, as she took in a deep breath while galloping onward.

"All I smell is the unforgettable lingering putrid odor of marsh mud," Rex mumbled in exhaustion as he lengthened his stride.

"What's that? Rex, you're not starting to get grumpy, are you?" Trissy asked although her keen sense of hearing had picked up every word her husband had uttered.

"I'm not *starting* to get grumpy, I'm already there. The only thing I can smell is the stench from the marsh. It's clinging to my nasal hairs and caked on my entire body," Rex complained vehemently as they hobbled toward Rula's.

"I'm starting to think that we're missing an outstanding opportunity. We could bottle that stinky mud and make a fortune. The 'Needless Markup' patrons would buy it by the gallon in their search for eternal beauty," Trissy announced rather convincingly.

"Absolutely, we could sell it as an anti-wrinkle cream. One application would make the consumer so malodorous that no one would come within ten feet of them. And from that distance, their wrinkles couldn't be noticed," Rex added while thinking that Trissy would be on her own if she decided to pursue that entrepreneurial venture. There was no way in hell Trissy was ever going to get him to help harvest mud.

"Excellent point," Trissy said as she slowed her pace, looking over her shoulder. "Rex, are you feeling all right, you're moving kind of slow and walking sort of funny? As a matter of fact, I don't remember you ever being bowlegged," she observed with a teeth-chattering chuckle.

"Very funny. You might assume that I'm saddle sore from riding a four-wheeler with broken struts for hours over rough terrain. However, in actuality, I'm trying to keep my fat thighs from rubbing together." Rex moaned as he continued to struggle with each step.

"Rex look, the black truck with a heavy chrome bumper!" Trissy shouted.

"Where?" Rex blurted, his eyes straining to pick out the vehicle.

"Over there," Trissy replied, pointing toward the barely noticeable truck at the far end of the parking lot.

"I see it! That must be the man-made battering ram that struck the police cruiser," Rex concluded as his eyes focused on the evil beast responsible for nearly taking their lives.

"Let's have a closer look," Rex insisted with renewed determination and vigor.

"Rex, I'm frozen and ravenous. When these two conditions coincide with PMS, the life expectancy of those in close proximity is believed to plummet," Trissy assured Rex in a subtle but effective effort to redirect his energy.

"Oh, in that case I suggest we see if our table is ready," Rex conceded as he surveyed the rustic two-story structure.

"How do you propose we enter this fortress?" Trissy asked, searching for a reasonable access point to the elevated, impenetrable improvement. The first level was windowless and constructed of stone. The second level, where the restaurant was situated, consisted of fixed, mosquito-proof, double-pane windows.

"I haven't a clue, but given all the external security cameras, our access is not going to go unnoticed," Rex assured Trissy.

"Rex, the cameras are probably there for show," Trissy suggested, bouncing up and down in an effort to stay warm.

"I don't know," Rex replied, while continuing to search for a point of entry.

"What do you mean, you don't know? You're the Navy SEAL!" Trissy reminded him.

"Yes, but I'm a SEAL with excruciatingly sore flippers," Rex admitted as he attempted to work out the soreness in his arms.

"That's a lame excuse, especially for someone who offered to buy me dinner. Well, what can a tired, battle-weary, sore SEAL offer?" Trissy asked candidly, jogging up the steps leading to the entrance.

"I'm afraid very little without a Jacuzzi, cocktails, and explosives. However, I am exceptional at barking and balancing a ball on the end of my nose, but only when my bald spot is rubbed," Rex chuckled, as he optimistically envisioned the tectonic plates shifting once again.

"Now Rex, our little ritual always stimulates Mr. Whale. Are you sure he can function out of water, and would it be safe?" Trissy questioned, although the thought of making love twice on the same night was rather appealing.

“Safety is a relative concept. Let me remind you that he’s a mammal equipped with a blowhole and sonar. He can breathe air. Thus, he’s functional both on land and at sea. Furthermore, with his highly sophisticated sonar, he can find someone with your beauty and charm in any condition and in total darkness,” Rex warned.

“Of course, that assumes that I haven’t hidden Mr. Whale’s happy pills,” Trissy said, looking in the front window. There were no lights on and no detectable movement in the restaurant.

“That’s cold and cruel. By the way, where have you stashed my pills this time?”

“Damn, it’s locked,” Trissy complained after attempting to turn the knob on the front door.

“Rex, that’s classified information only to be shared over a warm candlelight dinner. Most importantly, let me stress the words ‘warm’ and ‘dinner’!” Trissy confessed, scurrying back down the steps, rubbing her hands up and down her frozen arms.

“Well, now that you’ve raised the odds, let’s check around back. I think I remember a door on the first level at the far end of the structure.”

The door rattled and creaked as she pushed and pulled. “Look, Rex. You were right. It’s locked but the door is loose,” Trissy relayed enthusiastically.

“Let me see. Let’s just hope that there are no alarms,” Rex added, slamming his shoulder against the door.

There was a sudden loud snap as the bolt ripped through the termite infested wooden frame, and the heavy door gave way. Unable to stop his momentum, Rex was hurled face-first into a dark, cave-like enclosure.

“Good job, Rex,” Trissy praised as she reached for the light switch inside the door. “Wow, look at all the food!” Trissy gasped, her stomach grumbling. The large storage facility contained an assortment of canned and dry goods as well as an extensive selection of beverages in all flavors.

“Oh,” Rex moaned, sitting up while rubbing his head.

"Rex, are you all right? Trissy asked before noticing the contusion on Rex's forehead. "Nice goose egg on the coconut," she added.

"Thanks. What's life without a few bumps and bruises?" Rex replied as he attempted to move his right shoulder in a circular direction to ensure that it had not been dislocated.

"Rex, you're covered in mud," Trissy laughed. "Sweetheart, you're barely recognizable," she continued, not realizing that she was adding insult to injury.

"Come here, my love," Rex insisted as he pulled Trissy forward and held her in his arms. "The way I see it, we have two and only two options. We can either wallow in the mud or role in the hay," Rex offered as he navigated around the mud caked on her face to give her a passionate kiss.

"Rex, I've seen that insatiable sparkle in your eyes before. Most recently in the Jacuzzi, as I recall. You're not getting romantic, are you?"

"Hum, hum, HUM!" Rex snorted before licking Trissy's neck.

"Rex, not now but perhaps after dinner," Trissy sighed, fighting to control her emotions.

"Oh, Christ, that Louisiana marsh mud tastes as nasty as it smells," Rex complained as he attempted to expel large chunks of necrotic earth from his mouth.

"Rex, don't complain. At least it's warm in here. Now, let's see what's on the menu," Trissy announced, tapping her fingernails together in anticipation of a gourmet meal.

"While you're shopping, I'll see if there's access to the restaurant above," Rex said as he went off on his reconnaissance mission. Moments later, Rex returned but not empty-handed. "I regret to inform you that the door to the second floor is bolted shut. But I was able to find this," he added, dusting off a rare bottle of Château Lafite. He displayed and cradled the embodied creation of the gods with all the pride and joy of a father holding his newborn.

"Cabernet Sauvignon: nineteen twenty-eight. I would have preferred something a little stronger, but I suppose it will have to do," Trissy replied, as Rex gasped for air and clenched his chest at his wife's cavalier response.

"Trissy, we're not talking about a box of grapes, which have been fermented in some vintner's bathtub overnight. This wine has been nurtured and cared for by man for nearly a century," Rex emphasized.

"My apologies, now let's find some grub. I'm famished!" Trissy insisted, as her stomach continued to rumble.

Reluctantly, Rex sat the bottle of wine down on a small table in the center of the room. As he walked off to forage for food, he kept looking over his shoulder to ensure that his historic find had not walked off.

"Wahoo!" Rex shouted minutes later as he rolled a three-foot-wide slab of cheese into view.

"Wow, now that's a chunk of cheese!" Trissy said with surprise as her mouth started to water.

"Yes, I believe even the three blind mice could have found this monster."

"I wish I'd brought my camera. You're displaying all the pride of a great white hunter who has returned with enough food to feed his starving family, namely me," Trissy laughed.

"Yes, well, I was lucky enough to avoid the cannibals, malaria, and the dreaded titisee fly, but I'm disappointed that I couldn't bag the elusive kudu on this safari," Rex added as he began to embellish about his dangerous excursion and brush with death in the storage room.

"Well, my only regret is that I couldn't find an opener for these canned goods," Trissy complained as she dropped a large tin of candied yams onto the floor. "However, all is not lost." She grinned, holding up two wine glasses and a box of Ritz crackers.

"Let the festivities begin," Rex shouted with great emotion as he hoisted the fifty-pound block of cheese onto the rustic wooden table. Unexpectedly, the condensed cow's curd landed with such force that the table wobbled and one of the legs suddenly buckled.

"Oh my God!" Rex screamed after saving the bottle of Château Lafite in mid-flight.

"Good catch, Rex," Trissy responded gratefully, bracing the table with a nearby crate before digging through a drawer underneath.

"It looks like it's going to be trucker's night again. They're no plates or napkins, but I did find a knife and a corkscrew," Trissy announced as Rex began to salivate in anticipation of the moment yet to come.

"Bless you, my love," Rex announced as he held the exquisite bottle of wine tightly while kissing the dusty, moss-laden growth on the thick glass, which contained the crushed fermented grapes. "It's time to unleash this genie. Baucus would be most pleased!" he declared as the moist aromatic cork slowly slid out of the antique bottle. The subtle pop announced the arrival of a magnificent time, long, long ago.

Rex poured the wine as Trissy gorged on cheese and crackers.

"Rex, this is excellent cheese. Please, have some," Trissy insisted as she cut off a slab from the mother lode of cheddars and laid it in front of her husband.

Rex, however, was preoccupied initially with the cork and then with sniffing and swirling, swirling and sniffing the eighty-year-old wine.

"Um, ummm, now that's rather tasty," Trissy remarked after taking her first sip of the well-aged libation.

Rex did not hear her compliment. He sat mesmerized by the color and seduced by the bouquet of the romantic potion. Perhaps fatigue had caught up with him or maybe he had suffered a stroke, she thought. In any case, Trissy was determined to resolve this "silent husband syndrome," promptly.

"This grape juice actually goes quite well with the aged cheese," Trissy added in an attempt to break him out of his trance. Again, there was no meaningful response. After a moment of hesitation, Trissy decided that a more direct approach was in order.

"Rex, drink the damn wine, would you please?" Trissy growled, before taking another swig.

Rex brought the glass to his lips and raised the stem. The magnificent liquid rolled forth into his mouth and he slowly swished it about.

"Sensational!" Rex declared minutes later after actually swallowing the wine.

"Rex, our dinner conversation this morning has been rather one-sided, wouldn't you say?" Trissy complained as she firmly planted the knife in the remaining block of cheese. Again, her frustration went unnoticed.

"Rex, I'm going on a walkabout," Trissy announced as she picked up her glass and stood. There was no response from Rex, who appeared to be stuck in the sniffing/swirling mode, once again.

"Rex, be sure to let me know if Mr. Whale needs a pat on the back or access to a cozier cave," Trissy offered in one last attempt to stir tranquil waters and rekindle the robust romantic surge. Yet Rex sat quietly, oblivious to the arousing temptation.

"Obviously, it's time to hide the wine and break out a happy pill," Trissy mumbled before meandering off.

"Yes, dear," her hypnotized husband whispered moments after she had left to explore their newly adopted shelter.

"Those barrels look oddly out of place," Trissy noticed as she studied one wall of the storage room. After negotiating the many boxes and crates stacked in her way, she reached the wall. "These barrels are plastic. I should've known. But why would a penny-pinching North Korean go to the expense of building such a facade in this dingy damp space?" Trissy wondered as she examined the barrels more closely. It was then that she noticed the vertical hinges. "All dungeons need a secret passage leading to a closet full of skeletons," she rationalized.

"Open sesame," she commanded, attempting to gain entry by pushing on the opposite side of the barrel.

Immediately, a small door sprung open revealing a clandestine space crammed full of computers and sophisticated electronic gear all stacked on a narrow rectangular desk.

"Good God!" she gasped as she surveyed the equipment she had unexpectedly uncovered. "Rex, put down your sippy cup. You'd better come have a look at this!" Trissy shouted.

Rex was still in a semiconscious state but soon realized he was being beckoned. He gently placed the cork back in the incredible bottle and walked over to see what all the commotion was about.

"Wow, this ain't ya mama's play cave," Rex concluded.

"Brilliant observation Rex. What is all this?" Trissy asked as she placed her glass of wine on the desk and continued to survey her find with amazement.

"The majority of the electronics appear to be sophisticated telecommunication equipment necessary for uploading and downloading information bounced off satellites. And this," Rex said as he pointed to a sleek black box with an oddly configured keyboard, "appears to be an encryption device of some sort. In fact, it looks like a modern version of the enigma machine developed by the Germans prior to World War II."

"Look at all these security monitors. Chum has every inch of her restaurant and the perimeter under surveillance," Trissy said, watching the flickering screens and focusing on the images.

"So much for show. By the way, how's your Korean?" Rex asked after examining a computer keyboard emblazoned with bizarre little characters.

"Not as good as Wan's, but after a cocktail, quite acceptable, actually," Trissy replied confidently while sitting in a ratty chair, scrutinizing what appeared to be an email. "I'll bet I could access the Internet and quickly have this message translated within a matter of minutes," Trissy declared.

"I'm sure you're up to the task, but I believe you'll find that it's encrypted," Rex concluded as his attention became focused on the narrow wall to his left, which contained two pictures; one of which was a staged mug shot of the evil murderous North Korean dictator, Kim Jung-Il, and the other a picture of a cargo ship.

"Why in the world would anyone have the picture of this rust bucket on their wall?" Rex wondered. "*Il-sung*," he whispered, reading the name of the ship.

"Rex, I'm still hungry," Trissy complained while attempting to access the Internet.

"I know. I can hear your stomach growling," Rex admitted as he looked closer at the picture of the ship. "Captain Asaki," Rex said aloud, noticing the autograph in the lower right-hand corner. "He's probably another North Korean cutthroat," Rex concluded before surveying the closed-circuit security monitors. "Trissy, it's time to go," he announced abruptly.

"Rex, not now, I'm making progress. I'll have this North Korean mystery cracked in no time," Trissy assured him with a growing sense of excitement.

"No, you don't understand. We have some unwanted company and it's not Charlie Chan," Rex said, watching a stocky Asian male moving about in the restaurant above.

"Oh no, he's got a gun!" Trissy shouted, looking at the monitor and observing the big man who had suddenly appeared at the door leading to the storage room. Moments later, the bolt was thrown back and the door began to moan as it was opened, slowly and cautiously.

"Up," Rex whispered, looking at the rafters above. While cupping his hands, Trissy placed her foot in Rex's handy man-made ladder and extended her leg. She was able to grab a wooden beam and lift herself up and out of sight. Rex stood on the desk and hoisted himself up.

They waited in silence. Each could feel their pulses race as they heard intermittent creaking sounds emanating from the wooden stairwell and the large man began to descend. Time appeared to stand still, but in actuality it had only been a matter of moments before the door to the communications room was opened and the small stocky Asian man stepped in.

"He certainly looked bigger on the small screen," Rex thought to himself before noticing the glass of wine which had been left on the desk. Suddenly, there was a muted "poof," followed by a small shower of dust as a dried mound of dirt fell from Trissy's shoe, striking and exploding next to the glass.

The startled North Korean looked up and instinctively raised his gun. Rex knew that this was no time for indecision. He held onto one of the rafters and swung down quickly, attempting to create as much forward momentum as his mass would allow. Without question, he had to deliver a decisive blow—in one fluid motion, Rex kicked the man on the side of his face. There was a loud explosion and the shattering of glass as the weapon discharged, the bullet striking the computer Trissy had been working on. The man fell to the ground unconscious and the gun tumbled from his hand. Rex immediately jumped down and grabbed the weapon.

"I hate to eat and run, but I think we had better be going, Trissy," Rex said as Trissy eased herself down into his waiting arms.

"Good idea," Trissy responded as she leaped over the fallen man's body and back into the storage room.

Rex could see that he had broken the man's jaw. The stocky dude lay motionless with blood oozing from his mouth. Rex searched his pockets for a passport out of this dungeon.

"Ah-ha, keys," Rex exclaimed.

"It's hard to get good service," Trissy observed. Rex handed her the gun as he grabbed the bottle of wine.

"Come my love, let me show you the way out of Chum's house of horrors," Rex insisted.

"Rex, are you talking to me or the bottle of wine?" Trissy asked as Rex took her hand and led her out of the storage facility.

"Why, the wine of course."

"I thought so. Rex, I don't mean to complain about dinner. The food was great, the wine acceptable, and the company so-so, but the basement was void of any ambience," Trissy joked as they scrambled outside, back into the cold and toward the black truck with the heavy chrome bumper.

"I agree, that's why I didn't leave a tip," Rex chuckled as he depressed the electronic door opener on the key ring. The lights inside the black truck came on and the locks rose.

"Damn, it's cold," Trissy complained after hopping in. "Please, fire this bad boy up and crank up the heat," she insisted.

"Good idea. Would you be so kind as to hold our liquid 'pride and joy'?" Rex requested as he handed Trissy their bottle of wine. "By the way, I'm sorry we didn't get a doggy bag for the cheese," Rex apologized as the truck roared to life.

"Heat, Rex, HEAT!" Trissy urged. Rex turned on the interior overhead light so he could better see how to adjust the controls.

"Clearly, its time that we go on the offensive," Rex reassured Trissy with renewed determination.

"Agreed, but let's head back to our *hacienda* where we can at least lie down and recharge the batteries. SAC Richter would never suspect that we would head back home," Trissy declared as she reached for a note on the consul.

"And he most likely has roadblocks everywhere. Now, if I could just remember where we live," Rex joked as he placed the truck in reverse and started backing up.

"Oh, for Christ's sake!" Trissy shouted in anger.

"What?" Rex asked, slamming on the brakes before turning to Trissy.

"Well, we won't have any trouble getting home," Trissy declared as she handed her husband the note on which was scribbled their address and the directions to their home on Mallard Drive.

"My, my. It appears that we're quite popular," Rex replied nonchalantly as he hit the gas and popped the clutch.

Chapter 12

The black truck slowly crept forward as Rex cautiously approached the intersection of Hunters Grove and Mallard Drive. It was nearly 5:00 a.m. Both he and Trissy were exhausted. Over the last thirty-six hours, their relatively ideal world had been shattered by events beyond their control. They desperately needed to find a safe haven before sunrise. Food and sleep were now of the utmost importance in their battle to clear their good names, and what better place to look for these basic necessities than their home, which had been raided only hours before?

"Thank goodness. It appears that our less-than-hospitable guests have left!" Trissy exclaimed with a tremendous sense of relief as she surveyed their property from a distance.

"Yes, SAC and the boys were even kind enough to leave the Mustang. What amazes me is that the goons had the manners to shut the car door after dragging me from my high-spirited motor coach," Rex replied as he turned onto Mallard Drive.

"Well, let's hope they left some food in the house because my stomach is starting to rumble like a ravenous sports car on empty," Trissy growled.

"You mean to tell me that the wine and the cheese at our dinner party wasn't enough to squelch your hunger pains? I'll have to complain to the management at Rula's," Rex quiped, pretending to be disappointed.

"My stomach ulcer absorbed the wine and my tapeworm devoured the cheese before I had a chance to truly enjoy the nourishing meal."

"Well then, perhaps we should rustle up some grub, assuming we can get into our home," Rex suggested as he eased the truck over the curb and onto the driveway.

"We'll get in, even if I have to crawl through the cat door," Trissy replied without hesitation.

"Trissy, remind me again why we have the cat door?"

"Because it came with the house and you refused to pay for a new door," his wife snapped back, wondering why she would even respond to the ridiculous question.

"Ah, that's right. Now I remember."

"Rex, perhaps we should pull this rough-riding black beast into the carport so it's out of sight," Trissy suggested.

"Excellent idea, my love," Rex replied, coming to a full stop next to the remains of Trissy's once magnificent Mercedes.

"Rectal Richter and his bevy of broke back, butt-bumping bozos would never expect to find us here," Rex added confidently without restraining his sarcasm or anger as he placed the vehicle in park.

"Now Rex, was that analogy absolutely necessary?" Trissy asked, rolling her eyes as Rex killed the engine.

"Damn right!" Rex growled as he and Trissy exited the commandeered black beast.

Trissy gazed in silence at her unrecognizable SL 500. The smell of charred metal and burnt rubber continued to permeate the air in the partially enclosed space. She shook her head in disgust before refocusing her attention on their objective.

"Look, Trissy, someone has gone to the effort to wrap our home with a beautiful yellow ribbon. I thought they were supposed to tie such colorful wrappings around oak trees. By the way, what exactly do the words 'Crime Scene' actually mean?" Rex asked, hoping to elicit a smile.

"Obviously Rex, the FBI ran out of 'Welcome Home' ribbons," Trissy responded with a sneer before realizing that what appeared to be a delusional moment was, in actuality, a reflection of Rex's playful spirit.

"Well, let's hope that the Feds have also run out of shackles," Rex wished as he examined the damaged door while twisting the doorknob.

"Locked. How in the hell could the FBI destroy the door with a battering ram and then have it fixed so quickly?" Rex complained as he lay down on his back, placing his hand and arm through the cat door. Farther and farther he extended his reach until he had wedged his shoulder through the small opening. The plastic liner popped off as he strained to reach the doorknob. He could feel the tip of his middle finger brush against the outer circumference of the slippery brass knob but could progress no farther.

"Christ!" Rex shouted in frusration.

"Rex, let me try," Trissy suggested.

"I was so close, but I can't seem to reach the damn doorknob," Rex complained as he withdrew his arm from the small opening before tossing the plastic liner aside.

After abandoning his effort, he sat on the garage floor with his legs folded and his arms resting on his knees, his anguish more than evident. However, Trissy could see the wheels turning, or perhaps she could hear the gears grinding, in his mind.

"Now that I think of it, I may have dropped the keys to the Mustang when I was so rudely pulled from the vehicle and planted in the ground by those beefy hoodlums," Rex said as he stood up and walked down the driveway toward the front of the house.

As he approached the Mustang, he could see beads of moisture clinging to the red paint while a light frost glazed the windows.

"Unlocked, I can't believe it," Rex blurted optimistically as he opened the door. He placed his hand on the seat, leaned inside, and looked around. "Damn," he whispered as soon as he realized that the keys were not in the ignition. He quickly searched the adjacent ground. His eyes soon focused on a small but colorful rectangular ornament.

"Thank God! Come to me, my beauty," Rex insisted with great pleasure as he picked the magnificent pony-emblazoned medallion up off the ground. The car and house keys remained attached. Rex scurried back to the carport, invigorated.

"Excellent job, Rex. I want you to know that I never lost confidence in you," Trissy praised as Rex proudly dangled the key to their home.

"That's certainly reassuring. By the way, please accept my apology for growling," Rex replied sincerely.

"Apology accepted," Trissy replied as she opened the door.

"How in the world…"

"Rex, I'm smaller and more agile then you," Trissy answered as she motioned for her husband to enter.

"After such a long and grueling ordeal, I'm tempted to carry you across the threshold. However, I'm afraid you'd stick to the police tape," Rex replied with a smirk.

"Good thinking, Rex, perhaps another day," Trissy said as she ducked under the fluorescent ribbon and entered their home. With a flick of her wrist, the lights came on and she continued her trek toward the kitchen.

"What can I get you…?" Trissy asked as she turned around, but Rex had vanished.

Rex had made a beeline to the back of the house. He dashed through their master bedroom and into the concealed safe room built adjacent to Trissy's walk-in closet. He spun the tumbler to the safe to the right, the left and then back again, to the right. When the levered handle was depressed, there was a loud deep "clunk" followed by a low-pitched groaning sound as the heavy metal door swung open. Rex grabbed two smoke bombs and a large backpack containing all the bells and whistles from a deadly but noble profession, which he had abandoned long, long ago.

"There's nothing like a little high-powered weaponry and a few toys," Rex whispered with great satisfaction, closing the safe and spinning the tumbler. He scurried down the hall and placed the smoke bombs adjacent to the air-conditioning intake before making his way back to the kitchen. In a flash, he was out the back door before being noticed.

Minutes later, the backpack had been securely placed in the trunk of his sports car along with two coats. A deep, throaty growl and the rhythmic vibration of the walls of their home left no doubt that the

Mustang had come to life. Trissy knew where her husband could be found. As she looked around her kitchen, she flashed back to the horror of SAC Richer's intrusion into their lives. For a brief moment her hunger subsided.

"Ah-ha!" Trissy exclaimed as she focused on the lifeless radio. With a press of the magic button her favorite CD was ignited. Instantaneously, her spirits soared.

"I, I, I, I'm, stayin' alive, stayin' alive…" the Bee Gees blared.

"Now, that's an appropriate song," Rex announced, watching his beautiful wife move rhythmically to the beat. However, Trissy was so engrossed in the music that his comment fell on deaf ears.

"There's no place like home," Rex continued as he ducked under the yellow tape before shutting and locking the back door. "The alarm's activated," Rex declared. Although Trissy was preoccupied, she sensed movement and immediately looked to her left.

"Oh Rex, you scared me!" Trissy gasped after her trance was broken so abruptly. She soon regained her composure and turned down the volume. "Rex, where did you go?" she asked as he entered the kitchen.

"I stashed the Mustang in the woods one block over just in case we need access to a sporty escape vehicle."

"And just how do we get to the Mustang should the need arise?"

"I can't give away all my secrets. Trust me, I is a grad-u-ate of the Jethro Bodine School of Escape for Hardened Criminals," Rex declared with pride.

"Now I'm really worried. But fear and concern be damned, it's time to pig out. What would you like to eat?" Trissy asked, rubbing her hands together in anticipation of a gourmet meal.

"Do we have any tuna left?"

"TUNA?! This could very well be our last chance for a warm meal on this planet and you want tuna? Are you sure?" Trissy asked with amazement, as her salivating tastebuds suddenly became dry holes.

"Absolutely, I'm addicted to the flavorful mercury in each can."

"Well, perhaps you should develop a more sophisticated taste. Avian flu and mad cow disease have become extremely popular you know," Trissy suggested with more than a hint of sarcasm.

"Personally, I'm not in the mood for anything that clucks or moos. However, after our invigorating trip down the Cajun River, I have a hankering for fish."

"As you wish, but let me warn you that the stuff in the refrigerator is a week old. Even one day out of the can, 'Star Krust' is questionable."

"That's okay, it's relatively fresh," Rex assured Trissy.

"Well, if it passes the sniff test, I'll gladly throw together a couple sandwiches," a less than enthusiastic Trissy assured her husband as she reached into the refrigerator and pulled out a plastic dish containing the rather pungent grey chunky substance swimming in mayo.

"Excellent," Rex responded before heading to the living room.

"Don't mention it."

"Well, let's see if the reporters have made the fake news any more interesting than earlier this evening," Rex asked as he turned on the TV.

"All I'd like to know is when they plan to hang us so I can arrange to have my hair done."

"I wouldn't be overly concerned. Today, the grunge thing is in full swing. So you don't have to look your best on your trip to the gallows."

"That's reassuring Rex, thank you. By the way, the milk smelled sour so I took the liberty of pouring the last two glasses of Château Lafite," Trissy announced as she brought the wine and two rather stinky sandwiches into the living room.

"Did you add the 'Tony's?" Rex asked, although he knew that she sprinkled the addictive Cajun spice on everything she prepared.

"Yes, dear," Trissy huffed in frustration.

The sandwiches were devoured before the picture on the TV even came into focus. Rex's mug suddenly flashed across the screen. He was startled and choked on his wine. As Trissy increased the volume, Rex continued to cough in an attempt to rid his lungs of the liquid potion, which had been meant for his stomach.

"Dr. Rex Bent and his wife, Trissy, were arrested last evening and charged with treason. On their way to jail, they overpowered the guard and escaped. They're considered armed and dangerous. The FBI and the CIA, as well as state and local authorities, have launched an unprecedented manhunt in the little town of Carencrow, Louisiana. They fully expect to have these suspects apprehended within hours. Isn't that correct, Diane?" the ravishing veteran newscaster, often referred to as "Pocahontas," asked her reporter in the field.

"Yes, that's what we're being told," the reporter replied.

"Surely the Bents were searched after being cuffed, so exactly why are they now considered to be armed and dangerous?" Pocahontas quiered.

"That's a good question, but I don't have an answer. The only information we've been given is that they hit the state trooper over the head and then attempted to drown him. Perhaps they were successful in securing the officer's pistol. Or an even more frightening scenario is that they got their hands on the explosives or biological weapons, which were stashed away on their property," the reporter suggested after deciding to embellish her story.

"My God! One last question before I let you go. Is it true that the FBI has authorized and is overseeing a militia?" Pocahontas asked with great concern.

"Absolutely. In an unprecedented action, hundreds of local men and women have been recruited and deputized. They're now armed with every weapon imaginable and roaming the streets with instructions to take Dr. and Mrs. Bent 'Dead or Alive,'" the astonished reporter replied.

"It appears that the Wild West has returned. All that's missing are a bounty on their heads, a noose around their necks, and a tall oak tree. It will be interesting to see what the authorities and the ever-present ACLU will have to say about this issue," Pocahontas concluded as she shook her head and her silky jet black hair swirled across her soft brown cheek.

With the nod of agreement, the picture of the field reporter faded and Pocahontas reappeared.

"Well, I'd say that we just had our fifteen minutes of fame," Rex quipped.

"Rex, how can you be so nonchalant? The entire world believes that we're intent on destroying America with WMDs, and now we're accused of assaulting a police officer!" Trissy gasped.

"Let's not forget the charge of treason," Rex added, wondering how this story had grown so bizarre.

"Rex, not that I want to raise any concerns mind you, but being labeled as 'armed and dangerous' is bubba slang for 'shoot on sight,'" Trissy stressed as she turned toward her husband.

"That's the media for you," Rex replied without giving the ludicrous accusations another thought.

"Other stories we will be covering in the next half hour include the proposed easing of the immigration laws, the much-anticipated Affordable Care Act, and yesterday's sinking of the cargo ship *Il-sung* and North Korea's subsequent protest," Pocahontas said with a smile before a commercial appeared.

"Rex, we've been out of touch for one day and look at the important stories we've missed," Trissy mumbled, her eyes starting to close.

"Nothing like a healthy daily dose of sensationalism," Rex conceded. He took another sip of wine and thought about their next move, realizing that they had to stay one step ahead of the jackass, Rectal Richter. A dozen or so commercials later, the news anchor returned.

"Yesterday, the North Korean cargo ship *Il-sung* was fired upon and sunk by the *USS Kidd*. The North Korean government has launched a protest and has been so bold as to threaten military action if answers aren't immediately forthcoming. The saber-waving nation contends that the attack occurred in the Caribbean, in international waters, and was unprovoked. Twenty-five of their countrymen are dead and the ship now rests on the seabed. The North Koreans want to know why. There has been no response from the United States government. However, through confidential sources we've learned that the ship refused a request to be boarded and searched," Diane "Pocahontas" Davis emphasized.

"No way! There was a picture of that ship in Chum's dungeon!" Rex shouted as he started to yawn.

"Hum," Trissy mumbled as her head fell back onto the couch.

"I think we've had just about enough bad news for today," Rex concluded after noticing Trissy falling asleep. "Let's turn in," Rex added as he flicked off the TV before assisting Trissy to their bedroom.

"Rex, have you locked the doors?" Trissy whispered.

"All the doors are locked and bolted and the alarm is set. We'll have just enough time to get into our safe room should the need arise," Rex assured his wife.

After staggering to the bedroom, Rex and Trissy collapsed onto their king-size bed. There was a rush of air as the thick down comforter gently molded around their bodies. Neither had the time nor the energy to pull down the covers or undress. Moments later, both were fast asleep. Their troubles were now distant memories relegated to the subconscious.

However, the brief moment of peace and tranquility was soon to be rudely interrupted. Their nextdoor neighbor, Mr. Haney, had spotted Rex in the dim morning light moving the Mustang. The grumpy old fart promptly notified SAC Richter of the fugitives' location.

Chapter 13

It was a stormy, wintry morning on the San Francisco Bay. Most citizens remained sound asleep in their warm beds, oblivious to the wicked weather and the disastrous commute yet to come.

An ominous layer of fog engulfed the city and shrouded the Golden Gate Bridge while above, a dense, low-lying cloud bank assured that the brilliant light from the heavens would never be seen on this godforsaken day. The visibility was no greater than one hundred yards and the few lights evident within that radius swung violently as they cast an ominuous, pulsating glow. The winds gusted at speeds more than forty knots and the resultant turbulence generated horizontal swirling sheets of rain, attacking violently from all directions. The water within the bay was jet black but mysteriously sprang to life as four-foot swells launched a multitude of whitecaps that leaped skyward in an alluring motion, beckoning all to challenge the power of the sea. As thunderous waves crashed against the shore, the winds continued to howl.

On the north side of the bay, the quiet, one-horse town of Tiburon continued to be pummeled by the relentless storm. Once a major rail station and vast seaport from which all goods and services flowed to northern California, the town was now a sleepy little bedroom community. Gone were wharf rats, hookers, thieves, and scoundrels. An even more dangerous animal had replaced them: the all-knowing, all-seeing, ornery, tree-hugging Progressive. In addition to this motley cast of characters, the town itself had changed dramatically over the years. All that remained of the heyday was a local watering hole named Sam's, the Arthur Barr Harbor Master Building, and the dilapidated Agnes Dollar restaurant.

Situated on a rocky prominence and extending out over the water overlooking Raccoon Straits, Angel Island, and the Golden Gate Bridge, the Agnes Dollar had fallen into disrepair years before when the federal government had seized the property after uncovering an extensive money-laundering operation. But, despite its seedy past, the historic structure reflected the pride of a time gone by. The two-story building seemed to defy gravity. One end was anchored to a bluff twenty feet above the water while the other end was supported by spindly rusting pilings. Beneath the bowing wooden structure a small cave had been carved out of the granite and enclosed on all sides. Portholes cut into the metal walls provided an excellent vantage point from which to clandestinely observe all traffic on the bay. Additionally, access to the rocky shore would remain undetected through a watertight hatch. Most importantly, the restaurant was in close proximity to their first target, the harbormaster building.

Late the night before, five men had gathered in the man-made cave beneath the Agnes Dollar. Each was prepared to execute the plans they had so carefully war-gamed for months. As morning approached, they donned three-millimeter black wetsuits and slipped thick-soled rubber booties onto their feet.

"Damn, I can't see a thing," Achmed complained, staring out one of the portholes toward town, impatiently waiting for the fog to lift.

"It's okay, Achmed, the harbor pilot's boat has not left the dock. Of that, I'm sure," Sahib assured his comrade as he listened to the static coming across the shortwave radio.

"I'm ready to die for Mohammad," Achmed assured Sahib, worrying that their plan would be scrubbed because of the weather.

"Yes, we all are. Allah is great and our mission has been blessed by this storm," Sahib replied calmly as the other men in the group continuously paced the room, whispering religious mantras. Each was oblivious to the violence of the storm as well as the nerve-rattling squeaking sound coming from their boots as they rubbed against the wooden floor.

As the light from the single candle flickered, monstrous shadows were cast on the cold walls. Suddenly, the static cleared and the shortwave radio came to life.

"Harbormaster, this is *Dynasty*, do you copy? Over," the mammoth oil tanker bound from Singapore inquired, announcing the ship's arrival.

The men in the smugglers den erupted with joy and began jumping up and down, aggressively beating their chests.

"Silence!" Sahib shouted.

The celebration came to an abrupt halt as static returned to the airwaves.

"This is the harbormaster. What's your position, *Dynasty*?" Gunter Zank requested in a thick German accent.

"Praise be to Allah," Sahib whispered.

"Harbormaster, this is Captain Wei. We're ten miles due west of the Golden Gate. We're experiencing fifteen-foot seas, strong winds with gusts up to fifty knots, and less than one half-mile visibility. Is it possible for your harbor pilot to board in such conditions?" Captain Wei asked with great concern.

"Absolutely," Gunter answered without hesitation. "This is merely a tropical storm. Rest assured, Captain, we can board *Dynasty* and safely navigate your ship through the narrow channel in these conditions," Gunter Zank assured him.

"Very well," Captain Wei replied cautiously, shaking his head in amazement at the boldness of the American harbor pilots.

"Captain, our harbor pilot will be leaving the dock at oh-five-hundred and will rendezvous with *Dynasty* one mile west of the harbor entrance at oh-five-forty-five. Enjoy your stay in our beautiful city. This is the harbormaster, over and out."

The chanting erupted again as the Islamic killers within the smugglers' den donned black neoprene hoods, strapped on their backpacks laden with incendiary explosives, and made their weapons ready. Sahib, as well, was overcome with joy. Checking his watch, he let the celebration continue for several minutes.

"Our time has come, my young Muslim brothers," Sahib announced as his men anxiously awaited their orders.

"The infidels will soon experience the power of Allah. Achmed and Mujue, take out the harbormaster and kill all those within the headquarters. Set the explosives to detonate at oh-five-forty-five. Tatwo and Redo, come with me. We shall feed the harbor pilot to the sharks after we've commandeered his vessel," Sahib growled gleefully as he slung open the watertight door exposing all to the harsh elements. Quickly, the terrorists exited the smugglers' den beneath the abandoned Agnes Dollar.

"Mother of Allah!" Sahib shouted into the wind, as he and his men fought to stay upright.

He had not anticipated the ferocity of the storm. Slowly and cautiously the assassins progressed down a treacherous rocky path toward the harbormaster's headquarters. All along the way, they battled heavy wind gusts, brutal whipping sheets of rain, and massive waves that seemed to explode along the shoreline, engulfing and obscuring the path.

"Mohammad is Great!" Sahib screamed defiantly as he felt a powerful surge of jet-black water grab at his legs, as if attempting to knock him off his feet and pull him out to sea. "No!" Sahib shouted as he tenaciously held on to his weapon and fought off the tentacles of a watery demon. Suddenly, the water tumbled down the rocks and rushed back into the bay. A moment later, the partially submerged path cleared. Sahib looked behind him. All of his men had survived nature's wrath.

Achmed and Mujue peered through the window of the harbormaster's headquarters.

"Three lambs, ready for slaughter," Achmed chuckled as he observed Gunter and the harbor pilot, Billy Look, drinking coffee and evaluating the Doppler radar. His eyes had also noticed Ms. Pam Gainey, a beautiful young lady and Billy Look's mistress, standing beside a window watching the harbormaster's boat being violently tossed about.

"Baaa," Mujue shouted joyfully in anticipation of slaughtering the infidels. As he turned the handle, the front door flew open, striking the adjacent wall with tremendous force. Gunter, Billy, and Pam were taken by complete surprise. They turned simultaneously and were suddenly confronted by two young men in black wetsuits walking through the doorway. Immediately, they were distracted by a brilliant flash, followed by the thunderous sound of lightning striking nearby. Then, their senses were overwhelmed by the sweet smell of rain and a sudden gush of numbing cold."What in the…" Gunter started to say after noticing that the strangers had weapons. He never finished his sentence—his words were cut short by the roar of gunfire. No one had time to react before the projectiles started flying. There was an explosive thud as the bullets struck each victim, tumbled, and then exited their bodies, carrying massive amounts of blood and tissue which splattered against the walls and windows. The force of the impact was so strong that each body was thrown backward before falling to the floor, dead.

"I love the smell of fresh gunpowder!" Achmed screamed as he released his grip on the trigger of his automatic weapon.

"And the smell of fresh blood," Mujue added, also ceasing fire.

As the smoke cleared, the terrorists could see their victims more clearly. There was no movement, no moaning or sounds of lingering death.

"Well done," Achmed announced as he and Mujue smiled, giving one another a high five.

"This has been an excellent morning, Achmed," Mujue shouted with pride.

"Yes, Mujue, and as predicted each infidel died like a spineless sheep," Achmed added.

"I thoroughly enjoyed watching the fear in their eyes as Allah delivered their sentence for being nonbelievers," Mujue stressed with enthusiasm as he pulled an explosive device from his backpack and set the timer.

"The first phase of our mission has been accomplished. It's time we join our comrades," Achmed insisted as both men took one last moment to briefly admire their work.

Sahib and the others raced down the pier where they boarded the harbor pilot's boat. They easily located two deck hands and the captain, all hard at work. There were several instantaneous bursts of light as flames leaped from the barrels of the automatic weapons, but the sounds of gunfire were engulfed by the storm. Once again, bodies fell as the murderous rampage on San Francisco Bay continued.

"That was too easy, Sahib," Redo shouted as he tossed the bodies into the frigid water.

"Yes indeed, but a greater victory is yet to come. Within a few short hours Allah and Muslims around the world will have much to celebrate. There will be tears of joy!" Sahib shouted into the wind, assuring Redo as he looked toward the pier.

"Excellent!" Sahib shouted in response as he watched Achmed and Mujue running toward the boat. He made his way to the bridge where Redo stood at the helm.

"Tatwo, cast off the lines when Achmed and Mujue are on board."

The small vessel pitched and heeled unpredictably in the swells and occasionally shook violently as the beam crashed against the sturdy fenders protecting the boat from the wooden pier.

"We have done well, Redo," Sahib shouted as he felt the engines throb.

Redo nodded and smiled as Sahib opened the door to the bridge.

"All lines have been cast off. Go, go, go!" Sahib shouted to Redo after Tatwo gave him the thumbs-up. Redo immediately opened the throttle and spun the wheel hard to port.

"I believe *Dynasty* is expecting us," Sahib announced, bracing himself for a rough ride.

The roar of the engines could not be heard, but the bow slowly turned to port and the small vessel began to shutter as she slammed into the waves on her way toward the open ocean. Achmed and Mujue stood on the stern extremely satisfied that the captain and his crew had met a violent death. They laughed as they watched the bodies that their comrades had just thrown overboard bob up and down on the swells.

"That's what the Americans refer to as 'body surfing,' Achmed!" Mujue shouted.

"Not a good idea in shark-infested waters," Achmed laughed as he remembered thrilling videos of great white sharks hunting and then devouring their helpless prey in this part of the world.

"Let's head to the bridge," Mujue suggested as he flipped his automatic weapon behind him and held on tightly to the shoulder strap.

The pilot boat pitched and rolled, while the bow at times appeared to submerge beneath the large waves. Thick sheets of jet black water rocketed over the bow and crashed against the windows on the bridge with such violence that the assassins felt sure the glass would shatter. All secured themselves as best they could to ensure that they were not tossed around the small bridge. Shortly after getting underway, an eerie glow could be seen ahead.

"Yes!" Sahib shouted. "We've reached the Golden Gate. Behold our target, my Muslim brothers."

A long, horizontal string of lights was rapidly coming into focus. The men looked on in awe as their boat passed the massive vertical concrete stanchions, which supported the magnificent bridge.

Minutes later, the *Dynasty* was visible in the distance.

"That's a huge ship," Achmed whispered.

"*Dynasty*, this is the San Francisco harbor pilot, we are one-half mile from your location. We intend to board you on your starboard side. Come to a heading at twenty-five and slow your speed to four knots, Captain," Sahib shouted into the shortwave.

"San Francisco harbor pilot, this *Dynasty*. All preparations have been made. We're coming at a heading of twenty-five and slowing to four knots," Captain Wei replied, silently praying that the leeward side of his vessel would afford enough protection for the harbor pilot's safe transfer in the extremely stormy seas.

"Very well, Captain, I shall see you momentarily," Sahib assured his next victim.

"Good luck. *Dynasty* standing by for further orders," Captain Wei concluded as he watched the spires of the Golden Gate Bridge loom closer.

"Redo, keep the boat as steady as you can on our approach to *Dynasty*. The bow needs to be as close as possible if we're to successfully board the vessel. But be prepared to throw the engines into reverse if the great vessel rolls toward us," Sahib warned.

"Yes, this small tug boat could be crushed and I can't swim," Tatwo added.

"Redo, be sure to stay closer to the vessel when we can make our escape. I can't swim either," Achmed chuckled.

"Achmed, after we have boarded *Dynasty*, make your way to the engine room. Wait for our signal from the bridge to increase the engine speed to flank. When you're sure that the engines are responding, kill everyone and plant your explosives. Set the timer for oh-six thirty and make your way to the bridge," Sahib ordered.

"Yes, Sahib," Achmed responded promptly as he adjusted his backpack.

"Mujue stay on deck. Once you see that we've entered *Dynasty's* bridge, kill everyone in sight and generously distribute your C-four explosives on the bow and on the stern over the oil compartments," Sahib ordered.

"Absolutely, Sahib, it will be done," Mujue confirmed.

"Tatwo, I want you with me on the bridge," Sahib requested as the harbor pilot's boat approached *Dynasty's* starboard side.

Suddenly, the winds and waves calmed. The boat was now adjacent to the leeward side of the large oil-laden vessel. Although the massive vessel was sitting low in the water, her hull afforded a good degree of protection from the elements.

Tatwo nodded to convey his understanding of his orders.

"Now, it's time," Sahib announced before opening the door to the bridge.

Sahib and the others quickly made there way to the bow and held on tightly to the rail. Redo directed a large floodlight at *Dynasty*, exposing a thick cargo net, draped over the side.

"Closer, Redo, closer!" Sahib shouted as he and the three others waited patiently for the right moment in which to leap.

The men could see the wet cargo net swing away from them and then toward the hull. Suddenly, the net slammed into the enormous vertical sheet of steel and began to vibrate violently after impact. Instantaneously, each man became keenly aware of the dangers they faced.

Sensing that the timing was right, Redo pushed the throttle forward, bringing the bow of the small boat so close that it nearly touched the great vessel.

"Wait, wait!" Sahib yelled as the *Dynasty* rose in the water and the net slowly swung toward their position on the bow.

"NOW!" Sahib screamed as he and the others leaped and snagged the slippery moving target.

Redo immediately hit reverse and backed the pilot boat away from potential danger as a rogue wave submerged the men and the net slammed back into the hull.

"Oh no!" Redo screamed, fearing the worst; yet somehow Sahib and the others held on and made their way up the net.

"I am Hue and this is Wong," *Dynasty's* first officer announced after assisting the harbor pilot and the others onto the deck of his ship. Hue immediately noticed that all the men were wearing wetsuits and caring backpacks, but no one had a life jacket on. Then, in the dim light, he caught a reflection of the automatic weapons and immediately became suspicious.

"Who are you people?" First Officer Hue insisted, his friendly demeanor suddenly changing.

"I'm the harbor pilot, Sahib Ganue," Sahib exclaimed with a smile as Tatwo drew his knife from its sheath and began to make his way behind Seaman Wong.

"I'd like to see some ID," Hue requested as he scrutinized the other men.

"Certainly, just as soon as we get to the bridge," Sahib shouted over the violence of the storm.

"Not acceptable. Hand me your weapons," the first officer demanded as Sahib drew his pistol and leveled the weapon. Suddenly, there were three muffled pops. The bullets struck First Officer Hue squarely in the chest over his heart. The dedicated merchant marine officer fell dead just as Tatwo grabbed Wong from behind. In one fluid motion, he placed his hand around the man's face and slit his throat. As the mortally wounded seaman fell to the deck, blood shot from his carotid arteries and he began to squirm uncontrollably, gasping for air.

"Tatwo, let's pay a visit to the captain. Achmed, Mujue, you have your orders," Sahib said as he stepped over the now motionless First Officer Hue on his way toward the bridge.

Achmed and Mujue nodded, grabbed the two dead bodies, and tossed them over the side before proceeding to their assigned tasks.

Sahib pulled back the hood of his wetsuit before entering the bridge. As soon as he opened the door, he quickly assessed the situation. There were only three men on the bridge: the captain, a lookout, and the helmsman.

"Good morning, Captain. I am Sahib, your harbor pilot. Welcome to San Francisco," Sahib said, extending his hand.

"Thank you. I'm Captain Wei," the captain of the *Dynasty* replied warmly while shaking Sahib's outstretched hand and wondering why he was in a wetsuit and not foul weather gear.

"Captain, speed is very critical given the intensity of this storm and the width of the channel. Please increase your engine speed to flank and make your heading thirty-five," Sahib requested. He located a pair of binoculars in a pocket alongside the bulkhead and slowly brought the navigational aid toward his eyes. He fully anticipated that Captain Wei would question his request.

"Is that wise, Sahib?" Captain Wei asked, knowing full well that the ship was his ultimate responsibility.

"Not to worry, Captain. As soon as we gain enough forward momentum, I'll reduce the engine speed to all ahead, two-thirds," Sahib assured him as he continued to look out the window.

"Helmsman, all ahead flank, come right to thirty-five," Captain Wei ordered against his better judgment after a moment of hesitation. Sahib smiled after hearing the new orders.

"Very well, sir" the helmsman responded just as Achmed reached the engine room.

Shortly after the new order rang up, the massive diesel engines began to roar. Achmed watched with great satisfaction. He pulled out his pistol and killed the two men manning the engine room before proceeding to the bridge as instructed. Mujue had also met with success. Despite the waves, the rain, and the ship being tossed about, he had finished placing the incendiary devices from bow to stern.

The large vessel slowly turned to starboard and gained speed as the *Dynasty* proceeded toward the inlet to the San Francisco Bay.

"Captain, how much fuel is your vessel carrying?" Sahib inquired.

"Three hundred thousand gallons of sweet crude from the finest offshore wells in Malaysia," Captain Wei responded.

"Excellent. Captain, you have been quite gracious and we're very appreciative."

"I don't understand, appreciative for what?" Captain Wei asked, trying to comprehend what Sahib was telling him.

"Why, we're appreciative of *Dynasty*'s contribution to our cause. Your vessel shall make a most excellent weapon," Sahib suddenly proclaimed.

As Sahib continued to gaze out the window through the binoculars, Tatwo slung his automatic weapon around.

"Left full rudder," Captain Wei ordered after realizing that *Dynasty* had been boarded and commandeered by pirates.

Tatwo opened fire and a hail of bullets struck the helmsman who slumped over the wheel, dead.

"One down, two to go," Tatwo announced with pride as he took aim at the lookout, who was scrambling to escape. But Tatwo was too quick. Several bullets struck the lookout in the back. He fell to the deck dead, just as Achmed and Mujue arrived on the bridge.

"Achmed, grab the wheel and aim toward the southernmost stanchion of the Golden Gate," Sahib ordered.

"Nice shooting, Tatwo," Achmed praised as he took the helm, while Captain Wei looked on in shock.

"Thank you. That leaves us with only one little Asian. I wonder what his fortune cookie has to offer?" Tatwo chuckled.

"Yes, Captain, we need to discuss your future. I'm sure that there's nothing quite so embarrassing as running your vessel aground. Now, wouldn't it be far more honorable to die than to live with the shame?" Sahib concluded while reaching for his pistol.

"I'll get you, Sahib!" Captain Wei screamed, leaping forward.

Sahib fired two shots into Captain Wei's chest just as his rough hands wrapped around his neck.

"Not today, Captain," Sahib declared as he quickly brought his arms up and out with a forceful movement, which broke the stranglehold. The captain fell forward, landing against Sahib's torso, but the terrorist did not yield.

"May I suggest a burial at sea?" Sahib said as he grabbed the captain by the hair and jerked his head backward. Sahib briefly gazed into the dying man's eyes before stepping aside and allowing the captain's lifeless body to fall to the deck. "I'm tempted to throw these bastards overboard, Tatwo, but in this case, I feel it important that the captain go down with his ship. Perhaps I'm becoming too sentimental in my old age," he quipped sarcastically as he watched *Dynasty* bear down on the Golden Gate Bridge.

"Tatwo, we have a rendezvous with destiny!" Sahib declared.

"Yes, sir," Tatwo sounded off.

"As always, our timing is superb, my friends. We shall strike our target on the incoming tide. In a matter of moments, the city by the bay will have one less bridge," Sahib announced proudly.

"Another symbol of Christianity will soon be obliterated," Achmed added as Tatwo continued to make slight course adjustments.

"To destroy a monument erected by the infidels, to kill these heathens and to create mass panic, is a great honor. Our cause is just and Allah is great. The crusades have returned," Sahib shouted as *Dynasty*, now traveling in excess of twenty knots, continued to gain speed.

"We really need to do something about the gridlock on the Golden Gate," Achmed chuckled as he observed a dense flickering of lights dancing across the bridge and watched as the morning rush hour traffic fought for access to the city.

"That bridge is huge," Mujue gasped.

"Brace yourselves," Sahib ordered when the *Dynasty* was one hundred yards from its target.

Sahib's eyes grew large and his heart started pounding in anticipation of the collision.

"Allah!" Sahib screamed as the massive ship struck the Golden Gate Bridge with such force that each man was ripped free of his position and slammed against the forward bulkhead. The ominous sound of metal twisting and grinding seemed surreal. *Dynasty*'s forward momentum abruptly halted and all electrical power was lost.

"Wow!" Sahib shouted from the darkened bridge as he picked himself up off of the deck to inspect the damage.

The bow and the entire forward section of the vessel were cut in half and peeled back. The ship appeared to be wrapped around the massive structural support. The Golden Gate's great pillar was now dangerously leaning toward the ship and was within fifty feet of *Dynasty*'s superstructure. Sahib looked skyward. He could see the roadway canted some twenty degrees. All movement had ceased and vehicles above clung to the bridge. For a brief moment there was silence, but then the Golden Gate started to sway. The twisting motion rapidly increased in magnitude as the force of the winds overwhelmed the damaged bridge. Suddenly, a rapid sequence of loud explosions could be heard as the tension cables started snapping. As if possessed by the devil, steam began billowing from the Golden Gate Bridge as the cold rain struck the stressed steel, superheated from the twisting motion.

"It's time to abandon ship. Come my Muslim warriors, our mission is complete!" Sahib shouted as his men staggered to their feet.

The assassins left *Dynasty*'s bridge and made their way to the starboard side of the ship. Even with the wind and the rain, all were overwhelmed by the pungent smell of oil.

"There are my brothers!" Redo shouted enthusiastically as he brought the pilot boat adjacent to the crippled stationary vessel.

"Be careful, the net is slippery," Sahib warned his men before all cautiously crawled over the side.

In short order, the terrorists were back on board the small harbor boat. Redo hit reverse and swung the wheel to the right as Sahib entered the bridge.

"Redo, stay parallel to the bridge and head toward the northern shore. Sausalito is our destination," Sahib ordered as the dedicated soldier of Allah shifted gears and placed the rudder amidships.

"Yes, Sahib," Redo replied. The Golden Gate was now fifty yards off the starboard beam. Sahib left the bridge and made his way aft where his men were anxiously watching.

"This is as exciting as waiting for the towers to fall on nine-eleven," Sahib declared as the haunting sounds of grinding metal penetrated the storm.

"Indeed!" Achmed responded as he and the other terrorists looked on in awe. The roadway above began twisting even more violently, ejecting vehicles and infidels from the bridge.

Mujue laughed as he watched cars and trucks fall from the sky. The headlights shot in all directions before being suddenly extinguished in a big splash, as the metal coffins struck the frigid water. There was much joy in his heart.

"Look, the infidels are being tossed into the sea!" Sahib shouted.

"Even the bridge knows the power of Allah, Sahib," Tatwo smirked.

Without warning, there was a loud snap and a five-hundred-foot section of the magnificent bridge fell into the Pacific, carrying thousands to their deaths. A large explosive plumb of steam marked the location where the bridge had entered its watery grave. Moments later, only the sounds of the storm could be heard.

"It's been in excellent morning, Sahib!" Achmed shouted.

Sahib just smiled. He was overcome with pride.

"Mujue, inform Redo that it's now safe to travel under the northern section of the remaining bridge. As planned, head for Sausalito," Sahib ordered.

"Very well, Sahib," Mujue responded as he made his way toward the bridge.

Sahib looked at his watch. It was 0629. The small pilot boat had transited under the bridge and was once again in the relative safety of the San Francisco Bay.

"Watch, my friends, as we deliver our *coup de grâce*."

Suddenly, several large flashes of light erupted in the darkened sky, followed seconds later by multiple loud explosions that sounded like rolling thunder. Fire erupted and began to race over the water toward the city as thousands of gallons of sweet crude ignited.

"You can now appreciate the value of the incoming tide. Nature can also be used to our advantage," Sahib declared.

As the pilot boat steamed toward safety, Sahib and his fellow assassins stood on the fantail in silence, watching in awe and dreaming of the accolades that would soon be theirs. A symbol of American pride lay in ruins and the city of San Francisco appeared to be engulfed in a raging inferno.

Chapter 14

It was a magnificent November morning in Bar Harbor, Maine. The sun was shining, the air was still, and the mainland could be seen with the naked eye. In stark contrast to the evening, Frenchman's Bay was now calm and tranquil. Old Man Winter had delivered a spectacular gift during last night's storm. The Bayview was now engulfed in a thick glistening bed of fresh snow, which the winds had sculptured in exotic ways. Earl Vassar was hard at work in his study, analyzing and reanalyzing information, which the National Security Agency and a number of other agencies had compiled. He truly missed his beautiful companion and confidant, Leslie Valentino. Her determination and strength gave him courage. Without her, the eighteen-hour days were starting to take a toll on him physically and mentally. The volume of data was unimaginable and his responsibility immense. It was one thing to decipher good from bad information, but identifying the misleading data planted by foreign governments made the task much more difficult. Most importantly, all conclusions as to what presented a real threat to national security and the probability of that threat coming to fruition had to be realized given unrealistic time constraints. However, Earl had no doubt that he was up to the challenge.

It was 9:50 a.m. An important security briefing was to be held in ten minutes, and he was determined to be prepared. His concentration was so intense that when his phone rang, he was startled and his heart began to race.

“Damn, my nerves must be shot,” Earl complained. After calming down and collecting his thoughts, he answered the persistently pesky phone.

“Earl Vassar,” the chief of staff for the National Security Agency announced.

“Earl, this is Leslie. There has been a new development in the Carencrow case. Do you have a minute?” Leslie asked in a polite but mission-oriented tone.

“Absolutely, Leslie, I can’t tell you how much I enjoy hearing your voice. By the way, it has been intolerable sleeping alone,” Earl confessed, placing the papers he was reviewing back onto his desk.

“I’ve missed you too, Earl. Hopefully, I can conclude our business in this bizarre little town in a day or two and head back north to ruffle your feathers,” Leslie promised.

“Trust me, I could stand to have my feathers ruffled.”

“Well then, it’s a date.”

“What have you uncovered in Carencrow?” Earl asked with great interest.

“Dr. and Mrs. Bent are alive!”

“I can’t believe it, I thought they had drowned,” Earl replied in a tone that reflected his doubt.

“I was convinced that they had drowned as well, but the preponderance of the evidence indicates otherwise.”

“What led you to this conclusion?”

“First of all, no bodies have been recovered, but given the history of the violent and unforgiving Cajun River, that’s not unusual. However, a home on the riverbank, several miles downstream from where the police cruiser rolled into the water, was broken into last night. Two crystal snifters were found on the coffee table and the fingerprints match those of the Bents. The home was surrounded, but somehow the Bents escaped right under SAC Richter’s nose. Later that night, two adults in green scrubs were spotted fleeing the area on a four-wheeler. They successfully evaded capture and remain at large. Lastly, the police cruiser was discovered approximately forty-five minutes ago. After digging through several feet of mud in the back seat, two sets of unlocked, unoccupied handcuffs were found."

"Well, I suppose anything is possible. Leslie, you must make every attempt to locate the elusive Dr. and Mrs. Bent as quickly as possible. I'm as convinced as you that the information they could provide would be invaluable," Earl emphasized.

"Without question, I'm on it." Leslie assured Earl.

"Leslie, my understanding is that Dr. Bent checks his email quite frequently. Obviously, he has your Internet address and enjoys communicating with you, although some of the messages are less than flattering."

"He can be rather abrasive. However, we need to flush him out and the Internet seems to be the only viable means at present. I'll forward a message that conveys my conviction that he and his wife are innocent and ask that they give themselves up," Leslie responded.

"Excellent idea. I believe I would appeal to his patriotism as well."

"Honestly Earl, Dr. Bent just doesn't fit the profile of either a terrorist or a traitor. And after scrutinizing the events surrounding the accusations, examining the evidence, and talking with his wife at length, I'm convinced that they were set up," Leslie shared without hesitation.

"I respect your intuition. In fact, the FBI's preliminary report on the vials found in Dr. Bent's home came across my desk earlier this morning. The fingerprints identified on the small glass ampules were indeed those of Dr. Bent. However, some of the vials contained multiple imprints of the pad of his left thumb and the left thumb only, whereas others were scattered with imprints of the pad of his right index finger and only the right index finger. The report concluded that at this early stage of their investigation, there was a high degree of suspicion that the fingerprints were planted."

"I knew it!" Leslie shouted.

"Not to dampen your enthusiasm or be too gruesome, but the FBI believes that the contents of the vials is a mixture of Ebola and anthrax. However, both the virus and the bacteria appear to have a very low virulence."

"Earl, that makes perfect sense. The vials most likely contain last year's nonproductive leftover terrorist concoction. If these biological weapons of mass destruction cannot kill or incapacitate tens of thousands, then why distribute the WMD, unless it could be used to indirectly achieve their goals or protect their ongoing operations?" Leslie rationalized.

"If the Bents know too much and have to be eliminated, why would the terrorists try to kill them first, and then reverse course by taking the time and making the effort to set them up?" Earl wondered, remembering that their Mercedes had been destroyed in some bizarre story of road rage.

"Because the terrorists came to the conclusion that killing the Bents would bring unwarranted attention and the risk of being uncovered."

"Possibly," Earl replied although not totally convinced.

"By planting these deadly vials in their home and then tipping off the FBI, the Bents would suddenly and mysteriously disappear from the face of the earth. The terrorists would cover their tracks while Rex and Trissy spend the rest of their lives rotting away in some dark dingy federal prison," Leslie added.

The prospect of this unjustified scenario sent a cold chill down Leslie's spine. During the short time she had spent questioning Trissy, she had grown to admire her. This admiration was undoubtedly accelerated by the anger she felt witnessing the aggressive and childish behavior exhibited by SAC Richter after his raid on their home.

"Leslie, I sense that we're quickly running out of time. We must find and question the Bents before the terrorists discover that they are indeed alive," Earl recommended, digesting Leslie's scenario.

"We're too late. The news hounds at the rinky-dink local paper, the *Carencrow Cajun Times*, know that the Bents are alive. In fact, to complicate matters, several reporters have already disclosed the contents found in the raid."

"Good God! How in the hell did that story get out?" Earl growled.

"I can only surmise that SAC Richter's ego and thirst for recognition festered his consistently irrational judgment."

"I take it that he's still having trouble adjusting to your leadership."

"That's an understatement, Earl. He's a loose cannon who's now purposely withholding valuable information. I would've never known about the police cruiser being found in the Cajun River if I had not been informed by one of his special agents. But rest assured, I will win this battle."

"I know you will. However, let me lend my assistance. I'll personally place a call to the FBI director to see if we can get Richter relocated to some desolate outpost. We can't afford to battle that renegade and the terrorists at the same time."

"That would be most helpful and greatly appreciated. At the very least, it would put Richter on notice."

"Does Richter know about the radiation?" Earl asked.

"The stupid jackass should, he was present when one of his agents scanned Mrs. Bent. The needle on the Geiger counter went wild and the machine buzzed loudly."

"I sure as hell hope he didn't disclose the nuclear aspect we have uncovered in our investigation. There would be total chaos in this country if the American people knew the danger they faced," Earl stressed.

"I don't believe he has, but it's not beyond the realm of possibility."

"My God, we've detected a high level of radiation on Mrs. Bent, the dead Asian sailors, and most recently, on board the *Il-sung*. Yet we appear no closer to finding the source."

"I disagree. We're getting closer and I can feel it," Leslie replied optimistically.

"The terrorists have smuggled a nuclear weapon into the United States and the Bents remain our only lead. Leslie, we must locate the terrorists and find the weapon before these madmen have a chance to execute their sinister plans."

"No worries, I'll find the Bents and we will secure the information we need to terminate this deadly game," Leslie assured her boss.

"Good hunting, Leslie. I have the greatest confidence in your abilities. I love you and I miss you. Hurry home."

"I love you too, Earl." Leslie replied before hanging up.

Suddenly, there was a loud knock at Earl's office door. Earl looked up. His secretary, Sandra, quickly opened the door and leaned inside. This was unusual behavior for someone so quiet and reserved. Earl could plainly see the concern in her eyes.

"San Francisco has been attacked and the Golden Gate Bridge destroyed! The story just broke on CNN," Sandra announced in a very somber tone.

"Oh, Christ, NO!" Earl shouted in disbelief as he reached for the remote control to his TV. Sandra stepped out and slowly shut the door as a picture of San Francisco Bay came into view.

"Of all the TV stations to break this story, why the liberal bastards at CNN," Earl complained bitterly.

A dense, low-lying fog engulfed the bay and all Earl could make out was a city under siege by a fierce winter storm. The water appeared to be boiling and whitecaps were everywhere. Large mounds of sea foam were whisked skyward by the violent winds where they mysteriously disappeared in the torrential downpour. In the foreground, small pleasure boats violently tugged at their moorings as they road enormous swells, while tattered flags whipped back and forth.

Earl could see the reporter covering the story struggling to keep his balance but he couldn't hear what he was saying as he pointed to the bay with his right hand. As the camera zoomed in, the visibility improved and the destruction soon became evident. Flames leaped skyward for hundreds of feet and a wall of fire extended for miles as the ignited crude oil gushing from the damaged tanker continued to roll in with the tide. The raging fires cast an orange glow in the low-lying white stream of clouds shrouding the city. From the north side of the bay, all of San Francisco appeared to be ablaze.

The camera then panned to the right in time to catch a massive mushroom-shaped ball of fire punch a hole through the dense fog. The remaining fuel oil on board the *Dynasty* had exploded and, in the light, it was clearly evident that the glorious Golden Gate was no more. The span extending from the city, to and including the first enormous stanchion, had simply vanished. Only a section of the bridge from the north side of the bay remained standing, but it appeared to be possessed as it twisted and swayed violently in the strong winds. Thousands of headlights were also visible on top of what remained of the bridge. They appeared to move rhythmically in sync with the resonating metal. Frequently, these beacons of light could be seen falling to Earth like shooting stars only to be extinguished in the cold Pacific waters. Then, in an instant, the north side of the bridge was gone. The savage and unforgiving ocean had consumed San Francisco's Golden Gate Bridge, a glorious and spectacular contribution to this magnificent city by the bay.

Earl looked on in horror as the reporter once again came into view. He strained to hear the commentary when his buzzer rang.

"Earl, it's time for your ten o'clock security briefing," Sandra reminded him.

Earl felt overwhelmed by sadness and self-doubt, but the moment of weakness was soon overcome by a burning rage. He sat for a moment in silence as his emotions surged and his anger swelled.

"We will catch these murderous Muslim bastards," Earl promised. He stood and quickly gathered the recent documents he had been reviewing before flinging open his office door, startling Sandra.

"Damn Democrats had the audacity to declare eavesdropping by satellite unconstitutional and then had the balls to challenge the Patriot Act!" he shouted, stomping past his loyal secretary and walking briskly down the hallway.

Earl rushed past the atrium containing the highly sensitive and very active operations division and into the parlor. Waiting for him in the conference room were the intelligence officers tasked with overseeing the National Security Agency's activities in North America and in a multitude of countries on various continents. All were seated around a magnificent hand-carved Italian mahogany table. The spectacular room was full of conversation, which ceased abruptly as soon as Earl entered. Only the crackling of wood and the roar of the fireplace could be heard as he made his way to the head of the table.

"Ladies and gentlemen, for those of you who have not heard, San Francisco was attacked moments ago. The Golden Gate Bridge, a symbol of American pride and prosperity, was destroyed and I am sure many lives were lost," Earl announced.

"Waleta, have you been able to ascertain any details?" Earl asked the department head overseeing operations within the United States.

"No, sir. However, moments ago I placed a call to our station chief, Chris Batini. I understand he's on the scene and I expect to hear from him shortly," Waleta replied. She had worked tirelessly to defend this great nation, but her intelligence never reflected any terrorist activities in the bay area and she now wondered why.

"Waleta, is there any information that we've gathered over the last few weeks which would've allowed us to foresee this tragedy?" Earl inquired, already knowing the answer.

"Absolutely not," Waleta replied without hesitation. "However, we will review our intelligence once again, this time with a fine-tooth comb."

"Every organization relies upon communication. It's imperative that we uncover the subtle signals, which not only activate these terrorist cells but also reveal future dastardly plans," Earl demanded.

Earl realized that he had to push his exhausted troops harder if they were to obtain that elusive element of luck, which would turn the tide on terrorism. However, he refused to threaten and intimidate his employees the way so many corporate managers do in their quest for short-term stellar results, which always conveyed the illusion that all was well. That was not his style.

"Well, we're all going to have to redouble our efforts because the nuclear threat is now a real and present danger," Earl emphasized, pausing for a moment. "Is there any additional information or unusual findings we've uncovered over the last twelve hours?" Earl asked the group.

"Yes, there appears to be more traffic to and from Carencrow. However, there's been no information alluding to an attack being launched from either Canada or Mexico, which we were originally led to believe was the real threat axis. I find this lack of chatter to be highly unusual," Waleta added.

"Earl, late last night we intercepted an interesting email from Pyongyang to Carencrow. It was addressed to a Colonel Chum congratulating the colonel on a job well done and some gibberish about honoring her ancestors," Frank, the department head overseeing operations in Asia, disclosed.

"That's the smoking gun!" Earl shouted. "The North Koreans not only provided the nuclear material but also the means of transportation. Unfortunately, the damn evidence is now buried in a watery grave," Earl added in disgust.

"Of course, the *Il-sung*," Frank replied as soon as he realized that what Earl had concluded made perfect sense. There was a moment of silence as everyone pondered the ramifications of what had been disclosed.

"I'll inform the president of this new discovery. Frank, notify Leslie of what you've found and have her get the FBI involved immediately. She has a close personal working relationship with the FBI's special agent in charge of operations in Carencrow. We need to find Chum and dig deeper into this North Korean connection," Earl ordered.

"Absolutely," Frank replied.

"Waleta, when Batini calls, tell him that I must know if the San Francisco Bay disaster contained any radioactive contamination. The explosion I witnessed this morning on TV was faintly reminiscent of the nuclear detonation on Bikini Atoll that the History channel frequently replays," Earl insisted, although he suspected that this was not the case.

"Will do," Waleta replied.

"Now, hear this. There is a new marching order. I want everyone to focus on Carencrow, Louisiana. Waleta, you're in charge of coordinating this effort until Leslie returns. Leave no stone unturned. I fear that San Francisco was a prelude to the terrorists unleashing a very unforgiving weapon of mass destruction," Earl said before standing and walking over to the window. It was obvious the briefing had been adjourned. The department heads quietly left the parlor.

"East Coast, West Coast, the distracting and emotionally disturbing reign of terror continues. However, the most dangerous threat from the south has yet to materialize. What have these ruthless bastards planned?" Earl wondered as he looked out over the grounds. He was too deep in thought to enjoy the tranquility the waves of deep, sparkling snow offered on this spectacular, sunshine-filled day.

Chapter 15

It was another cold, damp dismal morning in Carencrow. The air was filled with a pungent smell emanating from a nearby paper plant. The grey ominous clouds overhead appeared to be alive as herds of dastardly buzzards circled a site from which death could be sensed.

Rex and Trissy's home on Mallard Drive had been surrounded once again. No less than thirty law enforcement officers laid siege on their humble abode. Many were dressed in black and sporting the latest body armor. Sharpshooters were positioned at key locations with one eye each glued to their high-resolution scopes, waiting for the order to take out the suspects once they appeared. Other officers remained out of sight with their automatic weapons at the ready, fully anticipating a firefight. Additionally, two highly trained SWAT teams stood positioned to lead the assault. As with any dangerous mission, emotions ran high and adrenalin surged in anticipation of the operation. *Live by chance, love by choice, and kill by profession* was the motto of this close-knit, hair-trigger band of brothers.

"Dr. and Mrs. Bent, once again, I have you in my sights. Your house is surrounded. You have five minutes to come out with your hands up or we will come in after you," SAC Richter announced joyfully over the loudspeaker from behind his unmarked federal vehicle.

"Richter, I do not want these people harmed in any way. Do I make myself perfectly clear?" Leslie Valentino warned as she drew closer to the recalcitrant SAC.

"Yes, ma'am," the disobedient special agent sarcastically replied, although he had already made up his mind. He was determined to use all the force necessary to meet his objective swiftly and decisively. There was no way in hell that he would risk the lives of his men because some broad-assed bimbo from the National Security Agency insisted that he play the deadly game of Cat and Mouse by her rules.

Leslie shook her head in disgust. It was clear that her message had not sunk into the cavernous void that housed Richter's pea-sized brain. She now realized that the Bents very lives were in jeopardy. They could be terminated without so much as a second thought. Most importantly, the key opportunity to save the nation from death and destruction of an incomprehensible magnitude could be lost. Leslie looked over the hood of Richter's vehicle and surveyed the Bents' home. The wind was foul and she was ill at ease.

Rex and Trissy remained motionless in bed. Well into a deep sleep, they were oblivious to this new threat and SAC Richter's demands.

"The black Toyota truck reported stolen earlier this morning is parked in the Bents' carport," Sergeant Jones reported.

"How dumb could those two jackasses be to seek refuge in their own home without any hope of escape?" Richter asked.

"Pretty damn dumb," Sergeant Jones chuckled as he continued to watch for any sign of movement from within the house. Sergeant Schnapps, at his side, barked in agreement.

"This is the second time in twenty-four hours that we've had to raid this terrorist sanctuary. Sergeant, direct SWAT teams one and two to huff and puff and blow this seedy house down. It's time to get this show on the road and the Bents either behind bars or firmly planted in the ground," Richter proclaimed.

Minutes later, a five-man team stood ready at the front door while another was poised to enter the back door.

"The crime scene ribbon appears unbroken," the leader of SWAT team number one reported as he attempted to access the property under siege by turning the knob and pushing on the door.

However, the forceful jarring action set off the home alarm. The resultant ear-piercing oscillating sound was loud enough to wake their neighbors and, most likely, the dead. Yet Rex and Trissy were slow to stir. They had only been asleep for a few hours, not nearly enough time to recharge their batteries.

Rex moaned for a moment after being so rudely dragged out of REM.

"Trissy, honey, wake up, we have visitors!" he shouted over the siren, gently nudging his wife. "I thought the alarm was loud at Dr. Fubar's river camp, but this is worse," he moaned, staggering to his feet and covering his ears.

The plan that Rex had thought out for just such an occasion was hazy and unrealistic in his semiconscious state.

Boom, boom, boom, the dull, bone-jarring pounding could be heard intermittently at the front and back doors. As Rex staggered into the hallway, the sounds became louder.

Rex realized that he had to act quickly before the rectangular barriers were pulverized by the battering rams. He looked down and his eyes were drawn to the air vent located above the baseboard.

"Stay focused, Rex, stay focused," Rex whispered to himself as he quickly took the grate off and slipped out the large blue filter. The two smoke canisters were just where he had left them earlier this morning. In one fluid motion, the pins were pulled, unleashing the canned smoke, and the grate replaced. The thermostat was flipped to the Sahara Desert setting and the circulation fan to full. Rex dashed back to the bedroom where he found Trissy standing next to the bed, struggling to maintain her balance.

"Trissy, nap time's over," Rex insisted as he grabbed his wife by the arm and led her toward the bathroom. Suddenly, Rex became aware that the pounding had stopped. The hairs on the back of his neck started to rise as the magnitude of danger instantaneously became apparent. He had anticipated having more time for their escape, but it was far too late to second-guess his judgment. The front and back doors had been breached, and although the screeching siren continued to numb the senses, he felt he could hear the rapid shuffling of boots right behind them.

"Made it," Rex whispered as the façade, hiding their safe room closed, seconds before the SWAT team entered their bedroom.

Smoke billowed downward from the ceiling vents, quickly filling all the rooms in the home as the officers frantically searched the bathroom and the closets for their prey. Rex gazed at his security system monitor. Although somewhat dated, the screen reflected in real time the action that the outside cameras were capturing.

"Rex, it's awfully hot in here," Trissy complained, rubbing her eyes.

"Well then, we'll have to cool things off. Especially since it appears that a sizable angry posse has gathered right outside our door."

"Let me see," Trissy said, pushing Rex to one side.

"Oh my God, Rex, that's not a posse, it's half the United States Army!"

"Look Trissy, there's Richter. Even on the small screen his ego is definately inflated," Rex whispered as he flipped open his cell phone and dialed 911.

"Rex, have you gone mad? What in the world are you doing?"

"Would you believe that I'm in the mood for Chinese food and thought I'd place an order? Everything is quite good, with the exception of the Tiny Spicy Rectal Richter," Rex joked in the face of the overwhelming odds.

"Now, that's disgusting," Trissy replied, overcome by a sudden wave of nausea.

"You've got that..." Rex started to say before the operator came online.

"There's a fire at Fifty-One Thirty Mallard Drive. The house is engulfed in flames and there have been several explosions. My God, the owner just staggered from the house carrying his child. Both are on fire, please hurry," Rex pleaded, his voice reflecting a rapid pressured speech, capturing the horror of the moment.

"Rex, I can't believe you did that!"

"Time for a new set of duds," Rex announced with a smile as he handed Trissy a dark olive green slicker with "Carencrow Fire Department" emblazoned in large yellow letters across the back.

"For the fashionably conscious, I even have a matching hat," Rex added as he placed the oversized heavy metal protective gear on her head, which was embellished with the letters CFD on an ornate silver shield. Rex donned the same gear and placed a clear plastic tarp over the electronic surveillance monitor before pulling out his father's Zippo lighter from his coat pocket. He briefly gazed at the insignia, the bow of a submarine flanked by two dolphins and the enscription, USS *Greenfish* (SS-351). Memories of his mom and dad and growing up on Ohau came rushing back.

"Rex, it's really getting hot, especially in this heavy slicker," Trissy complained as beads of sweat rolled down her cheeks and the back of her neck.

"What, what?" Rex said in a startled manner before quickly letting go of the past. "Not to worry, relief is on the way," he assured her.

"I always wondered why you had these fire department hats and slickers stashed in the closet. I thought it was because either you liked to flash people or it was your costume of choice on Halloween."

"Close, but actually it's because I love smoke and fire," Rex admitted as he flipped up the lid on the lighter, exposing the thumbwheel. A few downward strokes were all it took to produce a bold beautiful flame.

"Perhaps I should change your moniker from 'Dr. Mai Tai' to 'Smokey,'" Trissy chuckled.

"Yuck yuck, very funny, but now it's time to get serious and make our guests as uncomfortable as possible. Our tropical oasis is about to be transformed into a frigid wasteland," Rex announced as he held the lighter up next to the fire sensor. The safe room, as well as every other room in the house, was immediately awash in a fine frigid spray. The sprinkler system had been ignited and the result was beyond expectation.

"Oh, that's cold!" Trissy whispered while shivering. She wrapped the rubber coat tightly around her torso as large drops rolled off the brim of her hat.

Even the resultant torrential downpour couldn't extinguish the flame. Rex flipped the lid shut and slipped the always reliable Zippo back into his pocket.

From all four cameras, it was evident that the activity outside had intensified. Smoke could be seen drifting from the front door as several large men dressed in black retreated. Moments later, two large fire engines arrived from the Carencrow Fire Department. One fire truck parked in front of the house and the other on Windamere Drive, the adjacent parallel street, which ran behind their home. The firefighters immediately leaped into action. Hoses were made ready as a group of men wielding large axes ran toward the home from both directions.

"It's time to go, Trissy. Let's make our way toward the back door. Walk briskly, don't look up, and don't stop for any reason," Rex said as he glanced at the screen one last time.

"Oh crap, Richter and his cronies are following the firefighters into the house," Rex announced with disgust.

But this was no time to hesitate. His diversion had created enough confusion to allow a brief window of opportunity for escape. It was now or never. Rex and Trissy opened the secret door and quickly exited the safe room.

Visibility was limited to only a few feet. Jets of frigid water continued shooting down from the ceiling as smoke billowed from all vents while the high-pitched squeal of the siren threatened to drive anyone within the home mad. Rex grabbed Trissy by the hand and rapidly walked down the hall. He collided with several firefighters traveling toward the bedroom and nearly lost his balance. He was vaguely aware of shouting and cursing yet continued onward into the living room and past SAC Richter.

"Look at the damn plates and the wine glasses! Every place I go those two traitors are eating and drinking. I know the bastards were here. Why can't we catch these fuckers?" Richter shouted.

Rex and Trissy felt as if they were swimming upstream as they scrambled into the kitchen and then out the back door. All along the way they bumped into and brushed against firefighters and FBI agents while successfully avoiding recognition by the human wave, which was intent upon making its way into their home.

"This way!" Rex shouted as he turned to his right, tugging at Trissy's hand. They scurried around the remains of the Mercedes, out the carport, and onto the back lawn. Moments later, they had successfully made their way beyond the sharpshooters and through the crowd of bloodthirsty spectators, who had gathered to witness the much-anticipated demise of their renegade neighbors. Rex looked up just in time before running into a large red fire truck, which had been so conspicuously parked in close proximity.

Trissy gasped as she bumped into Rex, who had come to an abrupt stop. Without saying a word, Rex tugged on Trissy's hand and led her around to the other side of the bright shiny fire engine. On the street side, all was quiet and they appeared to be relatively shielded from all prying eyes.

"It's time to resign from the fire department after a brief but illustrious career!" Rex said as he quickly took off his CFD slicker and hat.

"Let's just hope the greedy politicians don't muck with our healthcare benefits or pensions," Trissy added, placing her equipment on the truck's black, grit-lined running board.

"Unfortunately, that's inevitable," Rex replied as he looked down the street toward the dead end where he had stashed the Mustang earlier in the morning. Under the shadow cast by the large oak tree, he could vaguely make out the silhouette of his pride and joy.

"May I interest you in a Sunday drive through the Carencrow buzzard-infested countryside?"

"Now, that sounds rather romantic," Trissy replied as they walked briskly toward their getaway vehicle.

Minutes later, they were sitting inside the warmth and comfort of the sports car. The power plant had been ignited and the heater placed on full.

"Damn, I'm tired of being wet and cold," Trissy complained.

"Well then, perhaps we should consider a trip to the South Pacific. How does Fiji sound?"

"Can the Mustang make it to Fiji, Rex?"

"Can buzzards fly? Of course, but given my calculations we would have to refuel in flight well over thirty times. So it might be wiser booking a commercial flight but only after we've flushed out and exposed GeeHad, Chum, and their gaggle of fellow terrorists."

"Agreed. Where do we go from here?"

"Carencrow Regional Medical Center. We need to explore and quite possibly ransack GeeHad's office. Perhaps we can find the clue that will break this case wide open."

As Rex revved up the Mustang and eased up on the clutch, the vehicle started to roll forward.

"Oh, Christ, isn't that Mr. Haney?" Trissy gasped as her eyes caught a glimpse of the old-timer in a faded checkered shirt and torn stained overalls. Trissy slipped down deeper into her seat in a futile effort to hide, but his penetrating eyes were locked on, watching her every movement. The Mustang passed within feet of their nosy neighbor.

"It could be, but with all the inbreeding in this wretched little town, it's probably a cousin," Rex replied, stepping on the gas.

Seconds later, after shifting into third gear, Rex glanced into his rearview mirror. The fire truck, the crowds, and ever-present Mr. Haney were rapidly fading from view. For a brief moment, Rex and Trissy were out of harm's way and SAC Richter was destined to be left with more haunting memories.

Chapter 16

The Mustang glided into the nearly vacant parking lot behind Carencrow Regional Hospital, close to the ambulance entrance. It was late Sunday morning and the Holy Rollers were still in church. Once their souls had been somewhat cleansed and their pockets picked, many would migrate and descend upon the emergency room with a litany of vague, long-standing complaints. The parking lot would soon be filled to capacity. Such was the weekly and much dreaded but very predictable ritual.

"Well, it's clearly evident that the pastor hasn't let the flock free," Rex remarked as he placed the Mustang in park, shut off the engine, and popped open the trunk.

"Oddly enough, I don't see any smokers lingering outside. Now may be the right time to enter the hospital unnoticed," Trissy concluded after surveying the area.

"Trissy, don't you find it the least bit unusual that those crabby old tobacco-laden buzzards, Mean and Evil, aren't perched outside?"

"Now that you mention it, it's highly unusual indeed. And I know for a fact that they're working this shift. Thus, there are three and only three possibilities: Either the vultures are working their token five minutes per hour, they're inside watching a rerun of 'The Birds,' or we've been set up."

"It's the latter possibility that's concerning but we must press on, regardless of the danger," Rex insisted after shutting the car door. He reached into the trunk. "Ah, there it is, safe and sound," Rex said as he retrieved his backpack along with their coats. "Let's go, we have a rendezvous with destiny."

Rex and Trissy jogged past the empty ambulance loading/unloading dock. Upon reaching the back entrance, they attempted to blend into the adjacent brick wall. Rex peered through a sliding glass door marking the ambulance entrance. No one was in sight.

"It's showtime," Rex whispered as he pressed 911 into the adjacent keypad. The double doors opened automatically and they scurried in with no one the wiser.

"It certainly helps when you have the code," Trissy whispered.

"I should say."

They scrambled to the left and ducked into a stairwell adjacent to the elevator designated for those poor souls destined for the Cardiac Catheterization Lab. Once on the second floor, Rex and Trissy quickly made their way down several hallways, through the unoccupied surgeons' lounge, and into the men's locker room where they knew a multitude of freshly pressed scrubs, all arranged according to size, could easily be obtained.

"Practical, but certainly not fashionable. Well, at least management replaced the florescent pink with dark blue," Rex said appreciatively as he rapidly undressed.

"A shower is in order and would be greatly appreciated," Trissy suggested.

"Absolutely, let's definitely book one for next week," Rex replied as Trissy sniffed herself, clearly not pleased with the unpleasant odor oozing from her pores.

"Well at least they're clean. My only concern is being able find you in the dark," Trissy declared as she tossed her well-worn muddy jeans into the dirty laundry hamper. The quick-change act went smoothly. Trissy was still putting on her top when Rex slammed open the door that led back into the surgeons' lounge. He walked across the room, which was laden with years of discarded debris of all sorts.

"I'll bet the housekeeper is buried somewhere under these mounds of garbage," Rex concluded as he picked up a stack of crumpled newspapers from a plush leather chair. Without hesitation, he tossed the refuge onto the matted orange shag carpet, sat down, and immediately picked up the phone located on the adjacent side table.

"It's time we call in a marker," Rex announced with conviction as he dialed hospital extension 311.

Trissy eyed Friday's leftover cakes on the kitchen counter. The petrified morsels were daily gifts from a stingy management. Crumbs, if you will, meant to appease an emotionally volatile and frequently deranged specialty within the medical profession. For some reason they were always neatly placed adjacent to the sink, which was overflowing with moldy discarded tableware.

"Gross! Rex, this physician 'Fun Palace' is filthy," Trissy complained, dropping an eye-watering blueberry muffin while brushing a swarm of ants from her hand. Rex smiled and wondered if the roaches and the rats would come out from hiding to greet his beautiful wife.

"ER, Mofuze," Sheila, Queen of the Jungle, answered in a stern businesslike voice.

Rex was caught off guard. He hadn't expected the street-smart charge nurse to answer the phone. He paused for a moment to gather his thoughts.

"Is Terrence Foxx there?" Rex asked in an exaggerated and poorly executed ethnic tone.

"Welcome back from the dead. I'll get him for you," Sheila chuckled, shaking her head while pressing the hold button.

"Foxxman, poor white trash impersonating a sophisticated black man for you—line two," Sheila shouted after spotting the ER tech in the distance.

Rex stroked his forehead nervously as he waited patiently for Foxxman to come to the phone. He was worried that he had jeopardized their element of surprise.

"Foxx," Terry answered.

"Foxxman, this is Rex. I need a favor," the fugitive physician pleaded.

"Dr. Bent!" the Vietnam veteran and present-day ER tech warrior responded enthusiastically after hearing Rex's voice.

“Shush,” Rex pleaded. The inflection in his voice left no doubt that his identity was to remain anonymous. But Sheila’s ears perked up instantaneously. She glanced at the caller ID and knew immediately that the call was originating from within the hospital. She looked up and her eyes met Terry’s. After a brief uneasy moment of hesitation, Sheila turned away and carried out her duties as if nothing had happened. Unfortunately, as fate would have it, Mean was at the counter and started to slowly shuffle toward him. Aware of the approaching vulture, Terry turned his back and began to whisper, which made Mean even more suspicious. She looked down at the phone with curiosity. Seconds later, Mean motioned frantically to Evil, who was also standing nearby.

“Rex,” Mean whispered as she pointed at the base station for the receiver.

The nurse buzzards smiled and snickered in unison. They began salivating at the much-anticipated demise of their fellow coworkers.

“Dinner tonight at seven thirty, sounds wonderful,” Terry announced for all to hear before hanging up the phone.

“Well, that should be a cheap meal,” Sheila jabbed.

Terry walked over to room five where Susan, the only housekeeper for the entire hospital, was busy mopping pools of blood off the floor.

“Susan, I need your help. GeeHad’s office needs to be fumigated immediately. Could you be kind enough to open the door to his office?” Terry asked his cousin.

“I’m on my way, but I don’t think they make a pesticide strong enough to kill what lurks inside that room,” Susan fired back, leaning her mop against the wall.

“You’ve got that right,” Terry chuckled as he walked to a more secluded phone, away from prying eyes.

“Evil, do you recall the FBI’s ‘tips’ telephone number from the TV commercial?” Mean asked.

“Sure enough do,” Evil responded enthusiastically.

“Dial it. The terrorists are alive and well, roaming the halls of Carencrow Regional Hospital,” Mean insisted.

“My pleasure,” Evil snickered.

◆

"Dr. Bent, GeeHad's office will be opened within the next five minutes. However, be careful because I believe Mean and Evil are aware that you and Trissy are in the hospital," Foxxman warned.

"Oh, Christ!" Rex gasped.

"It would be my pleasure to take out those two ugly buzzards, if you wish. In fact, now that I think of it, Big Dog has been eyeing those two birds for an upcoming family gathering. Mimi turns eighty and Papa wants to have a hoedown at their camp on the Bayou. Big Dog desperately needs some meat to add to Saturday's gumbo and he can't seem to find any old roosters or fresh roadkill. So just give me the order. I can have those two skinned and stuffed in no time," the veteran offered without reservation.

"That's a very thoughtful gesture, Foxxman. However, that would result in the Dog family being ground zero for a deadly mutant bird virus. The human species could never survive a pandemic launched by stewing those two ornery H-five-N-one-infested buzzards."

"I never realized the danger those two pose to world health," Foxxman replied.

"The outcome would be catastrophic, trust me," Rex assured his loyal ER tech.

"Well, Big Dog and I stand ready to help in any way," Foxxman offered.

"Thanks, Foxxman, you've done more than enough. Trissy and I are most appreciative," Rex shot back before hanging up the phone. "Let's roll!" Rex said as he sprang to his feet.

"What in the world were you and the Foxxman talking about?" Trissy asked as Rex opened the door that led out of the physician's lounge.

"Mean and Evil know we're here," Rex confessed regretfully, surveying the hallway for signs of life.

"Oh no! Well, it's time to throw caution to the wind," Trissy replied, pushing Rex into the hallway.

Trissy grabbed Rex's hand as they ran down the hallway toward the bank of elevators that led to GeeHad's office. Suddenly, a soft bell rang, followed by a rumbling sound. There was no doubt in their minds that elevator doors were opening. They had just enough time to duck into a stairwell. Rex quietly shut the metal exit door.

"Security guard," Rex whispered as he peered through the glass window. Obviously, they had not been seen.

"That was close," Trissy replied quietly, breathing a sigh of relief.

Rex and Trissy scrambled up two flights of stairs to the fourth floor. Huffing and puffing, Rex opened the stairwell door just a few inches. There was no one down the hall to his right. He opened the door a little wider and looked around to his left.

"The coast is clear," Rex declared.

They walked briskly toward a fancy glass facade.

"Administrative offices," Trissy announced as she read the sign above the door. "This must be the sinister think tank."

"Yes indeed, this is the Devil's den where thugs, thieves, and terrorists reside. Please watch your step," Rex cautioned as he reached for the large brass doorknob. The door was unlocked. Foxxman had come through. He and Trissy entered the richly decorated foyer, nearly stumbling on the spongy plush carpet.

"Rex, don't look now, but we're on candid camera," Trissy announced, pointing to a small camera located adjacent to the ceiling on the far side of the room.

"Not to worry. More likely than not the guard charged with watching the screen is probably snoozing. But just in case," Rex added while grabbing a chair to stand on. Moments later, the camera was unplugged. "Trissy, lock the glass doors. We wouldn't want any unexpected surprises."

"Will do."

"Here we go."

GeeHad Bin-Sad

Founder, President, & Chief Executive Officer

"I'd say that GeeHad has a bigger ego than Richter," Trissy concluded after reading the title on the door.

"That's not humanly possible. An ego bigger than Rectal Richter's?

"Rex, would you please stop referring to the SAC in that manner? It's making me nauseous."

"Okay, okay, but they should've added 'Terrorist & Scoundrel' to GeeHad's title,"

Rex joked as he opened the door and entered the palatial office.

"Wow," Trissy blurted in amazement as she looked around GeeHad's executive crib.

"As long as you're comfortable stealing from your stockholders, excessive opulence is perfectly acceptable whether and not the company is making any money. Just ask the Wall Street fat cats. All received hefty bonuses after the bailout," Rex announced sarcastically.

"Why does he have so many pictures on the wall of Abdul?" Trissy asked before raising her hand to her mouth. Trissy's facial expression revealed shock and disbelief as she suddenly realized the answer.

"Yes, well, every camel jockey needs his water boy," Rex responded, taking off his backpack and tossing it onto the couch.

Trissy pretended to ignore Rex's comment.

"Let me see if I can access the files on his computer," Trissy said, sitting down at GeeHad's desk while Rex surveyed the room.

Rex looked high and low. He closely examined the walls for possible hidden access to clandestine rooms. He also scrutinized a large bookshelf, various pictures, and even the unique furnishings without finding anything suspicious.

"GeeHad's first mistake was leaving his computer on," Trissy remarked. Rex sat down in a chair and continued to survey the room. Moments later, the sound of Trissy's fingers tapping on the keyboard halted abruptly.

"Rex, look at this. GeeHad's last email is this clip from Al Jazeera," Trissy added, hitting *play* and watching several Arabic men celebrating a victory of some sort.

"What do you make of it?" Rex asked.

"I'm not sure, but there must be some significance or GeeHad would never have downloaded this video," Trissy replied while continuing to watch the clip closely.

"On the surface it appears to be one of a multitude of similar daily stories captured on film and beamed around the world, but there must be some subtle underlying message," Rex concluded as he searched for answers. Then, the thought struck him.

"Trissy, take GeeHad's last five emails as well as this news clip and forward them to your new friend Leslie at the National Security Agency. Perhaps they can make something out of this seemingly mundane information," Rex suggested before noticing the sliding glass door leading to a balcony. As he stepped outside, Rex could see that the balcony had been furnished with a large teak table and fancy chairs with colorful cushions.

"Excellent idea, Rex," Trissy replied, typing in Leslie's email address and attaching a copy of GeeHad's personal correspondence.

Rex looked over the rail.

"Trissy, I believe we have company," Rex announced, watching a caravan of large black cars screech to a halt in front of the hospital entrance. Several armed men, dressed in black, ran toward the front door.

"Done," Trissy announced with a great sense of accomplishment as her email containing the confidential data was successfully forwarded.

"Trissy, Richter is hot on our tail. It's time to *vámonos*," Rex announced with a sense of urgency.

"All right, all right, just a few more minutes. I think I'm on to something," Trissy answered with excitement.

"We're out of time," Rex reiterated, pulling the Beretta from his backpack before slipping his arms through the shoulder harness and tightening the straps. Still, Trissy failed to realize or acknowledge the requisite timeliness of their departure.

Chapter 17

SAC Richter, several of his men from the FBI, and the Carencrow Police Department ran into the main entrance at Carencrow Regional Hospital.

"Where in the hell are they?" Richter screamed at the drowsy security guard slouched over the booth in the main lobby of the hospital.

"What—what are you talking about?" the elderly guard asked, trying to wake up and make sense of the Sunday morning intrusion. SAC Richter rolled his eyes. Clearly the security guard would be of little help.

"George, have your men secure the perimeter. Additionally, I want two men to proceed directly to the emergency room to see what information we can squeeze out of the ER personnel. No one is to leave or enter Carencrow Regional without my specific approval. Is that understood?" Richter growled.

"Absolutely," the FBI agent responded.

"Jones, Freemen, guard the north entrance," Special Agent George Green ordered. "Toomey and Clark, secure the south entrance. Mossy and Frachtman, your post is here guarding the front door. Patrick and Dennis, head for the ER and pump anyone and everyone for information. I want the rest of you men to stay with SAC Richter and myself."

As the agents rushed to carry out their orders, Richter decided to approach the security guard one last time. "We're looking for two terrorists, Dr. Rex and Trissy Bent. Do—you—know—them?"

an impatient Richter shouted at the frail guard responsible for protecting all those within the institution of healing.

"What?" the guard shouted back, cupping his hand behind his right ear.

"I believe he's hard of hearing," Special Agent Green relayed after noticing two light brown plastic elliptical objects lying on the desk.

"Pops, put your fucking hearing aids in!" an angry Richter shouted, grabbing the guard's hearing aids and slapping them into the palm of his hand.

Richter paced the floor as he waited for the old-timer to comply. Minutes later, there was a loud screeching sound.

"Damn!" the guard shouted as he turned down the volume.

"Now, exactly what is it you need, young man?" the slightly more alert guard shouted, surveying the armed men who by now had surrounded his booth.

"Have you seen Dr. or Mrs. Bent or any suspicious characters this morning?" Richter asked loudly, cupping his hands in front of his mouth.

"Son, there's no need to shout. You're going to wake the dead," the security guard replied.

"I don't fucking believe this!" Richter screamed, throwing his hands into the air and walking away from the desk in disgust. By now, Richter's second-in-command was behind the booth and looking over the guard's shoulder.

"The security camera in zone sixteen is out," the special agent announced.

"Pops, was that camera working earlier?" Richter snapped as he turned around and approached the guard.

"I'm not sure. It could have been."

"Pops, where exactly is zone sixteen?" Richter asked, fully expecting a runaround from the senile old goat.

"That's GeeHad's office," the guard responded slowly.

"And who exactly is GeeHad?"

"He's the gentleman who runs this fantasy land," the guard replied.

"Now we're getting somewhere. Mr. Burns, could you please take us to GeeHad's office?" Richter requested after reading the guards name badge.

"Certainly young man, just hold your horses and let me get my keys."

"The keys are on your fucking belt, old-timer. Let's go!" Richter insisted.

"George, help Mr. Burns up, please!"

"I can do it, I can do it. Get your cotton-pickin' hands off of me, young fella," the now feisty and invigorated security guard shouted as he stood up and started to shuffle toward a bank of elevators.

"Dag nabbit, I forgot my gun, my badge, and my whistle." The eighty-five-year-old cachectic guard started to slowly turn around and head back toward his desk.

"Pops, we're out of time," Special Agent Green chuckled as he turned the security guard back around. Richter reached for his pistol just before the elevator doors opened. For a moment, he was overcome with the temptation to put the security guard out of his misery.

"Thank ya," the guard shouted as he slowly made his way into the ornate metal box, followed by six of Richter's handpicked men.

Mr. Burns pressed the button for the fourth floor and the elevator doors closed.

"I was born here," the guard announced in an attempt to strike up a conversation with the young, impatient whippersnapper.

"And you'll probably die here," Richter growled as his troops snickered in the background.

Again, there was a loud screeching sound and the security guard began to fiddle with his hearing aid. "And I'll probably die here," Mr. Burns added.

Finally, after what seemed to be a month-long journey, the elevator doors opened onto the fourth floor. The hunched-over, eighty-pound security guard slowly shuffled out with Richter and his troops in hot pursuit.

"Here we go, gentlemen," the guard announced, fumbling for his keys. "I just don't know which one opens the administrative offices," Burns complained, holding the five-pound cluster of keys closer to his face.

"Let me help you, Pops," Richter insisted as he took his gun and smashed the glass.

Hearing the glass shatter, Rex immediately rushed to lock GeeHad's office door before quickly sliding a large sofa in front of the door.

"Hopefully that buys us a little extra time," Rex announced, although not overly confident in the barrier he had so hastily constructed.

"Son of a bitch!" Trissy shouted, oblivious to the danger that was now only several yards away.

"Trissy, we have got to get out of here, honey—NOW!" Rex demanded.

"The answer was right in front of me, on GeeHad's calendar; Sunday, November tenth. He's scheduled to be in Whiskey Bay today at three p.m.," Trissy announced with a smile, looking up at her husband and wondering why he looked so frantic.

"Let's roll, doll!" Rex insisted, grabbing Trissy by the hand and leading her out onto the balcony. He looked over the rail from the fourth story of the hospital. "Well, we can't fly."

"Rex, on your right there's a ladder. It must lead to the roof," Trissy observed as her adrenaline started to surge.

SAC Richter continued to smash the large glass shards on the perimeter of the door as his special agents gently moved the security guard out of harm's way. Richter reached in and unlocked the door, and the metal frame swung open. He and his troops rushed in as the security guard continued to blindly search for the right key.

"Excellent. Up you go," Rex insisted, helping Trissy onto the ladder.

Trissy and Rex negotiated the twenty-foot climb without difficulty. Rex frantically looked around for some means of escape before his eyes focused on a gray pad on the deck emblazoned with a large yellow emblem.

"So this is where the helicopter pad was hidden. All these years and I never knew," Rex announced with a sense of discovery.

"Rex, stay focused," Trissy insisted, wondering momentarily if they had backed themselves into a corner. Then it dawned on her.

She immediately focused on a beige cinder block structure with a large gray metal door. Trissy had been through that door several times over the years as she assisted the Air Med paramedics transporting severely injured and critically ill patients down to the emergency room.

"This way, Rex!" Trissy shouted, grabbing his hand and scrambling toward what appeared to be the only viable option for accessing the street level. She turned the knob and pulled on the large metal door. It wouldn't budge.

"Damn, it's locked!"

"Here, let me try," Rex insisted, but he met with the same result.

"Stand back," he said loudly as he leveled his pistol at the door lock before pulling the trigger.

When the weapon discharged, the brass knob flew off and the door swung open.

"There, you see, we didn't even need a key," Rex announced proudly.

Rex and Trissy looked inside just in time to see the elevator doors open. A number of men in black were standing in front of several hospital personnel. Rex immediately slammed the door and leaned against it.

"It would appear that our situation has taken a turn for the worse. You wouldn't have any other suggestions for getting off this roof, besides jumping, of course, would you?" Rex asked in an attempt to make light of their precarious predicament.

Rex could feel the door being pounded with ever-increasing force. It would give way slightly and then slam shut. Trissy could see Rex's feet starting to slide as the metal door was rammed time and time again.

"It looks like you need some help," Trissy shouted as she added her weight, all 110 pounds, to the battle.

"I'd say," Rex replied as Trissy pushed against the door with all her might.

Suddenly, the winds began to pick up and they became aware of the sound of an engine. *Whoosh—whoosh—WHOosh—WHOOSH.* The intense churning quickly became louder as the blades dug into the cold morning air. The Air Med chopper was only twenty feet off the deck and attempting to land. Moments later, the skids touched down on the deck. Rex looked to his left. Fifty yards away, he could see a man in black negotiating the last rung of the ladder he and Trissy had just ascended. Without question, they were out of time and options.

"Christmas came early. When I say 'go,' stay low and run like hell!" Rex yelled over the sound of the helicopter engine as he watched the rear door slide open.

"We're not going up in that *Storm Chicken*, are we?" Trissy screamed.

"Hell yes, and we don't even need a ticket!" Rex yelled back.

"Oh, Lord!" Trissy was petrified of flying, and the idea of riding in a rickety tin box kept aloft by a metal blade secured to the frame by one nut, 'The Jesus nut,' was not sitting well.

"Now!" Rex screamed as he discharged two rounds at the base of the metal door in an attempt to delay any desire by special agents to persue from that direction.

Hunched over, Rex and Trissy sprinted toward the chopper. Rex was unaware of how close the blades had come to separating him from his backpack. A helmeted man dressed in an orange flight suit greeted them upon arrival. The male flight nurse extended his hand to assist Rex into the helicopter.

"What a kind offer," Rex shouted as he grabbed the man's arm and yanked him out of the flying titanium box. Trissy hopped in and slid the door shut. As the flight nurse continued to roll on the deck, Rex opened the copilot's door and climbed on board without hesitation.

"Take us up!" Rex screamed to the pilot while flashing his pistol. His message was received loud and clear. The roar of the engine intensified and the helicopter began to vibrate as it struggled to free itself from the bounds of gravity. Seconds later, they were airborne. Rex looked down. Richter had his arms extended holding back several of his men, each of whom had his weapon aimed at the ascending whirlybird.

As the life flight nurse who had been abruptly tossed from the *Storm Chicken* lay on the deck, Richter stood on the helicopter pad atop Carencrow Regional Hospital, seething as he watched the chopper slowly rise. For a brief moment, he was tempted to order his men to shoot the emergency medical helicopter from the sky, but he hesitated. Not for the fact that several innocent people would have to die but because the cameras were rolling and there would be too many witnesses. For now, the pilot and the passenger being transported in need of medical attention were hostages.

Once again, Dr. Rex Bent and his wife Trissy had slipped from his grasp. As his anger intensified exponentially, SAC Richter quickly lost sight of his directive to bring these alleged terrorists to justice and focused on a personal commitment to kill the fugitives from justice.

"Son of a bitch!" Richter growled, realizing that the Bents' much-anticipated demise would have to wait. Suddenly, his seething turned to rage. Dr. Rex Bent smiling and giving him the thumbs-up was just about all he could stand.

"I'll get you, you fucking bastards!" Richter declared, shaking his fist at the departing *Storm Chicken*.

The hunter and the hunted briefly locked eyes as the strong winds generated by the rotor whipped Richter's fatigues back and forth.

"Goddamn it! I'm going to rip that fucking maggot limb from limb," Richter promised himself as the chopper faded into the distance.

"SAC Richter, this is Lieutenant Vickers of the Carencrow Police Department," Special Agent Charlie Prejean told his superior as a dozen or more FBI agents shouldered their arms and awaited further orders.

"Lieutenant Vickers, can you get your police chopper up?" Richter demanded.

"Unfortunately, no, sir. It's grounded because of electrical problems," Lieutenant Vickers apologized.

"That's great, just fucking great!" Richter growled in disgust. The disappointment in Lieutenant Vickers' face was evident, but then he was immediately struck by an idea.

"Perhaps we can be of assistance in focusing our law enforcement efforts to capture these hijackers. The city has a command center adjacent to the airport, which was set up to coordinate efforts in case of a natural disaster. It's manned and avail...." Lieutenant Vickers said before Richter rather rudely interrupted.

"Lieutenant, this is more than just a piss-ant local yokel disaster. The escape of these terrorists has national consequences. Hundreds of thousands of Americans could be murdered, and our very way of life, destroyed. The United States of America could crumble if these traitors are not captured and killed. Do I make myself perfectly clear as to the magnitude of our problem?" Richter screamed.

"Yes, sir, but let me just say that our command center is top-notch. Logistically, it's ideally situated because the control tower can track their flight. More importantly, we could have an airplane available at a moment's notice to take you to any location," Lieutenant Vickers offered the frustrated FBI special agent.

"Well, I guess it will have to do," Richter growled as he shook his head in disgust.

"It sounds like an excellent idea," Special Agent Prejean concurred.

"Let's take my car," Lieutenant Vickers suggested, heading for the rooftop elevator, which allowed access to the street level.

"Prejean, you and your men stay here. I want GeeHad's office turned upside down and inside out," Richter ordered.

"Yes, sir, will do," the special agent affirmed. Richter and Lieutenant Vickers scrambled off the helicopter deck high atop Carencrow Regional Hospital.

Chapter 18

THE HELICOPTER CONTINUED TO gain altitude as the pilot stared at Rex in amazement. By now, the FBI agents had lowered their weapons and were standing motionless on the landing pad atop Carencrow Regional Hospital, while several nurses and Boom Boom Witherspoon waved what appeared to be a fond farewell.

"I can't believe this. What in the hell are you doing, Rex?" chopper pilot, Ralph 'Skinny' McKinney, demanded. However, given his high-pitched voice and his "baby boom gone bust" appearance, it was hard to take him seriously. Skinny was a stout fifty-year-old who looked like the proverbial olive that had swallowed a toothpick. Scrawny bird-like bowed legs supported his brawny beer-belly-taxed torso. Yet what was really bizarre and mystifying was the fact that he had no discernible forehead. Over the years, his unkempt salt-and-pepper hairline had merged with bushy black eyebrows which, in turn, had engulfed and obscured the bridge of his nose. There was no doubt that Skinny epitomized all that could go wrong when using *homo sapiens* as guinea pigs in uncontrolled government-sponsored experiments.

Skinny and Dr. Bent had exchanged many war stories over the last decade. During long monotonous shifts, while awaiting orders to fly, Skinny would become bored late at night and stroll through the emergency room searching for companionship and conversation. He had always enjoyed talking with the recalcitrant physician. In turn,

Rex took great pleasure in analyzing and attempting to decipher what chromosomal defects had ravaged Skinny's double-stranded DNA.

"Sorry, Skinny, Trissy and I needed additional frequent flier miles," Rex replied with a chuckle as Trissy made her way to the front of the passenger compartment.

"As a matter of fact, that's true, Skinny," Trissy confirmed.

"For Christ's sake, there are easier and safer ways to obtain them," Skinny shot back while glaring at Rex's Beretta.

"Well, if you must know, we were looking for a little adventure as well," Rex clarified.

"I am, too, but I don't hijack helicopters at gunpoint," Skinny growled.

"I prefer to use the word 'commandeer.' 'Hijack' is just too hostile and more appropriately used when describing terrorists and murderers, not patriotic swashbucklers such as ourselves," Rex rationalized, waving around the pistol to emphasize his view.

"Agreed. Using our names in the same sentence with 'hijack' is not only offensive, it's down right insulting," Trissy stressed in no uncertain terms as her southern accent suddenly became more pronounced.

"Huh, you're both truly delusional," the chopper pilot concluded as a bead of sweat rolled down his cheek.

"That may be, but we all get our jollies in different ways," Rex replied before taking one last look at Carencrow Regional.

"Now, if you would Skinny, please head south-southeast. New Orleans is our destination," Rex announced, much to Trissy's dismay. However, she remained silent, realizing that Rex had a plan and not wanting to tip his hand.

"I'm not sure we have enough fuel," the now rebellious pilot complained.

"Skinny, let me remind you that we chartered this chopper," Rex emphasized, looking at the gas gauge, which indicated that the tank was nearly full.

"That's rather meaningless since I'm the pilot," Skinny snarled, believing he had the upper hand.

"As the pilot, I'm sure you're open to suggestions. Since fuel is an issue, we could always increase the range of the *Storm Chicken* by jettisoning any dead weight, and I believe it's only appropriate to start with the heaviest object," Rex chuckled, tapping the barrel of his gun against Skinny's belly.

"You wouldn't dare!" the chopper pilot growled defiantly.

"Skinny, you may have your pilot's wings, but without feathers, you're going to drop like a rock. So I suggest you stretch the gas or it's bye-bye birdie. Have I made myself perfectly clear?" Rex stated forcefully in an attempt to head off any thought of a mutiny.

"Rex, you're a son of a bitch," the chopper pilot uttered in disgust, his eyebrows twitching.

"Don't worry, Skinny, I'll make sure Rex doesn't throw you out," Trissy assured the nervous pilot after seeing the fear in his eyes.

"Rex, the thought of tossing the pilot out of this *Storm Chicken* is not one of your brighter ideas, especially since neither one of us can fly a helicopter," she reminded her husband as she tried to break the tension in the air.

"Good point, Trissy. Sorry about that, Skinny. Please accept my apology."

"Huh," Skinny mumbled in anger as he changed course and increased his altitude to one thousand feet. Clearly, the apology was not accepted.

"Well, no one wants to fly with two grumpy men," Trissy exclaimed, as once again, she made an attempt to lighten the mood.

"Rex, on the helipad, you were supposed to yell 'go!' Not 'now,'" Trissy complained after recalling Rex's implicit instructions given before dashing to the helicopter.

"It's just a question of semantics," Rex replied. He turned around and looked at his wife. She could see the sparkle in his eyes.

"I suppose 'charge' and 'retreat' are words which are also interchangeable," Trissy chuckled.

"Under our Dem-o-Rat commander in chief, yes, they are interchangeable," Rex replied affirmatively.

"Well, I'll forgive you this time. But don't let it happen again," Trissy smiled, kissing Rex on the cheek.

"Yes, dear. By the way, who's your new friend?" Rex asked, noticing an elderly black woman sitting up on a stretcher with a non-rebreather on.

"I'm not sure, but if she's in any distress, I think we should call nine one one," Trissy suggested jokingly.

"Trissy, we *are* nine one one."

"Oh, that's right," Trissy responded playfully. "Well then, I'd better find out how we may be of assistance because she's in for a long ride."

"Good idea, and while you're at it, see if she can fly this damn *Storm Chicken*. I'm not sure how much longer Skinny will last," Rex insisted, much to the chopper pilot's dismay.

Trissy looked at the patient and then hesitated for a moment. She felt that it was important to set the record straight with Rex, since he had created this rather unusual medical scenario.

"You realize that normally I would insist upon receiving a report with regard to this patient, her condition, and the treatment she's received thus far from the offgoing nurse. However, being that the flight nurse was so unexpectedly launched from the helicopter and is probably still dazed and rolling on the flight deck, I'll forgo this formality and forgive this breach in continuity of care."

"Please accept my profuse apology for the aggressiveness I displayed toward one of your fellow nurses, but we were limited on space and simply ran out of time."

"Not to worry. That flight nurse has always been a self-centered, egotistical jackass. Please consider your apology accepted," Trissy replied before turning to approach her new patient.

Rex felt confident that Skinny was not a threat, so he holstered the Beretta. Digging into his backpack, he retrieved his handheld GPS device and a pair of binoculars. Rex always insisted upon being prepared. It was time they go on the offensive and take the fight to the radical Islamic terrorists.

Trissy quickly assessed the situation as only a seasoned nurse could. She looked at the patient's vital signs, cardiac rhythm, and oxygen saturation on the monitor. Her vital signs were stable. The patient was in normal sinus rhythm and her oxygen saturation was 100 percent.

"I'm Trissy, your new flight nurse. What your name?" Trissy asked, removing the patient's facemask and revealing a far younger woman than she had expected. Her patient had short gray hair but, oddly enough, no discernible wrinkles. Her face was round and jovial and she had a broad radiant smile.

"My name is Zeila, Zeila 'Katrina' Washington," the patient responded without any noticeable respiratory difficulty. Trissy immediately placed her on a nasal cannula delivering oxygen at two liters per minute. As she was doing so, Trissy noticed a metal clipboard lying on the patient's lap. It contained the nurse's notes, which told the story:

Zeila Washington was eighty years of age. She was five feet four inches tall and weighed 150 pounds. Remarkably, all her home medications were listed. Miss Zeila had been picked up at her home in Turkey Creek at 8:35 a.m. after complaining of respiratory difficulty, which had gone on for several days but became worse this morning. An eighteen-gauge hep-lock had been placed in her right hand and she had been given eighty milligrams of Lasix IV push.

"You're not having any chest pain, are you?" Trissy asked, picking up a stethoscope draped across a defibrillator.

"No, ma'am, just a little trouble breathing, but it's a whole lot better now," Zeila confessed as Trissy listened to her heart and lungs.

"Take some deep breaths for me, please," Trissy requested. Even with all the noise generated by the *Storm Chicken*, she expected the patient's lungs to be wet, but they were clear. Her neck veins were not distended and there was no lower-extremity pitting edema. If Zeila was in congestive heart failure, it was mild.

"Katrina, now that's an unusual name," Trissy remarked while continuing to elevate the patient into a more upright position.

"Yes, ma'am. God told me to take that name after surviving the breach in the levees. He sure did. After running out of food and water,

I had to fend off the robbers and the rapists. I damn near ran out of ammunition," Zeila stated emphatically.

"What do you mean, you nearly ran out of ammunition?" Trissy asked.

"In the Naw-leans heat, some of those young boys got a little frisky, so I peppered their asses with buckshot. I could put up with the floods and the gators but no one was going to abuse this beautiful body. Unless of course there's cold hard cash on the line," Zeila replied with a sparkle in her eyes.

"I see," Trissy acknowledged, shaking her head in disbelief. The story seemed incredible and the implications even more bizarre. Surely, Zesty Zeila wasn't supplementing her social security check by engaging in prostitution.

"So you're from New Orleans?" she asked in an attempt to redirect the enlightening conversation.

"Born and raised," Zeila blurted with pride.

"Well, I'm pleased to know you, Miss Zeila. Rest assured, we're here to help. By the way, what were you doing in Turkey Creek?" Trissy asked.

"I live there with my great-great-granddaughter. My home in the ninth ward was destroyed but the insurance company, the mayor, and the governor won't let me rebuild," Zeila complained.

"I'm sorry to hear that," Trissy empathized, wondering if Zeila had thrown one too many "greats" in front of "granddaughter."

"Zeila, I'm glad to hear that you're breathing better." Trissy removed the oxygen to access her O2 saturation on room air.

"Yes, indeed."

"Well, I need to ask you some more questions, so bear with me," Trissy said, knowing that she had to get a more complete picture of Zeila's present medical condition and her history.

"That's okay, honey child," Zeila replied with a smile.

"How long have you been short of breath?"

"For the last eighty years or so," Zeila answered candidly.

"I thought you were eighty years old."

"No, I'm closer to one hundred and twenty."

"You can't be one hundred and twenty," Trissy remarked, thinking that Zeila might be confused from hypoxia. She looked up at the pulse oximeter, which read 99 percent. Obviously, Zeila was getting enough oxygen to her brain.

"I sure am," Zeila replied without hesitation.

"When were you born?" Trissy asked cautiously, deciding to pursue the age issue.

"Eighteen eighty-three. It was a great year," Zeila chuckled.

"Well, you look fantastic. What's your secret to a long, healthy life?" Trissy asked as she played along. Surely Zeila was not 120. There was no way, Trissy assured herself.

"Moonshine, but only my grandpa's moonshine. It gave me life! However, the first swig was so strong that it would take your breath away and cause your skin to peel. But after that, it became real smooth," Zeila confessed.

Trissy looked on in disbelief. For a moment, Trissy thought that maybe Zeila's grandpa had invented the fountain of youth or at least a concoction worthy of a decent chemical peel. In either case, Trissy intended to pursue this line of questioning later.

"What other medical problems do you have?" Trissy asked.

"I have high blood pressure, congestive heart failure, and the 'gouch,' but I don't have 'skizures' like my uncle Waldo," Miss Zeila responded promptly.

"That's comforting," Trissy chuckled.

"Damn sure is, uh-huh," Zeila replied.

"You don't have 'sugar,' do you?"

"No, indeed!" Miss Zeila shot back.

"Zeila, do you have any allergies?"

"Yes, bad whiskey and cheap men."

"Huh!" Trissy chuckled. "I know exactly what you're saying. I've met a few bad apples along the way myself, as a matter of fact," Trissy confessed, looking at Zeila in amazement. What a character, she thought to herself.

"Trissy?" Rex shouted loudly.

"Yes, Rex."

"How's our patient?"

"She's doing fine, and probably in better shape than our pilot," Trissy replied, handing him the nurse's notes.

"What's her chief complaint?" Rex asked reviewing the notes and the medicines she'd been given.

"Shortness of breath, but she denied chest pain," Trissy answered.

"From the notes, it looks like Miss Zeila has congestive heart failure. Does she sound wet?" Rex asked.

"No, but they gave eighty milligrams of Lasix."

"Could you put in a Foley?" Rex requested, winking at his beautiful wife while handing the nursing notes back.

"Now Rex, really, where am I going to find a Foley catheter in the *Storm Chicken*? Furthermore, even if I could find a Foley, there's no room to maneuver in this flying sardine can, unless Skinny wants to hold the patient's legs apart," Trissy chuckled.

"I don't think that's an option. Skinny's already in a foul mood," Rex smiled as they both became aware that urine was starting to drip from the stretcher.

"It looks like the Lasix is working," Trissy added.

"Skinny, who in the hell stocked this flying death trap?" Rex insisted.

There was no reply to Rex's query. The chopper pilot was in no mood for banter.

"Come on Skinny, lighten up," Rex requested.

"How can I lighten up? I've been hijacked, I'm hungry, I'm tired, and my shift is up," the chopper pilot complained, sniffing the air.

"Well, I'll be sure to make it up to you. How about dinner tonight at 'Commanders Palace,' on me? You know they have twenty-five-cent martinis," Rex suggested, although he had no intention of following through.

"What's that smell?" the chopper pilot asked, looking around the cabin.

"I'm sorry to report that we have a leaky bladder. Grandma is just going to have to wee, wee, wee all the way home," Rex replied articulately as he delivered the bad news.

"Oh, Christ, what a stench, I think I'm going to vomit," the chopper pilot complained bitterly, holding his nose and breathing through his mouth.

Chapter 19

Lieutenant Vickers and SAC Richter raced toward the command center in the lieutenant's rather dated police vehicle.

"Tony, this is Vickers. Did you have any luck reaching Jim Crowell?" Lieutenant Vickers asked over the police radio as SAC Richter looked around the 1990 Ford Explorer.

"We sure did, Lieutenant. He's here now," Tony replied.

"Excellent. We're on our way and will see you soon. Vickers out," Lieutenant Vickers concluded before sliding the radio back into its silver pronged holster.

"The helicopter will stick out like a sore thumb. There's no way the Bents can escape," he assured SAC Richter. But there was no response. The SAC remained deep in thought as Vickers drove on.

"I'm confident we'll have these bozos captured and booked by nightfall," Vickers added in an attempt to strike up a conversation with the preoccupied FBI agent. Again, there was no response. "And I just know that your men will be successful squeezing those two traitors for information. I've heard your techniques of interrogation can be quite persuasive," he added.

Once again, SAC Richter ignored the police lieutenant's words of praise.

"What an arrogant SOB," Lieutenant Vickers mumbled after all his efforts to elicit a dialogue were met by silence. He slammed on the brakes, the police cruiser came to a screeching halt, and both men quickly exited the vehicle.

"Well, here we are," he announced.

"This way, sir." Vickers directed the speechless FBI agent into the dreary concrete building that housed the command center.

"What architectural genius designed this damn ugly structure?" Richter grumbled loudly.

"I'm not sure, but I believe it was the mayor's son," Lieutenant Vickers chuckled. He was now cautiously optimistic that SAC Richter was starting to open up. Possibly the two could develop some element of rapport, he assumed unrealistically.

"Well obviously, corruption flourishes on all levels of government within this mosquito-infested state," Richter keenly observed.

"I'm not sure I could disagree. Here we are, sir," Lieutenant Vickers announced, opening the door to the command center.

Vickers was convinced that the level of sophistication his fair city had achieved would impress SAC Richter. In the center of the spacious room were rows of tables adorned with computers and telephones. There were dozens of men and women in uniform, ready and eager to expeditiously execute Richter's orders. Surrounding the beehive of activity were walls adorned with a multitude of maps of all sizes. There were even schematics reflecting the entire infrastructure of the city.

"I half expected a 'Green Acres' interior," Richter blurted as Lieutenant Vickers rolled his eyes at the insult.

"SAC Richter, this is Jim Crowell. He's a pilot and the owner of Air Med," Lieutenant Vickers said as he introduced the white-haired elderly gentleman with a voice so squeaky that he sounded like Mickey Mouse.

"I'm pleased to meet you, Jim Crowell," the successful businessman said as he reached out to shake SAC Richter's hand, but the special agent ignored the warm gesture and walked right past him.

"Yes, well," Jim Crowell muttered discouragingly. However, he quickly sucked up his pride and shrugged off the blatant snub. He was a can-do guy who was there to assist the FBI and the police department in any way he could. There was an important mission to accomplish and he wanted to be a part of it. Jim rolled up his sleeves as he turned to follow Richter.

"Ladies and gentleman, your obligation is to find that hijacked helicopter. Now, get to work, damn it!" Richter barked before scrutinizing a map of the state that covered one wall of the expansive room.

"Crowell, what in the hell do we have here?" Richter asked as the owner of Air Med stepped in front of him.

"I've taken the liberty of giving you some idea of our chopper's range," Jim Crowell calmly replied, looking the SAC straight in the eye.

"When Air Med two-niner took off this morning on a nine-one-one call, she was fully loaded. Given the distance covered in that roundtrip, I estimate the chopper now has just over four hundred gallons a fuel on board. That would give her a range of approximately one hundred and fifty miles." Jim Crowell pointed to the red circle on the map, which reflected the maximum flight radius.

"Does that line extending out from Carencrow reflect their flight path?" Richter asked. The door of the command center opened and Leslie Valentino walked in, unbeknownst to him.

"Yes, sir, it does; current and projected. Every five minutes the control tower gives us an update as to the chopper's coordinates which we, in turn, plot on this map," Jim Crowell confirmed.

"Interesting, the bastards could even reach New Orleans, and it would appear that the wretched Crescent City is their intended destination," Richter surmised as he scratched at his chin.

"Yes, sir, but there are a multitude of desolate areas between their present location and New Orleans in which they could set down unnoticed and never be seen again," Jim Crowell shared.

"They'll never disappear! Not on my watch, Crowell!" Richter barked defiantly as he continued to examine the possibilities. He quickly realized that the helicopter could even make it offshore into the gulf.

"I wouldn't be too sure," Jim Crowell mumbled. He came to the conclusion that the SAC was an arrogant jackass.

"The Bell Chase Naval Air Station is in New Orleans, isn't it, Crowell?" Richter demanded.

"Yes sir, it is."

"Well, surely the Navy has a few goddamn helicopters, which the base commander could make available for our use and at my discretion," Richter asssumed.

"Unfortunately, the Navy did have a few helicopters attached to the base, but they were pulled out after last year's budget cuts," Jim Crowell informed the increasingly agitated SAC while anxiously awaiting a much-anticipated explosive reply.

"What kind of fucking base is the Navy running?" Richter growled, pounding his fist against the map.

Jim Crowell began to snicker but quickly regained his composure. He was starting to enjoy the comical antics of the volatile FBI agent.

"Well, what in the hell does the Navy have remaining at the base? Flightless goony birds or blue-footed boobies, perhaps?" Richter asked sarcastically.

"I believe there's an F-eighteen fighter squadron still attached to that base," Jim Crowell added rather reluctantly as his desire to assist the crazy-eyed abrasive FBI agent quickly waned.

"Excellent. Thank God!" Richter blurted loudly. "It would appear that Dr. Bent's fortunes are about to change," he announced joyfully.

"Lieutenant Vickers, have someone in this group of useless uniformed lookie loos put down their coffee cups and raise Bell Chase. I want to speak with the commanding officer, pronto."

"Yes, sir," Lieutenant Vickers replied, walking past Leslie and toward a fellow officer, whom he knew could promptly accomplish the task.

"Bell Chase, F-eighteen fighter jets? For what reason, SAC Richter?" Leslie Valentino queried.

Richter immediately recognized her voice and wheeled around quickly only to come face-to-face with his persistently nagging nemesis. Once again, he was speechless. Leslie could clearly see that he was wound up tighter than a drum. Even the muscles in his neck had contracted with such force that they were beginning to spasm. Moments later, his face turned beet red.

"How in the hell did you find me this time?" Richter asked in a tone, which clearly reflected that the word "bitch" had been grudgingly omitted.

"Honestly, it's getting easier and easier to track you. I can ask anyone on the street if they've seen a bowed-up, bull-frog-like man with a short temper and a simple mind. Lo and behold, that one query always leads to you," Leslie Valentino replied, watching Richter struggle for the fortitude to control his anger. "Again, what are your intentions in scrambling the F-eighteens?"

"None of your damn business," Richter growled. Jim Crowell slowly walked away and out of the line of fire.

"That's where you're wrong. Once again, let me remind you that I'm your superior and you answer to me," Leslie replied calmly. "You're not privy to all the intelligence that is available, Special Agent Richter. Dr. Bent and his wife have information that would prove invaluable to the security of this nation," she continued, a futile attempt to get a stubborn FBI agent to understand the consequences of his actions.

However, her words had the exact opposite effect. The emotionally labile Richter felt threatened and immediately went on the offensive.

"Bullshit! They're terrorists, pure and simple. Their lives have no value. Why in the hell can't you come to that logical conclusion?" Richter growled, moving within inches of Leslie's face. "Let's face it Missy, you don't have the tactical experience necessary to catch these turkeys or the balls to make the right decision once you've caught them."

"That may be, but after years of rather obvious steroid abuse, I'm sure you don't either. Furthermore, my actions are neither encumbered nor controlled by dangling, atrophied raisin-like appendages. Now, my question still stands. What are your intentions?" Leslie demanded to know, standing her ground.

"Why, to blast the fucking Bents from the skies, of course," Richter shot back with a smirk.

"No sir, not as long as I'm still in command of this operation," Leslie assured her recalcitrant subordinate.

"Lieutenant Vickers, has anyone tried to raise the aircraft?"

"Yes, ma'am, but there's been no response," the lieutenant replied as he walked around the conference room table and back toward the map.

"SAC Richter, I expect you to establish communications with the Air Med chopper and—" Leslie said firmly before being interrupted.

"I've raised Air Med two-niner!!" Sergeant Carrie Blades shouted.

The command control room suddenly went silent as the police sergeant patched the communication into the overhead speakers.

"This is Air Med two-niner. My altitude is one thousand and I am presently on a heading of one hundred ten. There are four on board and our destination is New Orleans," Skinny suddenly volunteered to air traffic control.

"Well, at least he's predictable," Rex said to himself, confident that his disinformation had been conveyed with total honesty and forthrightness.

"Dr. Bent, there's someone who is very interested in speaking with you," Skinny smiled, handing Rex his headset.

"You don't say. It's not Inspector Clouseau, is it?" Rex asked the less-than-amused pilot as he placed the headset over his ears.

"Hello," Rex whispered timidly.

"Dr. Bent, this is SAC Richter of the FBI. You have used up eight of your allotted nine lives. Several Air Force jets have been scrambled to your location. Not as escorts, mind you, but with explicit instructions to blow your sorry ass from the skies. Land that bird—NOW!"

"I'm not sure I remember how to land, comrade. I believe I push the stick away from me. Is that correct?" Rex asked in an attempt to ignite one of Richter's many volatile and easily located hot buttons.

"You fuckin' bas—!" Richter screamed as Rex yanked the connection to the headset free from the control panel.

"Mission accomplished," Rex snickered, handing Skinny the permanently disabled communication device.

"Skinny, I suppose we should descend to two hundred feet and head south-southwest toward Whiskey Bay, as Richter has requested," Rex ordered nonchalantly.

"Rex, who was that?" Trissy asked.

"I'd like to say that it was another persistent salesman with the wrong number, but in fact it was the villainous Rectal Richter," Rex replied before looking at the heli pilot.

"Damn it, Skinny, in the future may I recommend that you place your *Storm Chicken* on the 'National No Cluck List.' It's our only hope for flying the friendly skies without interruption," Rex complained constructively as the helicopter veered to the right and reduced altitude.

"Hum," Skinny snarled while shaking his head. "Whiskey Bay covers a one-hundred-square-mile area. Exactly where would you like to go?"

"Away from the 'Turbine-Free Zone' and into harm's way. Fly on, Skinny," Rex insisted, lifting the binoculars to his eyes and scanning the horizon.

Intrigued by Miss Zeila's spirit and captivated by her own curiosity, Trissy found the courage to ask her unpredictable patient one more question.

"Are you married, Miss Zeila?"

"Hell no, I ain't married to no old rooster! They're all trouble and the skinny ones are the worst. All they do is raise hell, crow, and run around the barnyard. There's no way this young hen is gonna ruffle her feathers for any bird struttin' his stuff. You best learn that while you're young, child," a street-smart Zeila huffed as she crossed her arms, but her tough demeanor soon gave way to a smile.

"Excellent advice, Miss Zeila, I'll be sure that the renegade rooster sitting in the copilot's seat is made fully aware of our stance on this issue," Trissy smiled with appreciation. She had never met anyone quite like Zeila 'Katrina' Washington.

Minutes later the commandeered helicopter had flown over Interstate 10 and was approaching the eastern edge of Whiskey Bay. There were multiple dense groupings of bald cypress trees interrupted by large irregular patches of floating greenery. However, from the air, this normally vibrant ecosystem appeared lifeless and the waters below, dark and foreboding. Not a sparkle, ripple, nor reflection could be detected for miles. It was as if all ambient light shining down on the swamp on this early afternoon had been swallowed up by an unforgiving black hole.

Rex continued to look intently through his binoculars. He was scanning the swamp when he caught a glimpse of a rectangular silhouette on a small peninsula off in the distance.

"Skinny, come right ten degrees and head in this direction," Rex requested, pointing toward the area that had drawn his interest. He continued to adjust his focus as the whirlybird came closer.

"What do you see, Rex?" Trissy asked, straining to look out the cockpit window.

"I'm not sure. Wait a minute. There appears to be three buildings, a dock, and several trucks, all crammed onto a small jut of land!" Rex relayed with excitement.

"Perhaps we've found the proverbial needle in the haystack," Trissy replied enthusiastically as she zeroed in on Rex's find.

Rex recorded the location on GPS. "How unusual—the owner of this handsome piece of property has amassed quite a number of U-Haul trucks. There must be seven or eight of the rickety rectangular beasts parked around the camp. I don't think there's any doubt that 'U' marks the spot!"

"Let's go in for a closer look. I'd like to see what we're up against," Trissy requested.

"I don't think so!" Skinny growled defiantly.

Chapter 20

The skies were bright blue and the sun was shining on a magnificent afternoon in southern Louisiana. A caravan of four cars suddenly slowed and took a right off State Highway 72 onto an obscure, unmarked gravel road nearly hidden by dense foliage. One by one, each vehicle vanished into the unknown as the long, bushy leaves parted briefly only to quickly swing back into place.

"I just know you'll love our camp on Whiskey Bay," GeeHad assured Dr. Cornelius Lyons, his henchman at Carencrow General Hospital notorious for his ruthless attacks on anyone and everyone who stood in the way of management or the hospital turning an obscene profit. The vehicle they were riding in proceeded cautiously onward.

"Undoubtedly, GeeHad. Are you sure it's still here?" Dr. Lyons asked facetiously, although the leaves engulfing the vehicle obscured the view ahead.

"Yes, as Mohammad is my witness," GeeHad declared with a sinister smile that went unnoticed.

"Let me assure you that we, your faithful Carencrow General followers, truly appreciate the invitation," Dr. Lyons said as the Bentley emerged from the brush.

"There, you see. Allah knows no bounds," GeeHad announced after entering a clearing lined with magnificent, old moss-laden cypress trees. He immediately stepped on the gas and his heavy luxury car responded instantaneously.

"That's my understanding and belief as well. I have been reading the Koran as you had suggested. Mohammad is truly an inspiration," Dr. Lyons announced with trepidation as he adjusted his seatbelt and held on tightly.

"As you continue to be enlightened and realize the immense power that Allah wields, you will become a true believer," GeeHad assured the doctor as the vehicle raced down the narrow road.

"As a Jew, I've always believed that the Christians were dogs. Your forefathers almost wiped out the Christian religion during the Crusades. Tell me, I'm interested in knowing if the religious wars have returned?" the scholarly but self-serving Dr. Lyons asked.

"Not at all," GeeHad replied as his grip on the steering wheel tightened. Then, in a somewhat calmer and more reserved tone, he continued. "Although many infidels believe otherwise, their words are false and their accusations filled with hate. We will defend our way of life, but Islam has always been, and will continue to be, a very peaceful religion," GeeHad shared convincingly with the greedy but suspicious doctor who analyzed his every word.

"Yes, indeed. Muslims are a kind and generous people who have been misunderstood by their oppressors throughout time," Dr. Lyons replied hesitantly and without sincerity as the Bentley slowed.

"Ah, here we are. Welcome to Camp Eagle," GeeHad announced enthusiastically. He rolled through a metal gate and passed several angry young men wielding automatic weapons. His spirits soared when he recognized Mohammad ahead in the distance standing next to the shale-covered circular drive.

The Bentley came to a stop in front of the command post just as two handheld surface-to-air missiles were discharged. The fiery rockets screamed skyward leaving trails of white smoke, which slowly dissipated in the light breeze.

◆

"Onward, Skinny, into the Valley of..." Rex began, but mid-sentence, the *Storm Chicken* was rocked by an explosion. There was a flash of light and smoke suddenly engulfed the cabin.

"Trissy, are you all right?" Rex screamed, straining to look into the rear passenger compartment. Instantaneously, the nose of the chopper pointed downward at a precarious angle and the tail rotor started to twist violently to the right.

"I think so, Rex. Miss Zeila, are you okay?" Trissy shouted, quickly examining her patient for wounds.

"I sure am, but let me tell you, this has been one hell of a bumpy ride," Zeila complained.

Rex looked to his left. Ralph 'Skinny' McKinney was slumped over and unresponsive. There was no time or need to check for a pulse. His mottled lifeless body left no doubt. The chopper pilot was dead and the *Storm Chicken* was going down.

◆

A brilliant flash of light preceded a loud explosion. As the two men exited the vehicle, they could see a shiny object nearly occluded by thick, black smoke falling from the skies.

"Uninvited visitors?" GeeHad smiled while asking Mohammad. Dr. Lyons, normally cool, calm, and collected, looked on with grave concern as a fire erupted onboard the crippled aircraft before it disappeared behind the trees.

"No, it's hunting season. You know, GeeHad, we do have a permit from Fish and Wildlife," Mohammad quipped sternly and without emotion as the two men hugged and symbolically kissed one another on the cheeks.

"I thought hunting season was over for airborne water fowl," Dr. Lyons replied slowly and apprehensively, his voice beginning to quiver. However, he soon became distracted as the three vehicles traveling in their caravan suddenly came to a rumbling stop on the loose gravel. He could hear car doors open and the occupants exiting. Dr. Lyons immediately turned away from the black smoke billowing skyward.

"It ended last week, but infidels are in season year-round," Mohammad responded with an evil grin. The cold and calculating Dr. Lyons suddenly started to break a sweat.

"Mohammad, this is Carencrow General's Medical Director. He is a true and trusted friend," GeeHad announced as he introduced the two men.

"I'm pleased to meet you, Mohammad," Dr. Lyons said with a great deal of reservation as he extended his hand.

"It's my pleasure to welcome you to our humble but well-fortified camp," Mohammad replied as the camp erupted with activity. Suddenly, several well-armed men dashed toward a wooden dock. Seconds later, a beautiful, sleek Glastron with twin 150-horsepower engines raced out of the tranquil inlet.

"What's all the excitement?" Dr. Lyons asked, although he felt certain that he knew the answer.

"Well, you can't hunt without retrieving and then displaying the kill," Mohammad responded with a jovial laugh that appeared to be out of character for the stodgy Muslim.

"Mohammad, unfortunately one of the members of our group, Dr. Gonzo Gonzales, our dedicated emergency department director, passed away rather unexpectedly a few days ago," GeeHad announced. "However, it's my pleasure to introduce you to the other loyal members of our hospital group. From left to right we have Ms. Teresa Talon, our emergency room director of nursing, Ms. Martha Mucker, Carencrow's chief operating officer, and Mr. Johnny Cinch, our chief financial officer." Each person introduced nodded in acknowledgment of their recognition.

"Oh, and I almost forgot Sheguano and Dungsha. They're registered nurses who work in the emergency department. They prefer to be called 'Mean' and 'Evil,'" GeeHad chuckled.

"Ah, what splendid monikers," Mohammad replied with a smirk.

"Pleased to meet you," Evil said, extending her hand, but Mohammad chose to ignore the insulting gesture. Although at first he was unsure if this buzzard was, in fact, the lowest form of life on the planet—a woman. Gritting his teeth, he quickly regained his composure and clasped his hands together.

"Welcome, one and all," Mohammad replied insincerely.

"GeeHad, we recently purchased a houseboat and have arranged a tour of spectacular Whiskey Bay for you and your distinguished guests. There are cocktails and hors d'oeuvres on board as well as a very knowledgeable guide who is intent on showing you the beauty of life and the reality of death in the swamp. So if you would, please proceed down to the dock," he requested as Yassar approached.

"I hope that's not dinner," Mean whispered to Evil after observing one of Mohammad's men wrestling an ornery goat tethered to a tree.

"We'll just have to drink a lot more if it is," Evil suggested as the goat fell to the ground and the man withdrew a large serrated knife from its leather sheath.

"I don't think that's humanly possible," Mean replied as her stomach growled. She was suddenly overwhelmed by wave of nausea.

"Maybe you're right," Evil conceded as the knife came down and the goat suddenly went limp.

No sooner had Yassar whispered into Mohammad's ear than a new flurry of activity erupted on the dock. Suddenly, two sleek high-powered speedboats and several waverunners raced off into the swamp.

"That's very kind of you," GeeHad replied to the leader of Camp Eagle as the group slowly filed past the reserved yet somehow elated Mohammad.

"By the way," Mohammad announced loudly as his guests stopped and turned around. "Yassar has arranged dinner for five o'clock. He assures me that it will be spectacular, so please refrain from being eaten by our scaly neighbors and don't be late." His unsuspecting guests chuckled.

Chapter 21

THE DISABLED HELICOPTER CONTINUED to plunge, nose-first, toward Earth at an ever-increasing speed while the gyration of the tail rotor began to violently spin the aircraft counterclockwise in tighter and tighter circles. The smoke within the cockpit eliminated all visual references while the spinning sensation added to the confusion and disorientation. Additionally, a multitude of alarms kept buzzing louder and louder. For those on board, fear and danger had been well surpassed by sheer terror, which increased exponentially with each beat of their hearts.

"I'm having trouble breathing again," Zeila complained after inhaling the noxious smoke from within the cabin.

"Rex, do something!" Trissy coughed as she briefly searched for the non-rebreather to place on Zeila's face: an impossible task with zero visibility.

"Hold on!" Rex yelled, grabbing the stick and placing his feet on the rotor control pads. Rex pulled back on the stick with all his might, attempting to lift the nose and slow their rapid descent. Concurrently, he depressed the right rotor pad, assuming it might eliminate the godawful, disorienting spinning.

"Rex, please hurry! I'm getting dizzy," Trissy complained as the force of gravity remained intent on screwing their crippled aircraft deeply into the ground.

"I'm dizzy too and I feel like I'm going to vomit," Zeila growled.

"Rex, what exactly is our PROBLEM?" Trissy screamed.

"We've been hit by a surface-to-air missile. The pilot is dead, the engine is out, the rotor is kaput, and we're falling like a rock!" Rex yelled, attempting to push Skinny back from the control stick, which was now lodged somewhere deep within several rolls of fat.

"You didn't have to be that honest!" Trissy shouted back.

Suddenly, the pilot and copilot's doors were flung open and ripped off by the tremendous escalating centrifugal force. As a cold wind rushed through, the smoke in the cabin began to clear. In the haze, Trissy could see Rex struggling.

"How can I help?" Trissy yelled.

"Skinny is slumped over the control stick and it won't budge. Try to pull him free!" Rex yelled, continuing to fight for control of the *Storm Chicken*. Rex assumed that the main blade was spinning (autorotating) at high speed because of the freefall. If he could pull back on the stick just above the ground, the main rotor would generate enough upward lift to slow their descent and possibly save their lives.

"What do you mean, pull him free? THROW HIS ASS OUT!" Trissy screamed, reaching over Skinny in a frantic attempt to find the circular mechanism that would release the pilot's shoulder harness.

"I thought you assured Skinny that he wouldn't have to flap his wings," Rex replied, feeling compelled to remind Trissy of her recent humanitarian guarantee.

"That's when he was still breathing. A lot's changed in the last thirty seconds!" Trissy yelled, continuing to struggle to remove the dead pilot from his seat.

"I see," Rex muttered, trying to shove Skinny closer to his emergency exit door and out into the freedom of the wild blue yonder.

"Rex, I can't find the harness release buckle!" Trissy yelled in frustration.

"Trissy, pull up on his gut," Rex insisted after realizing that there was no way to manhandle or coax Skinny from his seat.

"Damn, he's dead weight!" Trissy screamed, grabbing Skinny's jelly belly and pulling backward with all her might. Slowly, she made progress, dislodging Skinny's lifeless body from the control stick.

"That goes without saying," Rex laughed, pushing Skinny's rolls of layered fat upward toward Trissy.

"I'm still dizzy and my belly is rumbling!" Zeila yelled.

"Hang on, Zeila," Rex pleaded, just as Zeila started to vomit.

"Rex, the control panel is on fire!" Trissy screamed, watching flames leap from behind the console.

"Good God!" Rex gasped.

"Rex, please get us out of this mess!" Trissy screamed, maintaining a firm grip on Skinny while watching the windshield begin to melt.

"I'm trying, I'm trying!" Rex yelled, watching several black dials on the control panel spin out of control.

Without a visual reference, Rex was unsure as to the *Storm Chicken*'s attitude and, most importantly, altitude. However, he could sense that the cold, dark waters of Whiskey Bay were rapidly approaching. There was no doubt that the Earth's gravitational pull was about to claim another crippled victim.

Unexpectedly, Skinny gave way as the last roll of adipose tissue cleared the control stick. Trissy lost her grip and flew backward, landing on Zeila.

"Ooof," Zeila moaned, as her nurse slammed into her queasy abdomen without warning.

"Sorry, Zeila," Trissy apologized as Zeila continued to heave.

With the control stick free, it suddenly jerked backward with Rex's continued forceful pull.

"Yes!" Rex screamed.

Immediately, the nose of the aircraft started to lift and Rex could sense the rapid, uncontrolled descent start to slow. However, the spinning had become worse.

Suddenly, there was a loud explosion and a tremendous downward jolt. The Air Med chopper had splashed down in Whiskey Bay.

The main rotor blades shattered instantaneously upon impact and large shards flew hundreds of yards in all directions, churning up the placid waters and ripping through trees as well as the dense surrounding vegetation. Then all was quiet, with the exception of a loud hissing sound generated as the cold, brackish waters of the bayou rapidly cooled the hot aircraft engine. The chopper had come to rest on its left side in several feet of water. Flames flickered from within the console and from what remained of the mangled tail section while smoke and steam billowed skyward as the unforgiving swamp engulfed the downed chopper.

With the exception of the pilot, all had survived the helicopter crash. Rex and Trissy were badly shaken, but Zeila remained virtually unscathed.

"Thank you, Jesus! My stomach feels a whole lot better!" Zeila praised the Lord from the snug confines of her stretcher, which had remained dry and upright.

Trissy moaned, placing her hand on her head. After being so violently tossed about the cabin, she could feel a large scalp contusion.

"Are you all right, Trissy?" Zeila asked, calmly folding her arms on her lap.

"I'm not sure. Everything keeps spinning," Trissy complained, finding herself sitting in muddy water, surrounded by jagged tree stumps. By some miracle, she had not been impaled by the foreboding remains of the gnarly forest.

"You look fine except for that knot on your head," Zeila observed as Trissy slowly brushed away the floating debris.

"Oh no, cold water—not again!" Trissy complained.

"You best sit back down," Zeila recommended, watching Trissy struggled to maintain her balance.

"Thanks, Zeila," Trissy replied, fighting fiercely to stay upright, clearly not heeding Zeila's sound advice.

"No one listens to Zeila, a black beauty and the wisest medicine woman the world has ever known," Zeila grumbled, watching her stubborn nurse continuing to struggle.

Trissy's mind started to clear and her thoughts focused once again on her patient. "Zeila, are you all right?"

"Of course I'm all right, and I'm starting to breathe better again," Zeila replied zestfully.

"What happened?" Trissy asked, struggling to remember the events preceding the accident.

"Your husband wrecked the helicopter."

"I thought he knew how to fly," Trissy mumbled, shaking her head and blinking frequently, hoping that the dizziness and confusion would resolve.

"Well, he must have attended some sorry-ass Arab flying school where they teach the students how to take off but not how to land," Zeila concluded, recalling the terrorizing moments before the crash.

"I heard that, Zeila!" Rex shouted, finding himself sitting on the deceased helicopter pilot.

"Rex, are you all right?" Trissy asked, turning her attention to her husband.

"I'm not sure, but I'm still breathing, which is always a good sign," Rex replied as he cautiously wiped the blood from his brow and attempted to gather his thoughts. Trissy slowly made her way toward the forward compartment.

"As a certified heathen, you can't be dead. Unless of course, hell has frozen over," Trissy reassured her renegade husband as she started to shiver. "Rex, you're bleeding. Come closer and let me look at that rattled coconut," Trissy insisted.

"How did you and Miss Zeila fare?" Rex asked as Trissy looked for the source of blood dripping down his forehead and into his eyebrow.

"I'm a bit shaken, but I think Zeila is fine," Trissy replied optimistically. She parted his thinning hair and found a small two-centimeter laceration just within the hairline.

"Zeila, are you sure you're not hurt?" Rex shouted so their patient could hear him.

"Hell yes! It's gonna take more than a fall from the skies to kill Zeila 'Katrina' Washington. Um-umm! By the way, with all this water, it looks like the levees gave way again. I just knew those jackass Republicans couldn't rebuild our fine city as promised," Zeila observed.

"Zeila, we're in Whiskey Bay, not New Orleans," Rex sneered as Trissy unbuckled the straps that secured Zeila to the stretcher.

"Oh, Lord, not another conspiracy-minded, global-warming Dem-o-Rat," Rex mumbled loudly.

"What was that?" Zeila asked, detecting the sarcastic reply.

"I said that we're seventy-five miles from New Orleans," Rex clarified, cupping his hands and scooping up brackish water to throw onto the smoldering control panel fire.

"How do you know? You're not a pilot, and I'm starting to wonder if you're a healer or if you're just another snake oil salesman," Zeila said in no uncertain terms.

Rex shook his head in disgust and rapidly came to the conclusion that it was time to retreat from the verbal skirmish with this crazy woman.

"You didn't hit your head, did you?" Trissy asked softly, wondering if Zeila was confused.

"It damn sure looks like the ninth ward to me. Uh-huh, yes indeed," Zeila observed, ignoring Trissy's question while Rex retrieved his binoculars and GPS device.

"Now, let's get out of this flying body bag," Rex insisted, grabbing his backpack and climbing out onto the wreckage.

"You don't have to tell me twice," Trissy agreed, grasping the handle on the passenger side compartment door to slide it open.

"They just don't make these choppers like they used to," Rex whispered, observing the twisted remains of the *Storm Chicken* while balancing himself with one foot on the doorframe and the other on the helicopter skid.

"Zeila, it's time to go," Trissy said, assisting Zeila to her feet. She immediately noticed that Zeila had no respiratory difficulty.

"That's good, because I'm getting powerfully hungry."

"I'll go first and then help you up," Trissy instructed.

"Let's go ladies, *wikiwiki*!" Rex stressed, noticing that the fire on the fuselage had grown larger.

The noxious smell of the charred, burning metal filled his lungs and Rex began to cough while the smoke and steam impaired his vision. As the gentle breeze shifted direction, the air cleared and

Rex could see that Trissy had already opened the sliding passenger compartment door. Rex leaned over to give her a hand but she popped out without any assistance.

"My, you're athletic," Rex remarked after witnessing how easily Trissy had extricated herself.

"That comes from diet, exercise, and lots of Chardonnay," Trissy replied with a smile, examining their less-than-hospitable surroundings.

"No doubt," Rex agreed before looking into the passenger compartment and wondering how in the world they were going to get Zeila out.

"Where's Skinny?" Trissy asked, clearly not remembering the circumstances that had taken his life.

"Skinny is circling the heavens in search of a wing and a prayer," Rex replied, wondering how Trissy had forgotten that key detail. However, after noticing the large contusion on her forehead, he quickly assumed that she had probably sustained a mild concussion.

"What in the hell are you two doing up there? Where are your manners, Zeila is turning into a prune while you two reminisce. Now, get me out of this wet dungeon before I really get riled up," the patient demanded.

Trissy noticed a fast-moving object after scanning the horizon.

"Rex, it looks like there's a motorboat approaching."

"Oh, Christ," Rex gasped, looking in the direction where Trissy was pointing.

"Somehow, I don't think that's Papa Boudreaux's delivering a pizza to the local, swamp-dwelling yokels," Trissy surmised.

"No, one must assume that they are the owners of the surface-to-air missile that brought us down," Rex replied.

"Please, tell me that you have a plan," Trissy asked. Rex surveyed the area and thought for a moment.

"Yes, in fact I do. Zeila, the bad guys are coming. Stay put, don't move and don't say a word. We'll be back for you." Rex slid the passenger door shut on the demolished whirlybird.

"I'll get you Republican-loving honkies for this. This is patient abandonment, pure and simple! Don't leave me!" Zeila shouted at the top of her lungs as the door slammed shut.

"Damn, stuck in the back of the bus again. Wait until Jesse Jackson, Al Sharpton, and the Black Folks for Zeila coalition hear about this. I'm gonna be raising some hell!" Zeila started to shiver in the cold waters.

The downed chopper rocked when Trissy and Rex jumped into the brackish waters of Whiskey Bay. Each splash was followed by a soft landing.

"Damn that's cold," Rex complained. The water quickly rose above his waist as he sank further and further into the thick bayou sediment. Given her weight and her slender physique, Trissy fared far better. She didn't sink as deeply into the submerged tar-like terrain.

"My feet feel as if they're stuck in glue," Trissy complained, finding it extremely difficult to take her first step and break free of the unyielding bottom muck.

"That's for sure," Rex agreed, struggling as well.

"This way," he insisted.

They waded through nature's dangerous and unforgiving obstacle course toward a grouping of three large cypress trees fifty yards away.

"Rex, please tell me that there're no dangerous snakes or man-eating alligators in this pleasantly named bay," Trissy begged as the water rose above her chest and she dodged partially submerged tree limbs.

"It's entirely possible that all the ornery bayou critters are stewing in a large pot of Cajun gumbo, but highly unlikely," Rex replied while struggling through the muddy waters and occasionally stumbling over sunken unseen logs.

"That's comforting Rex, thank you," Trissy acknowledged with concern while increasing her stride and speed, making every attempt to walk on water.

Suddenly, the water became more shallow and the going far easier. They dashed the last ten yards to the cypress trees and were quickly out of sight.

"Trissy, hold this for me please," Rex requested, handing her his backpack. He unsnapped the top flap, threw it back, and reached in, withdrawing the barrel and stock of a high-powered rifle.

"Rex, I can hear the motorboat," Trissy cautioned moments before becoming aware of the engines throttling down. Slowly, she peered around the tree.

"Hurry, Rex!" Trissy stressed as she watched the boat approach the downed chopper. Seconds later, Rex had his weapon assembled and the scope attached.

Suddenly, there was great deal of shouting in Arabic. Rex fumbled for his ammunition.

"As a world traveler, I can assure you that they're saying, 'Come out with your hands up, you Yankee Dogs,'" Rex embellished while securing the loaded clip into the magazine.

"Rex, they aren't Japanese. They're Muslims. You've got the wrong war and the wrong enemy." Trissy exhaled loudly and quickly in a manner which revealed her growing frustration.

"AaaaSooo—so very sorry," Rex replied as he secured a round in the chamber before he and Trissy peered around the tree trunk.

The motorboat was now adjacent to the downed chopper. As the fire on the fuselage continued to rage, dense clouds of smoke and steam drifted skyward from the wreckage, occluding their field of vision.

"There are two men in the boat and a third has already boarded the body of the helicopter. All are armed," Trissy whispered after a gentle breeze momentarily whisked away the smoke and steam.

Rex leveled his rifle and looked through the scope. "Damn." In an instant the breeze had shifted. The smoke obscured his view.

Three loud shots rang out in quick succession. In the cool, dense afternoon air, the lethal sounds were hauntingly magnified.

"Good God!" Trissy gasped, clenching her chest and staggered backward slightly after being startled half to death.

When the smoke cleared, it was obvious that the gunman on top of the chopper had just discharged his weapon into the dead pilot.

"Skinny never stood a chance," Rex remarked grimly as he watched the killer intently.

"He's making his way back to the passenger compartment, Rex. My God, he's got his hand on the door," Trissy whispered loudly, the sound of her voice increasing several octaves.

Rex had the Arab terrorist in his sights and was squeezing the trigger when his target suddenly disappeared in an eerie blanket of grayish mist rising from the remains of Air Med two-niner. However, the sound of the passenger compartment door sliding open was unmistakable.

"Oh!" Zeila screamed, as the petrified patient realized her fate.

As luck would have it, a gentle wintry breeze redirected the smoke and steam just in time for Rex to see the gunman level his weapon.

"Smile for Allah," Rex whispered as he squeezed off a round.

Skinny's murderer was struck squarely in the forehead and the force of the blast hurled the man backward over the waiting boat. Almost simultaneously, the terrorist's automatic weapon started to discharge wildly into the air. There was a large splash as his body touched down and then disappeared beneath the calm waters of Whiskey Bay.

"Nice shot, Rex," Trissy whispered enthusiastically.

"Obviously, this is no time for hesitation, you sorry bastards," Rex lectured, taking aim at his next target.

The two terrorists in the boat froze momentarily as they tried to understand what had happened. Seconds later, their comrade's body surfaced from the dark, foreboding waters. Their faceless friend was now surrounded by a crimson halo, which was rapidly beginning to expand. Instantaneously, the obvious became even more apparent. But time was not on their side.

That brief moment was all Rex needed to squeeze off two more rounds. Each found their mark and the two men fell dead.

"That's one way of securing passage out of this God forsaken swamp. Come Trissy, our water taxi awaits," Rex announced triumphantly, throwing his backpack over his shoulder and wading back toward the remains of the *Storm Chicken*.

"Wow, Rex, I never knew you were such a good shot," Trissy praised, following closely behind, keeping a keen eye on any movement in the water which could very well reveal her worst nightmare, an oncoming, slimy, slithering reptilian predator.

"I'm not," Rex replied stoically, continuing onward through the brackish waters, while Navy SEAL missions in even more destitute areas flashed back from an era long, long ago.

"A Glastron with two big bad Mercury engines—sweet," Rex praised as he approached the speedboat. "Let's just hope this baby has enough gas," Rex added, tossing his backpack and rifle into the sleek motor craft.

"At least it floats," Trissy replied optimistically as Rex swam to the stern, lowered a small retractable metal ladder, and hopped on board.

"Rex, I need some help here," Trissy pleaded while placing her hands on the side of the boat and struggling to lift herself up and out of the swamp.

"Give me one minute. I need to do a little housekeeping. These two dirt balls are demanding an afternoon swim," Rex replied as he tossed the two lifeless bodies overboard. "Here we go," Rex said, lending Trissy a hand.

"Thanks."

The overcast skies were finally starting to clear and, for the first time on this eventful day, the sun shone through. But the brilliant, yellow, radiant ball of warmth was now low on the horizon and the temperature was starting to drop.

"Damn, it's cold," Trissy complained, "and we forgot our coats."

"Trissy, use this," Rex said, tossing her a towel he had noticed lying in the forward compartment.

"Much appreciated," Trissy responded gratefully as she wrapped the dry towel around her shoulders.

"I'll understand if you start to smell like day-old camel," Rex chuckled.

"That's reassuring, but I'm freezing and frost bitten beggars can't be choosy," Trissy shot back while deciding to examine the towel for coarse, tan hairs before sniffing for any pungent odors. "It does smell a little musty but it will have to do," Trissy added, vigorously rubbing her wet hair. The friction soon generated enough heat to rewarm hibernating coronal synapses and Trissy began to think more rationally. Finally, it dawned on her that in the mayhem, she had forgotten all about her patient.

"Zeila!" Trissy yelled as Zeila recognized two familiar voices in close proximity. "Rex, help Zeila," Trissy insisted as she dropped the towel to assist.

"It's about time you two cotton-pickin' rebels returned," Zeila blasted, poking her head out of the passenger compartment.

"Zeila, are you all right?" Rex asked, quickly pulling the boat parallel with the helicopter's exposed skid.

"Hell no! I'm not all right. You gave me medicine that made me piss all over myself, I got so dizzy that I vomited several times as your helicopter fell from the skies, and then some terrorist tried to shoot me. Now, I've done stained my only pair of underwear," Zeila growled as Trissy watched her once oxygen-starved patient nimbly climb from the wreckage. Trissy was clearly amazed at the agility of her feisty eighty-year-old Cajun patient. She wasn't even breathing hard.

"Yes, well, we'll be sure to buy you a new pair of bloomers, Grandma," Rex assured her as he assisted Zeila into the boat.

"You damn sure will. Now, what in Jesus's name took you so long to pull the trigger?" Zeila demanded, putting her hands on her hips and wiggling her upper torso and neck from side to side defiantly.

"I couldn't get a clear shot," an insulted Rex replied, placing his hands on his hips and leaning forward while looking Zeila straight in the eye.

"Oh yeah! I think your genteel ass froze. Well, that's what you get when you place a weapon into some psycho physician's hands—indecision!" Zeila fumed.

"Oh yeah! You don't know what the hell you're talking about, you unappreciative refugee from the ninth ward. I saved you from drowning in your own bodily fluids and then prevented your premature demise at the hands of a terrorist. The way I see it, I saved your rump from roasting, twice!" Rex shot back as he mimicked Zeila by wiggling his upper torso from side to side.

"Honey child, let me remind you that you stole my helicopter, rudely interrupted my right to free medical care, not to mention a complimentary hospital meal, and then nearly got me killed in some wild goose chase," Zeila growled, raising her voice.

"Wild goose chase? We're protecting the country from bad people and attempting to foil an evil plot," Rex replied loudly in an attempt to rationalize with Zeila.

"Well, Boy Wonder, all I say is that you'd better pray that Medicare and Medicaid ain't charged for that helo. Terrorism, my ass, huh," Zeila growled as she stood her ground and battled Rex in a war of words.

"You're delusional," Rex huffed, shaking his finger at his defiant patient.

"You lily-white Republican plantation boys are all the same. Who cares if the beautiful black plantation slave is killed in the heat of the battle?" Zeila fired back, trying to grab Rex's index finger.

"I can't believe this. I just can't believe this. Zeila, I should make you swim back…" Rex started to say when Trissy interrupted him.

"Oh Rex, we have company again," Trissy shouted, pointing toward three boats moving rapidly in their direction.

"Damn!" Rex groaned, watching the approaching threat.

"I'll bet you pissed off my people from Naw-leans and the brothers are coming to rescue me. Hallelujah! Set me free, set me free, God Almighty, set me free!" Zeila sang loudly, raising her fists in the air and beginning to dance.

"Zeila, put a lid on it and take a seat!" Rex demanded. He fired up the engines.

"Trissy, cast off the line. Let's get the hell out of here."

CHAPTER 22

REX THREW THE ENGINE into reverse as Trissy cast off the line from the downed chopper.

"Trissy, look in my backpack and bring me the GPS and my binoculars," Rex requested as he turned the wheel hard to port. The bow of the motorboat slowly swung around until it pointed toward what appeared to be deeper water.

"Will do."

"Hold on!" Rex shouted, shifting into gear. He glanced over his shoulder. Zeila was sitting down in the rear seat, adjacent to the port engine, looking forward with her arms folded, pouting. Trissy had taken the rear seat adjacent to the starboard engine and was rummaging through his backpack. Both appeared relatively safe for throttle up.

"Here we go!" Rex shouted, throwing the throttle forward.

"I've got it!" Trissy shouted, standing to hand Rex the global position locator.

"Oh—*ooof*!" Trissy moaned after immediately and unexpectedly being thrown backward into her seat. The engines dug in while the bow lifted high out of the water.

"Wow, this baby's got some power!" Rex shouted into the wind as the big black Mercury engines roared and the boat quickly gained speed.

"Here you go, Rex!" Trissy shouted as she stood and pulled herself forward, struggling to keep her balance.

"Thanks. I've got the terrorist camp located and I want to mark the position of the downed chopper," Rex shouted, locking in the coordinates and tossing the GPS device onto his seat.

Trissy stood next to Rex and looked over the bow. She remained standing and held on tightly to the death grips secured to the forward console.

"Good thinking. By the way, you don't have any idea how we can get out of this mess, do you?" Trissy asked, knowing full well that the answer would not be what she wanted to hear.

"I haven't the foggiest, but I'm open to suggestions," Rex replied, looking to his right and scrutinizing the terrorists' boats bearing down on them. Instinctively, he turned the Glastron away from the threat and scanned the horizon for any opportunity that would allow them to escape.

Trissy picked up the binoculars to get a closer look at the oncoming danger.

"Well, it looks as if we're in big trouble again, Rex. There are at least four waverunners and perhaps two larger boats, all closing in rapidly," Trissy reported.

"How original, a sinister turban-turning terrorist armada. Only in America could Muslim mobsters amass such a fleet," Rex surmised.

"That's not funny, Rex. Get us out of here."

"I'm trying, I'm trying!" Rex shouted, making sure the throttle was pushed all the way forward and the engines were running wide open.

"Rex, one of the boats seems to be veering off," Trissy added, redirecting her attention.

"The bastards must be trying to flank us," Rex concluded, watching the boat disappear behind a large peninsula.

"Rex, when I scan the horizon in every direction, it all looks the same. There are trees, shrubs, stumps, and water grass everywhere."

"Well, keep your eyes peeled for the Whiskey Bay Visitors' Center because I'd sure like to know where the hell we're going," Rex shouted, dodging a multitude of dead tree trunks protruding from the water.

"Rex, we appear to be heading toward a wide inlet," Trissy announced, adjusting the binoculars to magnify an area two points off the port bow.

"I see it," Rex replied as he scanned the horizon and looked over his shoulder. The terrorists were closing quickly.

"What do you think?" Trissy asked.

"It's worth a try since we appear to be rapidly running out of wide open swamp and the Muslim maggots seem intent on reclaiming their boat."

"Rex, turn left—fast! There's a large sandbar, dead ahead!" Trissy screamed after noticing that the barren jut of land, which appeared to be moving.

"Got ya," Rex replied as soon has he spotted one of nature's many obstacles.

"Gators, huge alligators," Trissy whispered, realizing that the movement that caught her eye was not a mirage.

However, no sooner had Rex turned the wheel hard to port than the danger escalated exponentially.

Whoosh, BOOM! A rocket-propelled grenade shot over the boat and detonated just above the water twenty yards away. Shards of metal whistled by and there were several low-pitched thumps as the shrapnel struck the fiberglass hull.

"Good God, that was close! Is everyone all right?" Rex yelled after the explosion rocked the boat. No one responded. Rex quickly looked around. Trissy stood her ground in the heat of the battle and continued to look forward, scanning the inlet through the binoculars for any other navigational dangers. She appeared not to have been injured, and neither did Zeila who sat stoically in the back, unfazed by the attack.

"Rex, hard right rudder!" Trissy shouted after identifying another treacherous low-lying gator-inhabited sandbar.

"I see it, but it looks more like mud than sand," Rex confirmed, turning the boat hard to starboard.

Whoosh, BOOM! Another grenade shot over the small boat and exploded a short distance off the port quarter. Rex ducked instinctively just as a cloud of shrapnel peppered the Glastron.

"Is everyone all right?" Rex yelled, taking a quick survey. Again, there was no reply.

Trissy had remained standing next to him, calm as a cucumber looking over the bow, while Zeila appeared quite relaxed in her seat as if on a Sunday afternoon drive. Once again, all on board were extremely lucky that the multitude of deadly metal projectiles had not claimed any flesh. However, the boat had not fared so well. The port engine was now starting to smoke.

"Oh, Christ, it looks as if we're about to lose an engine," Rex complained bitterly, turning the wheel to the left, clearing the second obstacle.

After having missed two low-lying alligator-inhabited sand/mudbanks that appeared to be guarding the inlet, their Glastron was now in the center of the channel running wide open and heading toward God knew where.

"That would certainly be unfortunate," Trissy replied as she turned around and surveyed the smoldering engine before looking over the stern at the terrorist armada, which remained in hot pursuit.

"Somehow I don't think that waverunner to the right is going to clear that first obstacle," Rex observed moments before the speedy and agile craft slammed into the unyielding mudbank. The terrorist was ejected over the handlebars. He flew at least fifteen yards, flipping several times in flight before coming to rest in the thick, dark brown muck.

"I hope he doesn't give those gators indigestion. Fish and Wildlife would not be pleased," Trissy surmised with a hint of sarcasm as several large carnivorous prehistoric diners gathered for an unexpected feast.

"Most assuredly, the gators are giving thanks to Allah for a gift from the heavens," Rex concluded.

"Rex, the inlet is getting narrower and it looks like we've entered a river system!" Trissy yelled, putting the binoculars down and looking over the bow.

"I think we have bigger problems," Rex yelled after noticing that the armada had cleared nature's obstacles and were quickly closing the distance.

"Oh, Christ, we're losing this race! Rex, open the throttle!" Trissy shouted, looking over her shoulder.

"The throttle is wide open," Rex growled as more and more smoke was whisked away from the damaged outboard engine.

"Trissy, take the wheel," Rex insisted.

Three waverunners were now within fifty yards and a small arms fire started to erupt. Trissy grabbed the wheel as Rex scrambled for his rifle. She immediately started to zigzag in an evasive maneuver.

"Zeila, stay down," Rex insisted. He snagged his rifle and quickly staggered aft, fighting to maintain his balance as the boat swung unexpectedly to the left and then the right.

"The hell I will! I can tell you right now that you're going to need my help," Zeila assured him.

"Not likely," Rex replied, injecting a round into the chamber and slamming the bolt shut.

"I know Whiskey Bay like the back of my hand," Zeila stated with confidence.

"What do you mean you know this swamp?" Rex asked. "Less than an hour ago you thought you were back in New Orleans, for Christ's sake!" But there was no time to wait for an answer. He leveled his gun and placed the first of three tattered turbine water foul in his crosshairs.

Rex squeezed off three shots in succession. There was an explosion as the third round struck and ignited the gas tank on the small watercraft. The singed terrorist preceded a bright orange ball of flame skyward.

"Wahoo! That'll teach these Turkey-fried terrorists never to straddle an American gas tank!" Rex shouted.

But his celebration was short-lived. Suddenly, a waverunner rammed forcefully into the side of their boat. The collision threw Rex from his seat and onto the deck.

"NO!" Trissy screamed as a tall lean terrorist leaped on board.

Rex was startled. In an instant, he found long, lanky fingers wrapping around his neck and small, beady snake-like eyes staring into his soul. But it was the yellow, frothy sputum and the stench from his foul breath that ignited Rex's fury and rekindled his energy. Rex quickly brought his forearms up and out, breaking the death grip. The two men wrestled for several minutes, exchanging punches. Both nearly fell overboard as their life-and-death struggle continued.

Twice, Trissy tried to turn the tide and pull the man off Rex, while Zeila sat idly by. But at each attempt, Trissy was forcefully knocked to the deck. At moments, each man appeared to have the upper hand; then Rex grabbed the terrorist by the shirt collar before rolling on top. He cocked his fist and punched the man in the face with all of his might. Rex could hear the bones shatter. The spattering of blood and the facial deformity left no doubt that his enemy's upper and lower jaws had been broken in several places. Most importantly, the enemy had been knocked out. An exhausted Rex stood and staggered forward.

"Trissy!" Zeila yelled, pointing to the starboard beam.

Trissy and Rex looked to their right. The remaining waverunner had pulled alongside. Rex had no time to reach for his rifle. However, before the terrorist could level his automatic weapon, Trissy instinctively turned hard to starboard and rammed the smaller craft. The waverunner veered off into a dense grouping of dead and nearly petrified trees. A thick, jagged, fallen tree lay angled and only a few feet above the water line. The rock-hard, waterlogged wood penetrated the terrorist's soft underbelly with ease. His body twitched briefly after being impaled by nature's own punji stick.

"I believe I just lost my appetite for kabobs," Rex freely admitted after witnessing the gruesome death. "No ma'am, no beef or burka kabobs or anything else skewered for me."

"Or me, either," Trissy replied, suddenly feeling nauseous.

"Rex, behind you!" Zeila screamed.

Rex turned around to find the terrorist he had knocked out moments ago coming at him like a raging bull. His attacker had withdrawn a large knife from a scabbard lashed to his waist.

He slashed wildly as he came toward Rex. Rex caught the man's wrist before the pig poker could plunge into his neck. The terrorist kicked Rex's legs out from under him and they both fell to the deck.

"Zeila, I could use a little help here," Rex pleaded as the terrorist lay on top of him and the knife came closer and closer to finding its mark.

"Well, why didn't you ask earlier?"

Zeila grabbed Rex's rifle by the barrel and swung it like a club. The butt of the gun came crashing down onto the terrorist's head, crushing his skull. The man dropped the knife and Rex rolled out from under the dying man.

"Well, you're no Tiger Woods, but I'm most appreciative. Thank you, Zeila," an exhausted Rex gasped as he struggled to his feet while extending his hand in gratitude.

"Don't mention it," Zeila replied as she shook Rex's hand. "You've got to learn how to fight, *boy*. I'd teach you but I fear you're a slow learner; sho' is!" she added, brushing off her hands and calmly taking her seat.

The windy inlet off Whiskey Bay continued to narrow with each turn. Suddenly, there were explosions in the water, and large plumes of water shot up in front of the boat.

"What the hell was that?" Rex asked as he wiped the spray from his face.

"It appears that our neighborhood terrorists are rather persistent," Trissy observed, noticing one last boat in hot pursuit.

"Well, that may be, but they should stick with one weapon. Those are the rules of engagement. You can't be shifting from rocket grenades to rifle grenades. It's just not appropriate," Rex criticized, straining to see the enemy in the dim light.

"Rex, please no more lessons on military ethics! Not now!" Trissy pleaded.

"Sorry, it's a force of habit," Rex chuckled as Trissy continued to look over the bow.

"Forgive me for being alarming, but what's that green mound in front of us?" Trissy shouted.

"I'm not sure, but I think I know someone who does," Rex replied as their speedboat rapidly approached the new obstacle.

"Zeila, you said you knew Whiskey Bay like the back of your hand. Where are we?"

"You're in the False River," Zeila answered without hesitation.

"I see, and where exactly does this False River end?"

"At the 'Not So False' levee," Zeila replied calmly as more explosions fell in close proximity, rocking the boat and showering sheets of water across the deck.

"Rex, you're going to have to ask your questions a little bit quicker," Trissy recommended as the green mound loomed larger.

"Absolutely," Rex replied. "Now Zeila, can we make it around the levee?"

"Not likely, but legend has it that a few boats have jumped over it. The trouble is you're going to end up on the forbidden side of the bay where poachers, bootleggers, and murderers lurk," Zeila stated matter-of-factly.

"Why do I suddenly feel as if I'm talking to 'Miss Cleo'?" Rex asked himself.

"I'm not sure, but you're going that have to find some way to deal with it. Hold on, we're going to jump," Trissy shouted, searching for a suitable last-minute launching point.

"Yes, well, give me a moment to jettison some dead weight," Rex requested before quickly making his way aft.

"No, Rex. We don't have…" Trissy started to say, but the body had been tossed overboard before she had a chance to finish her sentence and Rex had taken a seat next to Zeila.

"Hold on Zeila, we're taking flight. Please, fasten your seatbelt!" Rex shouted politely to their patient turned guide.

"It's about time. I sho' hope there's still water on the other side of this levee," an unshakable Zeila chuckled. The boat hit the embankment at just the right angle and soared, unscathed, over the centuries-old mound.

Chapter 23

As this unlikely bird flew, the propeller began to whine in a high pitch as it searched for a more familiar viscous medium. Trissy placed the engine in neutral as Rex turned toward Zeila. The feisty, elderly woman smiled with satisfaction as she observed the shock on his face and the bewilderment in his eyes. For the first time in hours, Rex fell silent as he braced himself for what lay ahead.

"Yes sir, this sho' do remind me of the good old days!" Zeila shouted into the wind as the Glastron flew past a forest of denuded trees standing vertical in the stagnant waters of the swamp. Suddenly, the bow started to rise, gradually at first, but then more and more rapidly. Rex was convinced that the boat was about to flip when the stern touched down, gently. However, a tranquil landing was not to be. Almost instantaneously, the bow came crashing down with a violent force. There was a big splash and several sudden powerful jolts to the left and then the right as the boat struck and glanced off tree after tree.

"WOW, let's do it again!" an exhilarated Zeila insisted as the boat began to slow. "Rex, you can release your death grip. The eagle has landed," she proclaimed with zeal.

"Zeila, you haven't been sipping any of this swamp water, have you? There are reports of people going mad," a nervous, gravity-oriented Rex asked as his racing heart began to slow.

Rex looked over his shoulder. Much to his relief, the port engine had stopped smoking and the terrorists had not decided to take the leap of faith. All was quiet and the air was still. Darkness had fallen.

"Rex, leave Zeila alone," Trissy requested, finding the switch to the side-mounted searchlight.

"If you don't ask, you don't learn," Rex replied in his own defense.

"Zeila, where are we?" Trissy inquired while placing the engine into gear before easing the throttle forward. Slowly and carefully she steered around natures many obstacles.

"In paradise, my child, in paradise. This was my old stompin' grounds, when Grandma Moses was around," Zeila shared enthusiastically while reflecting on a happier time in her life.

"Rather soggy stompin' grounds, wouldn't you say, Zeila?" Rex said with an air of suspicion as he observed the elderly woman.

"Memories from a well-spent youth," Zeila replied vigorously while making her way toward Trissy.

"Grandma Moses. Huh, I'll bet. She didn't by chance part the waters, did she?" Rex asked sarcastically as he suddenly became aware of a thick, hazy mist engulfing the boat.

"No, but she did filter them for the boys making moonshine, that is. In fact, after one sip of Grandma's moonshine, you damn sure wouldn't need to part the waters. You could walk on 'em!" Zeila answered without breaking stride, the pride more than evident in her voice.

"Zeila, all of a sudden the terrain has changed drastically and the air is unusually warm," Trissy said with surprise as her searchlight illuminated a forest of massive cypress trees, each of which had refused nature's request to drop their leaves and all with thick blankets of moss flowing from the limbs.

"It's the 'Enchanted Black Forest,' where all life begins and ends," Zeila replied, savoring the sweet night air.

"It looks like a water-logged cypress forest," Rex keenly observed, looking around in wonderment.

"This is breathtakingly beautiful," Trissy said with awe as she pushed a lush, low-lying branch aside.

"Trissy, not to worry you, but metamorphosis is a real possibility. If Zeila suddenly changes into some bizarre creature, I'm out of here," Rex whispered as the waters began to gently swirl and a chorus of hoot owls started to sing. Rex's comment was instantaneously met with a bone-chilling look, which could only originate from a displeased spouse. Trissy wisely chose to ignore her husband's concern.

"Hoo, hoo."

"Man, what a big owl!" Rex gasped, noticing a four-foot-tall brown owl perched on a low-lying limb of an adjacent cypress tree. "That beautiful bird reminds me of the owl that suddenly landed on a desolate dirt road at night in Kruger National Park, shortly after I lost my dad. His nickname was Al! Our jeep came to a sudden stop some twenty yards away. Illuminated by the high beams, the owl kept staring at us for several minutes before flying off," Rex added as the memory from a magical evening at the Mala Mala Game Reserve in South Africa came rushing back.

"That has to be the largest owl I've ever seen!" Trissy agreed as she examined the magnificent bird. "Wow, I never knew that story about your dad. How bizarre, an 'Al' landing on a dirt road in front of an oncoming jeep in the middle of nowhere. Obviously, your dad came down from the heavens just to say hi."

"Yep, big but dumb. Well, like father, like son," Zeila remarked, much to everyone's surprise.

"Zeila, you're cruising for a bruising! What do you mean 'dumb'?" Rex demanded to know after being bludgeoned with an unexpected insult.

"The damn bug-eyed bird should be in a warm barn fluffing its feathers and chasing rodents, not hanging out in a cold, damp, alligator-infested swamp."

"The owl just happens to be the smartest bird on the planet. Maybe it's just hanging around checking out all the action," Rex said in defense of the bird, which he had always admired.

"Hoo, hoo, hoo—Hoo are you foolin'? That scruffy, foul-tasting bird doesn't sing, doesn't chirp, and can't even say 'who's dare' or 'who's dat,'" Zeila criticized.

"Yeah, well, it's probably the only animal in the world smart enough to know 'Hoo's Ya Baby's Daddy,'" Rex chuckled.

"Watch it, buster!" Zeila warned.

"Rex, be nice," Trissy pleaded, continuing to slowly navigate through the enchanted forest.

"Now in Carencrow the buzzard is revered. So I suppose that in New Orleans the vulture is probably the most admired bird," Rex suggested, continuing to fuel the zoonotic battle.

"You're wrong, cowboy. In Naw-lean's ninth ward anyone with any street sense knows that the hummingbird is the smartest and bravest of the warm-blooded winged creatures. Not only are they lean and mean, just like me, but they also bring a great deal of luck," Zeila said in an attempt to educate her illiterate and rather obnoxious boating companion.

"You may be mean, but you certainly aren't lean," Rex chuckled.

"I should punch you right in the nose," Zeila said, fighting back the urge to strike the callous city boy.

"Would you two please stop arguing?" Trissy insisted.

"Damn woman keeps flapping her wings. 'Hummingbirds bring luck.' Ha, what's she been smoking?" Rex mumbled.

"What did you say?" Zeila snapped.

"Oh, nothing, Hummingbird," Rex replied sarcastically.

"Huh, damned owl-loving white boy!" Zeila grunted.

"Oh, Lord, is this ever going to be a long trip," Trissy whispered as she strained to look ahead into the darkness.

"Which direction, Zeila?" she asked, swinging the searchlight back and forth.

"This way," Zeila pointed, focusing her attention on the challenge at hand, her bickering with Rex now a distant memory.

"Open waters are only one hundred yards ahead, my child."

"Zeila, you wouldn't know where any of that world-famous moonshine is hidden, would you?" Rex asked. The hair on the back of his neck was beginning to rise as they traversed the spooky swamp.

"Grandma Moses drank the last drop before she died."

"Figures," Rex complained.

"Trissy, turn off the light," Zeila ordered before rubbing her forehead and closing her eyes.

"Why?" Trissy asked, dousing the searchlight.

"I sense danger. There's a boat waiting for us in the darkness," Zeila stated with certainty.

"Zeila, you're not using a foggy crystal ball, are you?" Rex snickered quietly. He reached for his rifle and searched his backpack for a fully loaded cartridge to insert into the magazine. He wanted to be prepared even though he was convinced that Zeila was one crazy old Cajun lady.

As soon as the bow of the boat emerged from the forest, Trissy stopped the engine and picked up the binoculars. She methodically scanned the southern waters of Whiskey Bay. The moon was nowhere to be seen and although the stars were bright, absolutely no light was cast on the dark, foreboding waters.

"To your left, Trissy," Zeila whispered.

"I don't see it," Trissy replied, straining to catch a glimpse of the terrorists waiting in ambush.

"Trissy, here're the night-vision goggles," Rex said, handing her the indispensable aid from his backpack.

"What else do you have in that bottomless knapsack, Rex?" Trissy asked nervously. Although she appeared cool, calm, and collected, her insides were churning. She felt compelled to make light of the moment as the tension began to mount.

"It's not a knapsack. It's fashionable yet functional backpack for anyone trying to save the world," Rex replied. "However, now that you've asked, I have a laptop computer, dozens of rounds of ammunition, detonators, and several pounds of plastics," Rex admitted.

"Plastics, surely they're not intended for cosmetic use," Trissy quipped.

"Kind of. These explosives have the power to change the course of nations and the face of time," Rex answered with great satisfaction.

"That's reassuring. Well, I suppose we should get after it!" Trissy suggested with renewed confidence.

Moments later, the bizarre ecosystem came to life as Trissy scanned her surroundings once again. Egrets, hoot owls, and raccoons could be seen in close proximity, as well as a half-dozen alligators, each of which lay silently and patiently awaiting the opportunity for an early evening snack. In all, a multitude of beady little eyes remained fixed on the eighteen-foot cigarette-shaped floating intruder. Off the bow and in the distance, the familiar shape of dead, debarked, limbless, and lifeless trees reaching skyward could be seen protruding from the pitch-black waters. To her left, the vegetation was lush. Spectacular trees and shrubs of all sizes and shapes were vivid. And there, hidden in the shadows cast by a large oak, was the enemy.

"Rex, Zeila was right. Those sorry bastards are two hundred yards off our port quarter," Trissy said, adjusting the fine focus. Zeila sat quietly as Rex strained to look into the darkness. "There appear to be three, no, four, on board," she added, continuing to study the threat.

"Well, that explains why the one boat veered off earlier in the chase," Rex concluded as Trissy handed him the goggles.

"We can't outrun them, and apparently we can't out-gun them. Zeila, do you have any idea how we can elude these vicious villains?" Rex asked, studying their precarious predicament.

"As a matter of fact, I do. To the right and one half-mile ahead, there is a narrow tributary lined with thick foliage. There are downed trees, low-lying lands, and many more dangerous, unexpected obstacles. I know that area quite well. In fact, I could take you through blindfolded. Uh huh, sho' do and sho' could," Zeila assured Rex.

Trissy snagged the night vision goggles from Rex's hand and looked in the direction affording their opportunity for escape.

"Rex, I see the area Zeila is talking about."

"Let's roll!" Rex insisted, snapping a fully loaded cartridge into his rifle.

"Hang on, Zeila. Here we go!" Trissy shouted before opening the throttle.

The hungry engine growled as a surge of fuel brought the powerful propellers to life. In an instant, they were off.

Chapter 24

GeeHad, Dr. Cornelius Lyons, and the other invited guests from Carencrow Regional Hospital had enjoyed a spectacular afternoon on Whiskey Bay. By the time the large pontoon boat glided back into Camp Eagle's calm inlet, the sun had set. Although rather inebriated, all on board could plainly see that an ornately decorated table had been set up on the lawn. The ambience was majestic. Tiki torches, the flames from which danced peacefully back and forth in the cool breeze, surrounded the table. Off to one side the coals from a large barbecue pit could be seen glowing. Up above the skies were clear and the stars exceptionally bright. The stage was set for an unforgettable evening.

"My, doesn't that smell good?" Dr. Lyons said as the aroma from a roasted goat wafted over the inlet. All of his well-founded concerns from earlier in the day had been long forgotten, as were his thoughts of Islam and his possible conversion: courtesy of copious amounts of Jim Beam.

"You won't be disappointed, of that I assure you," GeeHad replied as the boat gently bumped the dock.

"Welcome back," Yassar announced, securing the lines while the helmsman killed the engine.

Yassar graciously assisted everyone ashore. Each was immediately overwhelmed by the silence.

"Wow, that's some presentation," Teresa remarked, watching the light reflect off the highly polished silver.

"You certainly know how to throw a classy party," Martha Mucker added after realizing that her sense of sight and smell had been overwhelmed.

The roasted goat lay on a platter at the head of the table while a deep-fried turkey was basking on the other end. All these delicacies were surrounded by bowls of rice, black-eyed peas, greens, and cornbread, interspersed with numerous bottles of vintage wine.

"This looks like a Cajun Christmas," Evil blurted out, unaware of the dire consequences of citing what the Muslims believed to be nothing more than a pagan ritual.

"Hell no, girl, there ain't no 'Cajun Curl' on the table," Mean complained, noticing that the world-renowned and highly prized spice was conspicuously absent.

"Mean and Evil," Teresa whispered curtly. "I insist that you two old birds show some style and class. And for God's sake, don't offend our hosts."

"Sorry," Mean and Evil snickered in unison as they each lit up a cigarette.

"Damn, put those cancer sticks out, NOW!" Teresa insisted.

"Sorry," Mean and Evil replied as each frowned. The disappointment of not being allowed their nicotine fix was more than evident. However, their frustration and concern of withdrawal were only momentary.

"Look at all these good-looking young men," Evil crowed, observing a half-dozen waiters standing by, ready to grant the diners, every desire.

"I noticed! And they all have tight little butts. Girl, let's hope they're on the menu because they would make a fine dessert," Mean moaned in ecstasy, wiping the drool from her cheek.

"Please, everyone take a seat. However, I must insist that the women sit on this end," Yassar requested.

"Why that end?" Martha Mucker, alias Mushroom Head, asked in an abrasive tone, clearly displeased with the fact that she had to sit away from anyone who controlled her destiny.

"Simply because it's closest to the water. Should an alligator swim up and bite you on the ass, it would give the men time to run," Yassar joked, much to everyone's delight.

"There, you see. No worries," Johnny Cinch injected, addressing the men standing at the table. "Now I know we're safe. If the alligators got ahold of Martha's backside, they'd be eating for days." Everyone laughed with the notable exception of Martha Mucker, who put her hands on her distended hips and growled angrily. Seconds later, her penis-shaped hairdo turned beet red and started to shake while the wrinkled layers of foreskin around her neck began to expand. Dickhead had undoubtedly shifted into attack mode. Johnny beat a hasty retreat.

"Please, take a seat," Yassar requested again as Mohammad emerged from the shadows, taking his place at the head of the table. All the men, as well as the ravenous buzzards, Mean and Evil, sat down promptly, followed by Teresa and the reluctant Ms. Mucker.

"How was your tour of Whiskey Bay?" Mohammad asked the now jovial Dr. Lyons as the waiters poured wine to only the nonbelievers.

"It was excellent. I especially enjoyed watching your man feeding the alligators," Dr. Lyons replied with a gleam in his eye.

"I've always enjoyed watching the alligators feed as well, especially on live, helpless animals," GeeHad added with a chuckle.

"Mohammad, did you have any luck retrieving the quarry shot down earlier today?" Dr. Lyons inquired after GeeHad's comment suddenly reawakened his concerns.

"Not yet. But I believe the game was wounded and they're in hiding. I have no doubt that my men will find them soon."

"I see," Dr. Lyons replied nervously before taking a sip of wine.

"Let's hope they're retrieved alive," GeeHad added as Dr. Lyons suddenly noticed the U-Haul trucks parked in the shadows on the perimeter of the camp.

"Damn, there's no roasted pig," Evil snorted, suddenly realizing that the Cajun delicacy was noticeably absent.

"Evil, shush! Pigs are considered dirty animals and would never be eaten by anyone of Islamic faith," Teresa whispered.

"They may not eat them, but they certainly have no problem allowing chauvinistic pigs to sit at the table and wallow in tall stories," a livid Martha Mucker snarled, watching the men laughing and joking. Not only had she been relegated to a remote seat at the table, she also realized she was being ignored.

"Good point, Martha," Teresa agreed in an effort to appease her boss.

"Hell, there's no catfish or hush puppies, for that matter," Mean complained.

Mohammad snapped his fingers and the waiters quickly descended upon the table. As they began to serve up the sumptuous meal, a ravenous Evil took matters into her own hands.

"I ain't eatin' no goat, but I see what I want," Evil announced to her friend while leaning over their table and snatching the platter with the turkey on it. Quickly, she pulled a big bird toward her.

"Make a wish!" Mean howled as both she and Evil simultaneously grabbed a leg and ripped them from the carcass.

"Did you two grow up in a barn?" Ms. Mucker asked incredulously, watching the two buzzards gnawing on massive turkey legs.

"Don't get your hands too close to them, Martha, you're certain to lose a finger. I've seen these two buzzards when they're hungry," Teresa warned as a waiter slipped a slice of roasted goat onto her plate.

"It's horrifying! I've never seen such terrible manners," Ms. Mucker remarked.

"Mean, Evil, stop growling. Get your elbows off the table and chew with your mouths closed," Teresa ordered, but her demands fell on deaf ears. Teresa immediately reached for her wine to calm her nerves.

"Mohammad, I couldn't help but notice that you've amassed quite a collection of trucks," Dr. Lyons gently prodded.

There was a moment of silence in which Dr. Lyons could see that Mohammad was clearly uneasy and possibly agitated with his question.

"We had planned..." GeeHad started, but immediately fell silent as Mohammad discreetly waved his hand.

"Yes, GeeHad and I recently purchased the U-Haul franchise for Whiskey Bay," Mohammad explained nonchalantly. He reached across the table, popped one of the goat's eyeballs out, and began gnawing on the tasty morsel.

The normally unshakable physician was immediately overwhelmed by a wave of nausea. He took a sip of water and then wiped the beads of sweat from his forehead.

"We're always looking for new opportunities," GeeHad added in support.

"Is it a profitable business?" the suspicious Dr. Lyons inquired, placing his knife and fork across his plate to signal that he was done.

"That remains to be seen. How was your meal?" Mohammad asked, attempting to change the subject.

"Excellent, especially the rice. Unfortunately, however, my appetite has waned," Dr. Lyons replied while surveying the property.

"That's indeed unfortunate, for I've gone to great lengths to ensure that this is the finest meal you'll ever have," Mohammad assured his guest without any perceived sense of disappointment, as a waiter offered him more sliced goat.

"GeeHad, what do you think of our new chef?" Mohammad asked.

"Superb, and the food is succulent," GeeHad mumbled, continuing to stuff food into a mouth that was already filled well beyond capacity.

"Would it be possible to take a tour of your camp?" Dr. Lyons asked after scoping out three large, dimly lit wooden structures on the property.

"No, no it would not. Dr. Lyons, somehow you've ruined my appetite, as well," Mohammad complained bitterly. He clapped his hands twice and the waiters promptly removed every plate from the table. This was an especially dangerous act, given the fact that Mean and Evil had not finished their meals.

"How rude, I was still hungry!" Evil snarled.

"Maybe they'll give us a buzzard bag to take home," Mean giggled as her rotund belly jiggled.

"Forgive me, Mohammad. You have been most gracious," Dr. Lyons apologized as bizarre thoughts raced through his mind.

GeeHad and Carencrow General had made Dr. Lyons a very wealthy man over the years. In his scramble for riches, he had crushed many innocent men and women along the way, but their demise and destruction were of little concern. However, he wondered if he could live with himself if accused of the crime of treason as all of the pieces of the puzzle suddenly came together: The hints of unwavering loyalty to fellow Muslims, the financial skullduggery, and, most recently, the federal scrutiny of Carencrow General. GeeHad and Mohammad were terrorists and Camp Eagle was their clandestine base from which to launch their assault on America.

"Ah, dessert," the usually reserved Yassar exclaimed as plates of dark mounds arrived.

"This looks interesting. What is it?" Johnny asked as Mean and Evil sniffed the unfamiliar dessert.

"Chilled goat testicles," Yassar replied enthusiastically. He brushed off the sand and hair before bringing the walnut-sized morsel to his mouth and taking a bite. "Ummm, that sure is good," he sighed as the infidels looked on in shock.

"He's joking," Mohammad announced in an effort to lighten the mood.

"Basil, do you have our after-dinner drinks ready?" he inquired, suddenly appearing impatient.

"Yes, Mohammad."

"Then please, offer a glass to each of our honored guests," Mohammad ordered, pushing his chair back to stand.

"Ladies and gentlemen, you're about to receive a gift from the Gods." The shot glasses were distributed.

"What is it?" Ms. Mucker asked loudly.

"It's an after-dinner drink called Tiraq," Mohammad replied proudly, raising his empty glass and proposing a simple but effective toast.

"To the United States of America and our new Islamic brothers and sisters—Salud!"

"To the United States," the American guests at Camp Eagle mumbled.

"My God, that tastes terrible!" Johnny shouted.

"Well, it's a little unusual, but perhaps it's an acquired taste," Dr. Lyon's injected optimistically as the others around the table exhibited bizarre facial contortions as if attempting to dislodge the foul viscous liquid from their tongues.

Minutes later, GeeHad's faithful followers from Carencrow Regional began to exhibit the neuromuscular symptoms consistent with poisoning. Their speech began to slur and all staggered away from the table.

"What have you done to my people?" GeeHad screamed, realizing what was happening.

"Just giving the infidels a little incentive before their journey into Hell," Mohammad replied emotionlessly as one by one the victims fell to the ground.

"You're damn lucky we didn't poison you as well, GeeHad," Yassar growled.

"What are you talking about? What journey? They are my loyal friends. How dare you!" GeeHad yelled.

"They have outlived their usefulness. Their bodies will be found in the abandoned U-Haul trucks after we have deposited North Korean's nuclear waste in the chosen cities. Thus, Americans will be implicated in the downfall of their own heathen nation," Mohammad declared proudly.

"But that means that I will be implicated as well," GeeHad shouted as Yassar pulled his razor-sharp Bowie knife from its sheath.

"I'd say that you too have outlived your usefulness, GeeHad," Mohammad observed in his usual ruthless manner.

"Now, you can stay and watch your friends depart in the morning, or Yassar can cut your throat. Which destiny shall you choose, GeeHad?" Mohammad rose, turned, and walked away.

Chapter 25

After traveling through the Enchanted Black Forest nestled in a swamp, Rex, Trissy, and Zeila emerged in a small inlet within Whiskey Bay. However, all was not well. Lurking silently in the shadows, guarding the entrance and their only means of escape, was a powerboat with four terrorists on board.

As soon as Trissy opened the throttle, she could feel the power and the responsiveness in her hands. Even the damaged Mercury engines were performing flawlessly. Now was no time to worry about the shallow depth, floating logs, or partially submerged stumps in the restrictive inlet.

"Trissy, head toward the terrorist's boat before turning toward open waters," Rex yelled over the roar of the engines as their sleek cigarette boat shot through the darkness with reckless abandon.

"Will do!" Trissy yelled. She turned the wheel to the left until the bow was pointed directly at their enemy.

As the Glastron continued to rapidly gain speed, the bow started to level out. The anchored enemy boat was only two hundred yards away and they were closing in rapidly.

"Zeila, hit the searchlight and shine it on the terrorists!" Rex insisted, quickly making his way aft with his automatic rifle in hand.

"All right, all right, don't rush me! My word, I've never met anyone so demanding!" Zeila complained as she reached for the light.

"Rex, have you lost your mind? It's going to give away our position!" Trissy shouted.

"I'm afraid that the roar of the engines and the tall rooster tail have already done that!" Rex yelled, balancing himself on a seat at the back of the boat.

"Zeila, Rex is on the prowl. Hit the high beam!" Trissy requested as Rex leveled his weapon.

"All right, all right, good God, stop nagging!" Zeila growled while turning on the searchlight.

"Come on, Zeila," Rex whispered impatiently as Zeila struggled to light up his target.

Trissy turned the wheel sharply to the right to avoid an imminent collision. The Glastron responded immediately and heeled to starboard. As Rex struggled to regain his balance, he could see that the enemy boat was now only fifty yards off their port beam.

"Good job, Zeila!" Rex shouted as the floodlight illuminated his quarry.

Rex could plainly see the terrorists scrambling for their weapons. The confusion on board was more than evident as the men bumped into one another. Without question, they had been caught by surprise.

"Nice grouping," Rex said to himself, looking through his scope with satisfaction. The enemy was within a confined space with no place to run or hide. "This is your lucky day. It's time to visit your camel-faced, sand-cracked virgins," Rex added, looking through the crosshairs and squeezing the trigger.

Within seconds, Rex had emptied his entire magazine. He could see backs arch and arms flail helplessly as several bullets found their mark. The force of the explosion threw the targeted terrorists against their evil comrades standing behind them. As the high-velocity projectiles ripped through bone and flesh, Rex felt confident there was enough force to kill those who had been shielded. As a Navy SEAL and an emergency room physician, Rex had witnessed firsthand the killing power of rifles such as his. The entrance wound was usually the size of a quarter, whereas the cone-shaped exit wound could be as large as a deep-dish pizza pie.

As Rex took one last look at the enemy, he could clearly see that no one had been left standing and there was no activity on board.

"Zeila, douse the light!" Rex ordered, putting the rifle down and making his way forward.

"All right, all right!" Zeila replied, while shaking her head in frustration. Clearly, she was not pleased with being ordered around under any circumstances.

"Did you nail any of them, Rex?" Trissy asked excitedly, clearing nature's visible obstacles on her right and entering a wide expanse of Whiskey Bay.

"I'd say we were successful in eradicating at least a few of the menacing maggots," Rex replied with confidence as they raced toward their destination, now less than a mile away.

But no sooner had Rex finished his sentence than the sky came alive with a brilliant burst of intense light as a starburst shell exploded overhead. Now, the terrorists would have no difficulty zeroing in on their elusive target. Seconds later, a rocket grenade whistled by.

The explosion was so close that they could feel the intense force from the shock wave strike their chests. Instantaneously, a cloud of shrapnel showered the immediate area, ripping into the exposed hull and whistling through the water.

"Oh, Christ!" Trissy screamed, looking at the newly created holes in the boat. "Is everyone all right?" she yelled, navigating the motorboat at sixty knots through the dangerous waters.

"I'm okay. Zeila, are you all right?" Rex asked, searching for the direction from which the weapon had been launched.

"Hell yes, but that damn explosion nearly ripped off my dress," Zeila complained, inspecting her tattered garment.

"As long as those well-seasoned bloomers were spared, I think we're all right," Rex said jokingly.

"Bloomers? I tossed my stained skivvies overboard hours ago. The stench was making me sick to my stomach," Zeila confessed without shame.

"Oh, Lord, half the fish population must be floating on the surface gasping for air," Rex said to himself as he nudged closer to Trissy. For the first time he wasn't sure what he feared most, the rocket grenades or Zeila going Comanche.

"There must have been a second boat," Trissy surmised while starting to zigzag.

"Absolutely, but where?" Rex wondered as he scanned the horizon. "Christ, they're right behind us, Trissy! Five hundred yards dead astern and closing in rapidly!" Rex shouted, as the terrorists' boat jumped their wake.

"No worries, another quarter-mile and we'll be at the mouth of the inlet!" Trissy yelled, looking through the night vision goggles. Instinctively, she placed her hand on the throttle and pushed forward, but there was no give. The engines were running wide open.

"I sure as hell hope we find a gas station quickly. It looks like we're down to a quarter of a tank!" Rex shouted, tapping on the gas gauge.

Trissy nodded in agreement but remained intently focused on reaching the inlet. Another rocket grenade exploded twenty feet off the deck and fifteen yards off the port quarter. Once again, shards of shrapnel indiscriminately searched for flesh and blood. Rex quickly glanced at Zeila and Trissy. Remarkably, no one appeared injured.

"Damn, that was close!" Trissy yelled.

"And getting closer, where in the world did these maggots get all these grenades?" Rex wondered, thinking about alternative plans for eluding their pursuers.

"Most likely from Iran, courtesy of our sanction-repealing jackass politicians and our president, whom I've nicknamed 'The Shite Slider,'" Trissy suggested. "Rex, get Zeila up here before I run this baby aground!" Trissy shouted as Rex staggered aft.

"Zeila, we're entering the inlet. Help Trissy navigate," Rex insisted, helping Zeila from her seat.

"It's been over fifty years since I've been here. A lot's changed," Zeila complained as she staggered forward.

"What are you talking about? You said you knew this area like the back of your hand," Trissy reminded her, struggling with the temptation of reducing speed.

"Yes, but at my age, I've forgotten which hand," Zeila replied rather nonchalantly.

"Zeila, your starting act more and more like Rex. Please, don't yield to the *Demons of Dementia*," Trissy pleaded as the broad inlet quickly narrowed. The windy waterway was now a mere thirty yards in width and lined on either side by dense mangroves.

As they rounded a bend, Rex looked aft. The terrorist boat in hot pursuit was hidden behind the dense vegetation. Rex brought the night-vision goggles to his eyes and looked forward over the bow.

"Trissy, we've hit a dead end. Damn, there's nothing but thick brush up ahead."

"It can't be!" Trissy yelled in disbelief as she glanced at Zeila.

"Zeila, this was your plan. We didn't borrow a flying boat! Just how in the hell did you think we were going to escape from this dead end?" Rex yelled as Zeila sat calmly with her hands folded across her lap.

"I knew you didn't have any brains, but now it appears that you have no faith, either," Zeila snarled as she stood, pulled herself forward, and looked over the bow.

"Faith!" Rex yelled incredulously.

"God, please keep me from killing this bleached-out black man. And, if you can spare the time, please tell me how Darwin could have been so wrong. There's absolutely no way that the white race could have evolved from our beautiful and sophisticated African culture," Zeila prayed as she clasped her hands together.

"Zeila, we seem to be in a bit of a quandary, so stop praying and start thinking," Rex insisted.

"Don't you have any imagination?" Zeila asked as she shook her head.

"Imagination?" Rex screamed in frustration.

Suddenly, the pitch of the engine changed and the boat shuttered repeatedly.

"We're bouncing off the bottom!" Trissy yelled as a propeller guard struck shallow submerged objects, jerking the prop upward and slowing their speed.

"It's time to make a stand," Rex announced, watching the terrorist boat round the last bend.

"Hold your horses, General Custer. Ah, now I remember. Trissy, head toward that tall cypress tree," Zeila insisted, pointing to her right.

Trissy responded without haste.

"I can see a low-lying clearing adjacent to the tree!" Trissy shouted excitedly while turning the boat twenty degrees to starboard.

"It can't be! Is that a bonfire here in the middle of nowhere?" Rex asked in disbelief.

"Zeila, it looks like they're people up ahead," Trissy said, trying to understand what they were getting themselves into.

"They're probably poachers or bootleggers," Zeila concluded without giving Trissy's observation a second thought.

"Well, let's hope the bubbas are friendly. We're about to crash their party," Rex announced, watching the Neanderthals dancing in the firelight.

"Zeila, what are these poles in the water and what in the world is hanging from them?" Trissy asked as their boat raced forward toward the shoreline.

"Alligator traps," Zeila responded, observing several of Colonel Clucker's fine-feathered friends floating tethered to the vertical metal poles which had been pounded into the underwater muck.

"I do miss huntin' the swamps. As a matter of fact, the best bait I ever found were the remains of unwanted relatives, but chicken would always do quite nicely," Zeila added with delight as she reminisced.

"Surely you're joking," Trissy replied with shock, looking at her rather remarkable patient who radiated such wisdom and mystery.

"Trissy, this doesn't look good. There are several large objects swinging from that massive, bizarre-looking bald cypress!"

Rex yelled apprehensively. As he focused in on the tall, twisted, lifeless tree with gnarly branches, Rex could feel the hair on the back of his neck stand on end.

"That's the *Sacred Tree of Alli,*" Zeila responded with pride and respect.

"A sacred Muslim tree, in the middle of a godforsaken Louisiana swamp! Surely you're joking," Trissy shouted in disbelief.

"Will you city folk ever understand? 'Alli' stands for alligator. The Cajuns have been using this tree for skinning gators since the beginning of time. The tree has special powers, of that I'm sure. To damage or show disrespect to this tree will cause great 'Gre-Gre,'" Zeila assured Trissy without hesitation.

"Gre-Gre?" Trissy snickered, amused by the oddly sounding words, not knowing what they stood for.

"'Gre-Gre' is a Cajun curse which is not to be taken lightly," Zeila warned.

"Well then, I would assume that the boiling pots next to the 'Gre-Gre' Tree are not hot tubs after all. Perhaps they're for conjuring up the spirits inhabiting the 'Sacred Voodoo Tree,'" Rex added sarcastically.

"How can one man be wrong so many times! The bubbas are poaching like their uneducated trailer trash fathers before them. What you're seeing is a makeshift processing plant. The gators are gutted and skinned and the meat is placed on ice. All that remains is the head. How else are you going to get those snappers pearly white if you don't boil the flesh off the skull? Besides, the brew makes a good roux for the gumbo," Zeila said as her stomach started to growl and her mouth began to salivate at the thought of eating swamp-fresh gator.

"I hate to be the bearer of bad news, but it looks like the bubbas know we're coming," Rex announced, watching everyone on shore abruptly stop and stare.

Suddenly, two rocket grenades shot by in quick succession. The first struck the water just off the stern, exploding a few feet below the surface, briefly lifting the boat from the water and violently shaking it in the air. Shrapnel ripped into the fiberglass, penetrating the metal casings enclosing the outboard engines. Trissy and Rex were thrown to the deck, stunned. Only Zeila remained standing. Instinctively, she grabbed the wheel and maintained the boat on course.

Unfortunately, the second grenade locked onto the *Sacred Tree of Alli.* The massive explosion was followed by angry, twisting winds. Suddenly, the clouds parted and a bright light shown down from the dark skies above. A split second later, there was a tremendous fiery upsurge which lifted Trissy and Rex to their feet in time to see a twisting mass of energy whisk the remains of the *Sacred Tree of Alli* back to the heavens from which it had come. In an instant, the entire 'Gre-Gre' tree had been vaporized. Rex and Trissy could feel their skin crawl after witnessing the frightening spectacle.

"So you thought granny was blowing smoke, did you, my pretties?" Zeila cackled in a sinister tone as Trissy took the wheel.

"The thought had crossed my mind," Rex replied, wondering how long Zeila had been possessed.

"Well, let's hope a Cajun 'Gre-Gre' has just been placed on 'The Turban-a-tors,'" Rex wished, struggling to clear his mind from what he thought was a mild concussion.

"Wow, there's nothing left of the Sacred Tree; no limbs, no roots, and no charred remains. It's as if it never was," Trissy said in amazement as the shoreline rapidly approached.

"Trissy, step on it! The terrorists are gaining on us and the engines are damaged!" Rex shouted, looking aft and observing smoke billowing from the powerful Mercury engines.

"The throttle is wide open and we're just about to run out of watery wonderland. Hang on!" Trissy screamed as Zeila and Rex braced themselves.

Almost immediately, there was a jolt. The prop guard struck bottom, slamming the engines forward and lifting the shafts and propellers from the water. The engines whined as the hull grazed the bottom. The bow quickly began to lift as the boat rose from the murky waters. The forward momentum propelled the speedboat swiftly up onto the shoreline. As the landlocked craft slid across the low-lying slippery point, it seemed to gained speed. Yet, to Rex everything seemed to be moving in slow motion. There were bubbas to the left of him and bubbas to the right of him. All appeared to have the 'redeye', as they watched their unwelcome guests race by. There was no doubt that these angry yard dogs would be intent upon giving chase.

"Trissy, watch out!" Zeila screamed reactively, noticing a maze of metal tubing dead ahead. But there would be no avoiding this man-made obstacle on their way toward the body of water that lay on the other side of the narrow point. There was a low-pitched screeching sound as the bow of the boat slammed into and attempted to part the bizarre metal forest.

Instinctively, Rex, Trissy, and Zeila ducked as metal tubing flew over the top and bounced off the sides of the boat. Fortunately, all had avoided being impaled, but Rex and Trissy had not gone unscathed. They had been doused with the thick, foul-smelling warm liquid that had been running through the pipes.

"My God, what a stench!" Rex screamed in anguish, wiping the clear liquid from his face and smelling his hand.

"Pee-ew!" Trissy gasped as a pungent aroma left her with the sensation that her throat was closing. A feeling of impending doom immediately overwhelmed her as she coughed incessantly, struggling for a breath of fresh air.

"You two need to show a little backbone," Zeila chuckled with delight.

"That sweet-smelling nectar is moonshine, and from what I can tell, a rather good batch," she laughed, while licking the savory liquid from her saturated lips.

"That's not moonshine, its embalming fluid," Trissy complained after catching her breath. She was certain that the noxious brew had even singed the hairs in her nose.

"No way, that's Bubba's Best. Now, the greatest contribution of moonshine, besides making me immortal and curing my rheumatism, has been converting ruthless Republicans into do-goodin' Democrats." Zeila felt compelled to share as their Glastron splashed back into the water.

"Put a lid on it, Zeila, we're in big trouble," Rex insisted as their boat stopped dead in the water thirty yards from shore.

"Rex, the terrorists just passed through the toxic cloud. Either get those engines in the water or start paddling!" Trissy shouted as the pursuing boat splashed down in the lagoon.

"All right, all right, don't rush me!" Rex shouted over the whining of the engines as they raced uncontrollably in the cool night. Black smoke continued to bellow from the damaged Mercurys, but as soon as the props hit the water, their boat took off.

Two shots from a pistol suddenly rang out from the terrorist boat. Instinctively, Rex and Trissy ducked but Zeila stood fast.

"You'd think the toxic moonshine cloud would've killed some of those scraggly bearded bastards," Rex complained as their Glastron continued to gain speed.

"Well, it appears to have invigorated the not-so-do-goodin' bubbas," Trissy said, watching the poachers scramble for their boats.

"I remember when Granddad drank moonshine by the gallon," Zeila reminisced.

"The home-brewed 'motion potion' would take the lead out of Grandpa's ass, but only when Grandma chased him with a large wooden spoon. She must have chased Grandpa 'Sambo' around that hickory tree a thousand times. All the while, screaming, 'I ain't yo mama'; ah, what fond memories," Zeila recalled with great pleasure.

"'Sambo'? Zeila, are you sure Grandpa wasn't chased by a tiger?" Rex asked suspiciously as he wondered about Zeila's state of mind.

"Sho', I'm sho', but grandma did have one hell of a tiger in her tank. As a matter of fact, she gave birth to a whole pride; ten rambunctious and unruly cubs of which I was the oldest and the wisest. Now..." Zeila continued as Rex shook his head in disbelief.

"Yes, well, we all have memories, some more haunting than others," Rex interrupted, making his way forward.

"Rex, I'm not sure we have much life left in those engines. We're starting to lose speed," Trissy shouted after looking over her shoulder at the smoldering Mercury outboards.

"I'd say we need an element of luck and possibly a little gas," Rex replied as he tapped on the gas gauge, which now read *empty*.

"Zeila, we need your help. Do you have any ideas?" Trissy shouted nervously, scanning the open, treeless body of water.

"Personally, I think we're out of time and ideas," Rex shouted, reaching into his backpack to pull out of fully loaded magazine for his automatic rifle. The terrorists were now two hundred yards astern and closing rapidly. As he slammed the magazine into the butt of the gun, he realized that they had no choice but to shoot it out. A firefight was inevitable, and Rex was determined to take as many of the bastards down as he possibly could.

"Trissy, you and Zeila stay down," Rex insisted as he leveled his weapon and looked through the site.

"Nonsense," Zeila replied.

"Trissy, head toward that cloud hovering over the water," Zeila calmly suggested.

"What cloud?" Trissy yelled, frantically straining to peer into the darkness.

As the engines started to sputter, Rex lost his concentration. For some reason, he was intrigued by Zeila's recommendation. He stood and began to scan the waters of Whiskey Bay.

"I don't see a cloud either," he complained as their boat slowed dramatically.

"Has the moonshine left you both blind? The cloud is right over here, my child," Zeila said, placing her hand on the wheel. Trissy released her grip and, in an instant, they were engulfed within a dense white cloud.

Suddenly, the sound of the engines ceased and all forward momentum abruptly halted. The battered speedboat was motionless, neither in water nor on land but bathed in a magical rainbow of light.

Chapter 26

THE MYSTERIOUS LOW-LYING CLOUD on Whiskey Bay had provided timely refuge for Rex, Trissy, and Zeila from the terrorists and the bubbas. In this spectacular sanctuary, a magnificent rainbow of lights streaking overhead captivated each of them.

"Wow!" Rex shouted in amazement after looking over the side and seeing his reflection and the booty beyond. The murky bayou water was nowhere to be seen, but the battered speedboat lay stationary in a brilliant sea of diamonds and silver, which suddenly began to move clockwise. Faster and faster the sparkling slurry swirled until suddenly, from under the keel, bursts of radiant silvery light pulsated rhythmically in all directions.

"Unbelievable!" Trissy gasped, watching a glittery silver spray arch fifty yards before drifting off and disappearing within the dense cloud cover.

"The Earth has many wonders, but her treasures are only available to those who believe," Zeila preached.

"Well, you certainly captured my attention, Zeila. Now, old girl, I truly believe we should bring some of these treasures home," Rex suggested, rubbing his hands together in anticipation of gathering riches beyond his wildest imagination.

"To do so would anger the Gods. Torrential fiery winds would howl, scorching the Earth, and the seas would begin to rise," Zeila said without hesitation.

"Zeila, you're starting to sound like that con artist Al Gore and his herd of gloomy, global warming, donkey-loving environmentalists," Rex criticized as the boat suddenly began to move.

"Huh!" Zeila huffed, crossing her arms and tapping her foot angrily on the deck.

"Just one bucketful, that's all I ask," Rex pleaded.

"No!" Zeila growled emphatically.

"Just a handful of silver, then. Surely that shouldn't upset too many of the gods," Rex rationalized, struggling to reach a compromise.

"Read my lips! No means NO! And this big black donkey-loving, environmentally sensitive Democrat is not about to budge. Do I make myself perfectly clear?" an unyielding Zeila concluded before walking toward the back of the boat to sit down.

"Damn liberal jackass," Rex mumbled. The severely damaged Mercury outboard engines mysteriously roared back to life just as the Glastron settled back into the water.

"Not to worry, my knight in shining armor. Our riches lie elsewhere within another cloud with a silver lining," Trissy whispered soothingly into his ear before kissing him on the cheek.

"Perhaps, but it's the principle of the issue. If Jesse Jackson or Al Sharpton were here, I guarantee you that Zeila would have allowed those greedy self-serving carnival salesmen to line their pockets. Now, would an honorable, hardworking Republican be granted the same opportunity?" Rex snarled before looking aft. Zeila was still huffing and puffing and the engines were still smoking. However, unexpectedly, the magical cloud was nowhere to be seen.

"Rex, let it go," Trissy recommended, looking down at the gas gauge that still read empty.

"These engines must be running on fumes," Trissy assumed as she tapped on the gas gauge, hoping to change the subject.

"Well, we have something in common then, because I'm fuming as well," Rex declared as Trissy suddenly became distracted.

Over the sound of the engines idling, the waves slapping the side of the boat, and a brisk wind whipping over the bow, Trissy shouted,

"Good God, Rex! Look!" Rex turned around to find total darkness engulfing the massive body of water. "What happened to the bubbas, the terrorists, and the lights from the poachers' distillery?"

"All gone," Zeila simply replied.

"Gone where?" Rex blurted as he quickly lifted the night-vision goggles to his eyes and scanned the area. "I don't see a damn thing."

"Have either one of you heathens ever gone to church? Have some faith. Head toward that light," Zeila insisted as she pointed.

"What light?"

"I think I see it. Hold on," Trissy replied as she opened the throttle and followed Zeila's directions.

"Well, let's just hope it's a gas station and they're open," Rex said as Zeila shook her head in frustration.

"A restaurant with a restroom, a cold beer, and a warm bed would be greatly appreciated as well," Trissy added.

"Personally, I'd settle for a tank of gas and a snort of Grandpa Sambo's moonshine."

"You got that right. Sho' do," Zeila agreed.

"Perhaps two snorts are in order. It's been a rather long day. We've been arrested for no legitimate reason, nearly drowned during our escape, and shot down while attempting to rescue the nation from impending doom. Not to mention we were pursued by Richter's Rectal-lites from the FBI, radical Islamic jihadists, and ball-busting bubba-necks," Rex moaned, stretching, in an attempt to work the soreness out of his muscles.

Despite all their misfortune, safety appeared near until, fifty feet from the rickety old dock, the engines began to sputter and the boat began to slow. Smoke started billowing from the dying Mercury engines, which had been peppered by shrapnel. Suddenly, a small flame erupted on the starboard engine.

"I think our outboards are caput. Trissy, have you seen the fire extinguisher, by chance?" Rex asked, frantically searching for the canister of flame retardant.

"No," Trissy replied, looking around the boat.

"I can't believe it. There are no fire extinguishers or life vests on board. Don't terrorists know anything about boating safety?" Rex complained as the flames began to grow.

"Rex, terrorists like to travel light. Try using the bucket," Trissy suggested, noticing that water was sloshing over her shoes as the hull started settling deeper and deeper into the murky water.

"On second thought, Rex, forget the engine and start bailing! We're sinking!" Trissy shouted.

"Oh, Lordie, I can't swim!" an agitated Zeila yelled.

"All right, calm down," Rex insisted, scooping up a bucket of water from within the boat and tossing it on the engine.

There was a loud hissing sound, but the water only seemed to agitate the Goddess of Fire. After the steam cleared it was evident that the fire had spread, and quickly.

"Damn, that's why we're out of gas. Most of it leaked into the boat," Rex concluded after throwing liquid fuel onto the fire.

The entire stern was now ablaze and, to make matters worse, the speedboat's forward momentum had halted. The crippled boat bobbed helplessly on the water only ten feet from the dock and safety.

However, the danger had not gone unnoticed. From out of nowhere, a portly black man on the dock yelled, "Throw me a line!"

Trissy scrambled to the bow and tossed him the rope coiled on the deck. It fell short. She pulled the wet rope back and tossed it once again. This time the man snagged the line and pulled the boat closer. The bow slammed into the dock and the Good Samaritan looped the rope around a nearby cleat.

"Now hear this: Abandon ship, abandon ship!" Trissy yelled, cupping her hands to make sure she was heard.

"Sister, you don't have to tell me twice!" Zeila assured Trissy as the man on the dock helped her up onto a floating wooden platform.

"Hold on. I'm the captain. As such, I'm the only one authorized to give that order," Rex complained bitterly as Trissy jumped to safety.

"That may be, but I'm the admiral of the fleet," Trissy retorted.

"Sho' is," Zeila agreed.

"Appointed by whom?" Rex demanded, as the fuel-laden water surged above his knees.

"The 'Goddess of Sex' and the 'Goddess of Fire,'" Trissy replied proudly.

"Oh, now that makes sense, 'Great Lay' and 'Pelé'!" Rex freely admitted as the flames surged toward him, as the stern rapidly sank deeper.

"That boy's nuts," Zeila remarked as she watched Rex going down with his boat.

"It would appear so, Zeila," Trissy replied as her frustration began to mount.

"Come on, Rex! The boat is sinking!" Trissy insisted, watching the pending disaster unfolding from the relative safety of the dock.

"Damn!" Rex shouted in frustration as he grabbed his backpack and rifle before leaping onto the dock.

The friendly old salty dog placed his arm around Rex's shoulder. "Welcome to our world. I'm your harbormaster, Captain Coco," he said with a smile.

"You can't be a harbormaster. There's no harbor, just one rickety old dock," Rex felt compelled to share.

"Now may not be the best time, but we need to discuss tariffs, as it were. The docking fees are thirty dollars a day. Add another fifty dollars for the personal danger I faced in rescuing these lovely ladies from certain death, and twenty dollars for polluting our beautiful harbor. That comes to one hundred dollars—a reasonable sum, I assure you. Tips are not included, of course, and the entire amount is payable—now," Captain Coco announced proudly and without remorse as he held out the palm of his hand.

Rex looked at the remains of the speedboat they had confiscated from the terrorists. The entire boat was submerged, with the exception of two feet of the bow, which remained above the water line, tethered to the dock. Thankfully, all the flames had been extinguished by the watery grave.

"That's not my boat," Rex replied, looking the captain in the eye.

"As judge and jury in this parish, possession is nine-tenths of the law," Captain Coco stated, his tone unyielding.

"I see. Well, Captain Cuckoo, would there be any discount for declaring the boat an artificial reef?" Rex asked, reaching into the side pocket of his backpack and pulling out a wad of cash.

"That's Coco. Possibly, but not likely," the captain answered, tapping his fingers together in anticipation of a windfall while attempting to analyze how much cash Rex was carrying.

"Well then, will a hundred and fifty dollars cover your costs?" Rex asked, handing the captain several bills.

"Yes, that would do very nicely, very nicely indeed," Captain Coco replied before stuffing the bills into his shirt pocket. "May all your dreams come true," he added with a smile as he tipped his hat before bending over to pick up his fishing pole and sitting down in a tattered old chair.

"Captain, by the by, where in the world are we?" Trissy asked.

"You're in the middle of nowhere."

"And just how does one leave 'nowhere'?" Rex inquired, although he thought his question sounded rather odd.

"By boat, of course," Zeila assumed.

"Precisely, and I just happen to have my personal yacht available for lease."

"Good God, that!" Rex blurted. As he pointed, Trissy wondered how the old wooden boat was still afloat.

"We'll take it," Zeila interjected without hesitation. "Rex, pay Captain Coco," the feisty Cajun insisted as she hopped on board.

Chapter 27

It was late in the evening and the Carencrow Communications Center was bustling with activity. An additional ten men and women were brought in to man the desks. Traffic flowed into and out of the center at a feverish pace as everyone struggled to locate the missing Air Med chopper. Tensions were running high and there was no doubt that SAC Richter's sphincter tone had shot off the charts.

"I can't fucking believe it!" Richter shouted, throwing his arms in the air in frustration before slamming his fists on the desk in front of him. The room immediately went deathly silent. All eyes were now on the enraged SAC who was now starting to appear more and more psychotic with each passing hour.

"Why in the hell can't we find these sorry bastards?" Richter screamed, pounding the desk once again. Yet no one felt compelled to answer this madman's ludicrous question, which had been posed to all.

"The chopper is nothing more than a cumbersome, lumbering, airborne mule, which has surely run out of fuel by now. Where is that fucking contraption?" Richter yelled, his voice starting to crack.

"Everyone's giving it their all. Many have not even had a break since we started this morning," Lieutenant Vickers responded in a calm and collected manner as SAC Richter nervously paced the room.

"I don't give a damn. I don't want moaning and groaning or excuses, Lieutenant. I want results! Find the fucking helicopter!" FBI Special Agent Richter insisted as everyone reluctantly resumed their duties.

"When SAC of Shit Bligh demands that we walk the plank, my ass is out of here!" one of the officers whispered to Lieutenant Vickers.

"George, that's an excellent plan. Please let me know when it's time to abandon ship," Lieutenant Vickers insisted, placing his hand on the frustrated police officer's shoulder.

"Hell no! In this case, Lieutenant, I believe it's got to be every man for himself. Besides, that silver bar on your collar entitles you to go down with the ship," his comrade-in-arms chuckled. Lieutenant Vickers smiled and nodded, easing over to the wall map where SAC Richter and Jim Crowell were standing.

"I have plotted Air Med's last known location and have drawn several concentric rings around the site. The first ring reflects a radius of five miles, the second twenty miles, and the third fifty miles," Jim Crowell informed the agitated Richter.

"Great job, Crowell, but that information does little to reduce our search area," Richter barked sarcastically.

"We have at least twelve squad cars and forty men on scene. All roads leading into and out of the area have been secured at the five-mile perimeter. Additionally, there are two police helicopters in the air searching for the hijacked chopper," Lieutenant Vickers reminded an irritated special agent.

"There's no way in hell that we're going to find them at night in that densely forested area with so few men. Does that make sense, Lieutenant? Am I getting through to you?" Richter growled, attacking the only man in the room who didn't want to see him dead.

"Loud and clear. But you have to realize that our resources are limited. I expect to hear from the governor's office at any moment with regard to activating the National Guard," Lieutenant Vickers mentioned.

"Well let's just hope that Governor Bimbo pulls her fucking thumb out of her ass long enough to execute that order!" Richter shouted.

"For once, we agree, and let's hope she washes that thumb before signing the executive order," Lieutenant Vickers laughed. However, his humorous comment didn't even elicit a smile.

"The F-eighteens scrambled from Bell Chase Naval Air Station this morning didn't see a thing when they arrived on location. Therefore, we're going to have to expand the search to the twenty-mile range, and we need more men on the ground and birds in the air to do so," Richter demanded loudly, grinding his teeth.

"The governor will come through. She'll have to. It's an election year. I assure you that the old battle ax would sell her soul for a vote," Lieutenant Vickers concluded optimistically.

"Huh!" Richter snorted, crossing his arms and tapping his foot.

"We intend to work throughout the night and by morning I'm sure we'll have assembled an adequate team with which to do the job," Lieutenant Vickers reassured the angry FBI agent.

"There fuckin' better be!" Richter insisted in a low rumbling voice.

"There fucking will be!" Lieutenant Vickers added uncharacteristically after making a conscious decision to mimic the much-despised Special Agent in Charge Richter.

Then, suddenly for whatever reason, Lieutenant Vicker's misspent youth flashed in front of his eyes and it finally dawned on him who SAC Richter reminded him of: the cartoon character Yosemite Sam. All Lieutenant Vickers needed to make the connection and confirm his observation would be Captain Richter's use of the word "varmint," he thought to himself as he fought back the urge to chuckle.

"What the hell are you smiling about?" Richter demanded.

"Just a humorous thought."

"Well, wipe that damn smile off your face."

"Yes, sir. Why don't you step out for a bite to eat and catch a little shut-eye? It's going to be a big day tomorrow," Lieutenant Vickers suggested.

"Don't you think I know that?" Richter barked.

"It was just a suggestion," Lieutenant Vickers said in his own defense.

"I would, but the way the day's gone, I'd probably run into that wretched Valentino woman," Richter moaned.

"She's rather strong-willed, I must admit," Lieutenant Vickers replied as Leslie Valentino quietly entered the room unnoticed.

"Strong-willed, bullshit! She's a fucking bitch!" Richter snarled.

"That may be, but you wouldn't want me as your enemy," Leslie coolly fired back, unfazed by the Richter's crude remarks. She watched Richter's neck veins bulge and his face turn a fiery red.

"Now, where do we stand?"

"We have been unable to locate the helicopter within the five-mile area we've secured. However, if the governor authorizes the activation of the National Guard, we intend to expand the search out to twenty miles in the morning," Lieutenant Vickers replied.

"Have we contacted the CIA to see what the satellite hovering over this area picked up at the time the chopper disappeared?" Leslie asked the snarling SAC, who remained speechless yet projected the image of a volcano about to erupt.

To Lieutenant Vickers, it appeared that SAC Richter was choking, but neither he nor anyone else in the room consciously considered using the Heimlich maneuver. No, in this case destiny had to take its course and everyone hoped that the Richter's downward spiral would be short and painful.

"No, ma'am, we haven't. In fact, the thought never crossed our minds, but I think it's an excellent idea," Lieutenant Vickers agreed, very much impressed by the first rational course of action that had been suggested all day.

"I'm running this fucking show!" Richter shouted.

"I'm sure you are. Running it right into the ground! Now, why don't you step outside and get some fresh air before I'm tempted to order your execution?" Leslie insisted in no uncertain terms.

And then, in an instant, Lieutenant Vicker's dream came true.

"Fucking bitch—damn varmint!" SAC Richter snarled, stomping his foot.

"I knew it!" Lieutenant Vickers howled.

Unexpectedly, Richter stormed out of the command center. The battle-weary troops immediately leaped to their feet, clapping, laughing, and shouting with joy upon the tyrannical SAC's departure. And, for a brief moment, Lieutenant Vickers noticed Ms. Valentino's lips turn upward. He wondered—Had he detected a smile?

Chapter 28

"You have made a wise choice indeed. She's the pride of my fleet," Captain Coco shared openly with Zeila, pointing to the twenty-foot-long barnacle-encrusted pontoon boat, which had been modified to exacting specifications. The bow was enclosed with a rickety, weather-beaten wooden cabin. Half of the windows were broken and the other half glazed over with grime. The stern remained open but the deck was cluttered with all forms of debris. The fact that this floating nightmare was powered by an old tractor engine jury-rigged to begin a new life at sea, was equally concerning.

"Fleet? What fleet? Harbormaster Coco, all I see is one waterlogged wooden blob struggling to stay afloat," Rex stated as Zeila courageously walked the deck.

"It looks like a floating outhouse," Trissy laughed.

"Surely you're joking," Rex chuckled after examining the boat from stem to stern.

"I beg your pardon. I built this handsome craft myself. Not only does she have beauty but she has speed as well," Captain Coco boasted, choosing to ignore the criticism.

"Well, Captain..." Trissy began before losing her train of thought.

"We'll take it," Zeila confimed to the captain once again. She whispered the name of the boat boldly emblazoned on the stern.

Damned Gre-Gre

Whiskey Bay, LA

"Zeila, I don't think this is the right boat," Rex concluded.

"Nonsense, 'Damned Curse' is an excellent although somewhat unusual name," Zeila replied boldly, holding out her arm to assist Trissy onto the craft.

"How much are you charging for this spectacular yacht, Captain?" Rex inquired hesitantly and with a hint of sarcasm.

"As you know, my rates are quite reasonable," Captain Coco assured Rex with pride, rubbing his hands together in anticipation of yet another windfall. He had always enjoyed the feel of cold hard cash.

"Undoubtedly, but we're on a budget, you know," Rex replied rather bluntly in an effort to evoke the captain's lowest price. However, his bluff would not work. The capitalist captain was an expert at inflicting the maximum tolerable financial hardship, especially when sensing the urgency of his monopolistic services.

"Let's see, with taxes and insurance, as well as a late-night surcharge, the unsinkable *Damned Gre-Gre* can be yours for as little as fifteen hundred dollars a night. Your remittance is payable up front, of course," Captain Coco insisted as Rex cleared his throat and attempted to regain his composure.

"A thousand dollars and you pay for the gas," Trissy countered.

"I'm but a poor businessman struggling to support a multitude of children, several wives, and a rather robust and demanding bevy of beautiful concubines. Twelve hundred dollars and you pay the gas," Captain Coco countered, dangling the keys in front of Trissy.

"Captain, we have an accord," Rex said, handing the pirate the appropriate amount of cash.

"A wise choice indeed," Captain Coco replied, rapidly counting the payment before handing Rex the keys, which he then tossed to his wife.

Trissy entered the dark, foreboding cabin and placed the key into the ignition. There was an initial grinding sound, and the small boat shook violently as the rusty engine struggled to turn over. A minute or so later, there was a small explosion. A cloud of black soot shot into the air and the engine roared life as Rex hopped on board.

"Now, you will help us cast off, won't you, captain?" Trissy asked, leaning out of the cabin.

"Deck hand fees start at fifty dollars per line, but you can pay me when you get back," Captain Coco replied as he worked the lines free from the cleats and threw them on board.

"That's reassuring," Trissy shouted over the throbbing of the engine as she placed the boat in reverse and quickly backed out of the slip.

"Rex, we need a heading," Trissy requested as Rex looked at his GPS.

"Head north."

As Zeila ducked into the cabin, Trissy looked out the broken portside window. The cash-flow pirate Captain Coco had disappeared.

"Hold on, Zeila!" Trissy shouted while turning the wheel hard to port, placing the boat in gear and opening the throttle.

"Well, I'd say that we've had a rather exciting evening. Zeila are there any other sights in Whiskey Bay you feel compelled to show us?" Rex asked calmly but with grave concern.

"Sho' is."

"Rex take the wheel, I'm going to down below," Trissy requested before flicking on the cabin light and walking down a narrow ladder. She then turned around and yelled toward the pilothouse.

"Wow! Would you look at this! Zeila, come see."

Zeila carefully made her way down the ladder.

"Now, this is blingin'! Captain Coco sho' has his ride tricked out, Miss Trissy," Zeila concluded as she looked around the cabin. There were two wide beds side by side in the bow and a queen-size bed in the master bedroom. There was also a shower, a kitchen with a refrigerator, and a small, intricately laid wooden dining table. Brass portholes, beautiful wood veneer throughout, and rich fabrics completed the ambience.

"I have no idea what you just said, but this is spectacular. Captain Coco is certainly an unpredictable character. Topside, the superstructure looks like an old, condemned outhouse, while down below, the finish-out is a site to behold," Trissy concluded, looking around in amazement.

"Zeila, why don't you round up some grub and then lie down? We're going to have a long night ahead of us," Trissy suggested.

"You don't have to tell me twice. My stomach's growling and my eyes are closing," Zeila replied while rummaging through the kitchen cabinets.

"Trissy, could you please pull out the black wetsuit and rubber booties from my backpack?" Rex asked.

Trissy returned with a one-piece stretchy diving suit, which she handed to her husband.

"Christ, is this tight. I didn't think rubber shrank," Rex complained as he struggled to work his enlarged frame into the old tattered suit.

"The problem isn't the expandable wetsuit dear, it's the hotdogs, the cheese dip, the Mai Tais, and just possibly a sedentary lifestyle, all of which have caught up with you," Trissy giggled.

"No way," Rex responded, sucking in his gut.

"Ah, that's better," Rex added after struggling with the zipper. "Now, we have a mission to accomplish, just as soon as I catch my breath. Damn, this thing is tight," he complained. "Where's my backpack?"

"It's right next to you, Rex," Trissy replied, wondering if the wetsuit was cutting off blood and oxygen to her husband's cerebral cortex.

"Oh! If it were an alligator, it would have had my ass," Rex declared, opening the flap and reaching for his GPS.

"We have to be at least a hundred miles away from the terrorist camp," Trissy surmised as Rex turned on the device.

"No, as a matter of fact, we're only sixteen miles due south of their evil little hideaway. I think we can be there in just over two hours, assuming it's a straight shot," Rex surmised, looking at his watch.

"It's twelve thirty. Why don't you go down below and get some shuteye?" Rex suggested, opening the throttle halfway and placing his hands on the boat's wheel.

"Not a bad idea. I'm exhausted," Trissy confessed. "I trust you'll avoid any bootleggers or poachers you encounter along the way," she added with a smile.

"Rest assured, I believe we've far exceeded our 'bubba quota' and sure as hell wouldn't want the 'Swamp Rangers' citing us," Rex replied in kind.

"I love you," Trissy said softly, blowing Rex a goodnight kiss.

"I love you, too. Sleep well."

Shortly after Trissy made her way down below, the cabin lights were doused. As Rex stood at the helm, he looked at the compass before turning the rickety pontoon boat to a heading of ten.

"Well, I surely wouldn't want to run this luxury yacht aground," Rex mumbled as he reached for his night vision goggles. After quickly scanning ahead, he was comfortable that there were no trees or low-lying landmasses in close proximity. For the first time in days, Rex had a brief moment to relax. The stars above were bright and magical, and the rumbling of the engine, along with a gentle rolling of the boat, hypnotic. But the peace and tranquility were to be shortlived. Rex, Trissy, and Zeila were sailing into harm's way.

Chapter 29

After cruising peacefully for several hours on a calm starlit night, Rex could see dim lights up ahead. He glanced at his GPS. The position of the terrorist camp he had marked, just before the *Storm Chicken* was shot down, was only one half mile away. He immediately pulled back on the throttle and placed the boat in neutral before making a ten-degree turn to port. As the boat slowed, the stern swung around, giving Rex an unimpeded view. He brought the night vision goggles to his eyes. He could see a large deserted dock and three wooden buildings. There appeared to be no movement on shore. As he adjusted the magnification, the trucks he had seen from the air came into focus.

"Surely the terrorists aren't in the transportation business. Why in the world would they have collected so many U-Haul trucks?" Rex pondered before walking back into the cabin and killing the engine. With sound traveling so far over water, especially on a cold night, it was important to maintain the element of surprise. He would have to pole the boat to shore. The time had come for their all-important reconnaissance mission. Rex glanced at his watch.

"Two forty-five a.m. I had better wake the girls," Rex said to himself, making his way toward the ladder.

It was pitch black down below. With the exception of creaking wood and the unnerving intermittent sound of someone grinding their teeth while snoring, all was relatively quiet. Rex was certain he knew which direction Trissy lay as he flicked on the red overhead light.

"My word, Trissy wasn't joking. This is magnificent!" Rex whispered as he admired the finish-out.

He could see Zeila and Trissy racked out, both dead to the world. Oddly enough and to Rex's surprise, it was Zeila who was guilty of generating the ghastly sounds.

"Trissy, Trissy," Rex whispered, placing his hand on her hip and gently rocking her back and forth.

"Huh—what? Oh, Rex, it's you," Trissy sighed as she struggled to wake up. Her head came off the pillow momentarily before flopping back down.

"Zeila, time to get up," Rex pleaded, but she did not rouse. However, the snoring had turned into snorting. Thus, Rex felt confident he was making some headway in bringing her back from a deep sleep. "Zeila, wake up," Rex said as he shook her.

"I didn't drink your moonshine, Grandpa Sambo," Zeila mumbled, fighting the demons in her subconscious. "What—where am I?"

"Zeila, it's okay. It's Rex."

"What time is it?" Zeila asked, struggling to sit upright before swinging her feet over the side of the bed. She sat quietly for a moment to collect her thoughts.

"Almost three a.m.; time to rise and shine. I need you both on deck in five minutes," Rex insisted before scurrying up the ladder, ignoring the moaning and groaning of his weary cotravelers. He didn't notice Zeila pull her legs back up onto the bed. Moments later, she was drifting back off into la-la land. Once on deck, Rex grabbed a long wooden pole he had seen lying against the rail. He put the pole over the side and began pushing against the seabed with all his might.

He lost his balance and nearly fell overboard as the pole gave way and slipped deeper into the mud.

"Damn!" Rex growled. He was starting to break a sweat, but the boat slowly began to gain speed. He was aiming for a small grouping of large dense trees on the tip of the peninsula, which was in close proximity but out of sight of the camp. He found himself continually running to the helm to adjust the rudder in order to keep the boat on course.

"Trissy! Zeila! I need your help!" Rex shouted in frustration to his crew down below. "I just knew they'd go back to sleep."

"All right, all right, don't rush us!" a groggy Trissy shouted back several minutes later as she slowly crawled up the ladder.

It was now 3:15 a.m. The boat was one hundred yards from shore when Trissy made it topside.

"Trissy, grab the wheel. Steer toward those trees," Rex insisted, pointing to the area where he wanted to put in. He didn't wait for a response before scrambling aft to man his pole in an effort to silently propel the unusual craft forward.

"Gotcha," Trissy yawned, taking her hands off the wheel to rub her eyes.

"Zeila, hold on," Rex whispered after noticing her on deck. They were only yards from shore when the bow eased into the thick muddy bottom sediment. There was a subtle jolt as the boat's forward momentum suddenly stopped.

"All ashore who's going ashore," Rex proclaimed, withdrawing his laptop from his backpack and placing the device in a safe location within the cabin.

"Just what's the plan, Rex?" Trissy yawned as Rex swung his backpack over his shoulder after confirming that his plastic explosives and detonators were accounted for.

"The plan is two-fold. First, there are several trucks parked adjacent to this grouping of trees and perhaps a hundred yards away. I can only assume that the intended use is either to clear out and move to a new location or to somehow promote the terrorists' evil plans. So we need to rig those trucks to explode," Rex explained.

"Why don't you just slash the tires?" Zeila asked.

"Because the pop and the hissing sound would alert these maggots and we'd lose our element of surprise," Rex replied with a hint of frustration, wondering why Zeila would even question his brilliant plan.

"Rex, why don't we just pour sand into the gas tanks?" Trissy asked as Rex began to wonder if there was a subtle mutiny in the works.

"Because it would take too much time, and the possibility of the metal gas caps clanging against the side of the vehicles would also give away our position. Furthermore, we would lose our ability to decide when and where to disable the trucks," Rex replied, attempting to rationalize his position.

"Obviously, the boy's put too much thought into this hairbrained scheme. Sho' has," Zeila remarked, much to Rex's dismay as Trissy nodded in agreement.

"Well, why don't we..." Trissy started to say before Rex quickly interrupted.

"No, no, and no! We're going to do this my way," Rex insisted.

"Suit yourself," Zeila mumbled.

Rex dropped his head and slowly shook it, wondering where he had gone wrong. "We're running out of time! Are you two in or out?" Rex asked bluntly.

"I'll have to think about it. When can I get back to you?" Zeila asked.

"Oh, Lord," Rex grumbled.

"I'm in, Rex," Trissy replied calmly.

"Excellent. Now, as you know, I have plastic explosives in the backpack. We're going to take a small portion and ball it up to the size of a plum and stick it into the radiator of each truck along with a satellite-activated fuse. Our jumpin' GeeHad surprise can be detonated from anywhere in the world from the laptop computer. Next, we need to survey the camp, which appears to be situated on a small peninsula. If we can cut off their one and only escape route, perhaps we can trap these bastards before they have a chance to kill innocent Americans," Rex announced with pride.

"If you're gonna cut off their escape route, why do you have to booby-trap the trucks?" Zeila asked, wondering if the Louisiana mud Rex had been coated with earlier in the evening had somehow warped his semi-functional mind.

"Oh, Lord," Rex mumbled, looking up at the stars hoping for divine intervention. Surely the good Lord could restrain Zeila and her thoughts for just a few minutes.

"Rex, the plan sounds rather ambitious, wouldn't you say?" Trissy interjected, playing the Devil's advocate.

"Well, as they say: *no guts, no glory*," Rex replied in his own defense.

"Grandma had a similar saying. She'd chase Sambo around the house with a meat cleaver, screaming, '*No nuts, no trouble!*'" Zeila said as Trissy howled and Rex cringed.

"Zeila, I would have loved to meet your grandmother," Trissy confessed as Rex continued to stay focused.

"Now, any plan that saves the United States from Allah's Crazed Virgin-Seekers has to be bold," Rex announced after deciding to proceed with his plan, regardless of the unfound criticism.

"Dat Rex is clearly having delusions of grandeur," Zeila shared openly as Trissy thought about Rex's macho battle cry.

"I believe the 'guts and glory' saying can be traced back to Colonel Custer at the battle of Little Big Horn. All his 'guts and glory' did for him was to ensure the good colonel and his loyal men a shallow grave on a cold windswept grassy knoll," Trissy recalled in an attempt to make her point.

"Let's hope that Rex Bent, the great turbine-a-tor, doesn't suffer the same fate as he rams his Little Big Horn up some radical murderous Muslim butt!" Rex shot back with confidence, trying to make light of the danger they'd face. "Are you with me or not?"

"What the hell. Someone's got to keep you out of trouble," Trissy conceded grudgingly.

"Excellent!" Rex fired back.

"Don't do it, Miss Trissy. Although it's probably a Girl Scout camp, I sense great danger. Besides, who's going to rescue Rex when he does something stupid?" Zeila pleaded.

"Rex, you must admit, Zeila has a good point," Trissy admitted.

"Hogwash!" a rambunctious Rex shot back before turning to the wise old Cajun woman.

"Now, Zeila, wait for us here. If you're a good girl, I'll bring you back some cookies and moonshine. However, if we're not back by five a.m., fire up the engine and haul ass. Find help wherever you can," Rex insisted.

Zeila didn't acknowledge his order. In fact, she had turned her back and was ignoring him.

"Zeila, are you listening to me?" Rex asked with growing concern.

"I believe only the Reverend Louis Farrakhan could save us from this pre-dic-a-ment," Zeila proclaimed, looking up toward the heavens.

"Isn't he the one that beams up to his spaceship on occasion?" Trissy asked as she, too, began wondering about Zeila's bizarre choice of superheroes.

"Sho' is. That's how he talks to God," Zeila replied with unyielding confidence.

"Oh, Lord, please help," Rex pleaded, once again launching his own request for divine intervention.

"Trissy, Farrakhan is the radical Muslim maggot who can't count. 'The Million Man March'—huh! Furthermore, the anti-Semitic babbling bastard has the nerve to run around this great country preaching hatred and violence. For all we know, he could very well be the ringleader of this terrorist organization. Even more concerning is the fact that if Leaping Louis brought us to his spaceship, he'd probably chop off our heads and eat our brains," Rex voiced adamantly.

"Yes, but that's only the nonbelievers," Zeila replied in support before deciding to change the subject. "Now, how do I start up this engine?" she asked, looking at the control panel adjacent to the helm. Rex hesitated momentarily, trying to decide whose side Zeila was on.

"You turn this key to the right. When you hear a rumbling sound, you stop turning," Rex answered. "Do you understand?"

"Sho' do, but I don't want to be left alone. Either Trissy stays or you give me your rifle," Zeila insisted.

"Absolutely," a subdued, battle-weary Rex acknowledged as he handed Zeila his weapon.

"I'll need an extra magazine clip," Zeila added bluntly.

"It's in the left-hand side pocket," Rex said, turning around and allowing Zeila to reach into his backpack.

"Got it," Zeila announced.

"Zeila, be very careful with that rifle. The safety is off and the trigger is very sensitive," Rex added before slipping over the side and into the water.

"By the way, where's my wetsuit, Rambo?" Trissy asked as she dangled her feet over the side.

"You're a tough German. You'll be just fine."

"I hate cold water," Trissy complained.

"Nonsense, come on in. The water's lovely," Rex added in an attempt to entice Trissy as he slapped at a swarm of mosquitoes closing in for the kill.

"Brrr, rabbits, damn that's cold. Next time, I insist you pack my wetsuit," Trissy requested after slipping into the cold, brackish swamp.

"Yes, dear," Rex answered obediently as Trissy shivered.

"How will I know it's you rustling through the woods?" Zeila asked, looking down at Rex and Trissy. They were now knee-deep in the murky water.

"Three three-second red flashes from my penlight will signal our return," Rex answered.

Moments later, Rex and Trissy vanished into the woods. Zeila felt abandoned. She was alone in hostile waters, charged with defending the *Damned Gre-Gre* against all enemies foreign and domestic. For a moment, she fondly recalled the many nights she had spent camping on Whiskey Bay with Sambo and all their relatives. The snakes, the alligators, the frogs, and the birds were all her friends, especially after a snort of Grandpa's moonshine. But suddenly her thoughts turned to Uncle Rufus, Sambo's firstborn child.

Fifty years to the day, family and friends had been enjoying a wonderful weekend camping out next to the infamous *Sacred Tree of Alli*. Everyone had passed out with the exception of Rufus, the only man in the world born with two livers. He had insisted upon fishing on that fateful morning.

It had been three in the morning when he'd staggered down to the water, waded out a few feet, and placed his lantern on top of a partially submerged tree stump. Zeila remembered standing on the shore holding his fishing pole and a small bucket of night crawlers. As Rufus had waded back, he'd become aware of two fluorescent wide set eyes in the water only feet from Zeila.

Only a small ripple, barely noticeable, had marked the seasoned predator's position as the stealthy carnivore had stocked his unsuspecting prey. Zeila remembered Rufus screaming 'NO!' as he'd rushed to shore. He'd appeared to be running in slow motion and, from that point on, time stood still.

Zeila had looked to her right in time to see the fifteen-foot alligator spring at her. Its front claws and body had been several inches off the ground and its jaws wide open. There was no doubt that the ravenous reptile could have swallowed her whole. Zeila had frozen as she'd watched the large, shiny jagged teeth come in for the kill.

She'd held Rufus's fishing pole firmly. The snarly snout had struck the vertical pole, throwing Zeila several feet from the prehistoric predator. But the animal had continued to attack.

Rufus had arrived just in time to distract the gator, but in his drunken state her uncle's reflexes had been no match for the cunning, lightning-fast beast. The alligator had grabbed him by the leg and begun pulling him back into the swamp.

Rufus had let out a terrified scream that roused everyone in the camp. Zeila had grabbed his hands and pulled with all her might, but she, too, was being dragged into the water by the powerful reptile. Her hands had slipped as the alligator had violently thrown its body back and forth in an effort to stun its prey. Rufus had continued to fight even though he was being unmercifully and viciously slapped against the water.

Almost immediately, the dark murky waters had turned a crimson red and seemed to boil as the splashing intensified. Zeila could hear bones crunching and a final bloodcurdling scream just before Rufus had disappeared.

Zeila bowed her head and prayed as the recurrent nightmare began to fade. As tough as she was, tears streamed from her eyes as she vividly recalled the tragic event. Suddenly, there was a loud splash and the sounds of the swamp at night became very haunting. Zeila could feel the hair on the back of her neck rise as her eyes began to bulge. Uncharacteristically, she was now overcome by fear of the great unknown.

"Rex is nuts! This position is in-de-fence-able. I'm a sitting duck. There's no way I'm staying put. This ragin' Cajun black beauty is out of here!" Zeila blurted, firing up the engine and placing the boat in reverse.

Chapter 30

Massive tree trunks with undulating roots guarded the tip of the peninsula and the southern approach to Camp Eagle, the terrorist's stronghold, within Whiskey Bay. Rex and Trissy brushed away the dense layers of moss clinging to the branches of the century-old cypress trees and cautiously stepped over large roots as they entered this foreboding area. All ambient light was suddenly eliminated by the prolific and impenetrable canopy overhead.

In the darkness, their sense of smell and hearing immediately heightened. As they carefully waded through the swamp, they were overcome by a strong musty odor, which intensified as the water swirled with every step. Every sound was magnified and eerily reverberated within the haunting and often unforgiving ecosystem. Owls hooted, frogs croaked, snakes slithered, and branches rustled. There was an occasional unexpected splash and the ever-present pair of opportunity-driven fluorescent eyes just above the waterline, watching the intruder's every move.

They became keenly aware of their key bodily functions. Hearts raced and each forceful contraction resulted in a loud, thunderous beat, while pulses surged and respirations became more rapid.

"Rex, this is damn spooky and I can't see a thing. Do you have any idea where we're going?" Trissy whispered, fighting off the multitude of dive-bombing mosquitoes.

"Hell no, but I think we're headed in the right direction," Rex whispered, pushing forward.

Suddenly, Rex heard the faint roar of an engine but was unable to determine the direction from which the sound was coming. At first he was convinced that it was emanating from the camp, but soon he realized that was not the case.

"Damn, I though we told Zeila to stay put and wait for us," Rex growled.

"Well, she's rather independent," Trissy responded in her defense.

"Yes, but she could very well wake the terrorists and eliminate our element of surprise," Rex argued.

"Not to mention take away our means of escape," Trissy added.

"That's not very reassuring. Why did I leave that crazy old Cajun lady in charge of the boat?" Rex wondered.

"Obviously, you were overcome with swamp fever. But now there's no turning back," Trissy replied, coming to a halt.

"You're right. The mission must proceed, whatever the circumstances and/or inherent dangers."

"Rex, are those lights ahead?" Trissy asked as she looked over his shoulder.

"Absolutely, let's go," Rex whispered.

Rex and Trissy trudged another fifty yards before finally hitting dry land.

"Look, there's a clearing just ahead," Rex whispered.

"I see it."

Rex crouched down and brushed a thick bushy limb aside just in time to see a family of raccoons making their way across the clearing, presumably toward discarded tasty leftovers.

"Here are our trucks. There appear to be seven in all. How convenient, each is parked nose-first toward the swamp," Rex announced enthusiastically, surveying the area.

"Yes, but I can't see the camp with all those unsightly box-shaped vehicles in the way," Trissy complained.

"I know. Stay here for a moment," Rex whispered before dashing out into the open. He immediately sought refuge adjacent to the nearest truck and, with his back hugging the vehicle, he quietly crept around one side until his view was unobstructed. The moon was low on the horizon and thus the light cast long shadows throughout the camp. There was a large open area with patches of closely cropped grass. Walkways and a large circular drive were covered with a crushed limestone that glistened like ice in the dim light.

Rex could see a small domed concrete structure off to his right, adjacent to the dock. Straight ahead and to his left were three large Quonset-style wooden buildings raised on stilts, each with a corrugated tin roof. Between the buildings were several large antennae and numerous satellite dishes.

He could make out four guards. Each was armed with an automatic weapon. Two were standing on the dock smoking and two were patrolling the grounds. No one was close to the trucks and all appeared calm.

He was about to leave when his eye caught a familiar shape. Adjacent to one of the buildings and nestled in the shadows was a familiar crème-colored sedan, which looked suspiciously like GeeHad's Bentley.

"For Christ's sake! It was only a matter of time before Carencrow Regional's fearless leader reared his ugly head," Rex said to himself before running back toward the front of the truck, where he knelt down. He motioned to Trissy who scrambled out of the swamp and joined him.

"What did you find?" Trissy whispered.

"Only that God-fearing, Medicaid-embezzling GeeHad has sought refuge in this remote wilderness park," Rex disclosed.

"No! GeeHad, here?" Trissy replied with shock and disbelief.

"Yes. Can his booty buddies and band of cutthroats be far behind?" Rex wondered, loosening his backpack and swinging it over his shoulder before gently lowering it to the ground.

"Well, I would have never guessed. Do you think the evil North Korean Chum is with him?" Trissy asked as Rex pulled a large rectangular block of plastic explosive from his backpack.

"It's hard to say, but there has to be some connection," Rex replied, forming the plastic explosive into eight round balls before retrieving the fuses.

"Rex, are you having trouble counting? There are seven trucks and you've just formed eight explosive plums," Trissy asked.

"We couldn't possibly desert this camp without leaving GeeHad a memorable going-away present. It just wouldn't be appropriate," Rex replied sincerely.

"Excellent idea. You know, I'm starting to think that we'll actually get to the bottom of their evil plan," Trissy replied confidently.

"Let's hope so. Now, Trissy, there are four guards walking the compound, so be very quiet. Place the explosive through the grill of each truck, like this, and mash it into the radiator. Then, embed the fuse firmly into the plastic compound," Rex demonstrated. "I've already set the fuses."

"Got it, but is that enough explosive to do any harm?"

"Absolutely. It's enough to destroy the radiator, blow off the hood, and mangle the engine without harming the occupants," Rex assured her.

"Wow! Now that's a bang for your buck," Trissy replied in amazement, looking at the small round ball, which reminded her of a glob of Silly Putty.

"You rig the three vehicles to the left and I'll handle the three to the right. We'll meet back here in five minutes. Be careful," Rex whispered, handing Trissy the necessary explosives and detonators. He placed his very personal and touching gift to GeeHad back into his backpack for safekeeping, withdrew his pistol, and then slid the black satchel into the shadows cast by the front of the truck.

Trissy scrambled to the first truck, knelt down, and secured the explosive and detonator in the metal grill before continuing on with the rest of her mission. In short order, all was complete. Trissy turned back to meet Rex as planned, but she became distracted after noticing that the windshield of each truck was glazed over. She slowly approached the compartment of one of the dilapidated trucks.

"That's rather odd," Trissy said to herself, touching the front windshield. "The condensation is on the inside, not the outside." Trissy whispered as her curiosity grew.

Instinctively, she stepped up onto the rusted-out runner. Her slender 110-pound frame was just enough to tilt the truck ever so slightly toward her. Immediately, the shoddy shocks exuded a low-pitched prolonged groaning sound, which she ignored. Trissy cupped her hands firmly against the glass to eliminate any ambient light and placed her face as close as possible to the passenger window for a look inside.

Suddenly, there was a subtle thud as a bound, paralyzed body within the compartment shifted and a grotesquely distorted face fell against the glass, displacing the accumulated moisture. Trissy could make out a large blue nonreactive emotionless eye with streaks of jet-black eyeliner running down a flattened white cheek. She also vividly pictured engorged ruby red lips that appeared to extend from the nose to the chin. With the lipstick smeared in a wide erratic distribution. It was clearly evident that the sorry incapacitated soul was undoubtedly having more than just a manic moment. In a split second, Trissy recognized the ugly mug—it was none other than Teresa Talon, the evil nurse executioner charged with beating of all the rebellious ER employees enslaved in Carencrow Regional's sweatshop.

Trissy screamed and leaped backward. As she planted her foot on the uneven ground, her ankle twisted and she was unable to stop her momentum. Before falling to the ground, Trissy struck her head against the adjacent truck. Stunned by the blow and crippled with fear, Trissy sat motionless. She was easy prey for the nearby terrorist standing guard.

"Oh, no!" Rex moaned the instant he heard Trissy's scream pierce the cool night air. He drew his pistol and raced to her aid. As he rounded the second truck from the end, he watched as Trissy struggled to free herself from her captor's grasp.

There was screaming and yelling now coming from all directions. Seconds later, bright camp lights illuminated the grounds. Rex leveled his pistol, impatiently waiting for a clear shot. But the terrorist had spotted him. Using Trissy's body as a human shield, the radical Islamic terrorist fired off a burst from his automatic weapon. Rex ducked behind the front of the truck just in time. A spray of bullets peppered the ground and ricocheted off the metal hood.

Unfazed, Rex was even more determined. He leveled his weapon once again and slowly squeezed the trigger. He was confident he could make the shot that would free Trissy. His concentration was so intense that he never heard the terrorist approaching from behind.

"Ooof!" Rex moaned after being hit on the back of the head with the butt of a gun. He fell to the ground, unconscious, before he'd been able to discharge the round.

Chapter 31

It was early morning on Whiskey Bay. As always, the struggle for life and death continued as the hunters pursued the hunted. Yet at this hour there was normally a peaceful serenity seldom interrupted by a kill. In their struggle for survival, all of the animals in this remote swamp were keenly aware that the sun was about to rise. A new day was soon to begin. There would be an uneasy truce for all but man.

Suddenly, the tranquility was interrupted by a burst of gunfire, which was followed by the ringing of a loud bell. The alarm was sounded with maddening tyrannical zeal. Instantaneously, the floodlights came on, illuminating Camp Eagle. There was a great deal of shouting and a flurry of activity as dozens of men scrambled outside. Many were half-asleep and half-dressed, but all were armed.

"Rex!" Trissy screamed, watching her husband's limp body fall forward while the guard who had struck him with a butt of his rifle laughed.

"Let go of me!" Trissy demanded of her captor, fighting to free herself from the terrorist's iron grip. "Rex!" She looked on helplessly while blood cascaded from the back of his head. With her arms being held firmly behind her, she relentlessly stomped on her captor's foot and blindly kicked at his knees.

"That's quite enough," the man declared as he lifted Trissy up and firmly stomped her petite body into the ground.

Trissy gasped as all of the wind was suddenly knocked out of her. She lay stunned, face-down in the damp soil as her captor pulled out his hunting knife.

"Uozoo, what's the meaning of this?" an exhausted Mohammad shouted while rushing toward the U-Haul trucks.

"The infidels have paid us a visit, Mohammad," Uozoo declared, pressing his knee into the small of Trissy's back and grabbing her hair.

"I see," Mohammad replied, quickly surveying the scene. Yassar and GeeHad were now standing at his side while all the other terrorists gathered around.

"Shall I sacrifice this one to Allah?" Uozoo asked, yanking Trissy's head backward, exposing her slender neck.

"Yes—yes—yes!" the men chanted in unison. The anticipation of drawing fresh blood was all that was needed to fully awaken the band of heinous cutthroats.

"Were there just the two?" Mohammad inquired, noticing Rex's motionless body on the ground.

"Yes, sir," Uozoo responded as his large blade flashed in the light, ready to strike a fatal blow.

"Ooh," Trissy moaned.

"Were there any weapons?" Mohammad asked.

"Only this pistol," the guard who struck Rex proclaimed proudly, holding up the sparse catch.

Mohammad snickered as he looked at the sole weapon.

"You'd have to be insane to launch an assault on our heavily armed camp with that peashooter. Roll that idiot over and let me look at his face," he ordered.

Mohammad walked closer as one of his men planted his foot in Rex's ribs and with a swift kicking motion flipped him over onto his back. Rex remained unresponsive. His ribcage expanded and contracted ever so slightly while an expanding puddle of blood now surrounded his head. Mohammad knelt down and placed his hand on the side of Rex's neck.

"He still has a pulse," Mohammad announced without emotion.

"That's indeed unfortunate," GeeHad replied angrily as Mohammad grabbed Rex by the chin and moved his head back and forth.

"I don't recognize either the man or the woman. They're not possibly friends of yours, GeeHad?" Mohammad inquired sarcastically as he looked at the man responsible for financing terrorist activities within the United States. Mohammad remained convinced that GeeHad had blown their cover and thus jeopardized the success of the diabolical plan he had worked on for years. He did not hide the fact that he felt betrayed by his Muslim brother.

"The woman looks familiar, but I'm not sure who she is. The man is Rex Bent, the emergency room physician responsible for contacting the National Security Agency and the CDC. As you recall, Mohammad, I had ordered his execution but you intervened," a now seething GeeHad fired back in his own defense, raising his voice.

GeeHad and Mohammad were constantly at one another's throats. Their disagreements over the years were frequent, but last night their volatile relationship had taken a turn for the worse. GeeHad was appalled that Mohammad had invited his loyal employees down from Carencrow only to drug them during yesterday's celebratory victory feast. For now, he would remain quiet, but GeeHad vowed to avenge this travesty after their crippling blow to the United States had been executed.

Mohammad was tempted to lunge at GeeHad and strike him down for displaying such insubordination, but there were far more pressing matters to attend to. He would deal with GeeHad later, he thought, as he fought to control his anger.

"So this is the elusive Dr. Bent. You see, GeeHad, all is going as planned. Operation Uncle Slam will get underway in just a few hours. Within a matter of days, New York City, Washington, DC, Boston, San Francisco, Los Angeles, San Diego, and Houston will be contaminated with radioactive nuclear wastewater and the monuments to this pagan civilization rendered uninhabitable. Furthermore, Allah has delivered these infidels for our amusement," Mohammad announced joyfully as he stood and walked toward Trissy.

Mohammad smiled as he looked down at his new sacrificial lamb, her beautiful face now caked with splotches of grass, clay, and mud. The joy and anticipation in Uozoo's eyes were more than evident. He could tell that Uozoo relished the thought of taking her life. All he needed was Mohammad's nod of approval.

"No, Uozoo. Sheath your knife for now, my friend," Mohammad requested after much thought.

"We're one passenger short on our ride toward immortality. This whore, along with GeeHad's good friends from Carencrow Regional Hospital, shall be implicated in dealing America's fatal blow. All will witness the power of Allah and each will die a thousand deaths!" Mohammad shouted, shaking his fists above his head.

Mohammad's words and mannerisms were well received. The dancing and chanting erupted into a fever pitch. Uozoo disappointingly released his grip on Trissy's hair and her face fell back onto the ground. Then he too joined in the celebration, jumping up and down. However, Uozoo had no rhythm. With all body parts moving out of sync, he danced like a dysfunctional white boy with multiple chromosomal defects.

Mohammad turned away from GeeHad without saying another word and began walking back toward the command post with Yassar at his side.

GeeHad felt insulted. Both he and his loyal followers from Carencrow had been lured down to Whiskey Bay for a celebration to mark the success of their mission, one that he had financed for years. It was now evident that he was very much an outcast. His people had been drugged, bound, and gagged. They were now destined for a gruesome death in American cities far, far away. GeeHad's anger raged. He could remain silent no longer.

"Mohammad, I demand that you release my people immediately," GeeHad insisted after catching up with Mohammad and Yassar.

"Their death is Allah's will. Their destiny cannot and will not be changed," Mohammad replied without breaking stride.

“Then I shall free them myself,” GeeHad announced defiantly as Yassar reached for his stun gun.

Mohammad suddenly stopped and thought for a moment before turning to face GeeHad.

“That would be rather difficult to do from the gates of hell!” Mohammad replied before turning to Yassar.

“Yassar, bring this traitor to his knees.”

Yassar smiled as he pulled the trigger. There was a soft pop. Instantly, two small metal darts struck GeeHad squarely in the chest. Although the barbs penetrated the skin ever so slightly, the effect was overwhelming. Unmercifully, ten thousand volts were delivered over thin copper wires attached to the darts. GeeHad screamed in pain as he fell to the ground. His arms and legs contracted violently and his writhing was relentless, but Yassar was not satisfied with GeeHad’s mere submission. He turned up the voltage until all motion stopped. GeeHad lay unconscious at Mohammad’s feet.

“Excellent,” Mohammad announced with great satisfaction as Yassar turned off the weapon and detached two wire spools. The two men then started back on their journey toward the command post.

“Yassar, have the men search the grounds thoroughly and double the guards. However, I think our two guests dropped in unannounced after we downed their helicopter. They are probably responsible for the disappearance of our beloved freedom fighters we sent after them. My concern is that the authorities may not be far behind. Therefore, we need to adjust our timetable. The trucks are to leave no later than oh-eight hundred. Then we will promptly move our camp to the prearranged location,” Mohammad ordered.

“Yes, sir. And the infidels?” Yassar asked.

“I’m tempted to broadcast their torture and beheading, but time is now of the essence. String them up on the dock. In the morning, place the woman in the U-Haul truck destined for Washington, DC. Lastly, ensure that the troublesome Dr. Bent dines with the gators,” Mohammad commanded.

"It would be my pleasure to execute your wishes and desires, Mohammad," Yassar assured his supreme commander.

"Our 'Gator Guillotine' can easily accommodate two nonbelievers," he added.

"Of course. It would only be fitting for GeeHad to join Dr. Bent." Mohammad smiled.

"I will make it so," Yassar assured Mohammad with immense satisfaction.

Chapter 32

Zeila navigated the *Damned Gre-Gre* through a forest of trees, which lined a peninsula only a quarter-mile away from Camp Eagle. Nestled in the foliage and camouflaged by waves of dense clinging moss, the boat could not be seen, but Zeila now had a commanding view of Camp Eagle and the large wooden dock.

"This will do," Zeila proclaimed, cutting the engine.

"I'm gettin' rather good at navigating this floating outhouse, if I do say so myself... My word, either the engine is still on, or that's my stomach rumbling. Well then, it must be time for breakfast. Let's see what Captain Coco has stashed in the galley," she announced, carefully descending the steep ladder.

"Now, where's that damn light?"

Zeila wondered as she searched for the switch that would illuminate the pitch-black cabin. She rubbed her hand against every bulkhead several times before achieving success.

"Ah, there it is. Why didn't Captain Coco put these switches where you can find them? The salt air must make boat builders goofy," she concluded, frantically rummaging through all the cabinets.

"I sho' is powerfully hungry. There's nothing like being on the water to build an app-e-tite," the feisty Cajun declared.

She emptied the cabinets onto the small kitchen counter.

"What's all this damn health food doing here?" she complained. "Lookie here, 'Ain't-Ya-Mama's Pancakes,'" Zeila read out loud as she examined the unopened box.

"I'll be damned, the good-lookin' black woman on the box looks like me. Sambo would be proud," she announced with pride as she ripped open the box.

"Ah hell, it's all powder!"

Zeila launched the box into the sink.

As the clouds of pancake mix started to settle, Zeila found the mother lode.

"Now ya talkin', 'Thibodaux's Spicy Cracklin.'" If I could just find something nonpoisonous to wash down these crunchy pork-belly treats. Oh, Christ, where in the hell have they hidden the damn refrigerator in this Martha Stewart stinkhole?" Zeila complained as she continued to search for liquid sustenance.

Several minutes later, success was forthcoming.

"Wouldn't you know it, the refrigerator is right next to the toilet. What mental giant thought of that? Probably some old man with a small bladder and a leaky faucet," Zeila concluded after opening a wooden paneled door hiding the small rectangular cool box.

"Beer, beer, and more beer; perhaps I misjudged Captain Coco," she confessed as she attempted to stuff three twenty-four-ounce cans of liquid malt into her drooping brassiere.

Although the elastic had lost its memory long ago, Zeila quickly discovered that after stashing away the first can she had run out of room.

"You boobies have got to go. Mama needs more than one beer!" Zeila declared as she set her disciples free. The mammary glands descended without hesitation and at a speed that far exceeded the laws of physics. Zeila's breasts came to a sudden stop, dangling dangerously close to the deck.

"I half expected tea and lemonade," Zeila muttered. With the beers secured, she grabbed her bag of cracklins and headed topside.

It didn't take Zeila long to get comfortable on deck. In short order, she had eased into the captain's chair and had her feet propped up on the side rail. After inhaling multiple fried pigskins and washing them down with several large swigs of beer, she gazed out over the water at Camp Eagle.

"I don't remember all those lights being on, and what's all the commotion about?" Zeila asked herself as she reached for the binoculars lying adjacent to the night vision goggles. She could hear screaming and the roar of an engine as she adjusted the focus.

"What in the world are they dragging behind that truck?" she whispered, watching an old, dilapidated truck race in a circular pattern.

"Oh no! The terrorists must've caught Rex!"

Zeila frantically searched for Trissy. But her efforts were unsuccessful. The dust kicked up on the shale road quickly occluded her view.

"Damn! I sho' is getting tired of rescuing these renegade redneck Republicans. Old Lordie Jesus, forgive me Sister Michelle for I keep trying to reach across the aisle, but these white folk are nothing but trouble," Zeila complained, continuing her search of the grounds through the binoculars.

"Well, let me sit a spell and wait for the dust to settle."

Zeila lowered the binoculars and hoisted the ice-cold beer to her lips.

"Ah, now that's a dead soldier," Zeila declared as the empty can tumbled to the deck. "I sho' is tired," she concluded, popping the tab on her second beer and reaching for more cracklins.

"I still can't see a damn thing," she complained after scanning the terrorist camp, this time with her naked eye.

"Doggone it, I'm out of pigskins," a less-than-pleased Zeila remarked as she looked into the bottom of the empty king-size bag before tossing it onto the deck.

"Let me just rest my eyes for a minute."

Zeila placed her head on the back of the chair rest and folded her arms around her partially consumed can of beer. Seconds later, she was out.

Rex and Trissy had been captured and tortured by the Islamic terrorists. Their only hope for escape was now in the hands of feisty Zeila 'Katrina' Washington, who was sound asleep. It would soon be light and, unquestionably, a gruesome death awaited Rex and Trissy Bent.

Chapter 33

From the Carencrow command center, the FBI, the state police, and a slew of officials representing the governor, as well as other elected scoundrels, continued to pursue the hijacked Air Med helicopter. As expected, SAC Richter had arrived before sunrise to coordinate the search. However, much to everyone's surprise, he was less abrasive than usual. Naturally, it was assumed that he wasn't fully awake. Still, there was no sign of the hijacked chopper.

SAC Richter was seated at a long mahogany conference table with his hands folded behind his head and his feet propped up on the table. He looked very much like a man who was quite full of himself, to say the least.

"Good morning," Lieutenant Vickers said cheerfully. He had worked until midnight but had been fortunate enough to sleep soundly for five hours—a record for him, given the stress inherent with his job.

"Ah, Lieutenant Vickers, it's about time you returned to work," a grumpy and agitated Richter announced as he looked at his watch. It was 6:00 a.m.

"Pardon me, but I had to get some sleep," Lieutenant Vickers replied with a nod and a smile. He was determined that 'Yosemite Sam' would not get under his skin. No one was going to ruin his day, or so he thought.

"Well, that's good to know. As you slept, our quarry escaped. By now they're probably on some remote Caribbean island, drinking rum and thumbing their noses at us all," Richter surmised, dropping his feet off the table and rocking his chair forward.

"That's highly likely, and quite frankly, it's comforting to know that someone has escaped your wrath," Lieutenant Vickers chuckled, thinking about the joy Richter derived from crushing all the little people in his life.

"Just whose fucking side are you on?" Richter growled as he stood up and placed his face within inches of Lieutenant Vickers'.

"You can beat your chest all you want, but please save your egotistical game of intimidation for someone else," Lieutenant Vickers shot back with determination, refusing to yield an inch to the abrasive and emotionally unstable FBI agent.

"Gentlemen, you need to take a look at this," Jim Crowell reported in an effort to diffuse the heated early-morning Mexican standoff.

"State troopers report talking to farmers in this area." He pointed to two blue dots he had placed on the map just inside the fifty-mile radius. "One reported hearing a loud thrashing noise that scared his cows, while another actually saw a low-flying helicopter. When the Air Med chopper disappeared at this last known location, she was at an altitude of fifteen hundred feet. It would appear that the chopper dropped to less than three hundred feet off a deck, an altitude below our radar, and then turned south-southwest. I'm convinced they were heading for Whiskey Bay," Jim Crowell surmised with confidence.

"Now we're fucking getting somewhere!" Richter shouted enthusiastically.

"Did we ever get the satellite data I requested last night?" Lieutenant Vickers asked.

"You're the one who was supposed to follow up on that lead. If you're going to work for me, you need to learn how to follow through," Richter admonished, continuing his unprovoked assault on the police lieutenant.

"Forgive me, Master. I incorrectly assumed that this was a team effort," Lieutenant Vickers replied, his stomach starting to churn.

"It is a fucking team effort, but you have to realize that I'm the team leader. How was I made the team leader you might ask? Simply because I'm a winner!" Richter stated with pride.

Enough was enough. 'Yosemite Sam' clearly needed a bloody nose. Lieutenant Vickers realized that it was time he took off the gloves.

"That's unusual, because everyone thinks of you as a weenie and a whiner, but certainly not a winner. And that's not just a question of semantics. Quite frankly, to set the record straight, I have no doubt that you're a fucking dickhead who stumbled into the position, sir," Lieutenant Vickers shared openly and honestly with the horse's ass.

Once again, the room went silent. Although in agreement, everyone was quite shocked with Lieutenant Vickers' bold response. SAC Richter could sense that all eyes were on him. He would not retreat from this battle. Immediately, he realized that he had to put Lieutenant Vickers in his place before the bastard created a mutiny and jeopardized the success of his operation. Over the years, Richter had climbed the ranks by putting the fear of God into his troops and this would be no exception.

"Your fucking insubordination will not be tolerated." Richter assured the lieutenant as his neck veins began to bulge and pulsate.

"You can have my badge, but not until this job is done," Lieutenant Vickers stated emphatically.

"George, have we had any luck with the satellite data from the National Security Agency?" Lieutenant Vickers asked over the dull roar of the multiple conversations, which had erupted throughout the room shortly after the verbal skirmish.

"The information came across just minutes ago. Our satellite did indeed pick up a helicopter at approximately the same coordinates given by the farmers. However, two hours later, after the satellite had completed another orbit, the chopper was nowhere to be seen," Officer George stated.

"Interesting," Lieutenant Vickers replied. "I suggest we refocus our efforts and concentrate on Whiskey Bay."

"I'd have to agree," Jim Crowell confirmed.

"How long would it take to get down to Whiskey Bay?" Richter inquired.

"Three hours by auto or forty-five minutes by air," Jim Crowell responded.

"Well, it's obviously time to close in for the kill. Now, Mr. Crowell, I need to take you up on your offer to provide transportation," Richter insisted.

"I'll have a chopper ready for you in twenty minutes. By the time you get down to Whiskey Bay, it will be daylight," Jim Crowell said. He picked up a phone to activate the ground crew and pilot who were standing by.

"Excellent."

"George, please inform Ms. Valentino of the Richter's intentions," Lieutenant Vickers whispered to his old friend.

"It would be my pleasure, Lieutenant. By the way, I was most impressed by your decisive actions earlier. After your highly praised display of alleged 'insubordination,' I give you my word that I will do everything in my power to ensure that your burial is with full honors," George assured the rebellious lieutenant with a wink.

"That's comforting indeed, George, and most thoughtful."

"Once again, I have the elusive Dr. Bent in my sights," Richter proclaimed, rubbing his hands together in anticipation.

"That assumes that he and the others are still alive. Whiskey Bay is teeming with large alligators with notoriously ferocious appetites," Lieutenant Vickers relayed.

"No fucking prehistoric animal would dare eat my quarry," Richter assured the brash lieutenant.

"Would you like me to join you? My family had a camp on Whiskey Bay. I know that area quite well," Lieutenant Vickers queried, although he had no intention of joining Richter on his wild goose chase. The bay covered at least a hundred square miles. Finding anyone or anything in that inhospitable swamp would require more than just an element of luck.

"No, Vickers, I think I can handle this myself. Subduing a middle-aged, out-of-shape man and his hundred-and-ten-pound wife will be a piece of cake," Richter replied with unshakable arrogance.

"That remains to be seen. Of course, you'll have to find them first and that will not be easy. Just don't get too close to the water," Lieutenant Vickers cautioned knowing how unpredictable and cunning the alligators were.

"Lieutenant Vickers, you need to be a leader and project some element of confidence. You're starting to sound like a fucking pessimistic pussy," Richter remarked, evoking his keen sense of observation.

"On second thought, might I recommend a swim in Whiskey Bay? I understand that the waters are quite refreshing," Lieutenant Vickers suggested, realizing that he could never win a battle with the evil, irrational, cartoon-mimicking character.

"Now, I expect you to stay at this command center day and night. You will keep me fully informed of the latest developments. Do I make myself perfectly clear?" Richter demanded.

"Perfectly. Please have a safe and prosperous trip," Lieutenant Vickers replied without one shred of sincerity as Richter put on his coat.

"With daylight hours so limited this time of year, I've taken the liberty to book you at the nicest hotel on Whiskey Bay. Of course, it's the only hotel on the bay," Jim Crowell announced.

"And what's the name of this hotel?" Richter asked, grabbing his briefcase.

"Frankly, I'm not sure anymore, but the locals refer to it as the 'Water's Wedgie,' so named because, after paying the bill, you feel like your shorts have been yanked up forcefully and wedged between your butt cheeks," Jim Crowell laughed.

"That sounds like your kind of hotel, SAC. May I suggest that before picking up your tab, you swing everything to one side so your nuts aren't crushed in the wedgie?" the astute Lieutenant Vickers recommended.

"That's not even fucking funny!" Richter barked before he and Jim Crowell dashed out of the command center.

When the door slammed shut, everyone in the room jumped up and shouted. As Richter waited for the elevator, he chose to ignore the spontaneous celebration.

"Fucking juvenile bastards!" Richter growled as the elevator doors opened and the two men walked in. Jim Crowell felt like busting out with laughter, but somehow found the strength to maintain his composure. As the elevator doors closed, he turned the other way to avoid having his broad smile detected.

Several minutes later, both men arrived at the helicopter. The pilot was on board. Having finished his preflight check, the rotor was turning and he was ready to lift off as soon as his distinguished passenger arrived. Jim Crowell and SAC Richter bent over and ran toward the chopper. Jim opened the sliding rear door and the FBI agent hopped in.

"Perhaps you should check into the hotel before starting your hunt," Jim Crowell suggested.

"Fuck no!" Richter replied, utilizing his rather limited vocabulary.

"Well then, have a good flight," Jim Crowell said cheerfully before slamming the door shut. Once again, he bent down and ran toward the hangar, snickering all the way as he thought about the passenger who had boarded minutes earlier. It was one of those unique once-in-a-lifetime gifts, which he felt sure was capable of doing everything with the exception of cheering up the hostile special agent.

"You're really going to have to work on your language," Leslie suggested to a startled SAC Richter as she emerged from the shadows.

"What the in the hell are you doing here?" Richter growled as the rotor picked up speed and the aircraft lifted off the tarmac.

"My job, SAC, my job."

"I'm on a mission and I can't have you in my fucking way," Richter proclaimed without remorse.

"Well, that's just your bad luck. By the way, not to add insult to injury, but we have adjoining rooms at the hotel. That should give us a chance to bond and discuss the anger management course you will be attending in the near future," Leslie said with a smile as SAC Richter's face turned red and his body started shaking uncontrollably.

Chapter 34

THERE WAS A FLURRY of activity in Camp Eagle as the sun rose on Whiskey Bay. All the soldiers of Allah were working furiously, disassembling gear, packing, and loading several unmarked trucks destined for a new, clandestine camp. Everything was to be taken, including the trash. Mohammad wanted to ensure that they left no trace of their existence behind.

Mohammad walked into the command center, which he and his men had utilized so effectively over the past year. The computers, the communication equipment, and the various tactical displays were all gone. As he looked around the empty room, he was overwhelmed by the silence. Briefly, his memory flashed back to a time when this invaluable command post had been bustling with activity. His reflection lasted only momentarily before he refocused on his mission. There was much to do, Mohammad thought, as he walked out onto the porch. He placed his hands on the rail and looked out over the grounds, watching intently as the work progressed. His loyal and fateful number-two man, Yassar, soon joined him.

"I'm pleased to report that we're ahead of schedule, Mohammad. As instructed everything has been loaded," Yassar announced confidently.

"Excellent, and I see that you've taken good care of our unwanted guests," Mohammad chuckled.

Trissy was lashed to a wooden piling on the dock. Rex and GeeHad were in a more perilous position, suspended from a small crane located on the dock. They were bound, gagged, and dangling upside down only a few feet above the tranquil waters of the lagoon.

"Even the traitorous GeeHad insisted upon hanging around. By the way, here are the keys to his Bentley," Yassar added.

"Many thanks. Again, well done, Yassar," Mohammad praised as he took the keys and placed them in his pocket.

"Thank you, but I must confess that I have been quite angry with the Louisiana alligators. Usually, within an hour of temptation, several twelve-footers gather around their quarry and leap from the water to snatch their pound of flesh," Yassar relayed.

"I can see your disappointment with the 'Gator Guillotine.' Surely, someone should've lost their head by now. Perhaps you should lower Dr. Bent and GeeHad into the water," Mohammad suggested.

"I'm tempted, but that just wouldn't be sporting. Besides, the men enjoy seeing the fear in the eyes of the victims just after the alligator grabs them by the head. Myself, I enjoy watching the large prehistoric animals thrashing about, twisting and turning before ripping the head and neck from the torso. The blood gushing into the water after the event is just an added bonus," Yassar replied in rather graphic detail as Mohammad smiled with pleasure.

"As you please, Yassar, just make sure we retrieve the crane after you've had your fun with these decadent and unholy heathens," Mohammad requested.

"Absolutely."

"It's time to proceed to our new camp."

Yassar lifted his forearm and with his index finger extended, made a twirling motion with his hand. The signal was understood and, within seconds, several diesel engines came to life. Soon, three large unmarked trucks were underway, slowly rumbling down the drive toward the seldom-used highway.

"Is it time to launch our massive assault on the infidels?" Yassar inquired with a sense of unbridled anticipation.

Mohammad looked at his watch. It was 7:45 a.m. "Yes, my friend, now is the time."

Yassar made the same swirling motion with his hand and the diesel engines powering the seven U-Haul trucks spewed clouds of oil and gas as they struggled to come to life. Yassar pointed toward the dock. Uozoo immediately understood that it was time to load the last remnant of human cargo.

From her position on the dock, Trissy had an excellent view of the cove. On this cool morning, a hazy white patchy mist rose from the placid waters. As she struggled to free herself, her eyes caught a glimpse of movement in the water. Soon, ripples appeared which quickly grew into several large triangular wakes. Shortly thereafter, the lifeless eyes of giant reptilian man-eaters surfaced. All were rapidly closing in on the position from which GeeHad and Rex hung precariously like overstuffed piñatas. It was clearly time for breakfast. Trissy could see GeeHad struggling to free himself, but Rex remained motionless. He had never regained consciousness after sustaining the blow to the head during their assault on the terrorist camp.

"Rex, Rex!" Trissy screamed in a vain attempt to warn him of the imminent danger, but Rex didn't respond.

The water suddenly became turbulent as the alligators fought for position. Soon, the dominant beast won the first attempt to draw blood. The thousand-pound killer leaped several feet from the water, bumping GeeHad and knocking him into Rex. Both men now swung back and forth over the diners that had gathered.

Trissy watched in horror as a second assault was launched. A massive gator shot from the water with such force that the animal seemed to defy gravity.

Trissy screamed as the animal clamped down its unforgiving jaws on its helpless prey.

"R-E-X!" Trissy screamed at the top of her lungs as the animal began to twist violently. The death roll was quickly followed by a snapping sound. Then, in an instant, the scaly prehistoric carnivore disappeared into the murky water. GeeHad's head had been severed at the neck. Blood spewed downward, splashing into the water and creating an ever-expanding crimson slick, which served to excite the other diners.

Suddenly everything went gray. The gruesome sight was too much for Trissy to bear.

"I knew the alligators would come through. We just had to give them a little extra time," Uozoo laughed before hitting Trissy over the head with his pistol. He then dragged her limp body to the truck. Bound and gagged, she was thrown into the passenger seat of a dilapidated truck destined for Islamic glory. "Take her to Washington," Uozoo said as he slapped his hand against the passenger door just before the vehicle started to roll.

Chapter 35

The sound of the diesel engines roaring to life carried across the still waters.

"What, what, where am I?" Zeila asked after so rudely being awakened from a deep sleep. Suddenly, the beer she had been nursing hours earlier fell to the deck with a thud and began spewing an amber froth.

"What's this?" she blurted.

Zeila brushed a multitude of cracklin crumbs from her damp dress. She was engulfed in an aromatic cloud of hops, malt, and barley, which had successfully recharged shaky neurons within her dormant gray matter. As her thoughts cleared, the painful events of the early morning hours were vividly relived.

"Oh no, Rex and Trissy!" Zeila shouted, reaching for the binoculars.

Zeila watched a cream-colored Bentley and the last truck in the U-Haul caravan roll out of sight. The camp looked deserted with the exception of two men standing on the dock.

"They're clearing out," Zeila whispered. She adjusted focus. "What in the world is that hanging over the water? … My God! Those are bodies, and it looks like they're being devoured by the gators!"

Zeila put down the binoculars and grabbed Rex's assault rifle. She slid a round into the chamber and ensured that the safety was off before looking through the scope. Initially, she zeroed in on one of the alligators, but then she instinctively switched her target. The crosshairs were placed on the first terrorist's forehead. She squeezed the trigger.

The shot rang out and the man fell dead instantly. His friend ran to his fallen comrade's aid. Zeila pulled back the bolt, expelling the empty shell, before slamming another round into the chamber.

"I feel like I'm back in the ninth ward protecting my pets, my property, and my ass," Zeila said loudly. The remaining terrorist stood, trying to assess the direction from which the shot had come. This was all the hesitation that Zeila needed to lock onto her target.

"Smile for Zeila, you murderous camel jockey!"

Zeila squeezed off a second round, which struck the man squarely in the chest.

"Annie Oakley couldn't have done any better," Zeila announced with pride. She put down the rifle and fired up *Damned Gre-Gre*'s engines.

"Ain't no herd of virgins where I sent those boys. They're destined for hell!" Zeila assured herself as she placed the engines in reverse and opened the throttle. When she was free of the moss-laden trees that had provided cover, she threw the wheel to starboard and shifted the engine into forward gear. The bow quickly swung around and Zeila gave the engines more gas. The propellers dug in and the boat surged forward.

With her naked eye, Zeila could see the gators in the distance continuing to leap out of the water. Clearly they had grown fond of human flesh and remained undeterred by the sound of gunfire.

"Hang on, Trissy, hang on, Rex! Zeila's coming!" the black bombshell announced with pride as she raced to the aid of her newly adopted friends.

As the distance quickly closed, Zeila could make out Rex but not the other figure bound next to him.

"What have those bastards done with Trissy?" Zeila wondered, throwing the engines into reverse to slow the boat.

The bow of the boat slammed into the tandem alligator hors d'oeuvres.

"Sorry about that, Rex. Just when I thought I was getting the hang of this boat. No pun intended, of course," Zeila announced, placing the boat in neutral.

The bodies swung over the port beam. Zeila could see that Rex appeared unharmed with the exception a large gash on his head and a multitude of deep abrasions.

"Christ you're heavy, and filthy too, boy!" Zeila complained. She reached over the side and grabbing Rex by the rope, securing his hands to his waist.

Unexpectedly, one of the persistent diners with an insatiable appetite leaped from the water, catching her by surprise.

"Damn, you is big!" Zeila declared, falling backward to avoid being captured in the jaws of this wild and unforgiving beast.

Even before she hit the deck, Zeila's eyes had widened well beyond the restrictive bounds afforded by the globes. As she rose to her feet, her heart suddenly began to race and she could feel the hairs on the back of her head stand on end. Zeila's fear only made her stronger and more determined.

"No, sir! You may have nabbed Uncle Rufus when he wasn't lookin', but this tough old black woman ain't on your diet!" Zeila declared as she reached over the rail once again and drew Rex closer to safety.

"Gotcha—Wow, you've gotta lose some weight, boy!" Zeila strongly recommended while working the torsos of both men up and over the side rail.

It was then that she noticed that Rex's friend had not fared so well. She stared at the headless man as the few remaining clumps of coagulated blood oozed from his lifeless body onto the deck.

"Rex, your friend ain't lookin' good, but I suppose you're salvageable. Now, if I could only find a knife to cut you down," Zeila said, searching the cabin for a sharp utensil as the alligators kept churning up the water.

"Ah, here we go," she said, pulling a large serrated knife from its leather sheath. "This should do nicely."

A few minutes later Rex plopped onto the deck.

"Wake up and tell your friend to stop bleeding all over Captain Coco's floating outhouse," Zeila demanded, freeing him from his bonds. But Rex remained unresponsive.

"Damn, Rex, you need to spend more time in the sun. You've gone from lily white to ghostly white. I sure as hell hope you're not dead. No, you still have a pulse, but as with every delusional conservative Republican, I'm not so sure you have a heart," Zeila joked, hoping to arouse a response. However, Rex did not stir.

"Well, this has been a rather one-sided conversation. I just wish my husband had been so quiet and cooperative. Perhaps he would've lived another few years," Zeila confessed.

Zeila looked at Rex and then his headless friend before scanning the deserted terrorist camp.

"What the hell am I going to do now? … I've got to rescue Trissy, but I can't do it without Rex's help." As she planned her next move, Zeila was distracted by the sound of an airplane approaching.

"Well, I'd best get out of sight before the terrorists come back or the authorities capture your sorry ass."

Zeila put the boat into gear and opened the throttle. GeeHad still remained tethered to the crane and what remained of his body slipped back over the rail, much to the gators' delight. Minutes later, Zeila had successfully guided the *Damned Gre-Gre* back into the safe haven from where she could continue observing Camp Eagle.

"Wow, that was close," Zeila gasped as several helicopters and planes shot overhead.

"Either the terrorists have their own Air Force, or law enforcement has every available aircraft in the sky. Thank God they weren't looking for the two dead bodies on the dock. But it's only a matter of time before they find the downed Carencrow helicopter, which will lead them back to this camp," Zeila concluded.

"Boy, you and Trissy is in big trouble!" Zeila shared with Rex as he lay motionless, sprawled out on the deck.

Chapter 36

It was shortly before 6:00 a.m. on the West Coast. The sun had not yet begun to rise. A dense, brownish-gray malodorous layer of haze hundreds of feet thick blanketed the City of Angels. As usual, the magnificent San Bernardino Mountains to the east trapped the massive volume of self-generated pollution. Visibility was reduced to less than half a mile but in no way interfered with the flights departing from or arriving at Los Angeles International Airport (LAX).

Hundreds of thousands of commuters had begun their daily, mundane ritual of commuting to work. Interstate 405, which ran adjacent to the busy airport and looked like a parking lot. Row after row of headlights marked the undulations inherent to the serpentine concrete trail. The four lanes of traffic running both north toward downtown and south toward Long Beach were nearly at a standstill.

What was unusual on this dark and dreary November morning was the fact that there had been no accidents. Gridlock was the norm at this time of the day for the densely populated city. As each commuter endured the fatigue and frustration intrinsic in the weekday migration, no one noticed the beatup pickup truck towing a dilapidated wooden trailer stuffed with yard equipment. Nor did they pay any attention to the tanker truck laden with thirty thousand gallons of gasoline following closely behind. Both vehicles were in the outside lane heading north at a snail's pace.

Subdue turned on the overhead reading light in the Chevy S-10. He looked at his watch briefly, studying the schedule he held in his hands.

"Sanda, United Airlines jumbo jet flight fifty-nine is scheduled to depart at six-oh-five a.m. for the East Coast, while an American Airlines DC-ten, flight two twenty-five from Chicago, is scheduled to land at six-oh-seven a.m. Both planes are full," Subdue announced with pride.

"Our position is excellent. We're under the flight path, the high point in the freeway is only yards away, and the exit ramp to LAX is just ahead. It's time to execute our plan. Allah willing, we shall kill hundreds of the American infidels and wreak havoc across this unholy land," Subdue announced, reaching for his cell phone.

"The Americans have been given full warning," his driver Sanda replied sternly.

"Christians and Jews alike will die. Islam shall rule the world," Subdue added enthusiastically.

"Allah is great," Sanda whispered, gazing at the multitude of red taillights ahead.

Subdue flipped through several papers until he found his phone list. He quickly scrolled down through the names until he came to Khaos. The month and the day would indicate which prepaid cell phone number had been activated. Subdue quickly dialed the appropriate number.

The cell phone resting on the ripped vinyl seat rang loudly. The driver of the oil tanker took one hand off the wheel and reached for the vital communication device. He had been expecting the call.

"Khaos," he answered coldly, tapping the brakes.

"This is Subdue—execute."

"Executing—NOW!" Khaos confirmed as he hit *end* before slipping the phone into his shirt pocket. He looked at the shiny chrome-toxic Hummer, which had pulled abreast. He smiled at the young front-seat passenger briefly while gripping the steering wheel tightly with both hands. Khaos stepped on the gas and turned the wheel abruptly to the left. The oil tanker responded immediately by crunching the front end of the gaudy, ego-laden, rectangular contraption, effortlessly shoving it sideways. The other vehicles that lay in his path did not fare as well.

As Khaos continued toward the concrete median, the wheels of the massive tanker rolled up and over every obstacle. The heavy cylindrical body came crashing down with such force that any vehicles in the way were instantly crushed. Occupants were either killed or maimed. No driver had the time or the maneuverability to avoid the disaster.

"Excellent, Khaos, excellent!" Subdue praised, watching Khaos successfully lay down the impenetrable metal gauntlet.

"Is it time for our air show?" Sanda asked.

"That it is Sanda, that it is. Stop the truck," Subdue ordered.

"Look, the American fools continue onward on their mindless journey, oblivious as to what awaits," Sanda laughed.

The sea of red taillights continued to gain distance as the commuters proceeded north, undeterred. Sanda brought the truck to a stop and placed it in park. Subdue opened the passenger door and climbed out. He quickly scurried to the wooden trailer, lowered the tailgate, and stepped in. He threw a weed eater to the side and reached for a rope handle on a large, rectangular metal box. With one quick motion he flung open the lid, exposing the lethal weapons. In short order, Subdue had the first of two surface-to-air rocket launchers resting on his shoulder, the site locked in place, and the weapon activated. He waited patiently for his outbound flight.

"That was too easy. I always knew that the Americans had soft underbellies," Khaos snickered, opening the driver's side door. He stepped out and looked back, admiring the destruction he had wrought. A multitude of white headlights illuminated the result of his glorious excursion. The sides of the shiny tanker glistened as large plumes of steam emanated from damaged engines and drifted skyward. As overheated radiators leaked coolant, there was a loud hissing sound, which was intermittently drowned out by screams of anguish and despair. Soon, car horns started blaring.

"Impatient infidels!" Khaos growled, climbing down from the cab and calmly walking around to the passenger's side. He looked north and smiled. Now there was no doubt. As instructed, he had effectively cleared a large section of the busy freeway.

"I see that my bomb remains attached to the undercarriage of this cylindrical jewel. Well, I'd say it's time to heat things up a bit," Khaos chuckled, opening several valves under the tanker. Immediately, thousands of gallons of high-octane gasoline began pouring out. Waves of the highly flammable liquid rapidly washed down the gentle sloping section of the freeway.

Satisfied, Khaos turned and ran toward Subdue. When he was twenty yards from the trailer, he slowed to a walk. He was now a safe distance away. He withdrew his phone from a shirt pocket and dialed the number that would detonate the bomb. Subdue could sense his presence.

"Any moment now, Khaos," Subdue assured his trustworthy friend, intently surveying the intended flight path of the outbound United flight.

"Is it time to activate our warm and glowing diversion?" Khaos asked as more and more stranded motorists signaled their frustration.

"Absolutely. All that honking is getting on my nerves," Subdue complained as the blaring of the car horns intensified.

Khaos pressed the green *talk* button on his phone.

Instantly, there was an ear-shattering explosion. The tanker was lifted several feet into the air and a mushroom-shaped plume of bright flames shot fifty yards in all directions.

Within seconds, thousands of gallons of gasoline, which had been set free, ignited. A surging wall of fire immediately engulfed hundreds of vehicles unfortunate enough to be downstream and in the path of the flammable cascade. All were set ablaze. Drivers and passengers panicked but no one stood a chance either inside or outside their vehicles. The sound of the car horns was suddenly replaced by roaring flames, intermittent vehicle explosions, and the horrific screams of the nonbelievers being burned to death.

"Well, we've done our part to eliminate traffic congestion," Khaos joked, admiring the flames and watching the black smoke billow skyward.

"We could always do more," Subdue assured Khaos while patiently waiting for the United flight take off.

"There she is, right on time; 'United We Stand,'" he chuckled. He locked onto the jumbo jet. As the large plane struggled to gain altitude, Subdue firmly squeezed the trigger.

The surface-to-air missile shot skyward. In the blink of an eye, the plane was cut in half and a huge, rapidly expanding fireball raced across the hazy gray sky. The mid-section was nowhere to be seen. The nose of the plane appeared to continue onward and upward for a brief moment as a multitude of charred, flame-ridden remains of United flight 59 scattered in all directions before plummeting to Earth.

The explosion was massive, much to the delight of the terrorists.

Khaos raised his hands and started singing and dancing on the freeway as Subdue reached for the second handheld rocket launcher.

"How unusual, even American Airlines is on time," Subdue whispered as he activated the weapon and locked onto his second target. Suddenly, the plane veered to the left. Subdue was unsure if it was within range, but instinctively he knew he could no longer hesitate.

The second surface-to-air missile was away. A half-minute later, a small explosion just aft of the plane's tail could be seen.

"Damn!! A miss!" Subdue growled, watching the large plane continue its evasive maneuver. American Airlines flight 225 had escaped disaster. Disgusted, Subdue tossed the expended rocket launcher onto the freeway and climbed down from the trailer.

"We must go," a less-than-pleased Subdue ordered before detaching the trailer from the Chevy.

All three men quickly hopped into the truck.

"Allah is great. Once again we have defeated the infidels in this pagan wasteland called America," Sanda announced with pride, shifting the pickup truck into gear and hitting the gas. Subdue sat silently as the tires screeched briefly before gaining traction.

Minutes later, the terrorists exited the freeway. They would not be found in the sea of illegal immigrants, which inhabited this congested Muslim melting pot on the West Coast.

Chapter 37

It was another less-than-pleasant evening in Bar Harbor, Maine. The winds were gusting in excess of thirty knots and the temperature twenty below. The waves in Frenchman's Bay thrashed about violently. Yet the foam on the whitecaps appeared to freeze in flight. In stark contrast, the Bayview Estate was relatively protected from the predominant winds that night. Ashore, the headquarters for the National Security Agency was blanketed by a peacefully, serene layer of sparkling white snow several feet deep.

Earl Vassar had finished dinner hours earlier and had returned to his office to continue working. There was much yet to be done, but he felt his energy waning.

"A quarter till nine. It's seven forty-five p.m. in Louisiana. Leslie should be calling soon," Earl said, looking at his watch. He slowly got up from his chair and walked toward the fireplace, where he stoked the embers before throwing one more log on the fire.

"Perhaps one cocktail is in order and certainly well deserved," Earl rationalized as he proceeded toward his liquor cabinet. Such was his nightly ritual, which had been carried out every evening for the last few months.

"What an exhausting day," he concluded as he grabbed a glass and then reached for the Oban. He poured himself a tall Scotch, neat.

"I sure hope things are going well in Carencrow and Leslie has located the Bents," Earl whispered with the sense of subdued optimism.

Earl sat down and took a sip of the smooth, single-malt whiskey. Almost immediately, he felt his batteries recharge and his spirits soar.

"Christ, given all the recent attacks on our soil, and now the indication that a nuclear attack is planned and appears to be imminent, we desperately need any information the doctor and his wife would be able to provide," he reminded himself, taking another sip.

Then, as scheduled, the phone rang. Earl looked at the caller ID.

"My, you're punctual."

"I can't help myself. It's a habit I inherited from my rather disciplined and, as some would say, neurotic father," Leslie replied.

"Oh yes, one of the benefits of growing up in a military household," Earl remembered.

"How's the weather in Bar Harbor?"

"Damn cold! No, I take that back. It's bitterly and inhospitably fud-rucking frigid," Earl declared. He looked out between the frosted windowpanes and watched the strong winds whip snowflakes back and forth.

"Wow, now that does sound cold. Just make sure you keep those buns warm, young man," Leslie teased, looking out her window and into a stark courtyard on a damp, dreary Louisiana night.

"Excellent advice but highly impractical without you sleeping next to me," Earl teased in return.

"I'll take that as a compliment."

"As well you should, because there's no one else who gets me so hot and bothered," Earl growled romantically.

"I should certainly hope not. Now, you just hold onto that thought. When I get back to Bar Harbor, you're going to have to readjust your rheostat because I intend to take you well beyond the boiling point," Leslie purred.

"Promises, promises," Earl chuckled. "By the way, have you made much progress?" he asked while pouring himself another Scotch.

"SAC Richter and I arrived in Whiskey Bay around eight a.m. and then spent hours in the air looking for anything suspicious. It was getting dark so we knocked off around five p.m. Unfortunately, we were unable to locate the Air Med chopper that Dr. Bent and his wife Trissy 'borrowed' or see any sign of a suspicious camp," Leslie shared, the disappointment evident in her voice.

"Helicopters are lumbering tin cans with limited range. It just couldn't vanish," Earl replied, rubbing his forehead in frustration.

"Well, it has. The FBI set up search grids, which are being explored systematically, but they're hampered by the lack of personnel. However, we anticipate that the National Guard will be activated and on location in the a.m.," Leslie explained.

"The National Guard should have been brought in yesterday as soon as the helicopter disappeared. Don't they realize that time is of the essence?" Earl complained.

"They should, given the number of times I've stressed that very point. However, it's tough to know what registers with the arrogant knuckle-butt SAC Richter. My impression is that he's slow to act because he doesn't want to share the glory of apprehending the Bents," Leslie surmised.

"What?" Earl shrieked. "That's not the same jackass who gave you such a hard time at the Bent home, is it?"

"The one and only. Dealing with him is like watching the Earth's tectonic plates shift—the outcome is always explosive."

"I tried to have him replaced, but the FBI insists that he's their best man. But he doesn't sound too bright, from the all stories I've heard."

"That's an understatement. He's just another persistently irritating, bowed-up Bozo with a big neck and a small head. He looks anencephalic, but if he has a brain, he's probably fried it with steroids and growth hormones," Leslie relayed.

"He couldn't be that dumb," Earl replied.

"After having had the wonderful opportunity to share the last week with the narrow-minded Neanderthal, I'd have to respectfully disagree. I'll bet he couldn't spell the word 'ape' even if you gave him the A and the P," Leslie concluded.

Earl chuckled. "Oh, Christ, well I think you're just going to have to weather the storm and somehow find the fortitude to work with the SOB."

"That's easier said than done. He's not open to suggestions and fights me every step of the way. Furthermore, he's left no doubt that he intends to kill the Bents," Leslie relayed to emphasize just how bad the situation was.

"Good, God! Leslie, you must ensure that the Bents are not harmed. They remain our only viable lead capable of disclosing and crushing this surge in terrorism," Earl stressed. He tried to comprehend why a seasoned FBI veteran would jeopardize their vitally important operation when the nation's security was at sake.

"Earl, the terrorists and the delusional SAC Richter are out to get the Bents. Personally, I don't know how this couple could create so many enemies in such a short time, but I will do everything in my power to protect them," Leslie assured Earl, sitting down at her desk and flipping up the screen on her laptop computer.

"You're going to have to. The very survival of our nation is at stake. As you very well know, over the last ten days, the United States of America has come under attack several times both at home and abroad. We were humiliated in the Persian Gulf with the annihilation of the Stennis Carrier Strike Group; while on the East Coast, Grand Central station was reduced to rubble. Not to mention the recent destruction of the Golden Gate Bridge and the United Airlines plane shot down while departing LAX," Earl emphasized.

"You don't have to convince me of the importance of my mission. We've had failures, but we've also experienced tremendous success. Let me remind you that the container ship *Mecca* was destroyed off in the Atlantic before reaching her intended destination, Washington, DC, while the North Korean rust bucket *Il-sung* was given a one-way trip to Davy Jones' Locker," Leslie replied, as she was beginning to realize the stress that Earl was under.

"Yes, but we got to the *Il-sung* too late. Although high levels of radiation were detected on board, I believe the ship had already delivered her nuclear weapon," Earl argued.

"Earl, we're going to find that bomb and round up this murderous group of radical Islamic terrorists," Leslie assured her boss.

"I have the utmost belief in you, Leslie. Forgive me, the fair-weather politicians in Washington are screaming for blood and Secretary Anderson's head is on the chopping block," Earl relayed, gritting his teeth and pounding his desk with his fist.

"Apology accepted. The secretary is a man of steel. He'll withstand the pressure coming from either power-hungry politicians or the bloodsucking reporters. And one thing's for certain, given recent events: the public will soon realize that the Democrats need to ditch the donkey and cast the ostrich as the symbol representing their political prowess. Clearly, they have their heads in the sand and their butts…" Leslie complained bitterly as Earl chuckled.

"Leslie, I'm glad we had this conversation. Thanks for the pep talk. Let me assure you that you've done more to relieve my concerns than several swigs of scotch," Earl shared.

"That's comforting, I think. Forgive me for ranting and raving, but I'm on a mission to find the Bents and to save the nation, all while wiping out stupidity," Leslie snickered, beginning to calm down and lighten up.

"Yes, that's quite apparent. Now, let me bring you up to date with regard to our most pressing issue. All electronic correspondence suddenly plummeted unexpectedly this a.m. Traffic is down a good seventy percent. Secretary Anderson and the president are convinced that we're in the eye of the storm and that a nuclear attack is imminent. I concur," Earl relayed.

"That's concerning indeed," Leslie replied slowly as she absorbed the shocking news.

"In fact, it's been so disturbing that the president has lost faith in the intelligence community. She has personally gone to the United Nations to ask for help in persuading the Islamic terrorists not to unleash their weapon of mass destruction," Earl confided.

"That's unbelievable! What's next, monetary contributions and country club memberships for terrorists? Sharia Law, perhaps? Clearly, 'patient diplomacy' has failed and the United States is on the verge of giving in to murderous extortionists," Leslie concluded angrily.

"You're not far from the mark. But I've been led to believe that the military option still remains on the table. At this very moment we have two battle groups, the Nimitz and the Ronald Reagan, steaming toward the Indian Ocean. One battle group is prepared to launch an attack on Iran and bring her scrawny, beady-eyed nuclear defiant president to justice, while the other is tasked with wiping North Korea and the country's waddling potbellied prick-tator from the face of the earth. Indeed, the war drums are beating." Earl revealed as Leslie listened intently.

"Good God! Although well underway, World War III is soon to be formally declared," Leslie gasped, thinking of the horrific implications.

"Here again, I don't mean to burden you with undo pressure, or to place you in harm's way, my love, but it's rather important that we locate the elusive Dr. Bent and his wife—ASAP," Earl reiterated.

"Well, it would certainly help if you could get that SAC Richter off my ass," Leslie insisted.

"I'll contact the FBI powers once again and more forcefully request that he be reassigned to some desolate island," Earl promised.

"That would be most helpful and sincerely appreciated, assuming that the sorry bastard can't swim," Leslie quipped, looking down at her glowing computer screen.

"That's my girl, tough as nails and as feisty as ever," Earl replied with great admiration.

"Personally, this sweet, passionate country girl is tired of taking names. It's time to kick butt!" Leslie said as her adrenaline went into overdrive. She downloaded her email.

"Just make sure that it's terrorist tush that you're kicking," Earl remarked, in an effort to refocus Leslie's rage.

Leslie opened a new message in her inbox. "Incredible!" Leslie shouted into the phone.

"What? What you talking about?"

"Earl! Rex and Trissy are ALIVE!" Leslie shouted.

"What are you talking about? How do you know?"

"Rex sent me an email, dated today. He is alive and well in Whiskey Bay, but the terrorists have captured Trissy. He believes she's on a U-Haul truck destined for Washington, DC," Leslie relayed as she read on. "Oh no!" she gasped. "Several other U-Haul trucks are headed for major American cities, each loaded with RADIOACTIVE NUCLEAR WASTEWATER!" Leslie shouted.

"Good GOD! What cities?" Earl shouted as Leslie pulled the receiver away from her ear.

"Rex has listed New York, Washington, DC, Boston, San Francisco, Los Angeles, San Diego, and Houston as the intended destinations," Leslie replied. Earl realized the consequences of targeting these densely populated areas.

"Christ, those cities would instantly become ghost towns, uninhabitable for thousands of years. Overnight, our access to the Pacific, the Atlantic, and the Caribbean would be lost. The United States would become a dying landlocked nation, trapped within the North American continent. I'll inform Secretary Anderson immediately. The president needs to order a mass evacuation of those targeted cities," Earl added emphatically.

"Hang on, Earl. Rex said he was successful in planting plastic explosives on each vehicle prior to his capture. He says, and I quote: *Rest assured the U-Haul trucks will be destroyed before they reach their intended targets*. Dr. Bent's only request is that we do everything in our power to help his wife."

"To affect any rescue mission is not justified nor does it represent a viable option. We don't have the luxury of time to take that chance. Roadblocks need to be set up on the freeways leading into those cities. Any and all U-Haul trucks on those roads must be stopped and destroyed, immediately. Trissy Bent has become expendable!" Earl insisted as Leslie gasped.

"Moments ago you told me that, whatever the cost, it's imperative that we not only find but save the Bents. All roads continue to lead to Rex and Trissy, but we don't have all the answers. You can't just kill them!" Leslie shouted.

But the line suddenly went silent. Earl needed a moment to collect his thoughts. Without warning, he set the phone down and walked over to the liquor cabinet.

"Earl, Earl!" Leslie shouted, but there was no response.

Earl's hand started to shake as he poured himself one last drink. There was no doubt with regard to the order he had to issue. Earl walked back over to his desk and picked up the receiver.

"Leslie, Rex and Trissy Bent have outlived their usefulness. They are soon to become nothing more than another statistic in our war on terror," Earl insisted coldly, not waiting for response.

"Noooo!" Leslie screamed into the phone before the line went dead.

"God Almighty!—Rolling dirty bombs only miles away from major American cities!" Earl screamed as he frantically dialed Secretary Anderson's private number.

Chapter 38

The *Damned Gre-Gre* remained hidden in the dense foliage along the shores of Whiskey Bay. It had been several hours since Zeila had rescued Rex from the jaws of a rather determined alligator. He remained unresponsive even to the most painful of stimuli. Frequently, airplanes and helicopters could be heard in close proximity. Zeila was well aware that the manhunt continued and she sensed that the authorities were closing in.

"I'll be damned if I know why I'm helping a hypocritical Republican fugitive. I've got better things to do," Zeila complained as she continued to grind up the leaves and bark she had gathered from several magical trees.

"If it weren't for Trissy, I'd turn your hide in. Hell, whatever hide is left after you were dragged behind that truck. And now that I'm thinking about it, there's probably even a reward for ya, dead or alive."

Zeila squeezed the saliva from two large bullfrogs into the potion before placing the poisonous croaking amphibians back into a makeshift cage for safekeeping.

"You've gotta wake up, boy, so we can find that girl. I surely know Trissy is in trouble!" Zeila shouted in frustration as she stirred the mixture until it had the proper consistency. "Lordie, who would have ever thought that I would be your nurse?"

Zeila rubbed the concoction on Rex's open wounds before applying a generous layer of smelly swamp muck.

"You sure is looking shriveled, Rex. Grandpa Sambo always said that this was an indication for a hydrating enema, but I'm going to need a tall beer before I find the courage to shove anything up your butt," Zeila concluded as she wiped the gooey, malodorous mud from her hands and onto her dress.

"Thank God!" Rex whispered.

"What's that?" Zeila wasn't sure if she was hearing things.

"Zeila, please don't shove anything up my butt," Rex begged, struggling to sit up.

"It's about time you woke up."

"How long have I been out?"

"For about twenty-four hours. You woke up briefly, sent some woman an email, and then passed out. You'd best hope that Trissy doesn't find out about Leslie. Mercy, she treats you so well and you repay her by cattin' around on the Internet," Zeila criticized.

"I have no idea what you're babbling about, but it's nice to know that I've been semi-productive," Rex replied, yawning.

"Productive my behind. You has been a real burden."

"Well, that could very well be," Rex confessed, twisting and turning, ensuring that all his limbs were still intact.

"What's that smell and what in the hell do I have all over me?" Rex added, scooping some of the swamp muck from his wounds and sniffing the foul brown concoction.

"Well, that's all the thanks I get? That happens to be my secret healing salve," Zeila shot back, crossing her arms in anger.

"Is there a dog around here? This smells like…!" Rex concluded, attempting to wipe his hand clean with the corner of Zeila's dress.

"Well boy, if you think you're starting to smell like a dog, then I suggest you start acting like a dog. The first thing I want you to do, Rover Rex, is find Trissy," Zeila insisted.

"Trissy! Where's Trissy?" Rex asked while trying to remember what had happened.

"Don't you remember? You and Trissy were caught sneaking into the terrorist camp last night. You were destined to be gator bait and I can only assume Trissy that was thrown into a U-Haul truck," Zeila reminded Rex.

Rex started to recall what he and Trissy had been able to piece together about the terrorist camp. As he stood and struggled to maintain his balance, the memories of the early-morning assault on Camp Eagle came rushing back at an ever-increasing pace.

"U-Haul trucks, of course!" Rex reached for his tactical computer that he'd left on the boat and turned it on.

"Rover, you should be sniffing instead of surfing. Put the computer away, boy, and get your nose to the ground," Zeila insisted, wondering if Rex was of sound mind.

"Zeila, we weren't sure what the terrorists were going to use the U-Hauls for, so we rigged them with explosives, which I can detonate from anywhere in the world from this laptop. The fuses also act as a GPS," Rex informed Zeila as the screen came to life. "There, you see. There are seven blips on the screen. Each one represents a truck we had, well, modified, as it were," Rex added as Zeila looked at the screen a little closer.

"Look, some are headed east and some west," Zeila observed.

"But they all seem to be moving. Now, which truck did they put Trissy in?" Rex wondered.

"I'll be damned if I know! But you're running out of time. Didn't those fuses have cameras on them?" Zeila asked incredulously.

"Zeila, have you got a screw loose? Of course not," Rex replied, studying the screen.

Then Rex suddenly remembered Trissy's warnings followed by intense screams as she had been dragged away from the dock. He could vaguely recall hearing other voices, but he had no visual recollection.

"You mean to tell me that there are no cameras? Boy, even cell phones have cameras. You're the one with a loose screw," Zeila chided.

Rex ignored Zeila's comments as he briefly perused the email Zeila said he had sent to Leslie.

"Radioactive nuclear wastewater, what in the hell was I talking about?" Rex asked himself before beginning to pace the deck. "I even listed the cities to be targeted, stating that Trissy was probably on the U-Haul truck heading toward Washington, DC, but I don't even remember sending the email," Rex gasped. He wondered where in the world such detailed information had come from and, most importantly, the validity of the information given his state of mind at the time.

"Christ! Zeila, I truly have no idea where they took Trissy," Rex admitted. He looked over the tranquil inlet while racking his brain. "But maybe we can find the answer onshore. Zeila, fire up the engine and get this floating monstrosity underway. Let's take a look at that camp," Rex insisted after his eyes locked onto what appeared to be an abandoned Camp Eagle.

"Now you're talking! Cast off the line!" Zeila ordered, turning on the ignition.

"You've got it, Captain Z," Rex mumbled as he untied the line wrapped around a small tree branch.

As Zeila navigated out of the secluded section of swamp, Rex turned off the laptop, shut the cover, and slid the computer into his backpack. Shortly thereafter, his rifle had also been dismantled and stored for easy access. He had also collected his night vision goggles and binoculars.

"Why can't I remember?" Rex mumbled, placing his arm through the strap and swinging the backpack onto his shoulders. Once again, Rex was ready for action and hungry for a fight. He had to rescue Trissy.

Minutes later, the unlikely commandos glided by two thick ropes dangling over the water, each suspended by a crane. The scene was hauntingly familiar. GeeHad was long gone, but Rex's memory went into overdrive.

"Don't ask, Rover. Just remember that I saved your Republican rump from a gruesome death," Zeila blurted, noticing Rex staring at the ropes gently swaying in the breeze.

"Zeila, are you sure you're not losing your mind?

"Well, one of us isn't all there. Now, make sure the bow doesn't ram the dock. We wouldn't want to damage Captain Coco's pride and joy," Zeila insisted, assuming the demeanor of an old demanding sea dog.

"Zeila, driving the boat is starting to give you a big head," Rex observed as he secured the line to the cleat before helping Zeila ashore.

"Could be, but someone has to be in charge," Zeila replied rather nonchalantly.

"Wow, what's that stench?" Rex groaned while attempting to swat off a herd of flies.

Then Rex noticed two decaying bodies on the ground, each with a gruesome look and lying in an unnatural posture. One had been shot in the head and the other in the chest. Rex looked at Zeila in disbelief.

"Rather gratifying shots, if I don't say so myself. Now, Rover, it's good to know that you haven't lost your sense of smell, but it's time to look for clues," Zeila suggested before walking the grounds.

"Stop calling me Rover," Rex insisted, although he was certain Zeila would ignore his request.

Rex noticed shards of rope at the base of an extended piling on the dock. Trissy's screams of terror became louder, but he still couldn't paint a picture of what had happened or where they had taken her. He held his nose and took off running for the command post.

Fifteen minutes later, Rex had completed his survey of the camp. He stood next to a smoldering fire looking at the debris when Zeila approached.

"Well, I didn't notice anything unusual, but it looks like the two dead terrorists left us their truck," Zeila shared with Rex.

"Everything, absolutely everything, has been cleared out. There are three vacant Quonset huts and one dome-shaped concrete structure. If it weren't for the two dead bodies on the dock, the crane, and this smoldering pile of ash, you would assume no one had been here for years," Rex added while continuing to experience visual and auditory flashbacks.

"Well, we know it wasn't a Girl Scout camp as I had first assumed," Zeila added.

"Were there any papers in the trunk?" Rex asked.

"No, but the keys are in the ignition," Zeila replied. Rex walked over to the concrete structure for a closer look.

"There's not even a door, just some vent on the top and at least a fifty-foot section of thick, black tubing with some odd connector on the end. What terrorist yo-yo designed this storage bin?" Rex asked before noticing a pile of dingy thick yellow suits hidden in the brush adjacent to the structure.

"I don't know, but you certainly couldn't smoke alligators in it," Zeila concluded.

Rex brushed off the leaves covering a small rectangular wooden crate labeled:

프 러시안 블루

"I wonder what's in this box," Rex said as he pryed open the cover. It was stuffed with hundreds of small clear plastic wrappers, each with the same writing and each containung a small black pill. "Wait a minute. Foxxman showed me this wrapper, which, as I recall, he found in the pocket of one of the dying Asian sailors," Rex said in a moment of discovery.

"Add water and it probably turns into a stinky fish sauce," Zeila guessed as she examined a small packet.

"No, Wan translated the writing as 'Russian Screw,' but the next day, when I was running to the ICU to save Wanda, he blurted some correction, which was—Blue..." Rex said as he struggled to remember.

"Well then, genius, why is the pill black?" Zeila asked. She flipped the wrapper back and forth in her hand before opening it and taking a whiff. "Pee-yew! It stinks. I knew it was a concentrated fish sauce," Zeila added before throwing the wrapper on the ground. Rex stood next to her lost in thought.

Suddenly, one of the bizarre events that had occurred over the last horrific week started to make sense. The dead Asian sailors had been blue-tinged!

"Prussian Blue—Prussian BLUE—P R U S S I A N B L U E!" Rex shouted. "Zeila, I've got it!" Rex screamed.

"You're goofy. The pill is BLACK!" Zeila stressed.

"Here, swallow this and see if it turns you blue," Rex insisted as he handed Zeila a pill.

"No way. Beautiful black Zeila ain't no lab rat. Furthermore, how's you gonna be able to tell if I turn blue?" Zeila said as she placed her hands on her hips and her upper torso swayed back and forth in defiance. "Now, on the other hand, you're lily white. I'd certainly be able to tell which color you turn; blue, black, or black and blue. Here, you take the damn pill!" Zeila insisted as she handed the pill back to Rex.

"That's true, but I'm the brains of this operation. What happens if it makes me sick?" Rex asked as he shoved the pill back toward her.

"Uh, huh! Oh no, Mr. Owl, you're sadly mistaken. Anyone with a birdbrain is of little use to our mission. Besides, you're already sick, mentally and physically. Dr. Zeila saved you once. I'm on a streak. With any luck, I could save your sorry ass again, feathers and all," Zeila huffed as she pushed the pill away.

"Please accept my apology, Hummingbird," Rex said, knowing that he had been out of line.

"Apology accepted," Zeila replied, appreciative of Rex's sudden but sincere retreat.

"Well, we seem to have a crisis, but is it blue or black?" Rex wondered as he rolled the pill between his fingers. "Perhaps the active ingrediants oxidized, turning the pill back," he added.

"Yes, well, you may never know, Rover, but I have no doubt that the authorities are going to lock you up before you get a chance to conduct your experiment!" Zeila shouted while pointing skyward. A helicopter appeared from out of nowhere and quickly began to descend.

Rex looked up at the whirlybird intruder. The word POLICE was clearly emblazoned in red on the outside. Rex ran toward Zeila and grabbed her hand.

"We've worn out our welcome. This is no time to lollygag, Zeila! Get the lead out!" Rex insisted. He pulled her along across the shale drive and toward the rusted out 1950s-style model truck.

"I knew I should've tightened your leash when we came ashore, Rover," Zeila complained, slowly picking up her pace.

"This is not the time to express any regrets. Hop in," Rex insisted, yanking open the squeaky passenger side door before gently shoving Zeila's derriere into the truck. He shut the door, quickly scurried around to the driver's side, and hopped in.

"Damn it!" Rex yelled as he continued to turn the key without success.

"Rex, the whirlybird has landed," Zeila warned as Rex pumped on the gas pedal frantically.

"Why won't this damn engine turn over?" Rex screamed in frustration, pounding the steering wheel with his fist.

"Rover, this is no time to throw a tantrum. If you get the truck started, I'll give you a special treat," Zeila promised her agitated physician.

"That's reassuring! What kind of treat?" Rex growled angrily, turning the key once again.

"Rex, there are men with automatic weapons climbing out and they don't look very friendly!" Zeila shouted.

Chapter 39

THE POLICE HELICOPTER HAD touched down at Camp Eagle. Several FBI agents with automatic weapons were now on the ground, running toward the old truck.

"If you don't want to go to jail, I'd suggest you hurry, Rover," Zeila emphasized. "Orange and silver just aren't my colors but I'll bet the jumpsuit would look good on you. Throw in a shiny pair of shackles and you'd be styling," she added, much to Rex's dismay.

"Come on, baby!" Rex screamed, frantically pumping the gas pedal.

"Don't flood the damn thing, for Christ's sake," Zeila blurted.

"Wahoo, the sweet sound of success!" Rex shouted, tapping the gas pedal to ensure that the engine wouldn't die.

Rex smiled at Zeila defiantly and placed the truck into first gear. The dilapidated rusted-out relic slowly gained speed as Rex fought to change gears. The FBI's SWAT team was now less than twenty yards away and closing quickly.

"You know, you really shouldn't go from first gear to third until you've attained adequate speed," Zeila suggested as the truck intermittently leaped forward and then jerked backward.

"I can't get used to this clutch. Besides, all the numbers are gone from the knob," Rex complained as the fugitives finally started to open the distance between them and their determined captors. Rex looked in his rearview mirror. The men in black had stopped running. Their weapons were leveled, but for some reason they didn't shoot.

"These old trucks are quite forgiving, but I don't think this one is ever going to forgive you for grinding the gears. Would you like me to drive?" Zeila asked as they rambled down the dirt driveway.

"That's kind of you to offer, but I think I have the knack of it," Rex replied, gritting his teeth.

"You're making me sick. Please, do try to avoid the potholes," Zeila suggested, bouncing uncontrollably on the rock-hard seat.

"I'm trying, I'm trying!" Rex shouted, fighting to maintain control of the truck as it continued to gain speed.

"By the way, where are we going?" Zeila stuttered, reaching for the handle grip above her door.

"Away from the police and toward Trissy," Rex stated emphatically as the rickety old truck emerged from under the dense canopy.

"Good idea. You know, Grandpa Sambo could always find his way out of a mess like this," Zeila reminisced as a paved road quickly appeared.

"Blacktop, thank God!" Rex shouted while applying the brakes. The truck started to fishtail, but he quickly regained control and slid to a stop. "Zeila, come clean. Did you really have a grandpa named Sambo?" Rex asked after turning toward her and looking her in the eye.

"God's honest truth, but his real name was Samuel Washington," Zeila replied as the dust they had kicked up on the road rapidly engulfed their truck.

"He was the illegitimate son of President George Washington," she added as she coughed and gagged, attempting to fan away clouds of dirt.

"Ha—no way, Zeila. That's too bizarre for even the most gullible person to believe," Rex shot back as he looked down the deserted road.

Instinctively, he turned left and stepped on the gas. The old truck slid briefly before the tires grabbed hold of the rough asphalt.

"It's true, George was sleeping with my great-grandma Bo, a cotton-pickin' slave on his plantation. He liked the way she picked and she like the way he prodded. Lo and behold, Samuel was born, but for political reasons, he couldn't live in the White House. In fact, he never met his father George. Sambo grew up dirt poor but he had a heart of gold. He loved his family and friends and was always happy. However, to his dying day, Grandpa distrusted every politician," Zeila concluded, releasing her death grip on the overhead metal handle.

"And just what advice would Sambo Washington give us if he were still alive?" Rex asked sarcastically.

"After drinking gallons of moonshine, he would become very philosophical. In a drunken stupor, Sambo would simply reflect on his heritage. Whenever anyone asked him for directions or advice, his reply would always be the same: 'If you want to get screwed, all roads lead to Washington.'" Zeila replied without hesitation.

"Sounds like a wise man. You know, that's excellent advice, especially around tax season."

Zeila's family history was absolutely comical and incredulous but told with such commitment and emotion that Rex had to chuckle. She was certainly a master storyteller endowed with a magical gift of gab, but the longer he reflected on her words, the more he believed her tall tales. Suddenly, the garbled words Rex heard while hanging over "alligator haven" came through loud and clear: "Take her to Washington."

"Washington, Washington! Of course! That's it!" Rex shouted, slapping the palm of his hand against the steering wheel.

"Have you lost your mind, Rover? You keep telling me that you've 'got it,' but that's it. Just what are you fantasizing about now?" Zeila asked, not sure if she really wanted to know.

"Zeila, Trissy is on the U-Haul truck going to Washington, DC. I'm convinced that all the trucks are carrying nuclear waste. Each one is a rolling dirty bomb destined to wipe out a major city. Christ, these fanatical Muslim madmen could kill millions of innocent Americans and destroy our great nation," Rex stated with conviction.

"Sounds like you has been nippin' on Sambo's moonshine," Zeila concluded as the sound of a powerful engine slowly drowned out her words.

"No, but I could damn well use a snort right now. And without question, I would most certainly propose a toast to Grandpa Sambo!" Rex shouted over the noise as he raced onward.

"Rex, look out!" Zeila screamed as the police helicopter suddenly appeared in front of them, hovering only feet above the road.

Rex jerked the wheel to the left to avoid a collision. The truck briefly went up on the passenger side wheels before slamming back down on all fours. He had somehow managed to avoid a collision with a chopper and maintain control of the truck.

"Good God, that was close," Rex sighed, wiping the sweat from his palms.

"Rex, you're going to need a faster vehicle. And I don't want to be the bearer of bad tidings, but your gas gauge is on empty," Zeila stated calmly as they flew through an intersection toward civilization.

"Now you tell me," Rex replied as he tapped on the gas gauge, hoping that the needle in the old Ford relic was stuck.

"That's not going to help. Rover, we need gas," Zeila reminded him. "And there's a gas station," she added, pointing to the right just as a helicopter swooped down, barely missing the top of their truck.

"Well, just in case your buddy the dishonorable Louis 'Fanatical' Farra-Scam doesn't extend us an invitation to escape to his 'mother ship,' we'd better stop," Rex concluded as he slamming on the brakes.

Zeila grabbed the dashboard with both hands to brace herself while white smoke rose from the asphalt and layers of tread were ripped off. The truck began to fishtail, but once again Rex was able to maintain control.

"I love the smell of roasted rubber in the morning," Rex joked, noticing that Zeila was now fuming.

"If I told you once, I've told you a thousand times, the honorable Reverend Farrakhan would never beam up a nonbeliever," Zeila huffed.

"Not unless they were Muslim, hated the United States, and made a healthy contribution to his astronomical and frequently abused 'Bash Bush Fund,'" Rex replied. He quickly turned around and headed toward the filling station where he had noticed a shiny red sports car refueling.

"Rex, you're going too fast. Watch out, you're going to hit that car!" Zeila warned just before Rex slammed into the back of a shiny new Corvette ZR1.

"Zeila, we've landed. Unfortunately, there's no time for a potty break," Rex said, opening the door and hopped out to greet the enraged owner of the crumpled car.

"How could you?! You've ruined my beautiful Corvette!" the middle-aged portly man cried. He put his hands to his face, assuming the nightmare would somehow magically go away.

Zeila slowly and apprehensively climbed out to survey the damage.

"Look what you've done to my truck! You've knocked all the rust off my bumper!" Rex argued vehemently, pointing to the damage.

The distraught owner of the sports car brought his hands down and stared at the truck in disbelief. That was all the opportunity Rex needed. He clenched his fist, drew back his hand, and threw a punch that landed squarely on the unsuspecting man's jaw. The short, rotund man with the nice sports car and the incredibly bad luck fell backward, striking the oil-stained concrete with tremendous force.

"Zeila, as recommended, I've procured a faster car and one with plenty of gas. All aboard!" Rex announced with all the panache of a streetcar conductor.

"Rex, what have you done?" Zeila gasped.

"Sacrificed everything in the defense of this great nation," Rex replied, opening the passenger door and assisting Zeila into the low-riding vehicle.

"I'm not sure I can get into this thing," Zeila complained as she attempted to navigate the bucket seat.

"Sure you can—if not, 'Hummingbird,' I think I can find room for you on the hood," Rex grunted as he forcefully squeezed Zeila's tush into the confined cabin and shoved on her door until it shut.

With the tank full, Rex withdrew the nozzle and replaced the gas cap. Then he placed the nozzle into an adjacent trash receptacle and squeezed the handle. Several gallons of fuel quickly flowed into the metal container.

"Please replace the nozzle once you're finished pumping gas," the attendant announced over the loudspeaker as Rex went to the truck and grabbed his backpack.

"Good suggestion," Rex mumbled, pulling out a small fuse and setting the timer for two minutes. He could hear the helicopter hovering overhead and felt certain they were impatiently waiting for him to make the next move as they called in reinforcements. Rex threw the fuse into the trash bin, opened the car door, and eased into the Corvette.

"My, aren't we full of ourselves. How quickly you've forgotten that the 'Hummingbird' saved the 'Owl's' sorry ass. Now, fire up the car boy, and turn up the AC—birdbrain!" Zeila ordered.

"Yes, ma'am," Rex replied politely, although his feathers were ruffled by Zeila's comment. However, given the circumstances, there would be no time to pursue this skirmish. Rex depressed the gas pedal and pushed the *on* button. The powerful engine roared to life.

"Now that's a rather throaty growl, but I rather prefer my Mustang," Rex added as he placed the sports car in drive and turned toward Zeila.

"I trust you're comfortable?" Rex felt compelled to ask, although Zeila's facial expression and body posture left little doubt as to her response.

"Hell no. I feel like a damn sardine."

"I'm sorry about that. It's not as roomy as the truck. Oh well, hold on because I'll bet this baby can fly," Rex insisted as he eased out from under the large metal awning, which had obscured all intelligence-gathering from above.

Rex rolled slowly down the curb and onto the street so as not to arouse suspicion. When the light turned green, he pressed down on the gas pedal. The Corvette responded instantly and the acceleration was smooth.

"Damn, I forgot the receipt and I believe the new Dem-o-Rat administration now extends tax deductions to those on the lamb," Rex complained as several police vehicles shot by.

In his rearview mirror, Rex could see other police cruisers closing in from the opposite direction as a helicopter directed traffic. All converged on the lonely, desolate gas station in time to draw their weapons on the portly man who lay sprawled out, unconscious on the oil-stained concrete.

"Well, they're sure to get a bang out of the warm gift we've left. I trust the officers will be able to pull the owner of this fine vehicle from the impending flames in time to prevent injury."

"I can't believe it. Somehow you gave them the slip. I was never that successful when I was running moonshine," Zeila replied, adjusting the side mirror to maximize her view.

"I never knew you ran Sambo's moonshine," Rex remarked.

"Well of course, Rover. Someone had to distribute Sambo's fountain of youth," Zeila said with a smile.

"Now, let me guess. I'll bet you sold the moonshine to Joe Kennedy," Rex suggested, trying to embellish Zeila's bizarre story.

"Yes, in fact we did. He paid top dollar, don't you know," Zeila replied calmly, unfazed by Rex's sarcastic tone.

"Now, my resourceful moonshine-running partner, just how do you propose that we get to Washington, DC, in time to save Trissy and the nation?" Rex asked, not expecting a rational answer.

"Well, the spaceship is out of the question since you've gone ahead and upset my people. But a little sign back yonder said 'Airport This Way,'" Zeila suggested.

"Are you mad?! There's no way we can get on a commercial flight. We'd be arrested and cuffed before we made it through the first checkpoint," Rex assured her.

"You have to think big, boy. Who said anything about a commercial flight? We need to charter a jet."

"Hmmm, I never thought about that, but the guardians of the skies just aren't going to let us drive through the gate," Rex replied, searching for a more feasible scheme while following the small blue airport signs scattered along the highway.

"Of course they will. I'll just tell them that I'm Jesse Jackson's mother," Zeila suggested with unshakable confidence.

"No way, they wouldn't let you through the gate even if you said you're related to George Washington. However, I rather like your creativity," Rex chuckled as the chain-link fence securing the perimeter of the airport came into view. Rex could clearly see a multitude of nondescript, personal aircraft of all sizes and shapes parked on the tarmac. He was suddenly struck by a rather unique idea.

"Show a little imagination, would you, Rover? We're out of time and I doubt that you have a better suggestion," Zeila remarked as they approached the side gate.

"Unfortunately, you're right," Rex replied hesitantly.

Rex slowed the car as a flimsy, wooden barrier loomed larger. He came to a stop and lowered his window. An elderly guard stepped out from inside a small wooden shack and slowly shuffled forward.

"Can I help you, young man?" the friendly character asked in a southern drawl.

"I'm Rex Bent, Regional Director for FEMA," Rex responded in a deep, confident voice.

"Well, I'll have to see some ID," the guard requested politely, immediately becoming concerned that he was offending a high-ranking government official.

"You don't understand. My ID was lost saving the poor and the indigent during Katrina," Rex responded quite sincerely.

"I can attest to that. He rescued me and I'm poor and indecent," Zeila said as she leaned over the center console and looked at the thin, emaciated white guard.

"There you have it, an honest testimonial. I work for the United States government, for Christ's sake. Nothing happens quickly. All our new IDs have been on backorder for years. Surely you can relate to all the problems we're having," Rex emphasized.

"Yes, I believe I can," the elderly man agreed. "Well, I suppose it's okay," the guard voiced approvingly as he slowly staggered back toward his reclusive hut.

"Where have our practical-joking pilots parked the plane today?" Rex asked as the guard pressed the button that elevated the rickety wooden security bar.

"Third plane on your left, they've been waiting for you," the guard replied before closing a reflective sliding glass door.

"I believe that's our invitation," Rex concluded after the security guard disappeared within the confines of his hut.

"This was far too easy. By the way, it's not 'indecent,' it's 'indigent,'" he corrected.

"It was a test. I just want to see if you poor, overeducated, opportunity-laden white folks had attained a respectable grasp of the English language," Zeila huffed.

"We certainly have, it's just the Ebonics that we're having trouble with," Rex joked.

"Well, there you have it. The problem and the solution are quite evident. You can't learn Ebonics without first having a little soul," Zeila responded firmly, informing Rex of the little-known prerequisite.

"I see your point," Rex replied politely, placing the Corvette into first gear and tapping the gas pedal. The car slowly rolled onto the tarmac.

"There we go," Zeila announced enthusiastically, pointing toward a modern *Gulfstream* jet emblazoned with the acronym synonymous with waste and corruption: FEMA.

"Wow, what a sleek plane. The old-timer was right. It certainly does appear that they were expecting us," Rex proclaimed, watching the pilot walk up the portable ramp and enter the aircraft as a refueling tanker drove off.

"I hate airline food," Zeila confessed as the Corvette came to a stop only yards from the ramp.

"Zeila, be nice and please don't say anything to offend the pilots," Rex pleaded, opening his door and crawling out of the bucket seat. He walked around the car and opened Zeila's door, fully expecting he'd have to grease the seat just to get her out.

"I'm never going to be able to get out of this thing," Zeila complained as she gave Rex her hand.

"I was afraid of that, old girl," Rex said, giving Zeila a tug.

"Who're you'ze callin' old, Rover?" Zeila barked as Rex grabbed her other hand and pulled harder.

After several excruciating backbreaking minutes, Rex managed to get Zeila's rump out of the bucket seat and onto the door jam, where she was now precariously balanced.

"My apologies," Rex said while struggling to catch his breath. "It was just a figure of speech." He placed his hands under Zeila's armpits and tugged with all his might.

"Watch it, buster, and don't scrape my heinie!" Zeila warned as her rump touched down on the tarmac.

"Do you Dem-o-Rats complain about everything?" Rex groaned.

"No, just about greedy, 'Rob-Ya-Mama' Republicans," Zeila shot back while grunting in anguish. Rex shook his head as he turned his attention toward freeing Zeila's legs from the confines of the Corvette's cockpit.

"Finally, next time I'm going to smear you with KY Jelly! Now, let's get you to your feet," Rex insisted, helping Zeila up before retrieving his backpack.

"There won't be a next time and don't even think about smearing me with KKK jelly," Zeila warned as they walked toward the airplane ramp.

"Here, you may need this," Rex said as he pulled a loaded .45-caliber handgun from his backpack and handed it to Zeila.

"Oh, a toy pistol," Zeila remarked sarcastically, pulling the magazine from the handle to ensure that it was fully loaded.

"It's time that FEMA know of my personal displeasure with the way they handle disasters," she growled, slapping the magazine in place and ramming a round into the chamber. Rex looked on, shocked at how easily Zeila had handled his weapon.

Suddenly, the tarmac became extremely windy. There was a roar of a loud jet engine and the churning of blades. Rex and Zeila looked up as a hail of bullets rained down from the police helicopter.

"Look out!" Rex shouted, pushing Zeila toward the ramp just in time to avoid being struck by a shower of indiscriminate, cylindrical metal projectiles. The bullets struck the tarmac, kicking up wisps of cement dust. The marksman leaned out of the helicopter, readjusting his aim.

"No, you don't. Ticket or not, no one's going to ruin my flight," Zeila declared, firing two rounds at the helicopter. The chopper immediately took evasive action, which threw the marksman off balance.

"Go, go, go!" Rex screamed as he and Zeila scurried up the ramp.

"Zeila's on board!" the feisty Cajun woman announced loudly after entering the plush cabin from the rear of the plane. "Get this albatross in the air, NOW!" Zeila shouted, waving her pistol.

Chapter 40

At the Baton Rouge International Airport, the fancy FEMA *Gulfstream* jet sat idle on a remote section of the tarmac reserved for corporate and personal aircrafts. The pilot and copilot were on board busily completing their preflight checks while the stewardess, Ginger Hacker, made sure all preparations were ready for takeoff.

There were only two passengers heading for Washington, DC, on this fateful morning; the distinguished Mr. Joseph S. Dagerpont, Regional Director for FEMA, and his buxom blonde personal assistant, F. Firm. Mr. Dagerpont sat impatiently reviewing reams of useless paperwork while Ms. Firm sat quietly, flipping through *People* magazine and sipping on a mint julep. Neither the sound of the police helicopter nor the marksman's attempt to take out Zeila and Rex had been heard. Yet no one could have warned or prepared those on board for their unexpected guests.

"What in the hell are they shooting at us for? Wait until my congressman gets ahold of those trigger-happy jackasses," Zeila threatened, dashing into the rear of plane with white smoke slowly trickling from the barrel of her revolver.

The smell of gun smoke permeated the confined space, but no one in the front of the plane paid attention to the odor or the intrusion. Nor did anyone turn around to evaluate the loud ravings of the agitated Cajun moonshiner.

"That was a close call, Zeila! Are you okay?" Rex asked.

"Damn sho' is!" Zeila shot back.

"Well, I don't see any obvious gunshot wounds or blood dripping from you," Rex concluded after quickly examining Zeila for any noticeable structural defects.

"That's a darn good thing." Zeila replied.

"We're awfully lucky. The marksman had us in his sights. I think the whirlybird pilot panicked when you popped off a couple of rounds in his direction. That was good thinking, Annie Oakley," Rex praised his accomplice.

"Thanks Rex. I've got what you call 'in-stinks,'" Zeila declared with unyielding confidence as she blew the remaining smoke from the barrel of the revolver.

"Yes, well, I can believe it," Rex agreed.

"Furthermore, I know about survival and I know about repression. Now, it's time that our government knows that Hurricane Zeila is howlin' mad!" the enraged New Orleans evacuee insisted, her eyes glowing a fiery red.

"I agree but even though you're mad as hell, I never expected you to get on this plane. I thought you were deathly afraid of flying, especially after being shot down over Whiskey Bay," Rex reminded Zeila, while attempting to calm down his feisty fellow hijacker.

"I was, but this is a 'freedom flight.' No honky-tonky bureaucrat and no scrawny raghead terrorist is going to hold me back. My fears be damned, we're on a mission, boy!" Zeila shouted as Mr. Dagerpont and Ms. Firm finally looked around to see what in the world all the commotion was about.

"Well, I'm truly pleased that you've found the courage to slay your gravity-defying demons on this flight," Rex conveyed with sincerity while surveying the cabin.

"Damn sho' has!" Zeila snorted insistently. "Wow, this plane sho' is tricked out!" Zeila whispered as she looked around the cabin, admiring the exquisite finish-out.

There was an undulating plush couch against one bulkhead and an ornate wooden bar against the other. Forward, twenty or so overstuffed brown leather lounge chairs were arranged in various configurations around teak coffee tables. Through mahogany doors in the rear of the aircraft, Zeila could see a large room with a queen-size bed. Completing the ambience were highly polished wood paneling, spectacular sconces, and a thick, rich carpet throughout.

"Let's get this show on the road!" Rex insisted with renewed determination.

"Sho' will! I've never swiped a jet before, but there's a first time for everything," Zeila voiced her agreement before storming toward the front of the plane.

As Zeila's thundering footsteps grew louder, the stewardess stepped back from the forward galley and looked aft. She sensed the immediate danger and quickly roused the pilots, who were busy concluding their preflight checks.

"Gentlemen, we have a crazy, gun-toting old woman on board!" Ms. Hacker announced.

"What are you talking about, Ginger?" Captain Ruben Gomez asked calmly.

The concern in Ginger's voice did not register, so both he and the copilot kept working. Finally, both men sensed that all was not well and turned around. Ginger eased back into the galley and nonchalantly grabbed a pot, intending to strike the approaching intruder.

"Everyone, welcome Zeila on board. No need to stand, but please hold onto your hats and zip your flies," Zeila insisted, noticing the well-dressed FEMA chief sitting adjacent to a young, voluptuous doll.

"Captain, get this bureaucratic bling-thing into the air, NOW!" Zeila demanded, waving her pistol. The pilot and copilot looked on in horror and disbelief as the elderly, angry woman came storming down the aisle.

"You heard Zeila. Get this plane into the air!" Rex ordered, slamming the rear cabin door shut and locking the hatch.

"I'd put that pot down, Missy, if I were you," Zeila warned, pointing her pistol at the battle-worn stewardess. Ginger quickly complied with Zeila's request and placed the pot back onto the stove.

"I'm Captain Gomez. Put that gun down now and get off my plane!" the captain insisted in no uncertain terms.

Immediately, Rex became aware that Zeila needed his help and swiftly worked his way forward. But the captain's vain attempt to exert his authority did not faze the unyielding Cajun wild woman. Zeila held her ground and showed no fear. Rex soon realized that Zeila had the situation well in hand.

"Ooh, ooh… What's that's godawful smell? Has something died?" Mr. Dagerpont and Ms. Firm shrieked as each suddenly began to fan their noses in a futile attempt to search for an elusive pocket of fresh air.

Instinctively, Rex checked the soles of his feet and smelled his underarms before realizing the source of concern.

"Oh, that's just swamp salve from Zeila's secret herbs, spices, and decaying muck," Rex attempted to explain.

"It's medicine for my wounds. Trust me, you'll get use to the smell," he assured his fellow passengers although he chose to ignore their grimacing facial contortions.

"I don't see how that's possible," Mr. Dagerpont replied, holding his nose.

"Captain, take your seat. Missy, get to the back of the bus. We won't be needing your services for awhile," Zeila ordered as she locked the cockpit door open.

"Everyone stay calm," Rex announced, taking off his backpack and laying it down on an empty seat. "We're commandeering this plane for safe passage to Washington, DC. You'll find this hard to believe, but radical Islamic terrorists are on their way to our nation's capital with a dirty bomb. Most importantly, my wife, Trissy, is strapped to their deadly delivery truck. We need to save her and with any luck keep the herd of egotistical, power-hungry, indecisive, greedy, shithead (e-PIGS) politicians from being congressionally cooked." Ginger, Mr. Dagerpont and Ms. Firm looked on incredulously while frequently coughing and gagging.

"I'm quickly running out of patience," Zeila growled as she placed her foot on the engineer's seat, resting her forearm on her knee.

With her weapon clearly in sight and in close proximity to the pilots, the jet jockeys immediately began turning knobs and flipping switches in rapid succession.

"That's more like it, gentlemen," Zeila praised.

"Captain, when we're twenty miles from DC, I need you to decend to one thousand feet and follow I-ninety-five. I must be able to see the traffic on the interstate," Rex insisted.

The captain listened intently and then whispered into his microphone. Rex assumed that he was talking to control tower but was uncomfortable with the tone in his voice, mannerisms, and his unusual momentary pause.

"It will be just a few minutes. We need to take on additional fuel and we're having trouble finding a ground crew to remove the access ramp," the captain announced convincingly.

"Well then, that should give me just enough time to get your copilot and stewardess comfortable. I trust you'll find solutions to these problems promptly," Rex insisted, pulling out long plastic ties from his backpack and ushering the copilot, Terry Spencer, and Ginger to the rear of the cabin. Moments later, Rex could hear the whining of the jet engines as he finished binding wrists and legs.

"You'll never get away with this," Spencer warned as Rex secured a seatbelt around the waist of each disabled crewmember.

"You're probably right, but patriotism has no bounds," Rex conceded. But soon he realized that the plane was not moving.

"Damn," Rex blurted as he looked out the window. He quickly made his way forward to express his personal disappointment to the captain.

Zeila couldn't help but stare at Mr. Dagerpont and Ms. Firm in disbelief. Both went about their business and appeared unfazed by the recent turn of events. Mr. Dagerpont kept reviewing reams of papers while prissy Ms. Firm kept primping herself. Zeila's fascination with the two suspicious characters was soon interrupted by Rex's arrival.

"Captain, I'm not horsing around. Get this bird off the ground," Rex reiterated forcefully as the captain put his forefinger into the air before placing his hand on his earpiece.

"It's the control tower. There's a call for you," the captain announced without emotion, handing Rex his headset.

"What's your call signal?" Rex asked the captain as he climbed into the copilot's seat.

"Gulf Sierra seventy-six," the captain coughed before turning his head in an attempt to avoid the pungent odor, which had suddenly invaded the cockpit.

"Control tower, this is Gulf Sierra seventy-six requesting clearance for takeoff," Rex asked calmly.

"Ah, Dr. Bent, we had rather hoped you were dead," SAC Richter shared.

There was a moment of hesitation before Rex realized who was on the other line. The hostile tone and the raspy, nicotine-encrusted voice, coupled with the unbridled arrogance left no doubt.

"Richter, I was convinced that the FBI would have put you out to pasture by now. Surely the director has to wonder why I keep slipping through your slimy fingers," Rex chuckled, while watching a small army of motorized vehicles suddenly appear from out of nowhere.

Oddly enough, all of the vehicles stopped in a line one hundred yards in front of the nose of the plane. The police helicopter, which had tormented Rex and Zeila earlier, landed in the same vicinity shortly thereafter.

"Well, I've got you now, you son of a bitch!" Richter screamed so loudly that his voice could be heard throughout the cockpit.

Captain Gomez couldn't resist cracking a smile. At that precise moment, several men in black emerged from the vehicles with their automatic weapons leveled at the plane's cockpit.

"I certainly believe you do," Rex replied in an attempt to buy time, while checking out the controls.

"Rex, someone's at the back door," Zeila announced after hearing a loud knocking sound radiating from the secured cabin door.

"I've got to assume that members of Richter's swell SWAT team have come a-calling," Rex astutely concluded. "I'd say that's quite considerate," he added, placing his hands on the yoke.

"We'll show those bastards, won't we, Captain?" Rex assured the defiant pilot. He pushed the starboard throttle forward to 60 percent power, while applying firm pressure to the left brake and turning the yoke to the left. The engines responded immediately and the plane began to pivot. Slowly, the tail started to swing around away from the boarding ladder, while the nose rotated away from the newly established mechanical gauntlet.

"Captain, where are the guns and Sidewinder missiles on this damn thing?" Rex joked as he brought the yoke to midline.

The captain folded his arms in disgust. In a matter of seconds, Rex had managed to evade a number of insurmountable obstacles with only one casualty. Their shiny red Corvette had been singed unmercifully by the fire and heat generated from the exhaust spewing from the revved Pratt & Whitney jet engines.

"How unusual. I've seen sports cars fly and even crash, but never melt," Rex quipped as he watched the fiberglass chariot smoldering in the distance.

The sleek, powerful plane quickly gained speed as several military vehicles and police cars gave chase. Minutes later, the *Gulfstream V* was on the runway.

"Hold on!" an enthusiastic Zeila yelled as she took a seat in the row opposite Mr. Dagerpont and Ms. Firm.

"It's time to kick this wickedly winged beast in the ass!" Rex announced loudly, gunning the engines. The tires screeched briefly with the added thrust. Rex was thrown back into his seat as the plane rapidly gained speed.

"You need to reduce the thrust to ninety-three percent power," Captain Gomez warned.

"That's good to know, Captain," Rex agreed without heeding the warning. The throttle remained wide open.

There would be no time for formalities with the Baton Rouge control tower as the jet raced down the runway, but Rex could not resist one more stab at his hapless nemesis.

"Inspector Clouseau; pardon me, I meant Rectal Richter. At what point do you realize that you've lost, again?" Rex asked with little concern for Richter's emotional health.

"If that plane takes off, I will shoot you out of the skies!" the FBI SAC screamed.

"That's not sporting old chap, and you'll have to locate this bird first. Most importantly, you have to realize your limitations. It's readily apparent that you couldn't find your backside even with Ms. Cleo poking you in the bum!" Rex chuckled before taking off the headset.

"It's been a number of years since I've flown," Rex confessed as he faced the captain. "I'm not sure I remember how to takeoff. So feel free to jump in at any time." He extended the courtesy as the end of the runway rapidly grew neared, vividly revealing the iminent danger.

But the captain sat silently with his arms folded across his chest as the plane continued to roar down the runway at breakneck speed. Soon, the sleek *Gulfstream* began to methodically sway as her wings created enough upward lift to lighten the bonds of gravity.

"Now passing a hundred and fifty-five miles per hour," Rex announced, examining a gauge that reflected the plane's ground speed.

"Awe, lookie here, no more runway, just tall trees and plenty of thick brush." Hearing Rex's dialogue, Mr. Dagerpont's and Ms. Firm's knuckles turned white from the death grip each had placed on their armrests.

"Wow, ever since I tasted Sambo's moonshine I just knew I was born to fly," Zeila howled as she looked at her terrorized passengers.

"Okay, OKAY!" Captain Gomez screamed as he suddenly came to life, grabbing for the controls.

As the captain pulled back on the yoke, the nose of the plane rose immediately. In an instant, they were off. The plane climbed at an unusually steep angle. Thankfully, the landing gear narrowly missed clipping the tops of the pine trees.

"I'm proud of you, Captain. You came through in the clutch," Rex confessed with admiration.

"Excellent job, Rex. I didn't know you knew how to fly," Zeila praised, dazzled by Rex's aeronautic ability.

"I don't, but the captain was kind enough to give me a lesson," Rex replied as he watched Gomez wipe beads of sweat from his saturated brow.

"Well, it's not as responsive as a Tomcat, but it's a lot fancier. As you recall, our destination is Washington, DC. You will keep the wings level, Captain, won't you?" Rex requested as he climbed out of the copilot's seat.

CHAPTER 41

As the *Gulfstream V* continued to climb, the runway began to fade rapidly. Rex and Zeila had been within SAC Richter's grasp, but once again they had successfully evaded the long arm of the law. Time was now of the essence. As they raced toward Washington, DC, at four hundred knots, Rex remained confident that he could save Trissy but wondered if he would be able to prevent the destruction of the nation's capital.

"Hijacking is a federal offense," Captain Gomez barked in anger as Rex was leaving the cockpit.

"A stern warning, Captain, but having knowledge of a foreboding attack on American soil and doing nothing about it is as well. I'm just one patriot doing his duty, regardless of the consequences," Rex shot back, knowing his response would fall on deaf ears.

"Rex, I don't mean to sound offensive, but there's a shower in back and I do have a spare set of clothes, which you're more than welcome to borrow," Mr. Dagerpont kindly offered, clamping his nostrils shut in a vain attempt to ward off the noxious fumes. Ms. Firm gagged and giggled but said nothing.

"Do I really smell that bad?" Rex asked as he sniffed the air.

"YES!" was the resounding collective response.

"You're kidding," Rex responded in disbelief, examining his tattered wetsuit caked with thick layers of rock-hard swamp muck.

"Rex, I think you smell fine. You know, in some parts of the world my medicinal salve is considered an aphrodisiac," Zeila shared with the group in an effort to rebuild Rex's battered ego.

"Obviously not here. Well then, perhaps I should shower," Rex concluded.

"Captain, no more tricks. Zeila has already shot two men dead today," Rex warned the nervous pilot as Zeila kissed the barrel of her nine-millimeter pistol.

"Actually, that was yesterday and they deserved it," Zeila replied, correcting Rex.

"Furthermore, should we run low on fuel as you anticipate, I'll be the one to find us a gas station," Rex informed the captain as he grabbed his backpack.

"Zeila, are you comfortable watching this rebellious group?" he asked, although he knew the answer.

"Sho' is," Zeila responded as Rex walked aft.

"Oh, man. I really need to contact Leslie now before it's too late," Rex whispered, stopping halfway down the aisle. He looked at the comfortable leather couch and sat down.

Rex withdrew the laptop from his backpack and placed it on an ornate coffee table adjacent to the couch. After several strokes on the keypad and a few clicks, he was able to retrieve the live satellite data, which reflected the location and speed of each deadly U-Haul truck.

"Excellent, all the trucks are still moving, which means that the assault on these major cities has not yet been launched. I can only assume that the timing is set to coincide with some obscure Islamic event," Rex surmised as he zeroed in on the eastern seaboard.

"Trissy is a hundred and twenty-five miles south-southwest of Washington. Her U-Haul is probably traveling at seventy miles an hour and I assume we have an additional two hours of flying time. We're not going to make it without a little help," Rex concluded, the concern more than evident on his face.

"It's time to recruit the National Security Agency and I know just how to go about accomplishing this task." Rex felt certain as he typed an email.

Leslie—

Attached is the present location of the U-Haul trucks carrying dirty bombs destined for US cities.

Trissy is 125 miles from Washington, DC. FEMA has been kind enough to loan us their corporate jet to effect her rescue. I intend to detonate the preplanted explosive charges on all U-Hauls as soon as a visual on Trissy has been obtained.

I strongly suggest that the freeways leading to each targeted city be shut down!

—Rex

"That's a message even a bureaucrat can understand," Rex chuckled before hitting *send*. His confidence renewed, Rex was certain that he and Zeila would reach Trissy in time.

"Now for that shower," Rex announced, much to everyone's delight.

Rex left the computer on and walked aft, past the disgruntled and recently restrained crewmembers, toward a highly polished, wooden bulkhead in the center of which was a stained-glass door with a shiny brass knob. He turned the knob and entered a spectacular bedroom.

◆

"Wow, is this first class," Rex complimented the interior decorator as he peeled off what remained of his shredded wetsuit, tossing it onto the floor before heading into the bathroom.

"A marble shower and gold fixtures, fancy that. Obviously, our hard-earned tax dollars have been put to good use in this shining levee-tory," Rex observed while twisting the shower handle.

Instantaneously, the water came on at a precise, preset temperature. Rex hopped in without hesitation. Slowly and painfully he washed away the layers of muck, which had adhered like cement to his deep abrasions.

"Everyone needs a scam. I wonder how I can become part of FEMA's funding and freewheeling fiasco?" Rex wondered as he lathered up, transfixed on his irrational line of thought.

"Trissy and I aren't greedy by any means. We need only enough hardbacks to procure a shack on the beach and, of course, some very basic necessities such as an occasional barrel of rum and enough propane for the tiki torches. Surely the government wouldn't miss the paltry sum needed to sustain our reclusive low-profile lifestyle. In fact, they'd probably be so appreciative that they would grant me some highfalutin diplomatic title," Rex assured himself, reaching for a towel and stepping from the shower.

Rex's delusions of grandeur and visions of glory continued as he gently patted his wounds dry.

"Ah, that's better. I feel like a new man," Rex sighed, rummaging through the closet for a new set of duds. While perusing the limited selection of appropriate attire, Rex came across several very skimpy items, which thankfully weren't in Mr. Dagerpont's size.

"Ms. Firm certainly has a good eye, and Mr. Dagerpont, my admiration. He has a beautiful plane, a stunning assistant with sexy lingerie, and the time to enjoy both," Rex praised the FEMA director after briefly glancing at the seductive see-through lingerie, no doubt selected by Ms. Firm.

"This will do nicely," Rex said.He grabbed from the wardrobe a pair of brown slacks and a white designer shirt that he buttoned up."Thank God the pants fit, but this starched shirt is irritating my war wounds…

Well, I certainly look better, but I'm not sure I smell any better. However, this is change I can truly believe in," Rex observed as he glanced in a mirror and sniffed his underarms.

"Now, let me see what trouble Zeila's gotten herself into in my absence."

◆

Rex's senses were suddenly overwhelmed as soon as he stepped from the bedroom back into the cabin. The smell of fine food gently waffled through the air, while overhead a familiar tune was playing "Staying Alive..." "Now that's a rather irresistible mouth watering aroma," Rex concluded unexpectedly. "My word, if Trissy were here she'd be dancing in the aisle. The stars must have aligned," he concluded as he walked forward, more determined than ever to save his beautiful wife.

"I believe we're missing a prisoner," Rex whispered, looking around.

The copilot had remained bound in the back of the plane, but the stewardess had vanished. However, the mystery was soon solved when Rex noticed Ginger serving food and cocktails to Zeila and FEMA's famished guests.

"At least Zeila has her priorities straight," Rex said as he ambled down the aisle. Oddly enough, there were no snide remarks launched as Rex passed by the dejected copilot.

"Rex, Ginger didn't have any pork rinds or fried chicken, but the steak and lobster is excellent!" Zeila mumbled before stuffing another large succulent bite of butter-drenched lobster into her mouth.

"And the mint juleps aren't bad either," Ms. Firm declared without hesitation as Mr. Dagerpont stabbed his large steak with a fork and started to nibble around the edges. Although admiring Ms. Firm's style, Rex quietly wondered what barn the FEMA director had been reared in given his total absence of table manners.

"It appears that the iron maiden can not only cook but also pours a mean drink," Rex remarked as Ginger sneered.

Rex poked his head into the cockpit to check on the captain. Their altitude was forty-five thousand feet and the heading north-northeast.

"What's our ETA, Captain?" Rex asked, examining the instrument panel.

"One hour and thirty minutes. By the way, what's the plan when we arrive in Washington?" Captain Gomez wondered.

"Frankly, I'm not sure," Rex responded candidly.

"Zeila, how would Sambo get down from forty-five thousand feet?" Rex asked jokingly.

"Sambo wouldn't have a problem because he thought he could fly," Zeila replied without hesitation.

"That figures. After consuming several jugs of moonshine, I'd think I could probably fly as well," Rex agreed politely.

"We're heading straight for Reagan National Airport. Perhaps we could touch down there," the captain suggested.

"Well, I like that possibility more so than batting my wings and gliding to earth," Rex responded as he looked at Zeila. She had not broken stride and continued wolfing down every morsel of the gourmet meal.

"Man oh man, was I wrong about airplane food. This is wonderful," Zeila conceded after taking a large swig of a tall, ice-cold beer.

"I can see that," Rex responded.

"May I bring you lunch?" Ginger asked in a stern, sinister voice.

"No, thank you, not just yet," Rex replied politely.

"Rex, you certainly smell better," Mr. Dagerpont remarked, sipping on his champagne.

"That's for sure," Ms. Firm added, taking another sip of her cocktail.

"Well, thank you. In the future, I'll be sure to shower more often," Rex assured his critical traveling companions.

"I just hope you don't get those wounds infected," Zeila mumbled before a large piece of steak quickly vanished from her fork.

"Ms. Firm, you look awfully familiar," Rex noticed as he slowly eased back into the plush leather seat next to Zeila.

"Yes, I was...." she started to say before being drowned out by her boss.

"Um, um, UM," Mr. Dagerpont mumbled in an attempt to clear his throat.

"I was Miss November. Perhaps you saw me on the cover of *Playboy*," Ms. Firm confessed, giggling.

"That could be. What's your first name?" Rex asked, watching the FEMA director squirm.

"My first name is 'Undoubtedly.' I'm a stripper by profession, so it's a stage name, of course. My real name is Frangellica, but my friends call me Fanny," Frangellica 'Fanny' Firm rambled on, indulging in another sip of her whiskey cocktail.

"Fanny, forgive me for being nosy, but what is it that you do for FEMA?" Rex asked as Mr. Dagerpont brought his hand up to cover his face, sliding down deeper into his seat.

"I'm Mr. Dagerpont's personal assistant," Frangellica responded without reservation.

"I see. By the way, was that your lingerie I stumbled across in the back?" Rex asked innocently as Mr. Dagerpont suddenly turned beet red.

"Why, yes, and I have some real pretty pieces. Would you like me to model my collection?" Frangellica asked sincerely, arching her back and unconsciously thrusting her voluptuous breasts forward.

"I think we've had quite enough excitement for one day, Fanny, but thank you," Rex responded.

"Hell, I'll model the stuff for you," Zeila blurted after taking another swig of beer.

"Now there's a sobering thought," Rex whispered as a vision of Zeila in a see-through nightie suddenly made him nauseous. He quickly changed the subject.

"Mr. Dagerpont, what's your position with FEMA?" Rex asked as the seasoned executive slowly regained his composure.

"I'm FEMA's regional director," Mr. Dagerpont replied proudly, sitting back up in his seat.

Suddenly, the memories of Katrina came rushing back to Zeila and her demeanor changed instantly.

"FEMA, FEMA! Boy, do I have a bone to pick with you!" Zeila shouted, slamming her fork onto her plate.

"I'm from Naw-leans and I am sick and tired of living in a flimsy, overpriced, trashy trailer park in the middle of Louisiana's badlands.

I know that the government blew up the levees, but what I don't know is when can I move back home," Zeila growled.

"We've made substantial progress, but I can't give you an actual date," a startled Mr. Dagerpont responded, taking a healthy gulp of champagne.

"Progress—There's been no progress. None of my neighbors from the ninth ward have moved back because the 'Slippery Finger' insurance company has refused to honor any of our claims," Zeila complained.

"I feel your pain, but that's the state's fault. Governor Blanco should have been riding shotgun over the greedy insurance companies," Mr. Dagerpont explained to the highly agitated evacuee.

"Pain, you want to talk about pain? I've lost everything, and now that I've found the courage to rebuild, I find that there's no water or electrical services, and the fire and police departments are virtually nonexistent. Furthermore, any new structure must now be built twelve feet off the ground to get the city's blessing. Hell, I'll get a nosebleed at that altitude," Zeila complained vehemently, standing up and shaking her finger at the self-serving, politically appointed, Ivy League government employee.

"Again, I feel your pain, but that's the fault of the governor and the mayor," Mr. Dagerpont pleaded as a frightened Ms. Firm squirmed.

"Here we go again, with the 'pain and blame' game!" Zeila howled, throwing her hands in the air in sheer frustration.

"Zeila, please don't forget that the city still hasn't even buried their dead and it's been well over three years since Katrina," Rex added just to throw a little extra fuel on the fire.

"Those are issues that the governor and the mayor need to address. I'm here to make sure that the levees are sound. The president has already done everything in his power to assist the state of Louisiana, the city of New Orleans, and the Katrina evacuees. At some point you have to assume responsibility for your own health and well-being," Mr. Dagerpont lectured.

"Health and well-being—HA! I should wop you upside the head for being so cold and callous," Zeila threatened, pacing back and forth in the aisle.

"There's no doubt that FEMA has become a bird of prey," Rex interjected, just to stir the pot.

"Well, they should've prayed that Zeila didn't get her hands on them. Rex, open the cabin door. It's time for this 'pain and blame' bird to fly!" Zeila shouted as she forcefully grabbed Mr. Dagerpont's arm.

The Zeila rebellion was well underway as the feisty evacuee tugged Mr. Dagerpont in one direction while his faithful well-endowed assistant tugged him in the other.

Whoosh! Whoosh! Boom—B O O M! Suddenly, the wrestling match ended as quickly as it had begun.

"What the hell was that?" Rex shouted.

"Two F-sixteens. They just shot by our nose and tapped burner, going supersonic. The fighter aircraft must have been scrambled from Andrews Air Force Base," Captain Gomez concluded.

"It appears that we have a fighter escort and the sonic booms were meant as a warning. Zeila, stop horsing around with that political glad-hander. You can throw him out of the plane some other time or into the gumbo for all I care, but now it's time to get back to work," Rex insisted, looking at his computer screen. Trissy was only sixty miles away and they were closing in quickly on her position. Rex looked out the window and noticed multiple fighter aircrafts close abreast.

"Oh, Lord!" he gasped.

"Rex, you certainly attract a lot of attention, but this doesn't look good," Zeila concluded, gazing at the fighter jets.

"That's an understatement. We're fighting the terrorists, the United States Air Force, and now, more than ever, time."

"Rex, I hate to be the bearer of bad tidings, but the Air Force is insisting that we land at Reagan National Airport immediately, or they intend to shoot us down," Captain Gomez announced.

Chapter 42

The president had been briefed by the secretary of the National Security Agency, Andy Anderson, only hours before. In a conference call with a chairman of the Joint Chiefs of Staff, General Kirk Shulke, it was decided that it was far too dangerous not to accept Dr. Rex Bent's information. Decisions were made and implemented over the phone and both men were summoned to the White House. Effective immediately, all major freeways leading into the seven major cities targeted by the terrorists were to be shut down. Furthermore, all U-Haul trucks on any roadway in the United States were to be stopped and searched. There would be zero tolerance. Any resistance met by the occupants of these vehicles was to be dealt with swiftly and decisively.

The president was standing and looking out the magnificent bay window in the Oval Office. Six inches of fresh snow had fallen the previous evening and the White House grounds were blanketed in a spectacular rolling layer of white that sparkled vibrantly in the late afternoon sun. However, all was not as peaceful as it seemed, for the United States was under attack once again and tough decisions had to be made. The newly elected president was deep in thought when startled by loud knock on her door.

"Madam President, Secretary Anderson and General Shulke have arrived," Mrs. Heidi Barnes, the President's secretary and chief confidant, announced as she the door to her office.

"Very good, Heidi, please show them in," the president requested, keeping her hands clasped behind her back while continuing to stare out the window.

"Have you had any success contacting the secretary of state or the secretary of defense?"

"Yes, both Secretary Robert Sheppard and Secretary Mounang Desai will be here within the hour," Mrs. Barnes replied with the precision of a field commander who closely followed the ground troops.

"And the vice president?" the president inquired as Secretary Anderson and General Shulke entered the Oval Office and stood quietly.

"Unfortunately, I've been unable to locate Vice President Schumer. It's as if he's dropped off the face of the Earth," Mrs. Barnes replied with regret after her extensive efforts proved unfruitful.

"It figures that the aggressive, condescending thorn in my side has finally chosen this particular day in which to vanish. Well, we know that he's certainly not searching for his Little Red Riding Hood reading glasses because they're superglued to the end of his nose!"

"Knowing how much he loves the media, as long as they give him facetime, I've checked every TV station without success," Heidi added.

"No, Chuckles the Crying Clown is probably hiding in some underground brothel, eagerly anticipating my demise and his succession," the president replied angrily, much to the astonishment of all in the room. She turned around to greet the men she had summoned.

"Madam President, I'm truly sorry to meet under these harrowing circumstances," Secretary Anderson said apologetically as he bowed and shook the president's hand.

"Secretary Anderson, these are indeed unprecedented times. Although you have been scrutinized and ridiculed by the media, I have not lost faith in your leadership. You and those at the NSA have worked very hard to protect our great nation. It's important that we be together to resolve this crisis," the president replied with sincerity and confidence.

"Thank you, Madam President," Secretary Anderson replied. However, as he looked into the president's eyes, he could see her concern and self-doubt.

"Madam President," General Shulke said in greeting his commander in chief, firmly shaking her hand.

"General Shulke, thank you for coming. Gentlemen, please," the president requested. She motioned to both of them to take a seat in the plush chairs next to the fireplace while she remained standing.

"Madam President, once again I implore you to leave Washington. From what Secretary Anderson has uncovered, the danger is far too great for you to remain in this city," General Shulke pleaded.

"General, I do not intend to run and hide like my Republican predecessor during a crisis that he himself created. Our founding fathers and all those brave men and women who have fallen in the countless wars defending the United States of America would never run from battle, nor shall I. Retreat is not an option. Do I make myself perfectly clear?" the president asked loudly.

"Yes, Madam President," the general replied promptly and without bias in his voice. However, he thought the unfounded criticism of President Bush during 9/11 was outrageous and irresponsible.

"Secretary Anderson, upon assuming the presidency I had intended to focus my time on rebuilding an economy decimated by the Republicans, health care, wealth redistribution, and global warming. Yet, I've had to spend my valuable time cleaning up a war and mending diplomatic wounds created by a mindless war-mongering Texan," the president stated frankly while pacing the room.

"Madam President, may we focus on the present danger?" Secretary Anderson pleaded as General Shulke fought the urge to blast his commander in chief for such absurd accusations.

However, the president remained determined to express her views to her captive audience.

"After fulfilling my campaign promise to withdrawal our troops from Iraq, the Stennis Carrier Strike Group was destroyed by forces from Iran. Shortly thereafter, the United States came under attack. The terrorists have once again returned to our shores not only with conventional weapons but now with rolling dirty bombs supplied by the damn North Koreans. The glorious Democratic Party inherited this mess! I will not allow my presidency to be tarnished by Republican greed and incompetence. Is that fully understood, gentlemen?" the president shouted, insisting upon an answer.

"Yes, Madam President, fully," Secretary Anderson replied affirmatively, knowing that his submission was the only way to diffuse the volatile, tyrannical outburst.

"Good, now where do we stand on protecting Americans against these rolling dirty bombs?" the president queried.

"Madam President, all the freeways leading into the designated cities have been blocked. Several U-Haul trucks have been stopped and searched, but no weapons of mass destruction have yet been found," Secretary Anderson replied.

"Madam President, Homeland Security has raised the terrorist threat level to RED. All available Navy, Air Force, Coast Guard, and Army fighter aircrafts have been scrambled. Additionally, thousands of National Guard troops and police officers from local, state, and federal jurisdictions have joined in the effort to stop this attack," General Shulke assured the president.

"General, are you comfortable that everything humanly possible has been done?" the president asked, wondering about the competence of both men. There was no doubt in her mind that the numerous disasters that had befallen America in the last few weeks had taken place on their watch. However, the president had come to the conclusion that now was not the time to demand their resignations.

"Absolutely, Madam President," General Shulke replied.

"I concur, Madam President. We've implemented every possible means to thwart this attack. However, there's one question which remains: that of the hijacked *Gulfstream* FEMA jet bound for Washington, DC," Secretary Anderson stated.

"As you know, a renegade physician, Dr. Rex Bent, is behind this crime," General Shulke added.

"So I've heard, Mr. Secretary. Is Dr. Bent friend or foe?" the president asked as she paced the Oval Office.

"That remains to be seen, Madam President. However, we're quickly running out of time and to give him the benefit of the doubt is far too great a risk to bear," Secretary Anderson replied.

"I agree. Furthermore, this bizarre story about the doctor planting plastic explosives on the U-Haul trucks remains as far-fetched as does his insistence that he has the ability to detonate these weapons from the air," General Shulke added before pausing. "Without question, the FEMA jet should be blown from the skies," the general recommended.

"Madam President, I strongly concur," Secretary Anderson interjected.

"Gentlemen, it's my understanding that Dr. Bent was a highly decorated member of our armed services, a Navy SEAL as I recall," the president stated.

"That is indeed correct, Madam President," General Shulke confirmed.

"Why then does it appear to be unlikely that he possesses the ability to take out these trucks?" the president inquired, demanding an answer.

"It's not a question of possibility as much as it is a question of probability and feasibility. Most importantly, if he did possess the ability to stop these U-Haul trucks dead in their tracks, why has he not done so?" General Shulke asked rhetorically.

"It was my understanding that Dr. Bent's wife, Trissy, is bound and gagged and held captive on the U-Haul truck destined for Washington," the president stated, remembering the details from an earlier briefing.

"Yes, that appears to be the case, and Dr. Bent has adamantly refused to detonate the plastic explosives until her U-Haul truck is in sight. He's had the audacity to request our help to save his wife," Secretary Anderson relayed.

"That's preposterous! There must be hundreds of U-Haul trucks destined for this city at this very moment. How in the world is he going to know which truck it is, and then what in the Sam Hell does he think he's going to do once he finds it?" General Shulke argued.

"Perhaps he's intending to parachute from the skies," Secretary Anderson suggested as both men grew frustrated, rationalizing their positions on Dr. Bent's fate.

"No one would have the balls to parachute from a jet traveling at a low altitude at over four hundred miles per hour with the intention of landing on an eight-by-sixteen-foot bed of tin," General Shulke blurted before realizing, in retrospect, that the words he had chosen to express his views would be perceived as rather harsh.

"Forgive me, Mr. Secretary and Madam President," the general said apologetically as the door to the Oval Office opened and Mrs. Barnes stepped in.

"Madam President, I've just received a rather interesting call from the control tower at Reagan National Airport. It appears that the control tower is in contact with several F-sixteen fighter jets. They have the FEMA aircraft in sight and are requesting orders. The hijacked aircraft is now thirty miles out and closing quickly. Additionally, the air traffic controller stressed that the rogue plane is on a flight path which would take it straight over the White House," Ms. Barnes announced, much to everyone's surprise.

"Good God!" Secretary Anderson gasped.

"Madam President, may I instruct the Air Force to blow the FEMA jet from the skies?" General Shulke requested insistently.

"Just in case the F-sixteens can't achieve their objective, I would also instruct the Patriot missile batteries surrounding Washington to bring down that plane," Secretary Anderson interjected.

"Mr. Secretary, you're overstepping your bounds," the president chastised.

"Heidi, I trust that your kids and Tigger are safe," she assumed but wanted to confirm.

"Absolutely, Madam President," the secretary assured her commander in chief.

"Heidi, exactly how much time do we have before the FEMA jet flies overhead?"

"Madam President, they didn't say, but they're still on the line," Mrs. Barnes replied.

"At that speed, less than eight minutes," General Shulke estimated as he impatiently awaited an order.

Almost immediately, the Oval Office was filled with an eerie silence. The president clasped her hands behind her back and slowly walked around her desk toward the large bay window.

"Madam President, may I give that order?" General Shulke requested once again, the concern beginning to show on Secretary Anderson's face.

Heidi stood fast awaiting instructions, for she maintained unwavering confidence in the president's leadership.

"Mr. Secretary, have we implemented the deception which makes Chinese intelligence believe that their cyberwarefare group has hacked into the Pentagon's computers and can control there destiny in time of war?" the president asked, much to the secretary's surprise.

"Yes, Madam President," Secretary Anderson replied, wondering what had prompted the question.

"General, are our naval battle groups ready to launch an attack against Iran and North Korea?" the president queried in a calm yet authoritative manner.

"Absolutely, I spoke with Admiral Nelson Perett only hours ago. He has assured me that the United States Navy stands ready to execute your orders, Madam President," General Shulke affirmed with overwhelming confidence.

"And the ballistic missile submarines, are they on station?" the president asked.

"Yes, Madam President. The Trident ballistic missiles are ready for launch with each of the multiple independently targetable reentry vehicles (MIRV) locked onto the specific cities within the countries we have designated. With each MIRV containing a blast yield in excess four megatons, our enemies will be vaporized," General Shulke confirmed.

"We will have no more surprises. The Soviets and the Chinese will have neither the time nor the opportunity to enter this war," the president declared.

However, General Shulke wasn't sure that the president would live long enough to execute the order.

"Madam President, may I give the order to blow the FEMA jet from the skies?" General Shulke demanded.

"I believe we've given Dr. Bent ample opportunity to effect whatever countermeasures he had in place. Yes, General, give the order," the president directed reluctantly as she stared out over the White House lawn.

General Shulke sprang from his chair. Heidi quickly led him to her desk where he grabbed the phone and issued the order.

"Let's hope we're in time," General Shulke remarked as he walked back into the Oval Office.

"I'll have no insubordination, General," the president growled after hearing the remark.

"My apologies, Madam President," General Shulke replied, although he was clearly frustrated with the president's indecision.

General Shulke took his seat adjacent to Secretary Anderson and patiently awaited further orders.

Both General Shulke and the honorable secretary sat in a deafening silence, watching the president stare out the bay window.

Chapter 43

The commandeered FEMA *Gulfstream* jet was now only twenty miles from Washington, DC, and closing quickly on the nation's capital. The plush government aircraft was cruising at a speed of four hundred knots and her altitude was down to twelve thousand feet. Rex and Zeila were on a desperate mission to save Trissy and the nation. However, both objectives now appeared to be in jeopardy. A fighter escort had just ordered the hijacked plane to land immediately or risk being blown from the skies.

"Captain, let the Air Force know that we will meet their demands, but quickly come down to an altitude of one thousand feet," Rex instructed as the captain shook his head in frustration. He immediately realized that the request was totally unreasonable.

"I can't just abruptly change my altitude, and there's no way that the control tower at Reagan National Airport is going to allow me to come down to one thousand feet. It's just too dangerous with all the air traffic in this area," Captain Gomez replied, attempting to raise the fighter aircraft.

"I don't give a damn. Get this bird down, NOW! I must be able to see the vehicles on Interstate ninety-five," Rex growled, growing more and more determined. Success was everything. Failure was not an option.

"This is Gulf Sierra seventy-six to our fighter jet escort. We will comply with your request and land at Reagan National," the captain declared after establishing a three-way communication between the control tower and the fighter jets.

"This is Lieutenant Colonel Peder Cox from Fighter Squadron forty-six. I intend to keep you honest, Captain. Any hostile acts will be met with a sidewinder missile up your tailpipe. Of that, I assure you," the jet jockey replied sternly.

"Oh, Christ!" Captain Gomez shouted, hearing the no-nonsense response.

"Reagan National, this is Gulf Sierra seventy-six. My uninvited guest has requested an abrupt altitude change to one thousand feet," Captain Gomez shouted.

It was apparent to those on the ground that the captain was starting to lose his composure. They had no way of knowing that his palms were starting to sweat, but they were keenly aware that his speech was now rapid and pressured.

There was no response to the captain's request. The airway fell silent. Rex grew more and more impatient as he looked out his window and observed the fighter escort.

"Captain, let me remind you that we're both quickly running out of time!" Rex shouted as he continued to look at the screen on his computer. The U-Haul truck bound for Washington, DC, with Trissy on board was now a mere ten miles ahead.

"This is a suicide mission and you're going to get us all killed," Captain Gomez argued, reluctantly slowing the plane's speed and pushing the yoke forward.

The *Gulfstream* descended rapidly and everyone on board was lifted from their seat. Each could feel their ears pop with the change in altitude. Mr. Dagerpont and Ms. Firm looked at one another with growing trepidation. Seeing the fighter aircraft and hearing the communication, it was clearly evident that the danger was escalating with every passing moment. The FEMA contingency now had a death grip on their armrests as the *Gulfstream* continued its sharp angle of descent.

"That may be, Captain, but I like to think we are going into harm's way for God, country, and my beautiful wife. Now, which side of the plane is I-ninety-five going to be on?" Rex demanded.

"It's going to be off the port side," Captain Gomez answered defiantly.

"Zeila, come over here next to me," Rex requested, motioning her to the couch where he was sitting.

"Why?" Zeila asked suspiciously.

"I need you to look out the window. Let me know the minute you see a U-Haul truck on the freeway below," Rex insisted, sitting on the plush leather couch with his back to the window, focusing on his laptop computer screen.

"Sho' will," Zeila replied, cupping her hands against the window for a better view.

"My, there's a flock of jets just outside our window. They must know that Zeila is coming to Washington!" the elderly Cajun woman surmised.

"They're here at my request to ensure that you arrive at the nation's capital with 'style and class,'" Rex replied as he concentrated on the screen.

"Rex, you're full of more Louisiana muck than anyone I know," Zeila chuckled.

"Can we just land this damn plane? I'm starting to get very nervous!" Mr. Dagerpont yelled, looking out the window and realizing that his life expectancy had somewhat diminished.

"Not quite yet, Dager-dung," Rex answered calmly as he watched the distance between the *Gulfstream* and Trissy closing quickly.

"Dager-dung, we're on a mission, so keep your self-serving, bureaucratic trap shut," Zeila insisted.

The captain placed his hand up to his earpiece, listening to incoming communication as Rex and Zeila remained focused on their tasks.

"This is Reagan National. Do not come down to one thousand feet. I repeat, do NOT come down to one thousand feet. You're authorized to start your glide slope now. You will be landing on runway One Alpha, runway One Alpha. Is that understood, over?" the control tower ordered, requesting confirmation. But it was already too late. The *Gulfstream* jet was well below ten thousand feet and continuing its rapid descent. Interstate ninety-five was now clearly visible and the vehicles traveling the busy freeway recognizable.

Seconds later, a multitude of loud explosions erupted unexpectedly within the cabin and the *Gulfstream* began to shake violently.

"Goddamn it!" Gomez screamed, fighting to maintain control.

Shards of wood and metal shot in every direction. In an instant, all on board were exposed to a violent, frigid wind. The entire cabin was filled with swirling debree of all sizes and shapes and a rancid, irritating black smoke, which flowed from burning plastic.

"Christ!" Rex screamed, looking aft.

Just a few feet beyond the couch on which he was sitting, the cabin looked as if it had been hit by a cyclone. The port side was riddled with baseball-sized holes, which glowed a fiery red for an instant before expanding, as large sections of the surrounding structure continued to be ripped away by the high winds generated from the plane's velocity. Plush leather seats were now unrecognizable. Storage compartments above had been ripped from their foundations and dangled precariously, violently slapping against the overhead, while yards of singed wiring lay exposed and coiled in nest-like configurations. As the conduit continued to melt, there were frequent sparks, followed by small flash fires, which quickly burned out. Also noticeably absent was the bulkhead separating the cabin from the bedroom, as well as the bedroom itself. Both had simply vanished. Rex looked across the aisle at the copilot he had subdued and restrained earlier in the flight. The man was understandably startled but unhurt.

"That's not a very friendly escort service. Wait until I get a hold of that pilot. I'll slap him so hard his mama won't even recognize him!" Zeila yelled, while shaking her fist at the F-sixteen, which had just fired on them.

"Zeila, are you all right?" Rex shouted, turning back around only to find his accomplice staring at his computer.

"Sho' is, but it's a bit cold in here," Zeila responded, unfazed by the sudden turn of events.

"Zeila, I need you to look out the window and keep your eyes peeled on the traffic below," Rex reminded his tough, New Orleans–born companion.

"I will, just as soon as you stop playing with that damn computer. Zeila's not going to stand for any more indecision. Push the button, boy!" Zeila demanded, placing her hands on her hips and leaning forward until her face was within inches of Rex's.

"I happen to be waiting for the most opportune moment. Don't rush me!" Rex insisted, reevaluating his well thought out strategy.

"Give me that damn thing!" Zeila growled, reaching for the computer. But her skirmish with Rex was soon interrupted.

"NO!" Mr. Dagerpont screamed in a bloodcurdling tone as the sound of the explosions within the plane ripped at the remaining fragments of his frayed nerves. As he dodged the dangerous debris shooting around the cabin, the FEMA director started to cough violently as the foul smoke irritated his lungs.

"I knew you were going to get us all killed!" Captain Gomez screamed over the roar of the wind.

That was all the normally reserved, politically appointed jackass Dagerpont needed to hear to send him over the edge.

"No, NO—NO!" the FEMA director screamed hysterically, struggling to unbuckle his seatbelt while Ms. Firm sat quietly, sipping on her fourth mint julep.

"For Christ's sake, calm down!" the airline stewardess ordered, observing the agitated FEMA director flailing about.

"Where in the hell are the fucking parachutes?" Mr. Dagerpont demanded to know. He was now standing and visually examining the damage that the twenty-millimeter cannon fire had wrought. He appeared disoriented and confused, but even with the limited visibility, the fear in his eyes was more than evident.

"You must be joking. There are no parachutes, but I'm happy to bring you a bag of peanuts," a less-than-amused Ginger offered, although she remained glued to her seat.

"I don't want peanuts. I want off this fucking plane," Mr. Dagerpont insisted, beginning to gasp for breath as his sense of fear became overwhelming.

"For crying out loud, grow some balls, would you? Now sit down, shut up, and buckle up," the old flying battle ax insisted as she folded her arms and looked away from the frazzled FEMA executive.

"That's the Air Force for you, Captain. Obviously, the trigger-happy 'Zoomies' were not pleased with your flying!" Rex shouted. The captain was preoccupied trying to keep the wings level and the nose up.

The crippled *Gulfstream* was now only 1,500 feet above terra firma and continuing to lose speed and altitude. However, they were less than five miles from Trissy.

"Rex, Trissy's life is at stake and we are going down, so push that damn button before I punch you right in the nose!" Zeila screamed, clenching her fists.

Not wanting to tangle with the feisty Cajun, Rex immediately pressed the appropriate keys on the laptop, activating the explosives he and Trissy had planted on all the U-Haul trucks destined for his Islamic glory.

Seconds later, a red light began to flash on the screen. It was now or never. The decision had to be made, although the U-Haul truck and Trissy were nowhere in sight.

"I love you, Trissy, and I'm coming for you, baby. God bless!" Rex whispered as he depressed the button, detonating the charges. In an instant, all seven blips on his computer screen disappeared. The U-Haul trucks rolling with the dirty bombs had been stopped short of their intended targets and seven major American cities had been spared from certain disaster.

"Good Lord, it's about time!" Zeila shouted.

"My word, there's a lot of traffic down there. In fact, the freeway looks like a parking lot. It sort of reminds me of the day all the white folks abandoned the black folks in Naw-leans," Zeila observed candidly.

"Zeila, enough with the democratically-inspired nonsensical ravings, do you see the U-Haul truck?" Rex asked as the tension in the airplane continued to mount.

"Sho' don't," Zeila replied, mesmerized by the beauty of the magnificent capital.

"Damn!" Rex shouted in frustration. The plane shuttered and the engines whined as the pilot struggled to keep the damaged jet airborne.

"Is everything in this city white? Lord, even the monuments are white!" Zeila grumbled.

"Zeila, stay focused," Rex insisted, pressing his face against the window.

"Nothing yet," Zeila added as she examined the interstate.

"The outbound traffic is flowing, but the inbound traffic is gridlocked. The police must have set up one hell of a roadblock. Leslie received my message," Rex concluded optimistically while continuing to scan the traffic.

"Look, there's the truck!" Zeila shouted with joy.

"Where?" Rex screamed excitedly, frantically searching below.

"Yes, whoop, whoop, *whoop*! There she is, right before that bridge!" Zeila screamed back, pressing her index finger against the window.

Rex locked onto the U-Haul truck. It had been snared in an unyielding impenetrable maze just inside the beltway. The hood was twisted and white steam billowed from the engine compartment. They had found the needle in the haystack.

"Wahoo!" Rex yelled joyfully, springing to his feet.

An equally excited Zeila soon joined him in celebration.

"We did it!" Rex shouted, hugging and kissing his favorite New Orleans refugee on the lips.

"Damn sho' did!" Zeila howled, taking Rex by the arm. They began dancing in the aisle amongst the flying debris.

Suddenly, the *Gulfstream* shook violently once again and the celebration came to an abrupt halt.

"Captain, go ahead and set us down at Reagan National. I need to catch a cab. And be quick about it. My wife's waiting!" Rex barked as he rushed toward the cockpit.

"That is no longer a viable option!" Captain Gomez yelled.

"And just why not?" Rex asked, looking at the captain through the smoke-filled haze.

"Because we're losing altitude too quickly and I've lost control of the plane!" the captain yelled back, pushing the throttles forward in a last-ditch effort to gain altitude.

Chapter 44

"Madam President, may I suggest that we continue our discussion on our way to the basement?" General Shulke asked grudgingly, already knowing the answer.

"Now General, you know my position on that issue. I shall never retreat, but I would be most appreciative if you would assist Secretary Anderson and Mrs. Barnes to a more secure area, posthaste," the president of the United States requested as she stood firm, unwilling to yield. "I can clearly see the FEMA jet in flames and it's heading straight for us."

◆

Rex struggled into the cockpit, sat down in the copilot's seat, and strapped in. Suddenly, the F-16 fighter jets veered off. Rex could hear the *Gulfstream*'s powerful Pratt & Whitney engines struggling and knew they were about to seize.

"Oh, Christ, we're in trouble, big trouble!" Rex conceded, looking at the instruments. There speed was down to 250 knots and the altitude 1,000 feet. Only a miracle would keep them from crashing.

"Zeila, buckle up!" Rex screamed.

Zeila buckled her seatbelt and looked around briefly at her fellow passengers. Mr. Dagerpont had sat back down. He was pale and clearly petrified. Ms. Firm smiled and winked, while Ginger sat cold and stone-faced.

"We're in for a rough ride," Rex added.

"Look at all the fireworks!" Zeila shouted as she looked out the window. The Patriot missile batteries had opened fire.

"My God! Bent, you bastard, we're all going to die!" the captain shouted as missiles exploded all around the crippled jet.

"It's not my fault that the skies aren't friendly anymore," Rex shot back as the nose of the plane shuttered.

"The wing's on fire!" Zeila informed all on board.

"Well, it's time to kiss my ass goodbye," Ms. Firm chuckled as she finished her mint julep and watched the beads of sweat roll down Mr. Dagerpont's ghostly white cheeks. Obviously, the FEMA director was in no condition to respond to his lovely assistant's tempting offer.

"The tail's on fire, too!" Zeila shouted as all the dense dark smoke within the cabin was suddenly sucked out of the damaged rear section of the plane.

"Oh no, I've lost hydraulics!" the captain shouted, canting the yoke to the right and then the left. But there was no response. The plane wouldn't turn.

"Zeila, get up here!" Rex yelled.

"All right, all right, don't rush me!" Zeila shouted back while looking out the window, fascinated by the Jefferson Memorial.

"Damn, is that boy getting grumpy! My first trip to Washington and I don't even have time to appreciate the sights," she grumbled as she unbuckled and staggered forward, clenching the backs of the seats in an attempt to steady herself.

"Take your seat and strap in!" Ginger growled angrily, observing the flagrant FAA violation.

"All right, all right," Zeila conceded, taking a seat well short of the cockpit and fastening her seatbelt as instructed.

"Now, I suggest you all start praying!" Ginger insisted to her captive audience.

"Pray for what?" Ms. Firm asked, oblivious to the danger while the not-so-honorable Mr. Dagerpont remained frozen with fear.

"You could pray for either a FEMA trailer or the airline stewardess's timely death. However, in all probability, neither one will come to pass," Zeila suggested with a chuckle.

"Huh!" Ginger gasped, turning her head.

"Girl, you got that right. *So I'd like to pray for another drink. You know, you can't fly on one wing*!" Ms. Firm announced without reservation while rattling the ice in her empty glass in front of Ginger.

"I could use a shot of moonshine myself. Oh, stewardess, we're thirsty!" Zeila shouted, but her untimely request fell on deaf and maliciously sobering ears.

Suddenly, there was a violent explosion on the left side of the cockpit as a missile from the battery had found its mark. Rex was launched from the copilot's seat and slammed against the bulkhead, striking his head.

"Rex, are you all right?" Zeila screamed as air rushed into a gaping hole on the port side.

"Oh!" Rex moaned, fighting to maintain consciousness.

"Rex, are you all right?!" Zeila screamed again.

Rex brought his hand to the left side of his face only to find that his palm was covered in blood. Instantaneously, he found his energy surge, courtesy of an adrenaline rage rush.

"Hell yes!" Rex screamed into the turbulent wind. Captain Gomez was slumped over the center console, dead. He grabbed the yoke and pulled backward with all his might. However, the plane continued to drop just as a second explosion off the starboard side rocked the crippled FEMA jet.

"You're missing a wing!" Zeila shouted as the plane quickly heeled to the right and the nose started to roll downward.

"This can't be good," Rex gasped as the plane began a rapid death roll just as it passed the Washington Monument.

"Keep the nose up!" Zeila shouted.

"I'm trying, I'm trying! Damned rear cabin flyers!" Rex screamed as the plane continued to roll.

Suddenly, there was a loud, metallic grinding sound just before the entire fuselage was ripped away.

"Now, you've gone and lost your tail!" Zeila shouted.

Rex quickly looked around and was amazed to see that the last twenty feet of the plane were missing.

"Now our goose is really cooked!" Ms. Firm added in an attempt to make light conversation.

Mr. Dagerpont screamed hysterically, shaking his head from side to side.

"Everyone hold on, we're going down!" Rex screamed as the second wing broke free.

Suddenly, the plane stopped rolling and the nose began to lift.

"Oh no!" Rex moaned as the White House came into view through the cockpit window.

Zeila sat quietly, mesmerized by the barren trees that rushed by her window. An instant later, there was a tremendous jolt and everything went black. Seats were ripped from their foundations and everyone in the plane was thrown forward as the pride of the FEMA fleet slammed into the ground, belly-first.

The *Gulfstream* jet slid across the White House lawn and raced toward the West Wing before coming to rest in a dense patch of snow, only a few meters shy of the Oval Office.

An eerie silence was broken by a wicked hissing sound as hot metal was rapidly cooled in the surrounding snow and by the sound of flickering flames thriving off what remained of the rear section of the cabin. However, distant sirens soon began to wail as firefighters and police raced to the scene of the accident.

The cabin quickly filled with a dense, dark tenacious smoke. Slowly, signs of life returned within the downed aircraft. There was coughing followed by moans and groans and, finally, movement.

"Rex, you're going to have to work on that landing," Zeila suggested, unfastening her seatbelt.

"Excellent advice, but what do you expect for a flight that doesn't offer frequent flyer miles?" Rex replied, looking aft to assess the situation.

"Damn hijacker!" Ginger growled as she stood and scurried aft.

"Thank you for flying 'Obama Airlines,' where all your dreams are guaranteed to 'crash and burn,'" Rex announced with great fanfare.

"Jackass!" Ginger screamed, cracking the hatch on the cabin door and dragging the copilot to safety.

A disoriented Mr. Dagerpont stood up, and staggered aft while Rex attempted to rouse an unresponsive Ms. Firm.

"Zeila, get the hell out of here before this downed bird explodes!" Rex insisted.

"You don't have to tell me twice," Zeila replied, walking toward the exit in the rear of the aircraft.

"Wake up, Fanny, we've landed!" Rex shouted, slapping Ms. Firm and shaking her shoulders.

"What? What happened?" Ms. Firm mumbled as she fought to regain consciousness while Rex unfastened her seatbelt.

"Welcome to Washington," Rex announced, assisting her to her feet.

"Thanks," Ms. Firm mumbled, slowly making her way aft with Rex's assistance.

"Tell Michelle that Zeila's here!" Zeila shouted to all the world. She stood proudly at the hatch and posing much like General Douglas MacArthur upon his return to the Philippines.

"Damn, even the snow's white!" she complained, landing in a soft three-foot drift.

"Here we go, Fanny. Please mind your head and watch your step," Rex instructed as he assisted the FEMA assistant extraordinaire the few feet to the ground.

Zeila slowly ambulated away from the burning plane and toward a bewildered and exhausted Mr. Dagerpont who had plopped down next to a clump of trees adjacent to Ginger and the copilot. Rex took one last look at the cabin and wondered how in the world anyone had survived the crash. He thought about the captain momentarily before his thoughts focused on Trissy. He jumped to safety and scrambled toward the others.

"Zeila, are you all right?" Rex asked as he surveyed his fellow passengers and the remaining crew. All were bruised, battered, and badly shaken with the exception of his magical Cajun companion.

"Sho' is," Zeila replied, looking up at the Oval Office and waving while the police and fire sirens grew louder.

"Who dat?" Zeila asked, staring at the individual in the large bay window.

"Zeila, now really. There are two and only two possibilities: either it's the Menacing Raptor Michelle or the transparency scamming Barack-o-saurus Rex. In either case it's guaranteed to be a bad bird," Rex concluded without looking up at the newly elected president.

"For once, I agree with you. Anything with a word REX in it has got to be bad," Zeila responded without hesitation.

"Well thanks, Hummingbird," Rex exhaustingly replied as he held up his hand.

"Don't mention it, my ornery Owl," Zeila said as she slapped Rex's open palm. "But whoever's staring down at us can't be as bad as that uncompassionate turkey from FEMA. When I get through with him his head is going to roll right into my gumbo," Zeila declared, looking at Mr. Dagerpont and recalling his arrogant, self-serving demeanor.

"Don't you think that's going to spoil the gumbo?" Rex asked.

"Not if you cook him right."

"Well, just the same, please don't invite me to that dinner," Rex chuckled.

He and the other survivors were suddenly descended upon by herds of firemen and gaggles of police officers.

"Zeila, let's go find Trissy," Rex said, graciously extending his arm.

"Sho' should. I just know that girl's all right," Zeila assured Rex with a smile as she took his arm.

"That's the man who hijacked my plane and was threatening to blow up the White House!" Mr. Dagerpont shouted as the Capitol Police, the Secret Service, the FBI, and the CIA officers cocked their weapons and pointed them at Rex.

In an instant, Rex was face-planted in the snow by several large men. Within sixty seconds, he had been cuffed and yanked to his feet. Rex coughed, violently gasping for air after having had the wind knocked out of him.

"And that's the evil woman who was with him," Mr. Dagerpont added in a personal effort to round up the entire terrorist tribe.

Zeila looked at Mr. Dagerpont in disbelief while her hands were held behind her back as she was being cuffed.

"'Gumbo Joe,' you're soon to go!" Zeila assured the FEMA director with a snarl.

"Stop, I need to rescue my wife. The terrorists have her captive in a U-Haul truck on I-ninety-five at the beltway," Rex pleaded.

"Shut the hell up. You say one more word and I promise you it will be your last," an angry officer warned.

"What an idiot! That moron is sticking to his same delusional story. There's probably no one named Trissy," Mr. Dagerpont chuckled. "You know, FEMA is really on the front lines of every national disaster and no one appreciates our work, Ms. Firm." Mr. Dagerpont complained.

"That's tragic. Well, I could certainly make you feel better, but I seem to have lost all my nighties," the young and voluptuous Ms. Firm fussed.

"My wife's out of town and you just can't stay alone, not naked and not after what we've been through. Perhaps I could console you and we could talk about that raise," Mr. Dagerpont purred seductively.

"I'd like that," Ms. Firm sighed and giggled while rubbing his inner thigh.

"I'm going to put the 'Double Damned Gre-Gre' on that boy!" Zeila shouted as she and Rex were unwillingly dragged down the hill.

"You don't have to, I believe he's already been cursed!" Rex shouted back as he was blindfolded and tossed into an unmarked vehicle.

"Let go of me, before I whip your butts!" Zeila threatened as she was blindfolded and ushered into an unmarked car as well.

Moments later, sirens shrieked and tires screeched. The prisoners were whisked away toward destinations unknown.

Chapter 45

Clearly, the federal authorities were not pleased with the FEMA *Gulfstream* jet hijacking or Rex's choice of location in which to put the opulent bird down. After being handcuffed and dragged down the White House lawn, Rex had been blindfolded and thrown into an unmarked vehicle. En route, there had been absolutely no conversation and, after forty-five minutes of twists and turns, the vehicle came to a screeching halt. All Rex could think about during the tortuous transit was Trissy and her safety.

"I'm coming, Trissy, please forgive my slight detour," Rex whispered, struggling to pull his wrists free of the steel restraints.

Time was of the essence. Every minute Trissy was held in captivity gave the terrorists another opportunity to kill her. Rex was so lost in thought that he didn't hear the footsteps approaching. Suddenly, the car door was flung open. Rex was yanked out.

"Could you take it easy, fellas? I've been dragged behind a truck by Islamic terrorists, nearly eaten by Allah-gators, and I survived two aircraft accidents, none of which were my fault, mind you. Furthermore, I'm missing half my skin and every inch of my body hurts," Rex pleaded unsuccessfully.

There was no response.

"How long have you all been associated with this deaf mute colony?" Rex asked politely as two powerful men placed a death grip on each arm and ushered him forward. As Rex stumbled onward, he could hear a multitude of footsteps, far more than the footsteps generated by himself and the gorillas he had on either side. He assumed he was surrounded by a number of men. Yet no one uttered a word.

"I wish you would take the blindfold off and let me bail out of this jail. My wife is in great danger and I need to save her," Rex insisted.

Again, there was no response, just a silence broken by a stampede of haunting footsteps, which were now amplified by and echoed off sterile concrete walls. The farther Rex advanced, the more he became aware of a damp, musty odor in this barren lifeless downward-sloping corridor. Suddenly, his entourage came to an abrupt halt. It was then that his senses were overwhelmed by a bone-chilling screeching sound emitted from a heavy metal door as the impenetrable security barrier was forced open. Rex was dragged forward, the door slammed shut and locked. Rex had no doubt that he was traveling deeper and deeper beyond the point of no return.

"I don't know where you're taking me, but I want to apologize right here and now for my check to the Special Agent Association bouncing," Rex joked in an effort to strike up a conversation and ease the tension, since the possibility of escape appeared to be highly unlikely.

Once again, the gaggle of gorillas refused to break their silence.

Several minutes later, Rex came to another unexpected stop. He could hear metal rings clinking together and the snapping of fabric as a hanging curtain was thrown back just before a needle pierced his right deltoid.

"Take those cuffs off and get him on the bed, quickly," the doctor ordered after the sedative/hypnotic was injected.

"We can't leave the cuffs off, Doctor," the agent reminded the doctor as Rex collapsed.

"That's all right. Cuff whatever hand you deem appropriate to the bed rail," the doctor recommended as Rex was tossed onto the stretcher.

"The IV's in," the nurse announced, drawing several vials of dark blood.

"Put in a Foley and run our standard labs on the blood and urine," the doctor ordered.

"Doc, given this traitor's plans to kill Americans and destroy several major cities, I'd like to see this dirtball dead. But the thought of torturing his pathetic soul and breaking his legs first is rather appealing. Can we make that happen?" the agent requested with the utmost sincerity as the doctor nodded and smiled in agreement.

"Nurse, give Dr. Bent our infamous cocktail," the doctor ordered.

"One 'NSA special,' coming up," the nurse replied joyfully, squeezing a portion of the air out of the syringe before injecting the truth serum through the IV.

"And get him into a gown," the doctor added.

"Will do," the nurse responded, pulling a pair of scissors from her coat and cutting off Rex's clothes. "My God, look at all the cuts and abrasions. His skin looks like hamburger meat," the nurse noted as she slipped Rex's arms into a hospital gown.

"Well, it sure isn't lean ground round," the agent concluded, observing Rex's watermelon abs.

"I think it looks more like rump roast," one officer suggested, his stomach beginning to turn at the sight of blood.

"All right, gentlemen, that's quite enough. Please let the interrogation group know when their subject is ready. They're anxious to get started," the agent in charge ordered before leaving the infirmary.

◆

When Rex awakened several hours later, the blindfold was off. He was lying on a stretcher in a small, cold, sterile room bathed in a dull, red light. The ceiling contained an unusual array of large lights. The walls were concrete, devoid of any pictures, and there was no furniture. There appeared to be only one door leading in and out of this dungeon.

"Where in the hell am I?" Rex mumbled, grabbing his pounding head. Then he realized that his right wrist had been cuffed to the bed rail.

"That's not very friendly," he growled. "I wonder how long I've been out..." Rex slowly sat up, cautiously throwing his legs over the side of the stretcher.

"Has it been hours, days, weeks, or even years? I'm dizzy, my vision is blurry, my head hurts, and I've got to pee."

As Rex's vision continued to improve, he soon realized that he had been bestowed a number of gifts.

"Those sorry bastards!" Rex growled, noticing the hep-lock in his right arm, a rough gnarly gown, and an irritating Foley catheter. He placed his feet on the cold cement floor and stood up, struggling to maintain his balance.

"There's no doubt that I've been probed, prodded, and drugged," Rex concluded.

He held onto the stretcher tightly as he began to form a plan of action.

"First things first, the Foley has got to go!" Rex insisted. He searched the stretcher and then the room for a syringe with which to deflate the large, water-filled bulb that held the evil urine-capturing contraption firmly in place. However, there would be no such luck.

"Hell, I can't find a syringe, a knife, or even a bottle opener, for that matter. Surely these goons left something behind before taking their hourly smoke break," Rex complained.

He dragged the stretcher around the room and examining the floor for any tool capable of safely removing his irritating plastic penile implant.

"Well, that leaves me with one option," Rex concluded, ripping the small plastic valve off the rubber tubing.

"There we go," Rex announced joyfully as sterile water trickled out of the bulb.

Moments later, the barbaric bladder-bashing hose had been safely withdrawn without ripping his urethra to shreds.

"Ah, now that's better," he sighed, throwing the overfilled Foley bag onto the stretcher.

"Don't they ever empty these damn things?" Rex complained as he looked at the bag, which was now full with several liters of dark urine with solid particles floating about.

"Now, for the handcuff," Rex said, pulling at the steel bracelet, thinking of ways to extricate himself.

Suddenly, the bank of bright lights above turned on. Reflexively, Rex brought his left forearm up to shield his eyes, but his efforts were too late. Although he had adjusted to the dim red light, the intense white lights gained easy access to his dilated pupils, temporarily washing out the light-converting cones and rods within the retina. Everything now appeared to be bright white and extremely hazy. There was no contrast or color.

Rex could hear a metal door open, followed by the sound of methodical, slow-moving, heavy footsteps. But this time, he was certain that there was only one man who had entered the room.

"For what do I owe the pleasure of your company?" Rex asked sarcastically as he blinked excessively. He followed the man's movements as the door slammed shut with a loud thud.

The footsteps suddenly picked up in pace and grew nearer. Instinctively, Rex moved the stretcher in front of himself to impede the man's progress. But the rolling obstacle was of little use. The stranger immediately grabbed the front of Rex's gown, twisting it into a knot with such force that he was able to lift Rex off the floor and halfway over the stretcher.

"You're going to have to do something about your breath," Rex suggested, realizing that their faces were merely inches apart.

Rex attempted to push the man away with his only free hand but was unsuccessful. Struggling to free himself, his vision slowly returned. Rex was now able to see contrast and could make out the silhouette of his attacker, a short stocky man with wretched halitosis.

"Hello Dr. Bent, I'm very displeased that you didn't follow my explicit orders and stay in Baton Rouge," SAC Richter growled.

"Richter, you're like a bad dream. You knew I had a prior engagement," Rex replied as the two men continued to wrestle.

"If that's what you want to call it. However, unlike your prediction, you've now been apprehended and your ass is mine," Richter declared with a sense of pride and accomplishment.

"Come on, Richter, anyone with any common sense would realize that I'm not the bad guy. By the way, how did you get to Washington so fast?" Rex asked the renegade FBI agent as his color discrimination and depth perception started to improve.

"It wasn't difficult, but at one point I didn't think I'd make it here in time. However, I must admit it was quite easy tracking you down. All I had to do was to look for a path of death and destruction. It appears that a devil like you scorches the earth wherever he goes."

"It sounds like you had a bad flight. I, on the other hand, was on board a brand-new *Gulfstream* jet. The ambience was incredible, the food impeccable, and the service exceptional. We even had a stripper on board," Rex bragged to the emotionally unstable little man with a big ego.

"I'll bet you did, my delusional friend," Richter replied, releasing his grip and pushing Rex backward. "Dr. Bent, it's time for you to take a trip beyond your fantasies and even beyond the realm of bad dreams. You're now in a nightmare, and what information chemical coercion does not allow us to obtain, I've been authorized to beat out of you. And I'm sure looking forward to your pain, suffering, and prolonged agony," Special Agent in Charge Richter assured Rex, pounding the end of his billy club in is open hand.

"That's all well and good. Have you chosen the time of death?" Rex quipped, backing the stretcher away from the possessed agent.

"No, no, not as of yet. That would only spoil the surprise. Now, it's time that we get down to business. I want the names and addresses of all those terrorists in your cell," Richter demanded, advancing on his restrained target. Rex now had his back firmly planted against the wall.

"Whose side are you on, anyway?" Rex asked, forcefully thrusting the stretcher outward.

"Dr. Bent, I'm just a patriotic citizen and loving family man determined to rid the world of scum," Richter blurted, deflecting the stretcher while swinging the club. Rex could feel and hear a gush of air rush by as the solid wooden club barely missed his face.

"Richter, have you ever considered attending an anger management class? Of course, the first thing they would suggest to a bulked-up, no-neck bozo like you is to drop the steroids," Rex suggested in an effort to enrage his already disturbed attacker.

"Why would I need anger management when I can take out my frustrations killing you?" Richter growled, leaning forward and swinging the deadly weapon again.

"You know, in addition to steroids causing aggression, they can stunt your growth, cause your forehead to expand excessively, and, most certainly, result in testicular atrophy. In fact, over time you begin to look like a bull-faced horny toad with microscopic raisin-ettes," Rex openly shared with SAC Richter to ensure that he fully understood the consequences of his medicinal abuse.

"You don't say," an unconvinced Richter replied sarcastically. He smashed his billy club against the stretcher, bending the metal frame.

"Yes, and all you have to do to prove it is to look in the mirror. You'll see a short man with a big head and no nuts!" Rex added for clarification, giving his attacker his award-winning smile, thus ensuring that Richter's hot button had been fully engaged.

"You've pissed me off for the last time, Bent!" the SAC screamed, suddenly turning into a raging bull. Richter pushed the stretcher forward, pinning Rex against the wall, and then began swinging his club wildly.

As Rex dodged the life-threatening blows, he looked down on the stretcher where he found his one and only weapon: a large bag of his malodorous acidic urine. At the opportune moment, Rex picked up the long rubber tubing with his free hand and pointed it at Richter. He then came down on the distended Foley bag with all his weight.

"Now that's a poor choice of words!" Rex shouted as a crystallized dark brown stream shot forth, striking the unsuspecting victim in the face.

"Oh, Jesus Christ!" Richter screamed as his eyes immediately started to burn and water excessively. The blinded agent quickly broke off his attack and staggered backward. Rex could see that the SAC was off-balance. With all his might, Rex rammed the stretcher into his gut. Doubled over on the stretcher and gasping for air, the injured Richter dropped his war club. Now was the perfect time for Rex to go on the offensive.

"It appears that the playing field has been leveled," Rex announced, struggling to reach the club. However, the handcuff severely restricted his movements. He immediately realized that he would not have the luxury of time to gather the weapon.

"How convenient," Rex whispered, viewing the Foley catheter, which had remained on the stretcher despite the scuffle.

Suddenly, the memories of Rectal Richter roughing up Trissy came rushing back as did the hell the renegade FBI agent had put them both through. Instantly, he raced past the fine-line-dividing physician from warrior. Revenge would be sweet. His rage suppressed any sense of compassion and allowed his hunter/killer instincts to flourish unchecked. There was only one viable alternative and there could be only one outcome in this battle for life and death.

"Even maggots like you need oxygen, but let's find out," Rex suggested, wrapping the thick rubber Foley catheter twice around the Richter's broad neck and pulling it tight with all his might.

The SAC's head and neck quickly became cyanotic. He struggled briefly and suddenly went limp just as the door to the dungeon was thrown open.

"Rex, NO!" Leslie Valentino yelled as the metal door crashed against the concrete wall.

Leslie and several large men with automatic rifles rushed in to save the cyanotic, unresponsive Richter.

Rex froze and, for a moment, time stood still. He looked down the barrels of the weapons and then at Leslie.

"Trissy?" was all he asked as tears welled up in his eyes.

"She's safe and unharmed," Leslie replied. "We got your message," she added.

"Thank God," Rex whispered, slowly releasing his death grip.

Richter fell to the floor. Rex looked down and observed, rather discouragingly, that his nemesis was still breathing. Richter slowly regained a fine pink oxygenated color, but his eyes continued to tear excessively.

"For a moment I thought Richter might have been an anaerobe," Rex chuckled, lifting his left hand high into the air, signaling his surrender.

"Rex, you almost killed the arrogant bastard," Leslie concluded, conveying her animosity toward the agent who had given her so much grief.

"It wasn't me, it was my urine. Clearly, my kidneys successfully filtered Zeila's toxic swamp salve," Rex surmised. Richter rolled onto his side and started to cough excessively.

"Well, that explains the putred smell," Leslie replied as she motioned to one of the agents. The burly man immediately put down his weapon, walked over to Rex, and unlocked the handcuff that kept him bound to the stretcher.

"Rex, come with me, I have a surprise for you," Leslie said. She took Rex by the arm and led him out of the dungeon from which no one had ever escaped.

Chapter 46

"I feel a draft," Rex complained after leaving the dungeon and entering the cold damp passageway.

"That's understandable," Leslie conceded, watching Rex struggling to bring the small tattered hospital gown around far enough to cover his backside.

"Rex, pick up the pace, we have to cover a lot of ground," Leslie requested as she scurried down the dimly lit, narrow concrete corridor with its many twists and turns.

"All right, all right," Rex conceded, limping along. He started to fall farther behind.

"Are we there yet?"

"Almost!" Leslie shouted over her shoulder, walking even faster.

Several minutes later, Leslie finally arrived at a single elevator and inserted her security card into the authorization slot. The doors opened slowly and with a rumble. She walked in and waited impatiently for Rex to catch up.

"Hold on, Grandpa's coming!" Rex shouted as he hobbled toward the lift.

"It's about time, Grandpa," Leslie chuckled as Rex finally entered the elevator. She reinserted her security card and the doors closed.

"My, you're speedy," Rex remarked as Leslie punched the button that would take them to the fifth floor.

"In this business, if you snooze you lose."

"Understandable. Leslie, by the way, where in the hell are we?"

"NSA headquarters, Fort Meade, Maryland."

"And the date?"

"Thursday, November eleventh."

And the time?"

"I wish I knew. My watch stopped last week, but I believe it's around five p.m.," Leslie replied, wondering if Rex had suffered some traumatic brain injury along the way.

"I don't even know why I asked, because after being locked up in your clandestine amusement park and drugged, time has become irrelevant."

"I'm indeed sorry about that. SAC Richter was acting on his own. He's not with the NSA."

"Hum. You know, it was the North Korean cargo ship, *Il-Sung*, which brought the nuclear wastewater into the United States."

"Yes, we know," Leslie simply replied although she wondered how in the world Rex would have come to that conclusion.

An eternity later, the elevator doors rumbled open slowly and Leslie withdrew her card.

"Here we go," Leslie announced. She and Rex exited onto a small nondescript stuffy lobby with a dull blue carpet and a homely receptionist.

"Is the NSA having some sort of budget crisis? Rex inquired as they walked past the receptionist who never looked up, never moved, and didn't even appear to be breathing.

"Hardly," Leslie chuckled as they walked through an archway and into a smaller room with two doors. Rex noticed the gold lettering on one of the doors.

Director

National Security Agency

"So this is where the Big Kahuna hangs out," Rex observed in his subtly tactful manner.

"I should say, when he's not in Bar Harbor," Leslie agreed, opening the second door that had no identification. She motioned for Rex to enter. Hesitantly, Rex slowly walked into a large boardroom, in the center of which was a highly polished mahogany table, large enough to seat at least twenty comfortably.

"There's no one here," Rex keenly observed as he shuffled toward the bank of windows.

"You're smarter than people give you credit for," Leslie chuckled as Rex clasped his hands behind his back, a comfortable position given the extended period of time in which he had been cuffed.

"I'll take that as a compliment," Rex replied, looking out over the rolling hills with amazement.

All the leaves had fallen off the trees and there was a soft blanket of sparkling snow as far as the eye could see. Although the terrain looked barren and cold, there was a magnificent light which he thought he would never experience again. With the sun starting to set, the countryside took on a serene and spectacular glow. Once again, Rex felt there was hope for America and the world as long as the United States kept the light of freedom burning brightly.

"Rex, stay here and please don't wander off. You might set off a multitude of alarms, which could very well land you back in our cozy basement with the good SAC Richter. I'll be back momentarily," Leslie requested graciously as she smiled and closed the door.

"You don't have to tell me twice," Rex replied, looking out the bank of windows once again.

Several minutes passed. The room was intensely quiet, with the exception of the aggravating rhythmic ticking of an obnoxious wall clock. Suddenly, Rex heard the soft clicking sound of metal hardware and immediately wheeled around. The conference door opened quickly and in walked Trissy, beautiful as ever and uninjured.

"Rex, thank God! I thought I'd lost you!" Trissy yelled, running to her husband as they embraced and kissed with unbridled passion.

"Trissy, are you all right?" Rex asked, gently clasping her face between his hands and looking deeply into her radiant brown eyes.

"Yes," Trissy responded simply as they held one another tightly.

"Ough!" Rex suddenly blurted, as Trissy unknowingly rubbed his deep abrasions during their moment of ecstasy.

"Ough? What do you mean, ough?" Trissy prodded, continuing to hold him, but leaning back to see what the problem was.

"Dermabrasion isn't all that it's cracked up to be. I'm ground up from my head to my toes," Rex complained.

"That's right, I'm so sorry," Trissy apologized as the horrifying sequence of events over the last few days came rushing back.

"I don't remember attending any wild Democratic fund-raising parties and falling into one of their entitlement blenders," Rex replied honestly as he tried to recall exactly what Zeila had told him about how he had sustained the injuries.

"Rex, we were captured and tortured by the terrorists. They dragged you behind their truck just before dangling you over their alligator pit. Don't you remember?" Trissy asked her bewildered husband.

"Vaguely, it's just all the details that are a little fuzzy."

"This isn't one of those male selective memory moments, is it?" Trissy inquired suspiciously.

"Quite possibly. By the way, did we ever consummate our marriage?" Rex asked with a wink and a smile.

"Several dozen times, don't you remember?" Trissy asked as the tone of her voice deepened before quickly deciding to put an end this charade."By the way who's asking, you or Mr. Whale?" she added as her worries and fears began to subside.

"Well now that you mention it…"

"By the way, where's Zeila?" Trissy asked.

"I'm not sure. Leslie's friends whisked her away just as we arrived at the White House," Rex recalled.

"The White House!" Trissy blurted loudly, wondering what Rex and Zeila had been up to in her absence.

"Leslie, please tell me that our trusted traveling companion is all right," Trissy demanded.

"I should say. Zeila is presently in a limousine sipping champagne and touring the sites in Washington, DC."

"That doesn't sound like our Zeila. Whiskey, yes, beer, yes. Champagne, NO," Trissy replied with conviction. Surely Leslie was wrong.

"I'm not so sure we've seen the true Zeila, Trissy. I'm convinced it was that *Gulfstream* jet."

"What *Gulfstream* jet?" Trissy asked.

"I just knew the old gal had 'style and class,'" Rex relayed as the vision of the ninth ward evacuee/survivor delving into the treasures of the nation's capital brought a smile to his face.

"What *Gulfstream* jet?"

"FEMA was kind enough to give us a lift from Baton Rouge to Washington on their corporate jet. How do you think we got to you so quickly?" Rex replied, placing an acceptable spin on the story.

"I wasn't sure, but a FEMA jet? You're pulling my leg!" Trissy replied, realizing that the odds of Rex coming clean were quite minimal.

"Actually, they hijacked the jet at gunpoint and were later shot down by fighter jets and the Patriot missile defense battery. In fact, they crashed on the White House lawn," Leslie relayed, folding her arms and looking toward Rex, assuming that he would want the opportunity to clarify some of the facts.

"Rex, you didn't!" Trissy gasped as she brought her hands to her face in astonishment.

"It was a miracle anyone survived the encounter with the F-sixteens, not to mention the missile batteries," Leslie felt compelled to stress.

Trissy's jaw dropped. Rex could tell that his wife was overwhelmed by shock and disbelief as she attempted to come to grips with the magnitude of the alleged crime. In all their years of marriage, Rex had never seen her speechless before. Not willing to face the deadly turbulence that appeared inevitable, Rex wisely chose to break his silence.

"Zeila did it. I just went along the ride," Rex confessed, attempting to shift the blame to their elderly Cajun companion.

"Well, your joy ride cost the government in excess of fifty million dollars. That, of course, doesn't include the expenditure for the sidewinder or Patriot missiles. Furthermore, for that matter, it doesn't even include the cost of medical or psychiatric care that all those with whom you have come in contact with will undoubtedly require. By the way, I just heard that Mr. Dagerpont is heavily sedated and locked in a padded room. He keeps mumbling, *'Get Bent.'* Needless to say, his recovery is doubtful. As for the president, she was not pleased with your landscaping revisions or with your support of the Republican party but has decided to pardon you, Trissy, and Zeila for any and all crimes. Additionally, the government will cover any and all loss of life, limb, and/or property," Leslie announced with great pleasure.

"My God, you crashed on the White House lawn!" Trissy gasped as Rex rolled his eyes and searched his atrophied gray matter for a plausible explanation.

"Ah …" Rex started to mumble before thankfully being interrupted.

"In fact, the jet came to rest just twenty feet from the Oval Office," Leslie blurted.

"Was anyone injured?" Trissy asked.

"The pilot was killed," Leslie replied.

"Oh NO! Rex, that's the second pilot you've killed this week!" Trissy reminded him, looking down and slowly shaking her head in disgust.

"Ah…"

"Leslie, we gratefully accept the pardon."

"By the way, were you able to nab the North Koreans or the other radical Islamic terrorists?" Rex inquired.

"No, unfortunately even with your timely information, we arrived on the scene too late. They're on the run, while we remain on the hunt. However, we have reason to believe that Colonel Chum has set up a money-laundering business somewhere in San Francisco. It's a sanctuary city, you know," Leslie replied.

"No need to remind me of that inexcusable liberal-stamped anti-American status," Rex growled, as Trissy suddenly focused on her husband's stained white garment.

"Rex, what's with the hospital gown?"

"The NSA insisted that I have a physical."

"A physical? What in the world for?"

"They think I'd make a good agent," Rex responded, smiling. Leslie turned her head and looked up at the ceiling.

"If you're thinking about joining the National Security Agency, you need your head examined," Trissy stated emphatically.

"You're probably right, but not tonight. Let's go home," Rex suggested.

"Well then, all that remains is a pleasant surprise for the both of you, courtesy of a very grateful government. Air Force One is standing by at Andrews Air Force Base to take you two anywhere you would like to go in the world, with the exception of Iran and North Korea," Leslie disclosed admiringly.

"Well, there are quite a few additional countries where we have just plain worn out our welcome," Rex freely admitted, stroking his chin and thinking of other possibilities.

"I don't have a thing to wear and Rex is half-naked. We couldn't possibly go anywhere," Trissy concluded.

"Nonsense, I was born naked," Rex blurted. "Leslie, have the pilot chart a course for Vatulele, Fiji," Rex insisted.

"Fiji? It's halfway around the world. My God, Rex, have you lost your mind?" Trissy asked, forming a fist and gently wrapping her knuckles against her husband's skull. "Empty, just as I had suspected," Trissy added after hearing an echo from the hollowed-out structure.

"I may have lost my marbles and my ass, but we still have each other. What do you say to a warm beach, a snort of kava, and a barrel of rum?" Rex asked enthusiastically as he put his arm around his beautiful wife.

"Now that you put it that way, I'm interested. By the way, what else do you have to offer to entice me into this trip?" Trissy asked, the glow in her eyes returning.

"Why don't we lie down and I'll show you?" Rex responded passionately, giving his wife a kiss on the cheek.

"Hum," Leslie mumbled, attempting to clear her throat.

Sensing that it was time to retreat, the blushing operations officer for the National Security Agency opened the conference door.

"Promises, promises, you older men are always full of promises," Trissy complained, putting her arm around Rex as they walked toward the door.

"Huh, I'll just pop a few of my magic pills and we'll see who's chasing whom naked around Nooki Nooki Island, young lady," Rex threatened.

"I'd run like hell," Leslie advised, inserting her security card and depressing the elevator button.

"Someone's got to make this roughed-up old SEAL happy," Trissy sighed as the thought of running naked on the beach became rather appealing.

"Yes, well. You're going to the first floor where the director's chauffeur will be waiting to take you to the plane," Leslie instructed.

"Rex, close your robe. We have a flight to catch," Trissy insisted as the elevator doors closed behind them.

Chapter 47

Vatulele, Fiji—December 23 (Six Weeks Later):

It was another spectacular day. A few exotic cloud configurations roamed the skies while the sun bathed the remote island in the South Pacific with vibrant, life-giving energy, encouraging all to flourish. As the leaves on the tall coconut trees swayed in the tropical breeze, the warm azure waters within the magnificent lagoon gently lapped against the sparkling white sandy beach. Death and destruction had been reduced to abstract unimaginable crimes against humanity. In this tranquil environment, neither hatred nor religious intolerance existed. This was a life without worries.

It was 11:30 a.m. As usual, Rex and Trissy could be found relaxing outside their bure on teak lounge chairs, adjacent to a grand old Banyan tree, which was at least forty feet wide.

"Christmas in paradise; no snow, no slush, and no scum. How do you beat this?" Rex asked, admiring the nearly denuded palm tree he had proudly planted in the sand a week before.

"Your tree is looking a little scrawny if you ask me, Santa," Trissy observed after lowering her latest Heidi Barnes novel and briefly scrutinizing Rex's paltry palm tree before returning to *The New York Times* bestseller *The Bellman*. "I beg your pardon. Surely you're joking. Look at the way the strong sturdy limbs support those colorful glistening ornaments. Without question, ten years from now this tiny sapling will be larger than the mighty Banyan tree behind us," Rex assured Trissy with unyielding confidence.

"Rex, the tree only has three palm leaves, each of which is dead, by the way. Furthermore, the branches are brittle and the trunk is starting to rot. But I must admit, it does have personality," Trissy added at the last minute, in an effort to show her appreciation for Rex's thoughtful holiday contribution.

"I knew you'd find it irresistible. By the way, what would you like from Santa, little girl?" Rex snickered, waiting impatiently for her response.

"Not another coconut bra, that's for sure," Trissy quickly replied, setting her novel down and reaching for a bottle of tanning oil.

"Well then, how about a designer grass mini skirt from Goosie Goosie, perhaps?" Rex suggested as Trissy rolled her eyes.

"Good idea, Rex, but the dry grass irritates my thighs," Trissy confessed as she thought about what she would really like.

"Of course, you realize that I have a solution to that problem," Rex assured his beautiful wife.

"And just what's that?" Trissy asked apprehensively.

"Going native and running naked on the beach. Of course, only after I've had a chance to massage your firm, muscular thighs with that sweet-smelling seductive oil," Rex suggested innocently as he watched Trissy applying liberal amounts of suntan oil over her voluptuous body.

"Now you're starting to make sense," Trissy giggled.

"Let's see, Santa, I'd like three things for Christmas," she relayed after much consideration.

"The first is snow," Trissy requested.

"Already done. Just look around you, there are two white sparkling flakes on the beach!" Rex chuckled.

"Gotcha, gotcha. My, you're awfully quick at granting my wishes. My second wish is for a CD of the Bee Gee's greatest hits," Trissy added.

"I'll have it here tomorrow, although the high-pitched voices may cause the wildlife to seek refuge on another island," Rex voiced with great concern.

"Rex, that wasn't nice. Now, what I'd really want for Christmas is a puppy," Trissy pleaded as Rex rolled his eyes.

"I see, and what kind of puppy?"

"A Havanese."

"No, no, you need a real dog, not a ten-pound fluffball. Most importantly, you need a dog with personality. Growing up in the hills in Southern California, we had a German shorthair named Duke. That dog would drink Colorado Koolaid and play horseshoes all day. He would even eat avocados and spit out the pits!

"I don't want a dog that big and the Havanese are extremely smart."

"I see, and what are you going to name your dog?"

"Simba because he will have the heart of a lion."

"Nice name. Well, I'll do everything in my power to ensure that your wish comes true. But for now, let's just concentrate on covering every square inch of your body with oil. The sun's rays can be so damaging," Rex recommended, feeling compelled to warn his wife.

"Oh, is that so?" Trissy replied skeptically. "Well, you're a physician, so I'm sure you'd know," she added, flashing her alluring smile.

"Of course, now may I be of any assistance?" Rex inquired, watching the oil dripping between Trissy's thighs.

"Can you be trusted?" Trissy asked, lowering her sunglasses to the bridge of her nose and turning toward her husband.

"Of course not, but one must assess the danger," Rex growled as he quickly invaded Trissy's space.

"And just how should I do that, Dr. Big Bad Santa?" Trissy asked as Rex lowered the backrest on her lounge chair and strategically positioned himself behind her. She willingly handed Rex the bottle of oil, realizing that she was throwing fuel onto the simmering fire.

"Well, young Trissy, you must determine if your greatest threat is posed by the sun's damaging rays or an aroused Rex," her husband warned while massaging the fragrant tan-enhancing concoction into her shoulders.

"Oh, I see. Well, quite frankly, I'm not sure," Trissy purred seductively as she rapidly fell prey to Rex's award-winning technique. Rex rhythmically contracted his fingers while sliding his palms down her back.

"Oh, that does feel good," she moaned.

"Ummm, undoubtedly," Rex groaned, kissing Trissy on the nape of her neck, fantasizing about the moment yet to come.

"Rex, behave yourself," Trissy insisted as her top suddenly, but not unexpectedly, gave way. Instinctively, she brought her hands to her chest to prevent her breasts from being exposed.

"It's too late. You've titillated my wildest primitive instincts," Rex moaned, slipping his hands under hers and onto her breasts. He met little resistance and slowly began to rub her erect nipples.

"Wow. Rex, I've got to warn you that I'm quickly losing control," Trissy groaned as her pelvis began to rock to and fro, stimulating Rex's trusted and highly engorged companion. Trissy could feel her pulse race with the thought of making love on the beach.

"I don't know if you've been naughty or nice, but Santa has a present for you. I..." Rex began to reply as he suddenly became aware of palm leaves rustling. He looked to his right just in time to see a young native Fijian girl emerge from the dense jungle, carrying a silver tray on which rested two colorfully ornate Mai Tais.

"Tee hee hee," Mere giggled as she approached. Trissy remained unaware of the unexpected intrusion.

"I've been bad and am about to be very bad, Santa," Trissy confessed as her pelvis continued to thrust back and forth.

Rex gasped, scrambling to find the appropriate words that would disguise this romantic overture.

"Rex, don't stop now," Trissy complained loudly, sensing that Rex was losing interest in the sexual interlude he had launched.

"Trissy, I just don't know how in the world those hooks could've unsnapped," Rex announced as Mere placed the drinks onto a small glass table, while Rex struggled to thread several small hooks through even smaller metal loops.

"What are you talking..." Trissy gasped, quickly turning to find their trusted and loyal "bure girl" standing beside them. "Mere!" she shrieked. "Oh, how—how, thoughtful," she praised, trying to catch her breath while regaining her composure.

"Excellent idea, and just in time to ward off the heat of the morning sun, thank you," Rex said in appreciation as he retreated to his own lounge chair.

Mere smiled and bowed as she walked backward. In an instant, she disappeared behind the magnificent banyan tree. All that remained, as the giggling reverberated throughout the jungle, were two refreshing Mai Tais.

"Rex, our nightly skinny-dipping is done under the cover of darkness. I just knew this daytime sexual escapade wasn't a good idea," Trissy surmised as Rex handed her a glass filled with the addictive, rum-based potion.

"Obviously, from all the giggling and cackling, I'd say Mere rather enjoyed the show. I have no doubt that even at her young age she's witnessed more than a little hanky panky on this romantically intoxicating island," Rex observed.

"No worries, my love. Cheers. You're breathtakingly beautiful and absolutely irresistible," Rex added, raising his glass and tapping it against Trissy's.

"That's awfully sweet. Cheers. Well, perhaps you're right, but next time we need to be more careful," Trissy concluded as she retrieved a succulent chunk of pineapple and bit into the sweet juicy fruit, while Rex jettisoned the umbrella and the flower from his.

"Nonsense, I say we throw caution to the wind, rip off the tag, and let our passion run wild. However, if you insist, I'll bet I could procure an old ceremonial love drum that I could beat to warn the Fijians of an impending cataclysmic event," Rex suggested, smiling as he dove into his cocktail.

"Ah, now that's GOOD!" he sighed after surfacing. Trissy looked on in amazement as half of Rex's drink instantly vanished.

"That would scare the natives and, now that I think of it, you would most likely be beating the drum day and night," Trissy realized as she began rubbing her leg against Rex's.

"I bet you're right because I just can't keep my hands off of you," Rex replied, scooting his lounge chair closer to Trissy's.

"Dr. Bent, Dr. Bent!" a voice shouted from somewhere deep in the jungle. Rex and Trissy turned around to find Karalaini emerging from behind the banyan tree.

"Not another intrusion!" Trissy complained as she took a large sip from her drink.

"I'll bet the entire village is hiding behind that banyan tree," Rex concluded with some degree of frustration.

"Dr. Bent, there is a Dr. Witherspoon on the phone. He states that his call is most urgent," Karalaini remarked, lowering a shiny silver tray on which rested the nagging, untimely communication device. Rex looked at the cell phone and hesitated for a moment before picking it up.

"Rex, I know Dr. Witherspoon is a dear and trusted friend, but are you sure you want to answer that call?" Trissy asked.

Trissy could see that all of Rex's deep abrasions had healed nicely, but wondered if rekindling relationships in the evil little town of Carencrow might possibly bring back haunting memories of the hardships they had endured.

"What the hell," Rex replied, taking another gulp from his Mai Tai before setting down his nearly empty drink.

"Rum gives me great courage," he declared as he motioned to Karalaini to bring another round before picking up the phone.

"Boom Boom, how the hell are you?"

"Doing well, Rex. How's Trissy?" Boom Boom asked as he placed his finger in his other ear in an attempt to cut down on the deafening chatter created by rambunctious emergency room personnel letting loose at their Christmas party.

"Arousing. As beautiful and as sexy as ever," Rex replied, smiling at his gorgeous wife.

"That's good to hear. Rex, there were rumors that you were either incarcerated or dead," Dr. Emanuel Witherspoon chuckled.

"I was in a seedy jail briefly and feel as if I've risen from the dead, so both were true," Rex confessed, polishing off his Mai Tai.

"Well, that means that your close personal friend, Dr. Fubar, is the only Carencrow physician that's still in jail," Dr. Witherspoon shared with great joy.

"No doubt that Rectal Richter finally got the right man," Rex chuckled.

"There's also a rumor floating around that you and Trissy rearranged his expensive riverside camp."

"Possibly, but all I can admit to is a romantic interlude in his Jacuzzi," Rex shared realizing how quickly the story had spread in the small town. "Boom Boom, where in the hell are you? All I hear is shouting in the background."

"I'm standing in Rula's having a drink with at least thirty rather rowdy emergency room nurses and doctors. I'm not sure anyone is of sound mind because they've elected you to be our next emergency room director. I apologize for any intrusion, but they insisted I call. So please don't shoot the messenger," Boom Boom shouted over the roar of the crowd.

"I'm honored. What happened to Gonzalez?" Rex asked as Trissy sipped on her Mai Tai, attempting to make sense of the conversation.

"He's dead. Of course, you were accused of and praised for his early demise, but all is forgiven!" Boom Boom assured his admired emergency room companion.

"Speedy is dead, Fubar is in jail, and I have been offered the emergency room directorship," Rex whispered to Trissy with his hand over the receiver.

Rex gazed into his lover's eyes. The expression on her face and her body posture instantly conveyed the appropriate "there ain't no way in hell" response.

"Well, that's good to know, and I'm very appreciative for the vote of confidence, but I don't think Trissy and I care to return to civilization quite yet," Rex answered candidly as Trissy nodded her head in agreement and clapped her hands.

"That's what I figured and I don't blame you. There are far prettier places in the world, some of which aren't patrolled by flocks of incontinent buzzards," Boom Boom replied.

"Are you talking about the birds, or Mean and Evil?" Rex chuckled.

"Mean and Evil are hairy and flatulent, whereas the buzzards are feathery and incontinent," Boom Boom laughed, reminding Rex of this subtle but noticeable difference in the similar ornery species.

"Excellent observation and I appreciate the anatomy lesson," Rex shot back.

"Rex, get your butt back here!" Beemer shouted, leaning toward Dr. Witherspoon. Although somewhat inebriated, in the excitement and sensing the need to be heard, he was unaware that a generous portion of his libation had escaped the confines of his glass and splashed onto Dr. Witherspoon.

"Beemer, either drink it or swim in it. Just don't spill it on me," Dr. Witherspoon pleaded.

"Sorry, Boom Boom," Beemer apologized, putting his arm around one of his favorite emergency room physicians.

"Dr. B, it's been hell without you. Man, my extended Cajun family needs your help. Yeah, boy!" Big Dog yelped as he nudged closer to Dr. Witherspoon.

"Rex, if you change your mind, the position is yours," Dr. Witherspoon assured Rex in one last attempt to sway his decision to return home.

"Boom Boom, you'd make one hell of a motivational speaker. I'll take the offer under consideration. However, I can't make any promises without first consulting Trissy and the all-seeing and all-knowing Zeila the Magnificent," Rex conceded as Trissy bowed her head in a manner that reflected her displeasure with her husband's reply.

"Consult whomever you need to. We'll be waiting," Dr. Witherspoon said.

"Rex and Trissy, we love you and miss you!" Wanda shouted as the little Ewok cupped her hands in an effort to propel her voice toward the receiver, which was now being more closely guarded by Dr. Witherspoon.

"C'est si bon!" Wan snickered, holding his glass high in the air before wandering off.

"Rex, as you can hear, this get-together is out of control, but I have one more question before I let you go. How in the world did you and Trissy survive your ordeal in Carencrow? Everyone wanted you two dead," Dr. Witherspoon inquired.

"I took your advice and stayed focused!" Rex replied without hesitation.

Suddenly, the phone came alive with a rhythmic chant. Dr. Witherspoon's voice was now indiscernible. Rex depressed the button that activated the speakerphone and placed the evil electronic voice box onto the glass table.

"We want Rex. We—want—Rex! WE WANT REX…!!" the proud and fiercely independent Carencrow emergency room staff shouted in unison before the line went dead.

"Well, I suppose we should check on Zeila. I wonder how the old gal is making out," Rex insisted upon knowing.

"No telling with that feisty Cajun."

"After the call, may I suggest one more Mai Tai and then lunch on Nooki Nooki Island?" Rex recommended with a twinkle in his eye.

"Only if I can have my way with you," Trissy insisted, sitting on Rex's lap and putting her arms around him.

"I know that can be arranged," Rex replied confidently as he dialed Zeila's number.

Chapter 48

It was a balmy, overcast evening in the Crescent City. Dark clouds raced overhead, while off in the distance lightning could be seen streaking across the night sky. It was the calm before the storm, for a cold front was soon to descend upon the city of New Orleans. Yet nothing could dampen the spirits of the revelers who had gathered at Zeila's new home in the abandoned but not forgotten ninth ward. As the flames from the tiki torches swayed in the gentle breeze, the deep, rich sound of pounding drums could be heard.

Rizzi, Zeila's younger sister, had just arrived by taxi. She had received an invitation to the party but was unsure as to the location.

"Oh no, this must be the wrong street," Rizzi said to herself, standing on the sidewalk examining an oasis amongst all the devastation.

"What in the Sam Hell is going on here?" she wondered as she reexamined the street address where she had lived before Katrina had ravaged her childhood home. "And where's my mama's house?" Rizzi demanded to know.

But her questions and concerns were soon answered as she read a sign high above the intricate wrought iron gate:

Zeilaville

Population: One

Living the American Dream—Baby

"It can't be!" Rizzi gasped but as she walked through the gate.

Almost immediately Rizzi found herself seduced by the sound of music and joyous laughter. Through the lush trees and dense vegetation that encompassed the property, she caught a glimpse of a party, which had undoubtedly already shifted into high gear.

"Lord have mercy, Zeila's done lost her mind! There's no telling what trouble she's got herself into now!" Rizzi surmised, cautiously entering a magnificent wonderland.

"My word!" Rizzi exclaimed as she watched a herd of kids playing with a black lab.

"Here, Rexy!" the children shouted as the dog escaped. They chased the elusive and energetic canine around the yard, each attempting to pull up their baggy britches before stumbling forward and falling.

However, despite all the activity, Rizzi's arrival had not gone unnoticed. As the youngest of nine children, she was loved by all and immediately greeted by her rather extensive family.

"Rizzi, Rizzi, Rizzi!" a gaggle of winded great grandchildren screamed, descending upon the only other remaining family matriarch. "Rizzi!" the kids shouted in unison, holding her hands and gazing up into her sparkling eyes, while Rexy barked his approval.

"Hello children: Sambee, Billy Barr, Sissy, Boo Boo, Dor Dor, Ho and Joe, Esmeralda, and Leroy," Rizzi announced with a grand smile as she enthusiastically greeted all of the kids.

"My, my, MY, what has that Zeila been up to?" Rizzi asked as she surveyed the grounds, while a lively African band played a rhythm that stirred her soul.

"Rizzi, Rizzi!" the kids chanted, tugging their much beloved great grandmother down a windy cobblestone path. The mouthwatering smell of Cajun spices suddenly filled the air as they scurried past 'Dagerpoint,' a headless man standing next to a large vat of alligator gumbo.

"The gumbo sure was powerfully good!" Sambee admitted as he rubbed his protruding belly.

"I'll bet it was. By the way, has your great grandma been sipping on moonshine?"

"Yes-um," all replied in unison loudly and without hesitation.

Rizzi and her herd of young admirers ambled past a large grill made out of a shiny jet engine casing. As the lid was lifted, and an enormous puff of smoke rose before revealing mouthwatering racks of pork ribs and barbecued chicken.

"Children, where's dat Zeila?" Rizzi asked as she was pulled along the path past dozens of picnic tables stacked with row after row of side dishes and desserts.

"She's just up ahead, past 'Sambo's Swamp,'" the children assured her as they enthusiastically pushed and pulled her forward, before stopping at a makeshift bar.

"Zeila 'incest' you drink this," Sambee said with a smile, handing Rizzi a shot glass full of Zeila's elusive elixir from her personal stash.

"Why, Sambee?" Rizzi asked curiously, taking the glass from the little man's hand.

"Because Zeila said you're too white," Sambee relayed verbatim.

"No, Sambee, she said Rizzi was too uptight," Esmeralda corrected her little brother.

"She also said you're loose and need to sin up," Sambee added with a broad grin.

"No, she said Rizzi needs to loosen up," Esmeralda clarified, much to Sambee's displeasure.

"Who you gonna believe?" Sambee asked Rizzi as he shrugged his shoulders and flexed his elbows with his palms up.

"Leopold, is this safe to drink?" Rizzi asked her great cousin who was tending bar as she swirled the viscous clear liquid around in the shot glass.

"Should be, since it hasn't eaten through the glass. It's from Zeila's personal still and aged for more than twelve minutes. If it doesn't kill you, it's guar-on-teed to cure whatever ails you," Leopold relayed.

"Well, as long as it helps with my rheumatism, I'll give it a try," Rizzi announced with great bravery before downing the potent jungle juice.

"Yay!" the children shouted in unison.

"Woof, dat's bad!" Rizzi snorted moments before her body started tingling and she felt an unbridled surge of energy. "Now, this is a party!" Rizzi shouted as she suddenly picked up her pace.

"Slow down, Rizzi, we need to show you 'Sambo's Swamp,'" Sambee insisted, trying to put the brakes on his supercharged great-grandmother.

Ten feet off the cobblestone path and beneath a large gre-gre tree, a small swamp had been constructed. Adjacent to the swamp was a thin elderly black man in overalls sitting on a wooden bench feeding two massive alligators, each with its jaws wide open displaying their pearly white snappers. The tribute to Zeila and Rizzi's father simply read: "Sambo's Swamp. Alligators Welcome."

"Well, I'll be. That even looks like Sambo, except the jug of moonshine next to him is too small," Rizzi chuckled as wonderful childhood memories came rushing back.

"Come on, Rizzi!" the children shouted. As she and her entourage rounded a tall grouping of recently planted trees, a jazz band playing "Mardi Gras Mambo" came to life.

"Whoop, dare it is!" Sambee declared with pride, pointing toward Zeila's humble abode.

"Good God Almighty!" Rizzi shouted as she stopped and looked on in disbelief. In front of her, propped up on tall steel pilings, was a huge jet with wings but no tail. The wings had been turned into balconies lined by iron railings and the tail replaced by a large, multifaceted glass dome. With the green pulsating running lights and the accent lighting shooting up from the ground, the magnificent *Gulfstream* jet appeared as if it were still aloft and gliding effortlessly through the skies.

"Let's go Rizzi, Zeila's waitin'," Esmeralda insisted.

"Okay child," Rizzi replied, overwhelmed by it all.

"Yes-um, don't stop here, you're sure to get stampeded," Sambee cautioned as Rexy plowed into the children and started barking. Clearly, it was time to play.

Rizzi walked up a wide stairwell that led to the port wing where she was met by dozens of near and distant relatives who shook her hand and gave her hugs before returning to gaze over and admire the magnificent grounds.

"It's not possible," Rizzi gasped.

"Merry Christmas and welcome aboard, Rizzi. Don't be afraid. Please, step right on in," her cousin Sadie encouraged, taking her hand and walking her through the escape hatch that had conveniently been converted into the front door.

"Merry Christmas," Rizzi whispered as she struggled to believe what she was seeing.

"Zeila, you go girl, this is fine!" Rizzi shouted as she worked her way through all the relatives who had been invited to celebrate the glorious holiday.

Zeila was talking to her niece while nursing a large vat of sour mash that had been boiling on the stove. She immediately recognized the voice, dropped a large wooden ladle, and turned around to face Rizzi.

"So you like *Zeila's FEMA Cantina*? It's my new watering hole. Merry Christmas!" Zeila said with a big smile, her arms open wide.

The two matriarchs hugged as the extended family of aunts, cousins, nephews, and grandchildren looked on with admiration.

"Merry Christmas. You're not running moonshine again are you?" Rizzi asked.

"Hell no, but I'm still drinking it!" Zeila proclaimed with a joyous laugh. Everyone within earshot howled at Zeila's response, for her appreciation of the potent libation was well-known. She screwed the top onto the boiling pot of sour mash and attaching the copper coiled tubing that ran into a large ceramic jar.

"By the by, did you get the magic potion I left for you at the bar?" Zeila inquired as the clear liquid began to drip slowly from the end of the copper tubing.

"Wow, sho' did. I feel ninety years younger," Rizzi exclaimed with great appreciation.

"To Zeila's fountain of youth!" her nephew Royal shouted, holding his glass high.

"Here's to Zeila!" young cousin Kevin shouted as he searched for a glass with which to propose a toast.

"Zeila, Zeila, Z-e-i-l-a!" everyone shouted in unison, raising their glasses.

"I'm already rather toasted and roasted, but I want to tell you all how very appreciative I am for all the love. Here's to a wonderful evening and many more to come," Zeila replied graciously, holding her drink in the air briefly before turning up her glass.

Her great grandson, Tyrone, watched in awe as Zeila downed what he thought smelled like and looked like jet fuel siphoned from the FEMA jet's tanks.

"Tyrone, did you get enough to eat?" Zeila asked as she gazed down at the handsome, bright-eyed five-year-old.

"Yes, ma'am. I was as ravenous as the Almighty," the young man declared, rubbing his distended belly in a circular pattern.

"Well then, do you have enough energy to fetch me just one more glass of moonshine?" Zeila asked as she placed her arm over his shoulder and held him close.

"Yes-um," Tyrone shouted enthusiastically after being given the opportunity to help his great grandmother in her time of need.

"And you'd better bring a tall glass for Rizzi has well. She looks mighty thirsty," Zeila added.

"A very tall glass," Rizzi emphasized. "After what I've seen, one glass may not be enough," Rizzi added.

"Coming right up!" Tyrone exclaimed, escaping Zeila's bonds and darting off toward the liquor cabinet, a location the enthusiastic pint-sized bartender had grown quite familiar with over the evening.

"Now, ZiZi, there's no one besides you who has had the opportunity to move back into the ninth ward. Surely, you can tell Rizzi how this all became possible," her curiosity consumed sister inquired, with great interest.

"Of course, but there's no mystery. Beautiful Michelle offered to make a contribution to the 'Zeila Katrina Washington Foundation' after what I had done to help save our great nation," Zeila shared with her skeptical sister.

"Well then, how did you convince the mayor to reestablish water, sewage, and electrical services to this part of the city?" Rizzi asked.

"You have to know how to deal with that sly, slippery old dog. I simply told the 'bad man without a plan' that 'Zeilaville' was to be built or I would kick his butt. Also, the threat of an old black woman's Cajun curse may have had something to do with his decision," Zeila chuckled, continuing to skirt the issue.

"Tell me, you didn't sleep with the FEMA director, did you?" Rizzi asked as she continued to probe for answers.

"Absolutely not, he's locked up on a funny farm. However, as you know, I'm not without beauty or charm," Zeila confessed, tossing her hair to one side and striking a centerfold pose while watching her sister's eyes roll upward in frustration.

"Rizzi, you just have to know the right people," Zeila assured her sister.

"I'll bet," Rizzi replied, wondering if she'd ever have the opportunity to fulfill the American dream.

"In fact, now that you mention it, I was able to purchase a lot next door," Zeila disclosed with a twinkle in her eye as she handed Rizzi the deed to the property.

"You didn't!" Rizzi shouted incredulously.

"I damn sho'enough did. Although I wouldn't want you as my roommate again, I most assuredly want you as my neighbor," Zeila proclaimed as the two matriarchs of a proud, hardworking but dirt-poor dynasty hugged again.

"Great-Grandma, here're your drinks," Tyrone announced with pride, handing each of the ladies a large glass of moonshine.

"Well thank you, Rapper T."

"Just in time. Thank you, Tyrone," Rizzi added, praising the young man for his kindness and efficiency.

"Phone call, Great Grandma! He says tits real poor-tent," Sambee shouted over the roar of the crowd as the four-year-old approached Zeila.

"Well, it can't be the neighbors calling to complain about the noise, because there ain't no neighbors yet," Zeila said to Rizzi with a chuckle as the little man reached up to hand her the phone.

"Thanks Sambee, that was very nice," she added, taking a sip of her stout libation.

"Hello? Speak up, boy, I can't hear you," Zeila shouted into the phone.

"Rex, is that you?" she yelled over the roar of the crowd.

"Excuse me Rizzi, I'll be right back," she assured her sister.

"Hold your horses, let me step outside."

Zeila walked through the escape hatch and onto the winged balcony.

"Zeila, this is Rex. Trissy and I just wanted to check on you, but from all the noise, everything must be going quite well," Rex assumed.

"Rex, life is great! I just moved onto my new plantation yesterday, so I decided to throw a little Christmas/open house party. The turnout has been fantastic and everyone's having a great time," Zeila shared with joy.

"That's wonderful," Rex replied joyfully as Mere delivered another round of Mai Tais.

"Although I saved your ass and nursed you back to health, I can't thank you and Trissy enough for helping me bring my dream to life," Zeila replied as tears welled up in her eyes. "In fact, I'm so appreciative that I bought a dog and named him after you," Zeila shared.

"No way. Oh, Lord, you probably adopted a white, mindless Havanese and named him Rover," Rex envisioned as Trissy punched Rex in the arm for his comment.

"No, in fact he's a black lab and I named him 'Sexy Rexy.' I've got to tell you that the dog has personality and is very, very special," Zeila relayed.

"I should have known. I'm honored. What makes 'Sexy Rexy' so special?" Rex asked reluctantly, taking a sip of his refreshing Mai Tai.

"He's the smartest dog I've ever had and the only one I've successfully trained to growl at bill collectors and Republicans," Zeila chuckled, taking sip of her moonshine.

"How unique, a Dem-o-Dog. No doubt he barks with a lisp, drinks out of the entitlement bowl, and has his mind in the gutter," Rex replied candidly, putting his hand over the receiver.

"Trissy, wait until Sean Hannity, Rush Limbaugh, and Mark Levin hear about Zeila's Republican-bashing canine," Rex whispered as Trissy picked up her third sensual libation, sipping on the inhibition-releasing rum.

"By the way, do you have any neighbors?" Rex inquired.

"Not yet, but I'm working on it. I intend to be the spark of light that reignites the ray of hope in this forgotten city," Zeila announced with pride.

"Fantastic! Zeila, you're an inspiration," Rex declared as Zeila watched lightning fill the dark, ominous skies with flashes of intensely bright light.

"Thanks, Rex," Zeila replied, as the sound of distant rumbling thunder grew nearer.

"Don't mention it," Rex said, watching his beautiful wife quickly polish off her Mai Tai.

"Do you and Trissy intend to head my way soon? I'd like to show you my magnificent plantation," Zeila asked with anticipation.

"Oddly enough, that's the question we wanted to ask you. I have been offered the head honcho position in charge of the emergency department at Carencrow Regional Hospital. What do you think?" Rex asked the wise old Cajun.

"Well, let me gaze into my crystal ball," Zeila said, looking into her glass and sloshing the moonshine around in a circular pattern before taking a sip. "No, no. After misbehaving with my girlfriend, Leslie, in DC, I believe she intends to offer you a job. She mentioned something about needing your help with '*RED*.' That's your best bet."

"Surely you're joking! Taking a job with the National Security Agency is in my future?" Rex asked incredulously as Trissy shook her head in frustration.

"Yes, but hang loose. As I recall, you've only been in Fiji for about six weeks. My advice is to forget about *Crisis: Black*, stay in the sun, and work on your tan until spring."

"Excellent advice, but living on an island too long poses many dangers," Rex shared as Trissy stood up, stretching.

"Like what?" Zeila asked as lightning bolts shot down from the heavens.

"We could possibly wilt in the heat or lose our minds," Rex slurred, polishing off his Mai Tai while admiring the oil glistening off Trissy's radiant skin.

"You may be too late. You're already sounding a little squirrely. I would imagine that there's not very much to do on a desolate island," Zeila shared as the sound of thunder intensified.

"That's where you're wrong, Zeila," Rex shared honestly as Trissy suddenly took off her top and extended her hand.

"Wow, hubba, hubba!" Rex snarled excitedly after observing the waves of pulsating heat rising from the tanning oil on Trissy's firm, beautiful breasts.

"Rex, you're not making much sense," Zeila declared as Rex stood and embraced Trissy.

"I'm losing you, Zeila. Trissy sends her…" Rex said as he tossed the phone down onto the lounge chair and passionately kissed his wife.

"It's time for our swim, Mr. Whale," Trissy whispered seductively as she nibbled on Rex's ear before running hand in hand into the warm, azure waters of the tranquil lagoon.

"Rex, Rex, are you still there?" Zeila shouted, but the line was dead.

"I truly worry about those two," Zeila said, pushing the *off* button and leaning against the rail.

Zeila could feel the winds beginning to pick up and the temperature dropping. In this moment of solitude, she stood quietly and gazed over the devastation of the once vibrant ninth ward. Nothing had changed since Katrina. A multitude of abandoned homes stood lifeless while off in the distance the battered levee, once again, stood tall. Although the jazz band was playing a lively song and the beautifully decorated Christmas trees on her plantation swayed in the breeze, Zeila was struck by a feeling of sadness.

Suddenly, a hummingbird appeared from out of nowhere and hovered just a few feet from Zeila's face. Then, in an instant, it was gone.

"Ah, my fine feathered friend, you've made me tough and brought that elusive element of luck that my family and I so greatly deserve. There is indeed hope. Once again, I feel certain that all is achievable," Zeila whispered before taking one last swig of moonshine.

Rex & Trissy Bent Return in

Crisis: Red

About the Author

John is the cofounder of 5VS (5 Vital Signs), a start-up committed to saving the lives of wounded American soldiers by allowing the medic, or any other soldier within one hundred yards, to triage on the battlefield. He is a Board Certified Emergency Room physician.

He graduated from the United States Naval Academy (BS), in Annapolis, Maryland, and the University of Texas (MBA) in Austin, Texas. Later, he completed his Doctorate of Medicine (MD) at the University of Texas Medical Branch in Galveston, Texas, and finished the Louisiana State University (LSU) Emergency Medicine Program in Baton Rouge, Louisiana.

5VS FIVE VITAL SIGNS

www.fivevitalsigns.com